Yankee
Rogue

Yankee Rogue

Dana Fuller Ross

WHEELER
PUBLISHING, INC.

★ AN AMERICAN COMPANY ★

Published in Large Print by arrangement with Book
Creations, Inc. in the United States and Canada.

Wheeler Large Print Book Series.

Set in 16 pt. Plantin.

Library of Congress Cataloging-in-Publication Data

Ross, Dana Fuller.
    Yankee rogue / Dana Fuller Ross.
        p.   cm.—(Wheeler large print book series)
    ISBN 1-56895-066-7 : $22.95
    1. Man-woman relationships—United States—Fiction.   2. Indentured
servants—United States—Fiction.   3. Large type books.
I. Title.   II. Series.
[PS3613.C8879V66   1994]
813'.54—dc20
                                                                94-0217
                                                                CIP

Yankee
Rogue

CHAPTER ONE

The early morning sunlight filtered through the trees surrounding a small clearing just outside London. The spot was close to the city, but isolated. This was just as well, because it was apparent from a glance at the men gathered there that a duel was about to take place, and dueling was strictly forbidden under an edict issued earlier the same year, 1739, by King George II, the Hanoverian monarch who spoke English with a German accent so thick that most of his courtiers could not understand him.

The men were gathered in two groups at opposite sides of the clearing. Those on the far side spoke in quiet concerned tones to a tall man of about forty, who had stripped off his tailcoat and was slowly rolling up the sleeves of his white silk shirt.

"I beg you to reconsider, milord," one of them said earnestly. "Lieutenant Hale is the deadliest swordsman in all of England, and you'll be risking your life if you insist on going through with this engagement."

Lord Otto Richardson, whose absurdly stiff and pompous bearing never failed to evoke surreptitious amusement in court circles, shook his head firmly. He was as stubborn as his good friend King George, which meant that once he had made up his mind, he was unyielding. "My honor, it has already been badly soiled," he said, speaking in a

1

heavy German accent. "My life is not worth living without my honor!"

His seconds looked at each other and shook their heads, knowing that further argument was useless.

Nevertheless, one of them tried. "His Majesty has issued a very firm edict, milord, and as you know, he despises dueling. You'll be certain to lose favor at court."

"Ach, no!" Lord Richardson exclaimed. "When I tell the king what has happened, I am certain he will applaud the stand I have taken!"

The conversation at the opposite end of the clearing was equally spirited, but the speakers were having no better luck in persuading their champion to abandon the duel.

Lieutenant Jared Hale of the Royal Dragoons, lean, tall, and obviously athletic, still in his twenties, was practicing for his coming bout by dueling an imaginary adversary. The swishing sounds made by his expertly wielded blade punctuated the words of his seconds.

"Jared," one of them said, "I know that asking you to be sensible is like asking the sun to rise in the west and set in the east. I beg you, though, for once in your life, use your head! Lord Richardson is not only principal chamberlain to His Majesty, but he happens to be an intimate friend of the king's, perhaps the only real friend George has this side of Hanover. If you so much as scratch him, and the king learns about it, you'll be driven out of England. Indeed, you'll be lucky if you're not hanged on Tyburn Hill and your head put on a pike as an example to others who would ignore the royal ban on dueling!"

Jared Hale laughed aloud, and his sword sliced through the air even more menacingly. His laughter was robust and genuine, the laughter of a man who truly relished life and all that it offered him.

"I may be a bit rash, as my friends so often accuse me of being," he replied, "but I'm not a bloody fool. I have no intention of stretching the royal temper to a breaking point."

His other second, a brother officer in the dragoons, looked relieved. "You mean you'll apologize?" he said.

Jared snorted contemptuously. "Apologize? Whatever for? When I tried to seduce the wench, I thought she was his daughter, not his wife! Besides, if he'd been about two minutes later in his interruption, I'd have succeeded!"

The seconds looked at each other and sighed. "Fight, if you must," the older of them said, "but I plead with you—if you value your commission and the place you hold in London society, don't kill him! You're without equal as a swordsman anywhere, and I daresay he's a rank amateur."

The smile faded quickly from Jared's face. His friend had unwittingly touched a raw nerve and had come close to exposing the reasons for the young officer's consistently reckless behavior.

Jared preferred not to remember, but when he had first entered the dragoons, his conduct had been exemplary. Then, a year ago, his father had died—reportedly in a hunting accident, but Jared knew that the elder Hale had deliberately taken his own life after sinking the better part of his fortune in a shady financial enterprise.

The younger Hale had been severely shocked when he had discovered the scheme—a monumental hoax perpetrated by his father, involving nonexistent real estate sold to scores of gullible investors. Jared's mother had taken the news even harder. Already in poor health, she had collapsed and died shortly after learning of her husband's suicide. Subsequently Jared had grown to despise his father's memory; mere mention of protecting his family's "good name" was enough to send him galloping off to the nearest tavern or gambling hall—and London had plenty of both to offer, especially to a well-off young gentleman.

Money, of course, had never been of much concern to Jared, and it meant even less now. He didn't grieve for a moment over the loss of the better part of his inheritance. Instead, reconciled to being the last of his line, and quietly relieved that his father's suicide had prevented the outbreak of a scandal that would have destroyed his family's good name, he had launched himself on a campaign of reckless conduct that had left his friends and his colleagues in the dragoons open-mouthed.

A small group of horsemen now approached the clearing, drew to a halt, dismounted, and tethered their horses. The party was led by a tall, imposing gentleman who was the principal referee of the duel, a man who had been approved in advance by both participants and who obviously took his duty seriously.

He marched to the center of the clearing, then

4

announced, "The duelists will be good enough to surrender their weapons to their seconds and will approach me for the purpose of conferring."

Jared lightly threw his saber to his fellow lieutenant, and pushing his dark hair back off his forehead, he sauntered toward the referee, looking devil-may-care and confident.

Lord Richardson soon approached from the other side and remained sober-faced, his expression grim.

"Gentlemen, I call on you to reconcile your differences and to halt this engagement before blood is shed. What say you?"

"I bear His Lordship no ill will," Jared said easily, "nor have I at any time in the past."

Lord Richardson stood ramrod-straight and spoke stiffly, pompously. "To my deep regret," he said, "I came upon Lieutenant Hale making advances of a most intimate nature to my wife, and when I asked him the meaning of his conduct, he compounded the insult by replying impudently that he thought she was my daughter. I cannot tolerate such conduct!"

Stifling a laugh, Jared nodded, his lips twitching suspiciously.

The referee turned to him. "Are you willing to express your apologies to Lord Richardson, Lieutenant?"

Jared's humor vanished. He well appreciated the importance of the whole question of honor, because of what had happened to his father, but in some things he, too, could be rigid and unyielding. "I am aware of no need to issue an apology for my conduct, sir," he said crisply.

Lord Richardson stood unmoving, statuelike.

The referee had done his duty, and it was time now to get to the business at hand. "The seconds are witnesses to my attempt to reconcile the duelists," he said. "Unfortunately, I have failed. You may retrieve your weapons and rejoin me, gentlemen. And I beg you to remember," he added with a meaningful glance at Jared, "that the mere shedding of blood—the infliction of the slightest wound—will suffice. There is no need to incapacitate an opponent or to kill him."

As Jared grasped his dueling saber, it seemed to become an extension of his arm, of his being. It was not as heavy as the cavalry saber he was accustomed to; nevertheless, anyone who knew swordsmanship would have recognized at once, by the way Jared handled the sword, that he was a master bladesman.

The duel began, and Lord Richardson, true to form, betrayed his Germanic origins. He immediately tried to seize the initiative and fought methodically, each of his thrusts totally predictable.

Jared, twice decorated in battle for valor, the veteran of a dozen or more cavalry sorties, defended himself with negligent ease.

It was apparent to the onlookers that he was merely toying with Lord Richardson, but this surprised no one. His supporters and the friends of his foe alike could only hope that he didn't lose his notoriously quick temper. If that should happen, his opponent surely would die.

Suddenly, as though tiring of the sport, Jared reached out and with consummate ease inflicted a light wound on his opponent's forehead. Then, before Lord Richardson could strike again, Jared leaped back out of reach.

The referee immediately intervened, halting the duel and declaring that honor had been satisfied because blood had been shed.

The physician, who was in attendance, daubed brandywine on a pocket handkerchief and wiped His Lordship's wound.

Jared bowed low to Lord Richardson and his seconds, shook hands with the referee and the physician, and then mounted his horse. "Come along, lads," he said. "I'm starved." He and his two companions rode along the bank of the River Thames for a short distance, and then Jared said, "We'll stop at a tavern I know for breakfast. I'm in the mood for a plateful of finnan haddie and a half-dozen eggs." Suddenly he erupted with laughter.

His companions saw nothing humorous in his remark and looked at each other questioningly.

"You don't understand, lads," he said. "It serves the old goat right for being so stubborn!"

"What does?" his brother officer said.

"Sooner or later," Jared replied merrily, "it will occur to His high and mighty Lordship that I've carved the letter C in the center of his forehead. Lord Otto will be branded as a cuckold for all to see!"

The gaming club, located on a quiet side street between the busy Strand and the Thames Embankment, was reputedly one of the finest establishments of its kind in England. Just as the building itself, made of weathered gray stone, was unobtrusive, so the atmosphere was genteel. The guests, who played cards for very high stakes, came to the place exclusively by invitation and had good reason to be satisfied. The food, prepared by a French chef, was unusually good, the finest wines were served, and the female companionship offered was little short of extraordinary. Not only were the women dazzling, their beauty rarely matched in London, but—as a number of the more fortunate patrons had discovered to their delight—they were also discreetly available for after-hours dalliance.

Such was the fame of the establishment that scores of young women applied for positions on the staff every month, and those who were hired thought they were fortunate. Polly White, sitting alone at a small table at the rear of the main gaming room, could remember the day when she was elated to have been hired, and she was amused that she could have been so naive. A half smile touched the corners of her full mouth, a rich red thanks to her liberal use of lip rouge, and there were hints of humor in her emerald-green eyes, limpid and huge thanks to her expert use of cosmetics.

She paid no attention to the stir she created among the male customers, some of whom ogled her on the sly, while others eyed her boldly. She had come to expect their homage as her due.

The truth of the matter was that Polly was bored. Hence, she sat very still, at first glance resembling a statue. Ignoring the fashion that demanded the wearing of wigs, she had her own dark, luxuriant hair piled high on the crown of her head and emphasized by long, dangling earrings that further called attention to her delightfully rounded features. Her gown exposed liberal quantities of her delicate, ivory-white skin and further enhanced the illusion that she was a statue.

The reason for her boredom did not escape her: She spent night after night sitting at this same table until summoned by the management to act as an "escort" for a gentleman patron. Thereafter, her duties were plain: She was expected to accompany the man to the gaming tables and to sit close to him, to rub up against him, and otherwise distract his attention. If he gazed long and hard into her eyes or down the front of her exceptionally low-cut gown, so much the better, because that enabled the dealer to perform sleight of hand and cheat the customer.

If Polly liked a customer, and if there was any money left in his purse after the dealer was finished with him, she was free to go to his home or take him to hers, if she wished. The management of the club did not care what she did on her own time. As long as she was faithful in the discharge of her duties, they were eminently satisfied, and she saw to it that they had no cause for complaint.

Of course there were dangers involved with every customer, but Polly had a knack for staying well clear of trouble. She could almost always spot the clients of the establishment who would carry on loudly, make a fuss, or call in the constabulary if they thought they were being cheated, and she took care with such men. On infrequent occasions, when the courts of London received a complaint and sent bailiffs to investigate, Polly was innocence itself, and the bailiffs, admiring her beauty, thought of her as too stupid to be party to a scheme of fleecing clients.

Polly had no cause for complaint, and she well knew it. She had come a long way and had risen high in the world for a onetime ragged orphan who had begged for crusts of bread outside Saint Paul's Cathedral on Sunday mornings. She had even taught herself to read and write, which gave her rare talents, and she made it her business to be conversant with politics, the theater, and the state of literature, which made her of interest to her male companions. Realizing that she was well off, however, in no way mitigated her boredom.

Business was slow tonight, and although Polly disliked the taste of alcoholic beverages, she nevertheless sipped from her glass of wine.

Suddenly the gaming room came alive, seeming almost to explode, and she turned her head a fraction of an inch to examine the man responsible for the transformation without seeming to be looking at him.

She had to concede to herself that the man, chatting with several employees at the far end of the room, was a prime example of masculinity. He was tall, rugged, and lean, with something about him that attracted the attention of every woman in the room. Polly noticed that two of her colleagues sitting at another table were eyeing him surreptitiously. Small wonder, she thought, scrutinizing him again. There was something about him that made her want to tangle her own long, slender fingers in his dark hair.

"No, Polly, m'girl," a female voice said softly. "He's not for you!"

The startled Polly looked up, realizing she'd been so preoccupied that she hadn't noticed Sandra, a red-haired colleague, slip into the chair beside her.

"That, my dear," Sandra murmured, tossing her head so her red hair cascaded down across her bare shoulders, "is Lieutenant Jared Hale of the dragoons—*the* Lieutenant Hale."

Polly's attention continued to be riveted on the young man, who accepted a glass of liquor and began to drink it with evident pleasure. "I've never heard of him." she said. "Should I have?"

Sandra giggled. "Obviously," she said, "you don't have many of the military among your clients. They talk of no one else. It's Lieutenant Hale this, Lieutenant Hale that."

"Will one of us be called to escort him, do you suppose?" Polly asked hopefully.

Sandra's blue eyes became disdainful. "If you're called, use no tricks on him, Mistress White. I warn you! He'll gamble all through the night until his purse is bare—of that you can be sure. But no dealer in his right mind would cheat him. If Lieutenant Hale suspected he was being cheated, he'd run the scoundrel through without a second thought."

"Really?" Polly looked again at the young officer. He was sounding more and more intriguing.

Sandra was proud of her superior knowledge.

11

"He's the best swordsman, by far, in the Royal Dragoons," she said, "and he may be the very best in England. What's more, he's also a superb pistol shot, and he's not in the least shy about using his weapons. Anyone who deals with him has to take very good care not to offend him. I'm told he has a hair-trigger temper, as well." She giggled again. "But it's said there's one thing that always soothes him."

"What's that?" Polly demanded.

The other girl looked down her nose.

"Oh," Polly said.

Having made her point, Sandra proceeded to expand on it. "I haven't had the experience myself—" she said demurely, then added with great emphasis: "yet. But I'm informed on the best of authority that you've never been properly bounced, rolled, or jiggled until you've been bedded by Jared Hale."

Polly became aware that Lieutenant Hale was looking in the direction of their table. Following her usual custom, she fixed her gaze on the wall behind and slightly to one side of him, so that she could see him without appearing to be too forward.

In this instance, however, her tactics were useless, perhaps because Sandra made it manifest that his attentions were welcome. The red-haired woman favored the young officer with her most alluring smile, her eyes suggesting the hidden delights that would be his if he was fortunate enough to win her favor.

Lieutenant Hale reacted instantly, crooking a finger and beckoning.

A gentle sigh of anticipatory pleasure escaped from Sandra as she rose slowly to her feet and, hips swinging, crossed the room.

Polly was irritated by the rejection, feeling as though she had been slapped across the face. She could not help watching in fascination, however, and noted that when Sandra approached Lieutenant Hale, he reached out with both hands and drew her closer, in the process deftly managing to stroke her buttocks and her breasts. Perhaps it was just as well that the lieutenant had not selected her as his companion for the evening, Polly decided. If he was not to be cheated at cards, the dealer would give her no percentage of the house's earnings; and if what Sandra had indicated was true, he would be penniless, at least temporarily, by the time his night at the gaming table came to an end. There might be little to gain by an association with him.

All the same, she could not help but envy Sandra, and she was annoyed with herself for feeling as she did.

The colonelcy of the dragoons was an honorary position, customarily held by royalty, and currently the title belonged to no one less than King George II himself. The actual command of the regiment, however, was assumed by the executive officer, Lieutenant Colonel Sir Harry Barber. Himself the younger son of a high-ranking nobleman, Sir Harry was a professional officer who had spent his entire adult life in the army. A veteran of numerous campaigns, he was in his late forties, a martinet and a stickler for protocol.

13

Nevertheless, he was highly popular with both his officers and men because of his rigid sense of fairness and his sympathetic understanding of his subordinates.

So when he unexpectedly called a morning meeting of his officers—and on a Saturday, a day they usually had entirely to themselves—the men assumed he had important reasons, and none of them protested.

Sir Harry always demanded punctuality, so the officers assembled well ahead of the appointed hour. Only one of them was almost late, hurrying into the mess hall at the barracks off Whitehall just before the clock began to chime the hour.

Red-eyed and weary, Lieutenant Jared Hale was still closing the brass buttons on his scarlet tunic and fastening the clasp on his sword belt as he made his way to his seat.

A captain couldn't resist calling, "Congratulations, old boy! You actually made it on time!"

A number of officers chuckled, their attitude indicating that all of them were aware of Lieutenant Hale's peccadilloes.

"How much did you lose last night, Jared?" a fellow lieutenant demanded. "You were at the gaming table until all hours."

Jared was struggling with the high collar of his tunic, and his reply was only half-audible. "I'm damned if I know," he said. "I refuse to add up my losses, because it will be too depressing to find out."

The major who commanded his battalion peered at him, and there was envy as well as a teasing note in the senior officer's voice as he remarked, "I'm sure that the red-haired wench I saw leaving your quarters less than ten minutes ago was well worth whatever you may have lost, Hale. She's a real beauty."

An even larger number of officers joined in the laughter. Lieutenant Hale's success with the ladies was a standing joke in the officers' mess.

"Ten-shun!" the regimental adjutant called from the door at the rear.

The laughter died away, and the officers reacted as one man, jumping to their feet, their spurs jangling as they clicked their heels and stood at rigid attention.

Lieutenant Colonel Sir Harry Barber strolled from the rear of the assemblage to the front, taking his time, his glance resting briefly first on one officer, then on another. "I see that you were able to pry yourself out of bed in time this morning, Lieutenant Hale," he said. "Accept my congratulations."

Jared became red-faced but managed to hold his tongue.

Sir Harry reached the front of the hall. "You may sit down, gentlemen," he said pleasantly, and stood with his legs apart, his hands clasped behind his back, as his subordinates noisily seated themselves.

"I regret any inconvenience I may have caused you by summoning you to a Saturday morning meeting, gentlemen," he said, "but this regiment is renowned as the king's own, and we have been, once again, honored by His Majesty."

15

The officers sat expectantly, their expressions professionally blank and polite.

"As we've anticipated, gentlemen, we will take part in the parade honoring King George's birthday next week. I have just received word this morning from one of the palace chamberlains that, at the express command of His Majesty, we will supply the military entertainment for the edification of the king's guests and the diplomatic corps, as well."

Most of the junior officers were unable to conceal their dismay. Their more experienced elders remained blank-faced, however.

"I suggest," Colonel Barber said, "that we select fifty of our most accomplished horsemen, regardless of whether they come from this group or from the ranks of your enlisted men. I further suggest that this group ride at full tilt toward the spectators in the reviewing stand and that, on command, they draw their sabers, reach out with them, and bisect fifty melons that will be strategically placed upon the ground. Does anyone care to comment on my suggestion?"

No one in the hall seemed surprised. On the contrary, most of the officers looked slightly bored, and all of them remained silent.

Finally, Lieutenant Jared Hale slowly raised his hand.

"Ah, yes," Colonel Barber said. "You're recognized, Hale. For a moment I thought you'd disappoint me."

Jared rose to his feet and, standing at attention, addressed his commanding officer in a formal voice. "Sir," he said, "I've held my commission

16

in this regiment for the past five years, and for four of those five years, I've participated in the melon-slicing act on the king's birthday. With all due respect, Colonel, it strikes me that His Majesty is certain to be bored with our exhibition, and I daresay that the members of the court and the ambassadors and ministers of the diplomatic corps will feel the same way."

He was right, of course, as everyone in the room well knew. But the more experienced officers questioned his wisdom in challenging the plans of the regiment's executive officer.

Harry Barber was at his nastiest when he appeared to be genial. He chuckled, nodded, and then said quietly, "Your point is well taken, Hale. What do you suggest we do instead of slicing melons at a gallop?"

Most officers would have retreated hastily and taken refuge in silence. But that was not Jared Hale's way. His expression innocent, his voice bland, he replied, "It would be a novelty, Colonel, as well as a rattlin' good show, if we speared hen's eggs on our sabers at a full gallop. I don't think anything like that has ever been done before."

The suggestion was so outrageous, so ludicrous, that the officers hooted with laughter.

Sir Harry Barber joined in the laugh, but there was a dangerous gleam in his eyes as he signaled for silence. "A capital idea, Hale," he said heartily. "The other forty-nine will slice melons in half as they've done in the past. You, however, will enjoy the privilege of spearing a hard-boiled egg on your saber!"

A tense silence settled on the group as Colonel Barber started back down the center aisle.

The officers jumped to their feet and again stood at attention until the adjutant, who followed the executive officer, called from the back of the room, "As you were, gentlemen!"

The meeting had come to an end, and the group was strangely subdued. The major who commanded the first battalion spoke for everyone present when he said to Jared, "You've really done it now, Hale. You're never satisfied to leave well enough alone, are you? Well, this time, lad, the joke is on you, and I pity you when you bungle this assignment!"

Enlisted men assigned as servants to the corps of dragoon officers worked furiously, polishing boots, scouring brass, and scrubbing white cross-webbing until it was spotless. On the morning of the review, the officers were unusually somber as they gathered for breakfast in the mess hall, and there was little of the customary raillery. Those who were performing special functions in the review, particularly those who were assigned to the task of slicing melons in half, ate light meals and took care that nothing upset their digestive systems.

Lieutenant Jared Hale was the exception. His face was slightly flushed, his eyes were bloodshot, and his gait was somewhat unsteady as he belatedly made his way into the mess hall.

His colleagues looked at him in stunned silence.

"I believe I'll have an order of Scottish oatmeal, Corporal," he said, his voice husky from overindulgence and fatigue. "And let me see—I'll have a double ration of bacon, some toasted bread, and a pot of marmalade. Oh, yes, and while you're about it, you might ask the chef to fry me an order of Channel sole."

"Very good, sir," the corporal replied, and filled a steaming mug of coffee for him.

Jared drank it gratefully, exhaling slowly and belching between sips. Ultimately he became aware that the half-dozen other officers at his table were all watching him, and he grinned feebly at them.

The captain who commanded Jared's troop was the first to speak. "Do I gather, Hale," he asked, a note of disbelief in his voice, "that you were actually out roistering last night?"

Jared's grin broadened. "One thing led to another, you might say," he replied. "I went gaming for an hour and became caught up in the spirit of the cards. There was a perfectly charming young lady who was wishing me luck by sitting beside me as I played, and since I won for a change, I felt the least I could do was offer her some private entertainment afterward. You know how it is." He finished his coffee, and the corporal, looking sympathetic, appeared and refilled his mug.

His dumbfounded colleagues looked at each other.

Again the captain broke the silence. "You're amazing, Hale," he said. "In case you don't realize it, the colonel is trying to teach you a lesson by having you spear a hard-boiled egg at the review for His Majesty. It won't go well for you when you fail, as you surely must know. Yet you've deliberately made almost impossibly long odds even longer. Your hands are shaking, you know."

Jared's food arrived, and he took a deep breath, then began to eat, slowly and rather experimentally at first, and when the food apparently sat well, with increasing gusto. "I don't advise any of you to feel sorry for me, my friends," he said. "I assure you I'll have steady hands and a firm grip on the reins when I'm in the saddle."

Again they exchanged glances, and the consensus was that Lieutenant Hale was right. Somehow he was endowed with remarkable recuperative powers, and those who knew him best were convinced that he would make good his boast.

One or two of the junior officers at the table looked dubious, however, and their lack of faith infuriated Jared. "If anyone doubts that I shall spear the egg, as I have been commanded to do, I'll be glad to oblige him with a wager. For any amount, gentlemen. But if you're going to bet, let's make it worth our time and set a minimum limit of one hundred guineas."

The sum was enormous, as he well knew, and the doubtful officers backed down hastily.

By the time Jared had finished his breakfast and mounted the stairs to his own quarters to don his dress uniform for the review, he was almost completely recovered. His eyes were clear, the color in his face had returned to normal, and his step was steady. The night's excesses were forgotten, and he was prepared to go ahead with

20

the extraordinarily difficult assignment he had been given.

A reviewing stand had been erected at one end of the regimental parade ground. The hard wooden benches, however, were considered unsuitable for King George II, so a leather armchair had been placed in the center of the first row of seats for his use.

The arrival of the royal party created a flurry of excitement, and King George, duly attired in his full-dress uniform of colonel in chief of the Royal Dragoons, was conducted by Sir Harry Barber to the seat of honor. Sir Harry found it difficult to converse with His Majesty because the king, like his Hanoverian father before him, felt far more comfortable speaking German than he did wrestling with the intricacies of the English language. In fact, most members of the party that had accompanied him were Hanoverian rather than English nobles; George II preferred their company for the simple reason that he could speak with them easily and fluently.

The review began, and the regiment of Royal Dragoons passed smartly in review, with the king standing as he took the salute.

Then the formalities ended and the entertainment began. The officers and men who had been assigned the task of slicing melons with their sabers galloped in two waves down the field, with those in each row striking in unison at the melons that had been placed on the ground for them. Not one missed his target, and although the spectacle was not new, King George was pleased and applauded politely.

"Kindly inform His Majesty," Colonel Barber said to a German-speaking chamberlain, "that he is about to witness what we hope will be an exceptional and unusual event. A lieutenant of the dragoons will attempt the singular feat of trying to spear a hard-boiled egg on the point of his saber while riding at full gallop."

The chamberlain translated his words, and a grin appeared on the broad, fleshy face of George II. He chuckled appreciatively and settled back in his chair, obviously eager to witness this odd entertainment.

A sergeant came onto the parade ground carrying a hard-boiled egg, which he presented for the king's inspection.

George turned it over in his pudgy hand, still chuckling, and then returned it to the sergeant, who peeled it and balanced it sideways atop an eggcup, which he placed on the ground about fifty feet in front of the king.

Lieutenant Hale rode out onto the parade ground looking as though what he was about to do were an ordinary occurrence that required no special skills. He drew his saber and saluted the king with a flourish, then resheathed the weapon and cantered off to the far end of the parade ground, his expression and the way he carried himself plainly demonstrating that he was completely self-assured and in no way concerned about the outcome of the stunt he intended to perform.

Only his fellow officers who knew him best were aware of the subtle transformation that took place in his attitude. His humor vanished, and although he still seemed at ease, his apparent relaxation was deceptive. He was devoting his full powers of concentration to the task at hand, and he studied the egg perched atop the tiny cup as he drew his saber again and twirled it above his head.

Suddenly he sprang into action, and as he spurred swiftly into a full gallop, there was no doubt in the mind of any member of his audience that he was a superb horseman. He had full control of his mount as he thundered down the length of the parade ground, heading straight for King George II.

At the appropriate moment Jared's sword flashed in a downward swoop, and to the amazement and delight of the entire royal party, he reined in smartly before the reviewing stand, saber held aloft to demonstrate that he had indeed speared the egg, which was now impaled on the blade.

Sir Harry Barber, joining in the applause, didn't know whether to be overjoyed or chagrined. His subordinate had performed superbly, but the lesson that the active head of the regiment had tried to teach the young lieutenant was totally lost.

The entertainment, however, had not yet ended. Urging his mount to a sedate walk, Jared approached the king's leather chair and extended the hard-boiled egg on the end of his saber. "Would Your Majesty care for a bite?" he inquired politely. "I'm afraid I can't offer you any salt with it, although the taste is much improved by salt."

"*Nein, danke!*" His Majesty appeared overcome with laughter.

Looking regretful, Jared brought the point of the saber to his own mouth and nibbled on the hard-boiled egg.

George II laughed so hard that he wept. *"Wo sind Sie gestern abend gewesen?"*

A chamberlain hastened to translate. "His Majesty," he said, "is inquiring as to your whereabouts last evening, Lieutenant."

Somehow the monarch had divined that Jared had engaged in a dissolute evening, and the young man had the grace to flush.

The king again spoke through his chamberlain, who again translated. "His Majesty is not only proud of his ability to read character in those of his subjects whom he admires, but he offers his congratulations to you, Lieutenant, on a job brilliantly done."

In order to salute with his sword, Jared first had to eat the rest of the hard-boiled egg, and George II continued to roar appreciatively. Then, after saluting, Jared withdrew, and the review of the Royal Dragoons came to an end.

Jared had no opportunity to celebrate his triumph, however. Less than a quarter of an hour later he was summoned to Sir Harry Barber's office, and he entered and stood at attention, his spurs jangling.

"Sit down, Hale." The colonel waved him to a chair.

Something in his superior's attitude indicated that he was not as delighted as he might otherwise have been.

"I'm obliged," Sir Harry said, "to offer you

24

felicitations on behalf of the regiment and on behalf of myself."

"Thank you, sir," Jared said, and wondered why he felt no sense of accomplishment.

"I deliberately gave you a virtually impossible assignment," the colonel told him, "because I was anxious to drive home a point to you. Unfortunately you've succeeded where I felt positive you'd fail, and in so doing you've destroyed my purpose."

Jared wanted to laugh, but a look at his superior's stern face convinced him he would be wise to contain his merriment.

The colonel sat back in his chair and looked earnestly at the young man. "Hale," he said, "you have natural endowments, and you've exhibited talents that are very rare. You have qualities that—when you bother to control them—are enviable in an officer. With the exercise of even a little self-discipline, it would be almost inevitable that in years to come you would end up sitting behind this desk."

"That's very kind of you, sir," Jared murmured.

"I'm not being kind," Sir Harry declared. "Far from it. In fact, if you must know the unfortunate truth, your conduct is such that you're heading toward certain ruin, sure self-destruction!"

Jared felt as though he had been slapped across the face, but his expression did not change, and he continued to regard his superior with a half smile on his lips.

"You've acquired a most notorious reputation in every sense of the word," Sir Harry continued.

25

"You're known throughout London as a reckless cardplayer who squanders huge sums of money that he can ill afford to lose. You've acquired a dreadful name for yourself among the ladies, so that no woman of stature would risk her reputation by being seen in public with you. And you've acquired dubious renown as a swordsman who has an insatiable bloodthirst. If His Majesty should learn of your penchant for dueling, I regret to say that you'll not only lose your commission in the dragoons instantly, but you'll be required to pay a very severe penalty under the law as well. Don't think your performance today is going to guarantee you a degree of royal protection that enables you to do what you please, where you please, and when you please to do it."

"I understand the point that you're making, sir," Jared said dryly.

The colonel looked at him intently. "Why are you behaving so outrageously, Hale?" he asked, almost pleading. "Why are you purposely squandering your chances for a brilliant future and assuring yourself of disgrace and failure?"

Jared did not quite know what to reply. Under no circumstances could he admit to Colonel Barber—or anyone else—that he was being driven and pursued by inner devils who had given him no peace since his father's disgrace and suicide and his mother's subsequent death. It was hard for him to admit even to himself that he had been robbed of all ambition and of all desire to do what society expected of him. What had happened to his parents had scarred his soul, and his life had been permanently changed as a result. That was,

26

however, his own very private secret, and he would never disclose it to anyone.

"Sir," he said, "I have only one life to live, and I'm afraid I must live it in my own way. If I can't enjoy each day and each night for its own sake, I see no point in human existence."

Sir Harry Barber knew it was useless to continue the conversation. Jared obviously would never live up to his potential as an officer, or as a human being.

CHAPTER TWO

Wilmington, a sleepy agricultural port on the Delaware River, dozed in the early spring sunlight. It was quiet everywhere, even on the river, where a brig was being loaded with corn and wheat being sent to England in return for precious currency from the mother country. The wits of Wilmington, like those of Dover and New Castle, the other principal towns of the area, often remarked that the state of quiet was not surprising, considering the fact that the very existence of the colony of Delaware was questionable.

The humor was not too exaggerated or farfetched. The people of the region, most of them farmers, liked to think of themselves as residents of Delaware—when in reality no such colony existed. Officially the region comprised the three administrative districts known as the Lower Counties of the royal colony of Pennsylvania. In fact, Delaware could not even call its name its own, having been named for one of the first gover-

27

nors of the neighboring colony of Virginia, Thomas West, Lord de la Warr.

In practice, to be sure, Delaware went its own way, paying neither taxes nor fealty of any kind to Pennsylvania. It raised its own militia and was developing its own system of roads, its own rules for distribution of land, and its own base of taxation.

Mostly country folk who lived by working the land day in and day out, the people of Delaware knew little excitement, and just about anything out of the ordinary aroused their interest. Certainly the sight of Caroline Murtagh created an immediate stir in the entire dock area when she made her appearance—but then Mistress Murtagh was well worth the interest she created.

Even those who knew her as a respectable married woman—the wife of Osman Murtagh, a wealthy local planter—had to admit she was unusually striking. Surely her beauty was incontestable. Tall and willowy, with broad shoulders and an incredibly tiny waist, she had long, wheat-blond hair that, when let down, fell below her waist, and her chiseled features were set off by a pair of luminous blue eyes that never failed to disturb any man on whom her gaze was fixed. She held herself proudly, as befitted an English heiress and wife of a leading colonial, yet her dignified bearing was always endowed with a natural and effortless grace.

Only a few who saw her, however, realized there was far more to Caroline Murtagh than the very attractive young lady who met the eye.

Though it was no secret that her husband was

overly fond of strong drink, it was not generally known that, as a result of his intemperance, she alone had managed their considerable estate for quite a long time—and managed it efficiently. She made good use of her staff of indentured servants, whom she treated sufficiently evenhandedly that they were loyal to her in return and worked more diligently than did most bonded servants. Also a shrewd judge of prices, she consistently managed to run the farm at a substantial annual profit; and yet it was said of her that she always kept her word and never cheated anyone with whom she did business out of so much as a ha'penny.

Dressed for travel in a plumed hat, a cloak thrown back across her shoulders, and beneath it a gown of yellow silk that rippled as she walked, showing off her perfectly proportioned figure to good advantage, she was followed by several indentured servants carrying her leather traveling boxes.

All activity on the docks came to an abrupt halt as Caroline Murtagh approached the brig. The farmers, who had been conversing quietly as they watched their produce being loaded into the hold of the ship, broke off their talk and surreptitiously followed her every move with their eyes. Crew members, being somewhat less reserved, stared equally hard but were far less subtle about their interest. Even the ship's mate, who stood on the quarterdeck, forgot his manners and blinked at the woman.

Caroline Murtagh pretended to be totally unaware of the commotion she caused. It was true she was accustomed to the reaction; everywhere she went males invariably greeted her in the same way.

What they failed to realize was that behind her expressionless facade, she was seething. How she hated them! How she loathed and despised all men! Without exception, they were all the same. They wanted only to use and abuse a woman sexually, and they cared nothing about her as a fellow human being!

Her experience was responsible for her bitterness, as she well knew. She had grown to womanhood in Cornwall, within sight of the sea, reared by a doting, well-to-do father, whom she had worshiped. He had arranged her marriage to Osman Murtagh, and even though he had died soon thereafter, leaving his entire fortune to his daughter and son-in-law, Caroline had never forgiven him.

Surely he must have known the true nature of the man he had persuaded her to marry. It was inconceivable that he could have been so naive, so ingenuous, that he was totally blind to the wickedness of the man who'd become her husband!

This, however, was not a moment to be thinking such things. She saw the ship's captain, who had been a guest at her home, approaching across the deck, and she assumed her public personality. As he removed his bicorn hat and bowed deeply before her, she gave him her most devastating smile.

"Mistress Murtagh! Your servant, ma'am!" He extended a hand and helped her across the short gang-plank onto the main deck of his ship.

"How good to see you again, Captain," Caroline said politely.

"You're alone, I see," Captain Arlegh said. "I hope nothing amiss has happened to Master Murtagh."

She shook her head and smiled sweetly. "Not at all," she said. "He had some private business to which he had to attend, and he'll be joining us here at any moment." She refrained from saying that the "private business" was nothing more than a visit to a local tavern for several drinks of the strong rum on which he depended so heavily.

The relieved captain directed a bo'sun's mate to attend the stowing of Caroline's luggage, and the sailor immediately led the indentured servants off down the deck.

"Your basket of fruit and other delicacies arrived a short time ago, and I've taken the liberty of having it held for you in the galley," Captain Arlegh said. "You can call on the cook for whatever you like."

"That's very kind of you, sir," she murmured.

He was proud of his ship and took his time leading her to her cabin, pausing every few feet to show off one or another feature of the vessel.

At last they came to her cabin. The indentured servants had just finished stowing her belongings beneath the bed; and pulling off their stocking caps, they wished her a safe and pleasant voyage, then withdrew.

After Captain Arlegh also took his leave, Caroline was alone in the cabin, and removing her cloak, which she hung on a peg that protruded from a bulkhead, she examined the quarters more intently.

The bunk, which emerged like a shelf from an inner bulkhead, was far bigger than she had expected. In fact, it was easily big enough to accommodate two people—and that, she thought, was certainly no blessing. There were also two small chairs in the cabin, both of them apparently nailed or screwed to the deck, and there was a writing table that folded out of the way when not in use. There were two oil lamps in permanent brackets attached to the outer bulkhead and, to her delight, a large, heavily shuttered porthole— apparently at one time used as a gunport. She went to it and with some difficulty forced it open, and knew at once that she would have a splendid view when the brig put to sea. But then something else caught her eye: It was her husband, coming on board, and she immediately lowered the shutter and braced herself.

A few moments later Osman Murtagh came into the cabin, which seemed to shrink in his presence. He was a great bear of a man, as dark as his wife was fair, with long arms, a barrel chest, and thighs and legs as sturdy as oak trees. He ran a hamlike hand through his black hair as he grinned at her.

"I seem to have lost my hat on my way to the waterfront," he said thickly, "but no matter."

"No matter, indeed," Caroline replied. "You have others in your luggage, and you won't really need them until we arrive in London."

"That's true," he replied brightly. "Besides, as long as I don't run out of rum, I'll be all right."

There was no chance that he would run out of rum, she thought bitterly.

"I couldn't, for the life of me, remember," he said, "whether I packed enough liquor for this voyage."

He had taken enough with him, she reflected, to last several ordinary people on a trip around the world.

"Anyway," he went on, "I decided not to take any chances, so I bought me a couple of kegs of rum at a Wilmington tavern—they're coming on board right now. And the captain is a gentleman, a real gentleman. He's actually finding space for both the kegs in the hold, and he's promised me that when I run out of rum here, he'll have the kegs brought to me one at a time."

"That's very obliging of him," she murmured.

Weaving unsteadily on his feet, Osman reached inside his swallow-tailed coat and produced a long and elegant silver flask, from which he removed the stopper and drank greedily. "Ah, that's good," he said, smacking his lips, then suddenly looking stricken as he remembered his manners. "So sorry. Would you care to join me in a little drink, my dear?"

There was nothing Caroline desired less, but still she took care to reply politely, "No, thank you."

His face fell, and then he suddenly became belligerent. "I might have known," he muttered. "Your Ladyship is too good to drink with us common folk."

Caroline was careful to make no reply, and in fact her expression remained quite unchanged, as though she hadn't heard a word he'd said. Her great fear was the nightmare that would inevitably spring into being if Osman drunkenly concluded that he'd been insulted and had to avenge his honor. Under no circumstances could she allow that to occur—not that she had that much choice in the matter; but to the extent that she could control it, she would do her best.

"I think we're about to sail," she said brightly, long experience with him having taught her to change the subject smoothly. "I think I'll go out on deck and watch us cast off. Would you like to come with me?"

He yawned, shook his head, and sat down heavily on the broad bunk. "I'm feeling a mite sleepy," he said. "I think I'll have me a little nap before supper." He fell back onto the bed.

"That's a good idea," Caroline said quickly, removing the coverlet and placing a pillow beneath his head, then struggling with his boots until she had removed them. She would have undone the stock at his throat, too; but by the time she had taken off his boots, he was already snoring, and she wanted to take no chance of awakening him before he drifted off into a deep sleep.

Relieved beyond measure because what she dreaded most had been postponed once again, Caroline knew that when Osman finally awakened—probably not until morning—he would feel the effects of the previous day's liquor so markedly that he would drink to excess again very quickly. This besotted cycle would be repeated for many days to come, during which time she could enjoy a peaceful reprieve and know that her worst fears would not materialize.

Ducking her head, she left the cabin and quietly closed the door behind her. As she came out onto the quarterdeck, she once again assumed what she liked to think of as her public expression—a look of self-controlled, amused tolerance of the world.

The captain and his mate both became aware of her presence instantly and tipped their hats to her.

She smiled and inclined her head in return, a perfect lady making a perfectly refined gesture.

As she strolled to the railing, she knew that all eyes on shore were fastened on her, but she pretended once again to be totally unaware of the stir that she had created, and she looked out into the distance.

The lines that held the ship to her berth were released, and the unfurled topsails filled as the vessel edged away from the dock. Slowly, the brig moved out into the broad waters of the Delaware River, which would carry them swiftly into Delaware Bay and then past Cape Henlopen into the open Atlantic beyond. Gulls were already circling overhead, and Caroline knew from previous voyages that they would accompany the brig far out to sea, happily living on the slops that the cook threw overboard each day.

The figures on the dock faded gradually and became smaller. A salt breeze was blowing off the bay, and the fresh, clean smell filled Caroline's nostrils as the breeze sent her hair flying behind her and pressed the thin fabric of her dress against her body, making every line of her superb figure stand out clearly.

She was going home to England, but the prospect gave her little pleasure. This was strictly a business trip, a journey to acquire more indentured servants, whose services she desperately needed on the farm. Besides, home—if she could call it that—was the large and comfortably furnished farmhouse that had been built in Delaware under her direction. But she could take little pride in that accomplishment, either.

Forcing herself to face the truth, she knew that her marriage to Osman Murtagh, constantly shadowed by the numbing fear of the nightmare that haunted her and that too often became reality, had soured her existence, and that no matter how successful and self-reliant she became, she found no joy in life.

For Caroline, the first weeks of the voyage across the Atlantic were a welcome relief from the daily routine of her life in Delaware.

She saw the sea in all its restless, changing moods. One day the water was a sparkling blue-green beneath a cloudless sky, with gentle breezes rippling the sails; the very next day it was wild and angry, with huge whitecapped waves causing the little vessel to bob like a helpless cork in the fury of a gale. No matter what the weather, however, Caroline thoroughly enjoyed the voyage. She spent the better part of each day alone— joining the ship's officers, and sometimes her husband, only at meals. The rest of the time she remained immersed in one of the many books she had brought with her, or stared out across the endless sea.

Valiantly trying to overcome the bitter frustration caused by the strange turns her life had taken, she made a supreme effort to become philosophical. She was still exceptionally attractive, as she well knew, and she had amply demonstrated her abilities as a business-woman. Her dowry had gone into the purchase of the farm in the Lower Counties, and she had transformed the venture into an extremely profitable operation. In the process she had won the unstinting admiration of every citizen of stature in the region that called itself Delaware.

All the same, her hatred of men was so intense that it often threatened to overwhelm her. She realized that logically her attitude made no sense. It was wrong to condemn all members of the sex because of the swinish behavior of the man who, unfortunately, was her husband.

She was grateful, at least, that she saw very little of Osman on the voyage. He busied himself with his casks of rum and began drinking as soon as he roused himself from his long night's stupor, usually shortly before noon. He missed as many meals in the mess as he attended, and by now the captain and the two mates surely knew that he was suffering from a severe addiction to alcohol. But they behaved liked gentlemen, and at no time did they mention the subject to Caroline.

She was grateful, too, that he was drinking so heavily that he had no time left to bother with her. There was at least that much to be said for his conduct.

One evening, like so many before it, Caroline was reading in bed, lulled by the gentle rocking of the ship and soothed by the creaking of her timbers. She was thoroughly relaxed and was enjoying a book.

Assuming that her husband was off drinking somewhere on the ship, she had left the door unbolted and had dismissed him from her mind. The story she was reading absorbed her, and she was more at ease than she had been in many days.

Suddenly the door burst open, and Osman's rugged body filled the frame.

Caroline took one quick look at him and knew from his belligerent stance, his legs apart, his thumbs hooked into his breeches, his eyes reddened and watery from drink, that the nightmare she had dreaded for so long was coming to life again.

Catching her breath, she reacted instinctively, without thinking, and drew her peignoir closed above the low décolletage of her nightgown.

"You're a lady, eh? You're too damn good for me, is that it?" He kicked the door shut behind him and began to lurch toward the bed.

Caroline shrank back beneath the covers. There would be no escape and she knew it, but still she was totally unprepared for the ordeal that she faced.

As always, the strong odor of rum on his breath nauseated her. Osman chuckled and, bending down, gripped her shoulders in his huge, powerful hands. His fingers bit through the thin fabric of her peignoir, and she knew that there would be black-and-blue marks on her body the following day. But that was the least of her concerns.

All at once he released her with his right hand

and cuffed her hard across the side of the head. He delivered one blow, then another, then yet a third, and the light of the oil lamp in the cabin seemed to explode before her eyes.

Long experience had taught her that if she did anything to protect herself, she would enrage him all the more and he would become increasingly dangerous. So she tolerated his abuse in silence. But when he began to shake her violently like a rag doll, she became genuinely frightened. "Please, Osman," she stammered, "I'm doing nothing to oppose you."

He laughed loudly, coarsely. "No," he said. "You're not dong a blame thing now, are you? That's because I'm going to teach you a lesson that you'll never forget."

She knew the nature of the "lesson" all too well and did her best to harden herself to the inevitable. But it was impossible not to feel a surge of loathing for this brutal, bestial creature.

Still laughing coarsely, his contempt obvious, he reached for the collar of her peignoir and night-gown and began to rip away the fabric.

Shamed beyond measure, Caroline knew better than to protest or raise her hand to halt him.

Osman did not stop until she was stretched completely nude on the bed below him. Muttering an obscenity under his breath, he stripped off his own clothes and threw himself at her, landing atop her with such force that he literally drove the air from her lungs.

Before Caroline could recover, he was making crude, violent love to her. The nightmare went on and on until it reached its horrid, inevitable climax. Her flesh crawled, and she prayed for release. But still there was no release. He seemed thoroughly to enjoy his violent mistreatment of her, and occasionally he added insult to physical injury by chortling and cursing her anew under his breath.

The physical pain Caroline endured was intense, but it was nothing compared to the mental anguish she was compelled to undergo. Osman was making a mockery of their marriage, a mockery of the very idea of marriage, and she was powerless to halt him, unable to do anything that would end the agony. She had never known it was possible for a husband to rape his wife, but she was sure that that was exactly the case every time she was forced to suffer Osman's intimacies.

Her whole world had narrowed to the brute who was having his way with her. The odor of rum was so strong that it almost suffocated her, and she was so distraught that she wanted to scream, to tear at his flesh with her long fingernails and make him suffer as he was causing her to suffer.

But she knew that if she dared to lift a hand against him he would become even more violent and abusive. She was fortunate, she told herself, that he hadn't marked her face with blows or broken her nose or her jaw. She would be wise to tolerate the horrendous experience as best she could, and eventually it would pass.

Finally Osman Murtagh was done. He climbed clumsily off his wife, then stumbled around the cabin as he fumbled with his clothes, dressing himself again.

Caroline took pains not to glance in his direction, and slowly, inch by inch, she drew the covers over herself to conceal her nudity. Her degradation was complete.

The bleary-eyed Osman stared at his wife, then spat in her direction and staggered out of the cabin into the rainy night. He slammed the door behind him, and the sound seemed to echo through the ship.

Somehow Caroline found the strength to haul herself wearily to her feet and to go to the door, which she bolted with a trembling hand. She knew what would happen next and was in no way surprised when she vomited into the slop jar.

The ship's cook had earlier prepared an enclosed tub of hot water for her, and she now lowered herself into it, not bothering to check to see whether it was cool enough for her to tolerate. Picking up a crock of yellow soft soap and a rough-textured washcloth, she scrubbed herself furiously, as though trying to wipe away the memory of the shame to which she had been subjected.

After drying herself, she opened a leather box, from which she removed another nightgown and robe. She donned them, shuddering violently and rubbing her arms, which felt lifeless and numb.

Shoving open the porthole so she could discard her torn peignoir and nightgown and empty the slop jar into the ocean, she listened briefly in the fog and drizzle. But she could hear no sign of Osman on deck. Quietly she removed the bolt from the door. His anger was spent now, and she wanted to do nothing that would again arouse him and make him violent.

Caroline extinguished the oil lamp, then

climbed beneath the covers and drew them over her head. She wanted to weep, but the tears would not come. She was too far gone even to cry.

Neither Caroline, the ship's officers, nor any member of the crew had the slightest idea of what befell Osman Murtagh. Weaving precariously from side to side as the ship pitched through rolling seas, he made his way to the taffrail, where he peered out over the stern into the fog. The mate and the helmsman at the foot of the quarterdeck were unaware of his presence and had no idea that he was only fifteen or twenty feet behind them.

As Osman leaned against the rail to disentangle his foot from a coil of rope he had stepped in, the ship dipped suddenly and violently, toppling him into the Atlantic below. Fortunately for him, his right leg was still entangled in the rope, which was attached to an anchor buoy stored nearby.

The shock of hitting the icy water numbed Osman, making it impossible for him to think clearly. But he reacted instinctively, pulling furiously on the rope until his fingers closed around one end of the buoy.

Somehow he managed to secure himself to the frail float, and he lay there panting and shivering. Not until much later did he realize that the ship's stern lanterns, barely visible at best in the fog, had faded away and left him to his own devices in the Atlantic Ocean.

Caroline's first feeling was one of great relief when she awakened the next morning to find the place beside her in bed empty. She was glad to be spared the ordeal of facing her husband again, and she assumed that, as had happened to him so often in the past, he had lost consciousness elsewhere and would reappear sometime before noon, much the worse for wear.

She dressed slowly, with care, and her obstinate pride compelled her to select an attractive silk gown that was none too appropriate for shipboard life. Staring at her reflection in a looking glass as she brushed her snarled, knotted hair, she saw with dismay the deep smudges beneath her blue eyes. Then, steeling herself for the next encounter with her husband, she went off to breakfast.

The ship's mess cabin was unoccupied, she was relieved to find. The confrontation with Osman, it seemed, would be postponed at least for a time.

The cook noted her arrival and hastily prepared her breakfast—broiled salted fish and a slab of toasted, freshly made bread, on which he had spread honey. She was immensely grateful to the cook, who knew she disliked the hard biscuits the ship's crew customarily ate at sea.

As Caroline began to eat, one of the mates came in, paused, staring at her for an instant, and then hastily departed again.

She thought his conduct peculiar but attached no special significance to it.

A few minutes later Captain Arlegh appeared, and he was far more jovial than usual. He sat opposite her and accepted a small beer from the cook, which he sipped slowly as he chatted.

He was a big eater, and Caroline was surprised. "Is that all you're having for breakfast, Captain?" she asked, "I hope you're not ill."

"No, indeed," he replied. "As a matter of fact, I had my breakfast some time ago, and I've come back here just to keep you company."

"That's very kind of you," she said, somewhat puzzled.

The captain spoke casually, almost too casually. "Master Murtagh didn't come to breakfast with you," he observed.

Caroline shook her head but did not elaborate.

"He doesn't happen to be in your cabin, either, I take it," he said.

It was clear to her that Captain Arlegh was fishing for information, and she saw no reason to refrain from admitting at least part of the truth. "I haven't seen my husband since last evening," she said, "when he returned to the cabin for a short time. He was under the influence of his rum, I'm afraid, so he didn't make too much sense." She forced a strained smile. "I suspect you'll find he's fallen asleep in some odd corner of the ship."

Captain Arlegh braced himself. "I regret to inform you, Mistress Murtagh," he said, "that we've already conducted a thorough search of the entire vessel, and Master Murtagh is nowhere to be seen. Not only has he disappeared, but so has one of the anchor buoys that we keep on the aft deck for a sea anchor. I can only assume that he vanished overboard at some time during the night."

Caroline's eyes widened, and a hand crept slowly to her mouth. But she made no comment. It would be wrong, she knew—terribly wrong— to admit that she felt as though a tremendous burden had been lifted from her. She wanted to

44

shout for joy but knew it would be unseemly, so she remained quiet.

"I can only assume," the captain said gravely, "that he fell overboard by accident while he was intoxicated. I've entered the information into the ship's log accordingly. I'm terribly sorry to be forced to inform you of this, ma'am, but I know of no other way. Please accept my sincere condolences."

Averting her face so he would have no chance to see the expression in her eyes, Caroline bowed her head in response. She knew she had to say something, and she searched her mind frantically before she finally found the right note to strike. "Perhaps, Captain, you'll be good enough to remove my husband's clothing boxes from my cabin."

"Of course, ma'am," he replied, reasoning that she would find the sight of them too painful.

"Perhaps you'll donate the contents, on my behalf, to the indigent seamen's fund," she suggested.

"By all means," he said.

Caroline felt lighthearted, actually giddy. She was removing Osman Murtagh from her life for all time and was ridding herself of all reminders of him. She had never consciously wished ill to any other person, but she knew that her prayers had been answered and that, as a widow, a whole new life was opening before her.

Arthur and Alvin Trevor were fishermen who made their home with their mother, Mary, in the Isles of Scilly, about thirty miles into the open

45

Atlantic off Land's End, the westernmost point in Cornwall and indeed in all of England. The Trevors were dour, silent men who practiced their craft assiduously and with great skill, earning a humble yet sufficient living, as befitted men who tended to business and expected few pleasures in life.

Mary Trevor was cut from the same bolt of cloth as were her sons, and her vegetable gardens were envied by her neighbors, who knew the back-breaking labor she put into growing the plants.

She was on her hands and knees in the carrot patch, weeding, when she looked up and saw her sons approaching. Alvin, the elder and huskier of the pair, was carrying the large, unconscious body of a man dressed in wet rags.

The woman's expression remained unchanged. "Be he alive or dead?" she demanded.

Alvin, as usual, wasted no words. "He's alive, Ma. Worse for wear because he's been battered by the sea, where we found him, wrapped to a buoy. But he's big and strong, and with a little care I think he'll be just fine."

The woman nodded, and a pleased expression crept into her hard eyes. "It may be," she said, "that the Almighty has listened to my prayers and has heeded them. Put him in the hired hand's room in the barn."

Alvin carried the unconscious Osman Murtagh to the barn and deposited him on the hard, thin mattress.

After a time, Mary Trevor appeared with a container filled with a rich, hot soup—a broth of beef and chicken into which she had cut up a number of vegetables as well. Propping up the unconscious man to a sitting position, she pried open his mouth and began to spoon in the soup.

Murtagh made no move, remaining barely conscious until he had unwittingly consumed about half the soup. Then he stirred and began to cough.

"Here, now, mind your manners," Mary Trevor said impatiently. "This broth will do ye no good unless ye get it inside ye. Spill it and it will be wasted."

He opened his eyes, saw his benefactress, and slowly took in the scene. The last thing he remembered was drifting interminably, clutching his frail raft, and he could not immediately grasp that he had been rescued. "Where—where am I?" he asked hoarsely.

"My sons be fishermen," the woman said, "and they brought you ashore here on the Isles of Scilly. You're off the coast of Cornwall, and lucky you are to be alive."

Her sons squeezed into the room and stood behind her, looking at the rescued man through narrowed eyes.

Osman Murtagh didn't know why he reacted as he did, but a wave of fear and discomfort swept over him. "I'm much obliged to you, gentlemen," he said. "You've saved my life."

"You'll have a chance to repay us, never fear." A faint smile showed at the corners of Mary Trevor's thin mouth.

Her sons chuckled appreciatively.

"We be poor folk who earn our living by the sweat of our brows," she went on, "and the same goes for you. You will need food to survive, and from the looks of ye, ye have a good appetite. You'll need new clothes, instead of the rags you're wearing, to cover your naked body. All of them things cost money. So you'll oblige us by workin' in the vegetable garden and relieving me of a chore that I have little time for of late."

Osman was moved to protest. "When I return to my own home," he said, "I can arrange to have funds transferred to you as a reward for rescuing me, and I'll always be grateful—"

"You'll have your chance to prove it," the woman interrupted, and raising her walking stick of roughhewn oak, she struck him as hard as she could across the soles of his bare feet.

Osman was stunned by her savage assault, and his pain was so great that he curled himself up in fear, unable to speak.

She held the walking stick shoulder-high, ready to strike him again if she felt it necessary. "You'll do what you're told," she said. "The Almighty sent ye to help me in my garden, and that's what you're going to do. After you've earned back what we have to spend on ye, we'll talk about you earnin' enough funds to pay for transportation back to your own home. Until then, you'll do as you're told!"

Weakened by his long ordeal on the raft, Osman Murtagh finally sank back onto the hard mattress. At least until he regained his strength, he was at the mercy of this woman and her brawny sons and would be required to do as they bid. The prospects for returning to his own home in the distant New World were remote, and for now he would have to be content with scheming and planning a way to escape.

CHAPTER THREE

The fragrance of Caroline Murtagh's scent obliterated, at least temporarily, the more pungent odors that usually filled the office of Newgate Prison's warden, and Harold Simpson was grateful. His life had been dreary in the three years since he had been appointed warden, but a few more visitors like Mistress Murtagh would cause him to reconsider resigning and leaving London for a simple existence in a country cottage.

Warden Simpson, long an admirer of the ladies, well knew there weren't many like Caroline Murtagh, and the longer he studied her—only when she wasn't looking, of course—the more readily he admitted to himself that she was indeed a rare beauty. Surely she was as lovely as any lady-in-waiting at the court of King George II; and her delicious figure, with her full breasts that she made little effort to conceal beneath her low-cut gown of fur-trimmed silk, literally left him aching with desire.

The warden's pulse quickened even more at the thought that she was single and, evidently, an heiress. It was unfortunate that she was also a colonial who lived in some godforsaken part of America known as Delaware, but that was her only drawback—aside from the undeniable fact that she was proving herself far too stubborn for the taste of any man.

49

"Ma'am," he said, "I hope you'll accept my sympathies on your recent, sad loss of your husband."

If there was any subject on earth that Caroline had no desire to discuss, it was the disappearance at sea of Osman Murtagh—a stroke of good fortune that had freed her at last from a tyranny under which she had suffered untold agonies. She was simply too forthright and honest to accept an expression of sympathy for an incident that in actuality made her want to rejoice. Besides, the warden was a man—a member of the sex she despised. She decided to cut short his protestations. "I'm very busy today," she said curtly, "so I'll appreciate a return to the business at hand."

Harold Simpson knew when he was rebuffed, but he recovered quickly and spoke in soothing tones. "My dear Mistress Murtagh," he said in the elegant manner he adopted when addressing members of the aristocracy, "I sell five or six indentured servants a week, and I've yet to hear a complaint from the ladies and gentlemen who buy them from me. They trust my judgment, and I fill their needs."

Caroline's full-lipped smile was sweet, but her eyes remained cool. "I'm sure you're a man of discernment, Warden, or you wouldn't hold your post. My needs, however, are unusual, so I must rely on my own judgment."

Simpson tried in vain to hide his exasperation. "You have already seen seven prisoners, ma'am, the best of the crop. If you'd like to wait until next month, now, when His Majesty goes out to Hampton Court for the summer, we'll be sure to have a new assortment of cutpurses and the like. The constables are busy, I can tell you, when Londoners gather by the thousands to watch the king and his court go in procession to their barges on the Thames."

Caroline shook her head, and her blond curls danced. "I've arranged passage to the colonies on a ship that sails in less than a fortnight, and I can't wait for another. If I must, I suppose, I can visit the jails in Edinburgh and Glasgow, but I'd much prefer an English prisoner."

Simpson's professional pride was wounded, and he leafed through some papers on his cluttered desk. "I can offer you one more, but mind you, ma'am, I don't recommend him too highly."

She tapped her satin-slippered foot impatiently and waited.

"He's a rough one and not reliable. Jared Hale is his name, ma'am, and among other things he has an unsavory reputation with the ladies—"

"Why is he in Newgate?" she asked crisply.

The warden sighed. "First, he couldn't pay his debts at cards. Next, he lost his commission in the dragoons after fighting a duel with a gentleman who happened to be a close friend of the king's. Somehow the king found out, and—"

"Why did they fight?"

He found her interruptions irritating. "It was over a lady—who was no lady."

Caroline smiled. "He sounds a trifle better than the ordinary highwayman or cutpurse."

"He's a dragoon," Simpson said with a shrug. "Or he was. All they care about are horses and fighting—and in Hale's case, gambling and

51

wenching as well, if you'll excuse my bluntness, ma'am. A rogue in gentleman's clothing is what he is, pure and simple."

Caroline was neither shocked nor perturbed. "I've had a slight acquaintance with the type," she said cryptically. "You may send for him."

Simpson sighed and reached for the bell rope. In spite of Mistress Murtagh's many assets, he thought, he would hate to be an indentured servant in her employ.

A quarter of an hour later two burly assistant wardens accompanied the prisoner into the office. Jared Hale insolently ignored them and, although they pressed close to him on either side, seemed unaware of their existence.

What immediately alarmed Caroline was the amazing fact that the prisoner was wearing a sword. A reassuring glance from the warden, however, assuaged her worst fears, and she proceeded to study the prisoner more closely.

A tall, slender man in his late twenties, Jared Hale carried himself with an air of one accustomed from birth to the respect due the gentry. He held one hand lightly on the hilt of his sword, and although his white satin breeches, plum silk coat, and ruffled shirt were soiled, he somehow managed to look elegant. His black hair, beneath the hat he doffed politely to Caroline, was shaggy and unkempt, however, and the deep lines at the corners of his dark eyes indicated that his attitude might be something of a pose.

Jared realized that he had no one but himself to blame for his present plight. By ignoring the advice of his military superiors and his friends and refusing to change his ways, he had brought about his own downfall. But his pride was still intact and his spirit was unbroken, and the sight of an exceptionally attractive young woman in the warden's office did not fail to arouse his spirits.

Caroline immediately pressed a heavily scented handkerchief to her nose.

Jared bowed to her as he removed a grimy handkerchief from his own sleeve. "Accept my apologies, madame," he said, mixing gallantry with irony, "but the bathing and laundering facilities at this inn leave something to be desired. They're a trifle old-fashioned here, I regret to say."

Caroline gave no indication she had heard him. "Warden," she demanded, "how does it happen that a convicted prisoner carries a sword?"

"It's a common courtesy permitted gentlemen who become our—ah—guests," Simpson replied.

"Well said, Master Simpson!" Jared bowed again. "Did you receive my complaint that the beef stew—if that's what it is—has been inedible again for the past week?"

"We'll hire a new cook," the warden said dryly. "Well, ma'am?"

Caroline looked the former dragoon officer up and down.

Jared, puzzled at her interest, boldly inspected her in return.

"Apparently you know horses," she said.

He grinned. "I assure you, madame, that I would have been dismissed from my regiment far sooner if I hadn't. If you're thinking of buying a mount, I'd be delighted to advise you. I regret the inconvenience to you, but you'd have to bring him here. Warden Simpson doesn't permit me to leave the confines of this charming place."

His humor fell flat. "Are you familiar with farms?" she demanded.

Jared sobered momentarily. "I was reared on the estate of my father—God rest him—and I thank the Almighty he didn't wait around to see me squander his fortune and sink so low." He stared still harder at her. "Who are you, madame, and why do you question me?"

Caroline paid no attention. "He's quick-witted, too. That could be useful, Warden."

"A little too quick-witted, if you want the truth," Simpson muttered.

The woman frowned and, again pressing her handkerchief to her nose, moved closer to Jared. Before he quite realized what she was doing, she felt his biceps and bent to test the strength of his thigh. Hastily backing away again, she nodded to the warden. "He's more muscular than he appears," she said impersonally.

"Oh, he's strong. The courtyard bullies avoid him." Simpson plainly disapproved of her interest.

She turned back to Jared. "Open your mouth," she commanded.

He blinked, astonished.

One of the assistant wardens clamped his hand on the prisoner's jaw, prying it open. "Do as the lady says!" he roared.

Caroline examined the inside of the mortified prisoner's mouth. "He has all his teeth, too. Better

54

and better. Those who have lost them are inclined to be slovenly."

The assistant warden released Jared, who stood very still for a moment, rubbing his jaw. Anger and embarrassment had made him livid, but recent experience had taught him he would regret it if he gave in to his impulse to strike the man.

Caroline seemed totally unaware of his reaction. "What will he cost, Master Simpson?"

"One hundred pounds as a token payment on his debts, and fifteen shillings to the Crown for housing and feeding him."

"He's expensive."

"More by far than anyone else would pay," Simpson said. It made him uneasy to see the calculating look in Jared's eyes as he studied the young woman who was humiliating him.

"I'll take him," she said calmly. "Can you have him bathed, dressed in clean clothes, and delivered to me on board my brig in eleven days?"

"A bath will cost a thruppence extra, ma'am. As for clothes, we have none that—"

"I'll provide him with some. I'll send them to you with his ankle chain after I've had the plate engraved. I trust, Warden, that you attach them at no additional fee?"

"Of course, ma'am."

"Then everything is settled. I'll send you the money by messenger this afternoon." She started for the door.

Jared took a single step forward, making certain he did not venture beyond the reach of the watchful guards. "One moment, my sweet," he said. "I hate to see you lose a fat purse. But I've never yet played the stud for a fee, and I don't intend to begin now."

Caroline whirled, her eyes blazing with anger. In one movement she stepped in front of him and slapped him viciously across the mouth, cutting his upper lip with a huge ring of brilliants she wore on her middle finger.

He lost his self-restraint and would have slapped her in return if the assistant wardens had not caught his arms.

"Let's understand each other at once," Caroline said acidly. "For the next fifteen years you will be my indentured servant and will submit yourself to my authority in accordance with the laws governing such relationships. You will *not* be my lover."

Jared licked the blood from his lip.

"You will obey me in all things," she continued. "You will speak only when I wish, and you will address me as 'ma'am.' Instead of rotting here, you're being given an opportunity to make a new and useful life, and I expect you to show appropriate gratitude for the chance."

He said nothing and returned her gaze with mock deference.

Her slipper tapped on the floor. "Well?"

"Although I'm an involuntary partner in this arrangement," Jared said, "I gather you want a candid expression of my opinion, *ma'am.*" His face was coldly expressionless. "Rather than enter your employ, I would prefer a slow Newgate death. But I've been given no choice, and I accept my fate."

56

No matter what the weather, the main court-yard of Newgate was always crowded. All prisoners except condemned murderers were released from the over-crowded buildings that fanned out from the square like the spokes of a wheel, and everyone was relieved to escape for a time from the foul-smelling cells and corridors. The veterans said that more business was conducted in the courtyard than in the London beyond the walls of the prison, and that was not far from the truth.

Thieves and pickpockets wandered with seeming aimlessness through the dense throngs, paying particular attention to the new arrivals who still carried watches, fobs, and wallets. Prostitutes sauntered with the casual care of their profession, seeking men who received food from relatives or who were influential enough to sleep on real feather beds in rooms that well-bribed jailers kept unlocked at night. Highway-men exchanged information on post schedules and the peculiarities of traffic conditions on lonely stretches of rural roads. And the swindlers, who considered them-selves a breed apart, concocted schemes to bilk their fellow inmates of food, silver, and special privileges.

The beggars were everywhere, as were brawlers from Southwark, the slum area directly across the Thames from London. Members of both groups were penniless, forced to eat the slop served to the completely indigent, and were ignored by everyone else. Occasionally a Southwark gang threatened or even attacked a prisoner of standing, but these assaults had become relatively rare since the majority had banded together for the purpose of resisting such terror. On the rare occasions when riots did occur, the warden invariably blamed the Southwark element and punished the offenders by locking them in underground cells, giving them neither water nor food for as long as ten days at a time. Not even the most callous of Southwark toughs enjoyed such treatment, and the gangs had lost much of their spirit.

Debtors were in a class by themselves. Virtually none had ever committed criminal offenses or associated with lawbreakers. Most were middle-class merchants and shopkeepers whose businesses had been forced into bankruptcy, while a few were aristocrats whose appetites had exceeded their incomes. One was the younger son of an earl, another was a baronet, and several were knights. Regardless of their previous stations, the debtors formed a solid, united group. Refusing to mingle with any of the other prisoners except an occasional trollop, they remained aloof from Newgate's communal life, and even at noon did not go into the main courtyard but instead strolled up and down a short road leading into it, called Gallows Lane.

Jared Hale was the exception and consequently was regarded with misgiving by his fellow debtors. He gave fencing instructions to a young highwayman who paid for the lessons in cash, delivered lectures on horsemanship to a pair of professional gamblers in return for card tricks that someday might prove useful, and incurred the envy of every male prisoner in Newgate by engaging in an affair with a courtesan whose wealthy lover had bought her the use of a private cottage and each week sent her baskets of wine, roast meats, and other delicacies.

So when Jared Hale appeared on Gallows Lane one bright midday in early June, approaching from the direction of the courtesan's snug house, the other debtors greeted him with reserve, if not open hostility. He seemed impervious to snubs, however, and greeted the others jovially.

"Why so glum, milord?" he asked, slapping the earl's son on the back. "The wench down the road can be yours now, provided you can convince her you'll establish her in a suite in your father's palace—someday. And you, Master Babcock," he continued, turning to a wool manufacturer who had lost his business in an expanding French market, "I have good news for you. This very night you can move out of your hovel into the room I'm vacating—the room I won at dice six weeks ago."

The debtors, sensing that something out of the ordinary was taking place, clustered around him.

"Master Morton," Jared said to a gunsmith who constantly bewailed his inability to protect himself in a place filled with criminals. "I'm making you a handsome gift." Removing his sword and belt, he handed them to the man with a flourish. "You claim you can use a blade. You shall have more chances, I promise you, at Newgate than anywhere else on earth."

The gunsmith looked at the sword, then at Jared. "What do you want in return for this?"

"Nothing but your remembrance. Perhaps,

when your fortunes improve, you might want to make me one of those splendid pistols with the shaved French hairspring triggers."

Morton remained dubious. "Have you come into an inheritance?"

"You might call it that," Jared replied evasively. "I'm leaving Newgate within the hour."

The debtors responded with a chorus of congratulations and questions, but the gunsmith was still unconvinced. "If you're being released, you'll need a sword."

"Not that one," Jared said scornfully, determined to keep hidden at all costs the fact that in his new, lowly capacity he would not be permitted to own or carry weapons of any kind. "If you don't want it, Morton, I'll give it to someone else."

The gunsmith clutched the sword more tightly. "It's mine now," he said stridently, "and the rest of you are witnesses. It was a free gift."

Jared caught a glimpse of two assistant wardens shouldering through the crowd of prisoners in the main courtyard and knew they were coming for him. "Good-bye, my friends," he said hastily. "May all of you enjoy luck like mine." Waving, he made his way toward the guards.

"There you are, Hale," one of them said. "We've been looking all over the grounds for you."

"We've found each other, then, and I'm quite capable of walking without help, thank you." Jared avoided the man's grasp, knowing the watching debtors would realize he was still a prisoner if the guards laid hands on him.

The men escorted him to a building directly

behind the warden's house. There other staff members were waiting, and Jared was ordered to strip off his clothes. In spite of his protests they cut short his shoulder-length hair, then smeared his entire head and body with a mixture of ashes, pine tar oil, and a white soap that stung painfully when it was applied. They scrubbed him with brushes of hogs' bristles until his skin was raw, then poured bucket after bucket of cold water over him to rinse him clean.

Finally, when he thought his ordeal had ended, they stretched him out on a table, and a band of iron was fitted around his ankle. A poker was placed in the grate until it became red-hot and then was held against the open ends of the band, permanently joining them. The searing pain in Jared's ankle quickly shot up his leg, but he refused to give the guards the satisfaction of hearing him cry aloud, so he clamped his teeth together and endured the torture in silence. More water, which made a hissing sound when it struck the iron, was poured over his leg, and the pain gradually faded.

Jared stared down at the symbol of his degradation. It had become part of him, and he winced when he saw the words engraved on the outside of the band: *Hale, indentured servant. Property of Mistress Caroline Murtagh.* The punishment he had endured ever since his gaming debts had overwhelmed him had been mild, it appeared. His future, by comparison, now seemed hopeless.

He had deserved imprisonment for his debts, he knew, and although he loathed Newgate, he felt his punishment had been just. On the other hand, he believed his dismissal from the dragoons had been cruelly unfair. He was willing to concede he had been something of a sinner, but certainly he deserved a fate better than that now in store for him.

Glumly donning the rough smallclothes and the shirt and stockings of thick, stiff wool that had been provided for him, Jared shuddered at the first full realization that he had become the actual slave of a capricious, spoiled, and bad-tempered young woman.

CHAPTER FOUR

The brig *Leona Anne* rode at anchor in the Thames, a dozen crewmen high in the rigging of her square-rigged masts, tightening lines preparatory to sailing. A sturdy merchantman of two hundred and eighty tons, she had been freshly painted and, her holds filled almost to overflowing with cargo, sat low in the water. A crowd of ladies and gentlemen had gathered on the shore to bid farewell to some of her passengers, and they were laughing and chatting, sharing an adventure with those who were about to sail.

Two of Newgate's assistant wardens moved slowly down the wharf with a drab figure whose hands and legs were manacled, the clanking of his chains contrasting sharply with the merriment of the throng. Jared, unable to walk rapidly because of the weight of the metal, could not bring himself to look in the direction of the passengers and their guests. It was possible that he was acquainted with some of them, and his burdens were already too heavy.

When he saw the brig, however, he turned to one of his guards in bewilderment. All he had known was that he was being delivered to a vessel, and he had assumed that the young woman who had bought him as an indentured servant was sailing for a visit to France or the Low Countries. It was obvious, however, that a heavily laden brig the size of the *Leona Anne* was making a longer voyage.

"Where am I being taken?" he asked.

The assistant warden was amused. "The way I heard it, the New World."

Jared felt as though he had been kicked in the pit of the stomach by a horse. He knew very little about America and had no desire to learn more. As he understood it, the colonies were populated exclusively by lower-class merchants trying to make fortunes for themselves and by the poverty stricken who preferred to take their chances in a wild, raw land rather than starve in England. He braced himself. "Where, exactly? Boston, or Port Royal in the West Indian Islands, perhaps?" His knowledge of New World geography was vague.

The guard shrugged.

They were rowed out to the brig in a small boat by two sailors whose indifference indicated that they were not unaccustomed to having passengers delivered in chains. The manacles made it difficult for Jared to climb on board, and after he finally made his way up a ladder, afraid he might fall into the river at any moment, he awkwardly fell to one knee when he stepped onto the deck.

Someone laughed, and he looked up to see a pretty wench of about twenty, with long, dark hair.

A look of genuine contrition appeared in her green eyes, however. "I'm sorry," she said. "You must be Mistress Murtagh's."

He loathed the casual way she referred to him as someone's property and was about to retort when, as he pulled himself to his feet, he saw an iron band around her left ankle. She, too, was an indentured servant.

"I'm Polly White," she told him, and her fleeting smile was warm before she added to the assistant wardens, "I'll get Mistress Murtagh. She's expecting you."

One of the guards nudged Jared as they watched the girl, her hips swaying beneath her snug-fitting skirt, walk quickly down the deck. "Maybe," the man said, "a few weeks at sea won't be too bad."

The same thought had already crossed Jared's mind.

After a short wait Caroline Murtagh appeared, elegant in a gown and matching seagoing bonnet of ivory silk. The indentured girl followed at a respectful distance, and the guard grunted approval. "Better and better," he muttered.

In this Jared violently disagreed. Never had he despised any woman as much as he did this self-satisfied, coldly efficient creature who had purchased and treated him as though he were an animal on sale at a farmer's market.

Caroline took charge at once. "I was beginning to wonder whether Master Simpson intended to keep his bargain. We sail very shortly." She looked Jared up and down critically. "He looks much improved. You may take him below—Polly will show you the way—and discard the chains. The ship's master tells me he can't escape." She did not deign to address Jared directly.

With the indentured girl leading them, the assistant wardens escorted Jared to what appeared to be a small suite of cabins. One was unusually large, and a glimpse through the open door showed that boxes, packages, and several kegs marked "Grain Seed" were lashed to the bulkhead. Opposite it was a tiny cabin, scarcely larger than a clothes cupboard, containing nothing but a narrow bunk and, on a shelf lowered from the bulkhead, a pitcher of water and several bowls.

In the dark passage connecting the two cabins there was a pallet on the deck, and here the girl stopped. "This is it," she said, her clipped words revealing a strong trace of London's lower-class Cockney accent.

The men produced a hammer and a steel chisel and, showing small regard for Jared, broke the chains. Eager to return to the open, they departed at once.

Jared rubbed his chafed, bruised wrists.

"The brutes did the same to me," Polly said, showing him the yellowing marks on her own slender wrists. How well she remembered him— the dashing young officer, the man she had so admired one evening at the gaming establishment where she had been employed! Now they were in the same boat—literally as well as figuratively— and indentured to the same mistress. "They took mine off three days ago, and I'm still hurting. They don't care how they treat you."

"Were you at Newgate?"

She nodded. "But not for the reason you think. I worked as a decoy, you might say, for some friends who earned their living sharing the riches of old lechers with fat wallets." Her quick smile was infectious. "But one night there were three constables, bold as you please." She shuddered. "I hated Newgate."

"I don't think that what's ahead will be much better."

"Oh, she's not so bloody awful. I've been with her a week now, and she only slaps me when I deserve it."

The cut Caroline had made on Jared's lip with her ring had not entirely healed.

"I know all about you," Polly said, leaning indolently against the bulkhead. "Everybody at Newgate talked about you, and I'd never have thought we'd belong to the same mistress."

"It's enchanting," he said acidly.

The girl looked at him blankly.

Obviously sarcasm was wasted on her, so he turned to more practical matters. "Where are we going?"

"America."

"It's a rather large land. Do you know anything more specific?"

"Yes. Mistress Murtagh owns a plantation in a colony called Delaware."

The future would be even worse than he had feared. Boston and Philadelphia were semicivilized places, from what he had heard, but a plantation far from the pleasures that made life worth living would be bleak. He tried to remember what little he knew of Delaware, but all he could recall was that it adjoined Pennsylvania and that it had a coastal area. He had no idea what crops were grown there and found it impossible to imagine day-to-day existence in such a remote spot.

Polly demonstrated unexpected shrewdness in reading his mind. "We'll do all right," she said comfortingly. "I've even heard tell that sometimes servants are set free before the end of their fifteen years."

No matter what became of him or what penalties he had to risk, Jared was determined to end his indenture long before a decade and a half expired.

Again Polly knew what he was thinking. "You'll have to take care," she said. "Mistress Murtagh can be strict when she sets her mind to it. And servants who try to run away have their ears cropped."

"Is that what she told you?" It would be typical, he thought, to frighten a newly purchased slave with threats.

"She didn't need to. Everybody in London knows it."

Not quite everyone, Jared thought, and he realized there was so much he didn't know that the lower classes took for granted. But he would have to learn, having become one of them.

"This," Polly said, pointing at the pallet on the deck, "is where you're to sleep."

He was being treated like a pet dog allowed the luxury of a rug outside its mistress's bedchamber,

67

but he was in no position to protest. "It could be worse," he murmured, thinking of his first weeks at Newgate.

Her green eyes reflected the discomfort that she, too, had known.

Even in dire circumstances, Jared had discovered during his past months of misfortune, a man did what he could to improve his lot. He grinned at the girl, noting that her plain dress of dark, thick wool could not fully hide the appeal of her ripe figure. "That bed," he said, indicating the bunk in the smaller of the cabins, "is no match for a four-poster in a duke's palace, but it might accommodate two now and again."

Polly warily retreated a few steps.

Jared's advance was gentle but firm.

Her back touched the bulkhead, and she could go no farther.

He brushed aside her upraised arms and embraced her, and when she tried to avert her face, he turned it toward him and kissed her.

Polly's lips parted, and for a moment she accepted him, but when his ardor increased, she wrenched free and shoved the heels of her hands against his chest with such force that she pushed him against the opposite bulkhead. "Mistress Murtagh won't stand for lollygagging," she said.

"Mistress Murtagh may go to blazes," Jared replied. "You like it."

She made no reply.

He saw her face was still flushed and that she had not yet regained control of her breathing. "It's going to be a long voyage," he said, "but you and I—together—can make it seem much shorter."

Polly wanted to clamp her hands over her ears in order to shut out the sound of his voice. He was suggesting what she had wanted so badly the first time she had seen him, and she was somewhat shocked to discover that she still yearned for his lovemaking. There was a magnetic quality to this man that drew her to him, and she found his charm almost irresistible.

Jared read her availability in her eyes and knew he could do what he pleased with her. Laughing quietly, he reached for her, and as he drew her to him and kissed her, pressing his tongue between her readily parted lips, his hands were busy caressing her.

In spite of the dangers involved, the certainty that she would be severely punished if they were apprehended, Polly felt powerless in his embrace and let him do what he pleased.

Suddenly he released her and took a single step backward.

She looked at him, her emerald eyes luminous, her fists clenched, as she regained her breath with great difficulty.

"This voyage," he said huskily, "is going to be one of the shortest on record."

Jared's prediction, unfortunately, proved far from accurate: For him the voyage across the Atlantic was interminably long. The two-masted vessel, similar in design and size to scores of merchantmen that plied the busy trade lanes between England and the colonies, had been constructed to hold cargo, at the sacrifice of speed. She crawled across the calm, early-summer seas.

And one day, after some of her cargo had shifted during a particularly nasty gale, she hove to in mid-ocean for a full day as the contents of her aft hold were rearranged.

Jared soon found that his hopes of seducing Polly White had to be postponed, at the very least, and that he would be wise to forget them. Caroline Murtagh, as he told Polly, had the soul and mind of a spinster, even though she was young and attractive. Surely she left nothing to chance in her attempts to protect what might be left of her female indentured servant's virtue. A light sleeper, she frequently came out into the corridor each night to assure herself that Jared had not left his pallet, and occasionally she crept past him to peer into Polly's tiny cabin.

The morals of her slaves were none of her concern, he indignantly told Polly, and he branded her as a frustrated busybody.

Polly disagreed. Hesitantly, and in some embarrassment, she explained the laws of the colonies to him. "Mistress Murtagh is thinking of the money," she said. "When a serving maid gives birth to a baby, the child is freeborn, and it must be brought up at the expense of the indentured woman's master or mistress. The ladies and gentlemen aren't allowed to stint, either. These children live in the big house and must be treated and schooled as gentry."

At first Jared found it difficult to believe that such a strange code really existed, but finally he solved the puzzle to his own satisfaction. Men of property, he realized, would deal less freely with their indentured women if forced to accept finan-

70

cial and social responsibility for their own bastards. The knowledge provided him with his first inkling that life in the New World might be more complicated and less primitive than he had assumed.

Until reaching America, however, he was suffering from excruciating boredom, and each day was almost exactly like that which preceded it. Since he had no way of knowing when day broke, he remained on his cramped pallet until Polly opened her door for an instant to tell him morning had come. Then he hurried to the forecastle, where the sailors allowed him to shave and wash before he made two trips to the cabins with water, a bucket of hot and one of cold for Caroline, and one of cold for Polly.

The next hours were his own. Weather permitting, he was allowed to go on the forecastle deck, where three other male indentured servants also congregated. All were former inmates of Newgate, but he had nothing else in common with them; they were crude products of London's gutters who had been imprisoned for petty misdemeanors, and their one aim in life was to obtain vengeance, in some vague and undefined way, on the system that had condemned them to long bondage and hard labor.

It was important to Jared that he keep in the best of physical condition, so he continued to practice a regimen he had developed while he was incarcerated at Newgate. Ignoring the other indentured servants, who stared at him in open-mouthed wonder, he engaged in a series of violent physical exercises for the better part of two hours.

Not sparing himself, he worked until his body was covered with sweat. Then he would return to his tiny pallet and bathe himself from a small, inadequate tub in time to hurry to breakfast.

The meals for everyone on board the ship were prepared in a galley in the stern, and each morning after the officers and the paying passengers had eaten in the mess cabin, the seven indentured servants were permitted to get their own breakfast from the galley and eat it on the forecastle deck. This meal invariably consisted of salt fish, watered wine, and hard biscuits from which it was necessary to tap weevils.

The three female indentured servants were kept busy the rest of the morning tending the wardrobes of their mistresses, but the men had nothing to do except stare out at the water. The first mate, Caleb Fleming, took an interest in Jared after discovering the indentured servant's background, and whenever his own duties permitted, he would explain to Jared the principles of navigation. But such interludes were rare.

Early in the afternoon, after the officers, passengers, and sailors had again eaten, the servants were given a somewhat smaller version of their morning meal. Then there were hours of inactivity again, followed by the one substantial meal of the day, usually dried beef or salt pork, varied on rare occasions by minced mutton that had been preserved in tubs of strained lard. With it was served the only hot food and drink of the day, porridge and tea, together with the usual hard biscuits, which Jared soon learned to detest.

After sundown the indentured servants were

sent to their quarters and not permitted on deck, a practice that had arisen on a previous voyage, following the attempt of a number of bonded men to seize possession of the ship. This proved to be the most difficult period of the day for Jared. For hours he found it impossible to drop off to sleep; and Caroline made frequent, irregular visits to the suite, deliberately interrupting whatever she was doing in order to look in on her servants. Polly, apprehensive of being caught dallying with Jared, took the precaution of keeping her door bolted.

Although it galled Jared to ask favors, he requested Caroline's permission to spend his evenings reading. But his simple wish could not be fulfilled. The ship's master ruled that it was dangerous to burn tapers in such confined quarters, and no spare lamps were available. Neither, for that matter, was there any reading matter to spare for the purpose, and Jared couldn't help wondering whether he was the first literate indentured servant ever to be sent to the colonies. Common sense told him there had been others, and he guessed that they, too, had sometimes wondered if they were going mad.

One early morning in the third week of the voyage, while Jared lay wide awake on his pallet, enduring the now customary torture of ennui, he heard shouts, the pounding of footsteps on the deck overhead, and the muffled sound of a woman's scream. The noises continued for at least a quarter of an hour, whetting his curiosity, and finally he heard the roar of a cannon in the distance.

Unable to resist his curiosity any longer, he

went to the hatch at the end of the corridor and stuck his head out. The sun had not yet come over the horizon, but a single look off the starboard bow told him all he needed to know.

A graceful sloop was bearing down on the *Leona Anne,* and a moment after Jared reached the deck there was a flash of fire, followed by another roar. An iron ball from what appeared to be a nine-pounder splashed into the sea about twenty yards from the starboard hull. As nearly as Jared could make out, there were at least four such cannon on board the enemy ship—only two of which they could bring to bear at any one time. As the smoke cleared, he could make out her name on a plaque at her bow. She was the *Attique*—undoubtedly a French privateer, Jared realized, a ship privately authorized to attack English merchantmen while the government of King Louis XV discreetly looked the other way.

In his years as a dragoon, Jared had been indoctrinated with an abiding, deep hatred of France, and something within him exploded. A dozen seamen were frantically hauling two small guns into place on the *Leona Anne*'s starboard deck, and the excited orders of the mate and those of the master, Peter Darwin, who was shouting from the quarterdeck, completely contradicted each other, with the results that the sailors didn't know what to do. It was plain that although Darwin and Fleming might be first-rate seamen, they knew little of gunnery.

Jared raced forward, ignoring the strict regulation that forced him to remain below until sunrise. "Here, lads," he called, the ring of authority in

74

his voice so sharp that the sailors instantly turned to him. "Concentrate on this gun first. You there—and you—start hauling ammunition. Bo'sun, stand by with your rammer. You, move clear with that swab."

In a few moments one of the guns was in place, and Jared swiftly directed its loading.

"What are you doing up here?" Fleming demanded above the uproar.

Jared paid no attention to him. "Don't pack your powder in too tightly! These six-pounders are delicate little guns. Now, bo'sun, give me the rammer and start moving up your other cannon. Right there."

Orderliness replaced confusion, and even Darwin stared in silent astonishment at the indentured servant who had taken charge.

"We'll need to come a bit closer." Jared squinted down the barrel and did not flinch when another shot from the *Attique* landed alarmingly nearby. "Mr. Fleming," he continued crisply, "I'll be obliged if you'll ask the captain to hold this ship steady on her course." He beckoned to the bo'sun's mate, who was standing a few feet away with a burning fuse. "Touch her off when I tell you."

The sailor came closer and held the fuse ready.

Jared moved back, still squinting down the barrel at the *Attique*. "Fire!"

At the first flash he stepped clear of the gun and covered his ears, and the others did the same. The gun roared and recoiled, belching smoke, and immediately all of them scrambled back to their stations, ready to reload.

Jared vaguely realized that the ladies and gentlemen watching the scene as they huddled together at the foot of the quarterdeck were cheering. But he did not share their joy. The shot had crashed into the prow of the *Attique,* and although it made a small ragged hole, it had done no substantial damage. The French privateer continued to bear down on the merchantman, and at close range her own more powerful cannon would do infinitely greater damage.

"Damnation, I'm not accustomed to these bobbing corks at sea! Step lively, lads. Bo'sun, reload this gun while I see if I can improve my luck with the other."

Jared brushed past the astonished Fleming as he ran to the second cannon and began the exacting task of aiming it.

The crew of the privateer had been spurred into more rapid action by the strike, and the women passengers screamed when a ball skidded across the deck a few yards in front of them, ripping a jagged furrow in the planking before dropping overboard into the sea.

"Not bad shooting," Jared said, and his calm quieted the jittery gun crew. "Ready, lads? That's it. Lively!" Again he summoned the bo'sun's mate. "Fire!"

When the smoke cleared away Jared joined in the cheers. His shot had smashed squarely into the privateer's gunwales directly amidships, leaving a gaping hole and causing several casualties. He did not pause to inspect the damage to the sloop but returned to the first gun, which the revitalized Fleming and the bo'sun had reloaded. For the

76

moment, at least, his expert gunnery had discouraged the captain of the *Attique* from closing further, so the *Leona Anne* was in no immediate danger. Therefore Jared was able to take a little longer aiming the six-pounder.

Not until he was entirely satisfied did he give the order to fire. The shot sliced through the sloop's rigging, bringing down a jib and crippling her sufficiently to cause her captain serious concern.

As Jared moved back to his other gun, the *Attique* began to veer away. Darwin and Fleming were relieved, as were the ladies and gentlemen, and the brig's master immediately ordered his mate to crowd on more sail in order to put as much distance as possible between the two ships.

Jared felt a sense of abrupt, bitter disappointment. Although the *Leona Anne* was inferior to her foe in both armament and speed, he had already demonstrated her ability to put up a fight and believed he had a reasonably good chance of sinking the privateer or battering her until she surrendered.

Peter Darwin had only one desire, however, and broke off the engagement. His brig continued on her westward voyage, and the last anyone on board saw of the *Attique,* men were swarming into her rigging. Mate Fleming put some of the *Leona Anne*'s crew to work, too, repairing the damage caused by the Frenchman's one strike, and the brig's master called Jared to the quarterdeck.

"Where did you learn gunnery?" He was still surprised and shaken.

Jared, once again conscious of the iron band on his ankle, had no desire to talk about his past. He shrugged, preferring not to mention that he had been an ensign in a Royal Artillery battery before transferring to the dragoons.

Darwin respected his silence. "No matter. Everyone on this ship is in your debt. The French have formed a habit of stealing cargo in the past year, and their treatment of English passengers has been none too pleasant."

Jared felt he had earned the right to learn more about the situation. "We aren't at war. Why are they behaving as though we are?"

The grizzled ship's master smiled. "After you've spent a few months in the New World you'll know. There's been no formal declaration of war by either London or Paris, but in the colonies the feud never ends. We're trying to expand, and so are they. There's a great empire at stake, and everyone in America realizes it, even if the governments in England and France don't understand there will be no real peace until one of us drives the other out of North America."

Jared reflected that as far as he was concerned, the French were welcome to the entire continent.

Darwin saw that the ladies and gentlemen had gathered around him and Jared.

Jared noted the master's glance and remembered his own place. "You have no further need of my help," he said sourly, "so I'll go below."

He walked past the passengers, and even though he did not look in their direction, he was conscious of their admiration. Even Caroline appeared to have thawed somewhat, but he had already learned that the relationship between proprietress and indentured servants was stiffly formal at all times. He opened the hatch, climbed down the ladder, and groped down the corridor toward his pallet.

Polly White opened the door of her tiny cabin the instant she heard his footsteps. She was so overwrought she had forgotten to put a robe over her nightdress of thin dimity. Her eyes wide, she anxiously asked what had happened.

Jared told her the story, not quite realizing how much he played down his own role in the affair. It had never occurred to him that in spite of the braggart's airs he assumed, he rarely boasted of his genuine accomplishments.

Polly heard more than he told her, and by the time he reached the climax of the tale her eyes were shining.

The proximity of an attractive wench, the flimsiness of her attire, and her obvious approval acted as a balm and a tonic. Jared had been feeling a sense of anticlimactic frustration after routing the privateer and had been irritated by the thought that the ladies and gentlemen were probably sitting in the mess cabin at this very moment, celebrating the victory he had won.

Finishing the story of the battle in a few words, he suddenly swept Polly into his arms and, lifting her from the deck, carried her into her cabin.

She immediately became conscious of her own vulnerability and began to protest. "No!" she cried. "We mustn't! We—"

Jared silenced her with a long kiss that was gentle at the outset but swiftly mounted in its intensity.

The girl stopped struggling and curled her own arms around his neck.

He kicked the door closed behind them and increased the pace of his lovemaking.

Polly made no attempt to escape when, still kissing her, he began to fondle her breasts.

Thoroughly aroused, Jared lowered her to the narrow bunk and quickly joined her. He began to caress her firmly but gently, and as her ardor was aroused, she responded in kind. They were two healthy young animals who had been cooped up in confined quarters, with no opportunity for emotional release. That opportunity was now at hand, and everything else faded from their consciousness. They knew only that they wanted each other, and both of them cast aside all inhibitions.

Neither was new at the art of lovemaking, and they did not hesitate to let their experience show. They employed lips and tongues, hands and bodies, in moves as intricate as the most complicated minuet. When one advanced, the other retreated, and they knew instinctively when to exchange roles.

All at once their desire became unbearable, and with one accord they joined and moved swiftly, violently toward an explosive climax.

At last they moved a short distance apart, and when Jared caught his breath, he murmured, "That was wonderful."

"I knew it would be," Polly replied, not caring in the least that she sounded smug.

The door opened, and they wrenched themselves to a sitting position, Jared almost tumbling to the deck.

Caroline Murtagh stood in the frame, her eyes cold. "Hale," she said, "you'll join me in Captain Darwin's quarters at once." The door slammed.

Polly began to weep. "She'll whip both of us."

Jared realized he had no way of exercising control of any sort over Caroline, but the circumstances impelled him to make the most rash of promises. "I will see to it that you won't suffer," he said. "If I must, I'll even claim I raped you."

He stamped into his boots, pulled his cumbersome wool shirt over his head, and for the second time that morning, went up onto the deck.

Darwin and a fuming Caroline were waiting for him in the master's cabin, by far the largest and most comfortable accommodation on the ship. The captain was sitting at a desk attached to the bulkhead, where he had been writing a report in his log on the encounter with the privateer, and Caroline, her foot tapping furiously, had seated herself in a comfortable chair beside him. Apparently Darwin had attempted to soothe her with a glass of sack, which stood near her on the desk.

The instant she saw Jared she jumped to her feet. "I insist the wretch be punished. Give him the full penalty—twenty lashes—and—"

Jared interrupted her. "If you please, sir," he said to the captain, "I accept full responsibility. The girl was without blame."

"Do you suppose we don't already know it?" Caroline cried. "Warden Simpson of Newgate

81

warned me you were lascivious, and I should have listened to him."

Trying to be fair, Jared made an attempt to tell himself he really couldn't blame her for being upset. If she herself were less attractive, he thought, it would be easier. He had to protect his own skin, however, and wondered what to offer as a defense.

Darwin folded his hands across his paunch and waited for the indentured servant to speak.

Excuses and rationalizations would be a waste of breath, Jared realized, and his months in Newgate had taught him there were occasions when it was wise for a man to appeal to the mercy of the court. "What can I say, sir?" he asked, speaking with deliberate calm. "I'm a man, and I was drawn to as luscious a wench as I've ever seen. I've spent almost a month on board ship, and until today's exercise against the French, I had nothing to occupy me. I'm fond of the lass; we simply had a few minutes' diversion."

His audacity made Caroline tremble. To think that she had gone after him to tell him that she was granting him more liberty because of what he had done to save the ship! Only when she had found his pallet empty had she gone to Polly's cabin and then—with good cause—lost her temper completely. "It's plain enough, Captain, just listening to him, that he plotted and schemed until he was able to seduce her. Our responsibility is clear: After he's been lashed, he must be made to marry her."

Jared was speechless. The thought of marriage—to anyone—had not crossed his mind.

82

Polly was appealing enough, but the prospect of taking any woman as a wife when his future was so precarious made him blanch.

Darwin shook his head and smiled. "Apparently you aren't completely familiar with the colonial law governing indentured servants, Mistress Murtagh. Single men and women who are bonded can't be made to marry against their will. That's one of the advantages they enjoy over slaves."

Jared averted his face so his feelings of triumph would not show.

"The few years you spent in the colonies haven't been enough to give you a real understanding of the way people in America think, Mistress Murtagh. They don't consider themselves their brothers' keepers, and everybody tends his own pasture."

The rebuke was gentle, but Caroline flushed. "My indentured servants aren't my brothers and sisters, Captain Darwin!"

Darwin remained unruffled. "All the same, they have feelings as well as legal rights."

"I can see," she snapped, "that I have to take better care of my maidservants hereafter to protect them from a lecher."

Jared, listening to the exchange but keeping silent, thought he detected a hint of amusement in the shipmaster's eyes.

Darwin, however, took care to speak solemnly. "As to lashing this fellow, I can't do it."

Caroline was so indignant that she sputtered inarticulately.

"For one thing, I have no real precedent. If men

were lashed for tumbling bonded girls, a brig's master would be kept busy for the whole of the voyage."

Caroline's eyes were baleful.

"What's more, Mistress Murtagh, I owe my life to Hale, and I hate to think of what would have become of you if the French privateer had captured us. I have an idea you'd be fighting this very minute to protect your own virtue instead of worrying about some other woman's. I myself am very grateful for what happened today. A talent that should be serving the Crown is being wasted."

Jared's relief at being spared a whipping was diminished by the realization that the woman who had the power to control his life for the next fifteen years was an unmitigated bitch.

"Of course," Darwin said, "we'll have to remove him from temptation for the rest of the voyage. Hale, there's an empty cabin forward on the port side, next to Mr. Fleming's. Move into it tonight, without delay, or I'll be forced to put you into irons." He winked lightly.

Jared knew the brig's master was offering him generous repayment for his efforts in the fight with the *Attique,* and the prospect of sleeping in a real bunk, in privacy, was irresistible. "I'll go there at once, sir," he said. "And you can depend on it, the women on the *Leona Anne* will be safe for the rest of the voyage."

CHAPTER FIVE

Jared did not know it, but the incident involving Polly marked a peculiar change in Caroline Murtagh's attitude toward him. Even Caroline herself was unaware of this change until early one morning when she wandered onto the deck while Jared was engaging in his regular exercises.

Seeing him naked to the waist, engrossed in his violent calisthenics, she retreated to the hatch from which she had emerged and started to descend the ladder that led to the cabins below. But curiosity impelled her to look at Jared again, and knowing she was unobserved, she examined him more carefully.

She had to admit that Jared, unlike her late husband, was trim, with no excess fat on his muscled frame. She had never known a man whose physique was so attractive.

What surprised her most, however, was the grace of his movements. He seemed to be endowed with the fluidity of a natural athlete, and forgetting herself completely, she became absorbed in observing him.

All at once it occurred to her that her cheeks were burning and that her whole face felt flushed.

"What nonsense!" she murmured aloud in annoyance. "He's just a bondsman, after all!"

After five and a half weeks at sea, the *Leona Anne* finally reached her destination, sailing up Delaware Bay into the Delaware River. On the west bank, across from the New Jersey shore, stood the town of New Castle, capital of Pennsylvania's three Lower Counties—which everyone on board ship, however, chose to call Delaware. Jared, standing on the deck of the brig, had never seen a more dismal little community. Giving New Castle the benefit of every doubt, he estimated that it had a maximum population of two thousand persons. Most homes were either crude log cabins or one-story houses of white-washed clapboard. Both types were drab.

A number of spires were clustered close together, and as Jared discovered from a crewman standing next to him, New Castle, for her size, boasted a remarkably large number of churches. The Anglicans had two, as did the Lutherans, while the Baptists, Roman Catholics, Dutch Reformed, and Congregationalists each had one. The Jews were building a synagogue, and at the far end of town from the other places of worship was a modest Society of Friends meetinghouse.

At the waterfront stood a strange old fort of stone and wood whose rusted cannon had not been touched in decades and looked as though they would explode if fired. The original fort, since expanded, had been built by Swedish settlers in 1638. Less than two decades later the Dutch had seized Delaware, and they had added two stone turrets that now would collapse if fired upon by the guns carried on board any self-respecting frigate. The English had done little to improve the town's defenses after driving out the Dutch, and eventually the Lower Counties had been ceded to William Penn as part of his proprietary colony.

He and his followers in the Society of Friends had been unalterably opposed to war, and the fort had been allowed to rot.

Only in recent years, when the descendants of Swedish, Dutch, and English settlers had banded together in an attempt to establish the independence of the Lower Counties from Pennsylvania, had old timbers been replaced and a new wing added. But Jared, observing it with the sharp eyes of a professional soldier, knew it could be demolished in a sea attack by no more than two frigates or captured in a land assault by a single battalion of about two hundred and fifty skilled sappers and infantrymen.

Directly south of New Castle lay the fields that supported the town and appeared to be the sole reason for its existence. As the *Leona Anne* maneuvered into her berth, Jared saw fields of wheat, barley, and rye and caught a glimpse, in the distance, of what appeared to be apple orchards. The region due west of the town presented a far different appearance and startled an Englishman accustomed to the neat farms and pastures of his native land. Here a vast forest formed an impenetrable-looking barrier that began no more than a few hundred feet from the houses on the western edge of the community.

Towering stands of oak and elm, maple and beech reached toward the sky, and intermingled with these trees were innumerable evergreens, including the tallest white pines Jared had ever seen. As a youth he had formed the conviction that woods should be trim, spare, and civilized, and the proximity of this raw wilderness to a colonial capital dismayed him.

The things he saw at close range when he finally struggled ashore, carrying some of Caroline Murtagh's heavier belongings, made him feel even worse about the life ahead. Not one of New Castle's roads was cobbled, the hall in which the Delaware assembly held its meetings resembled a dilapidated barn, and the Crown and Scepter, which Caleb Fleming had told him was New Castle's best tavern, was a rustic disgrace that no self-respecting yeoman farmer in England would patronize. But Jared had little time to brood.

Caroline's packages, boxes, and kegs were piled into two oxcarts, while Caroline and Polly climbed into what appeared to be the only carriage in town. The *Leona Anne*'s officers and some of her passengers had already bidden Jared farewell, thanking him again for saving them from the French pirates, and now, lonely and neglected, he began his real life as an indentured servant.

Adam Marshall, a painfully thin, laconic man of middle years, the overseer of Caroline's plantation, who was himself an indentured servant, stood by and directed the piling of the freight onto the carts. Although engaging in no physical labor himself, he repeatedly urged Jared and the coachman to work harder. Then, after Caroline had addressed a few words to him and driven off, he climbed onto the seat on the rear cart and instructed Jared to sit beside him.

The lumbering oxen were powerful and pulled the heavily laden cart with ease, but they were maddeningly slow, and the ride seemed endless.

Clouds of dust from the lead cart enveloped Jared, a hot sun beat down on his heavy wool clothing, and, jouncing on the rutted dirt road, he soon felt as though every tooth in his head were rattling.

"Too bad about Master Murtagh," Marshall said.

Jared tried in vain to make himself comfortable on the cart. "I didn't know there was a Master Murtagh," he replied.

Marshall seemed barely to hear him. "Drowned. Too bad. He never interfered with the help—too busy drinking. Now his wife will be in complete charge, and that'll be difficult. She's inclined to fuss about everything."

That view confirmed Jared's opinion of Caroline Murtagh, but he thought it best to keep his thoughts to himself. As for her deceased husband, he couldn't have cared less.

The road led them toward the southwest, skirting the edge of the forest, and they passed a number of farms far more extensive than any Jared had ever seen in England. In spite of his misery, he confirmed his first impression that the principal crops were grain and fruit, and he saw huge fields filled with high, growing stalks that he would learn to identify as American corn, which was called maize in England and was not yet appreciated in the Old World. The manor houses on these estates were baronial, although made of unadorned clapboard, and he saw as many outbuildings—among them kitchens, stables, granaries, barns, poultry sheds, and servants' huts—as there were on the grounds of any English farm.

Most of the properties were fenced along the

road but had no barriers dividing them, and both cattle and sheep apparently roamed at will. The cows looked sleek, the sheep were sturdy, and Jared grudgingly revised his opinions of the New World a trifle when he saw magnificent horses, far superior to those owned by the wealthiest of dragoon officers. Animals, at least, seemed to thrive in America.

After a ride that lasted about a half hour, the lead cart turned in at the gate of a large estate, and Jared whistled softly under his breath when he saw the white-painted main house at the end of the road. It was three stories high, with a massive chimney at either end, and must have contained at least thirty rooms.

The carts rumbled past the side of the house and continued toward the outbuildings. There six or seven other indentured men, all of them taciturn and heavily tanned, helped unload the freight. At last, the work completed, Marshall beckoned and led Jared past a line of small log cabins to one at the end of the row.

"This here," he said, "is where you'll live."

Jared looked inside and saw a bedstead with a straw mattress on it, a rickety homemade chair and table of pine—the latter with a candle stub on a broken saucer standing in the center—a water pitcher, and several iron cooking utensils.

"Mistress Murtagh told me she will inspect every Saturday," Marshall said. "If your house is not swept and clean, you get no Sunday dinner."

Jared was startled.

"Me," the overseer said with an unexpected grin, "I've been bonded for fourteen years, and come the end of next year I aim to get a place of my own down in Kent County. So I figure a little tidying won't kill me. Osman Murtagh, now, he didn't care if we slept with the pigs, but this here widow of his thinks she's a schoolmistress."

Jared laughed aloud for the first time in many days, and an immediate rapport with the overseer was established.

"Your knife is over yonder," Marshall said. "You use it for chores and skinning and the like, and I reckon you'll find it's easiest to carry in your boot top. That's within the law. But if you get your hands on firearms, be careful of what free men you let see you with them. And don't ever let Mistress Murtagh catch you with a rifle or a pistol. She'll have you flayed, for certain."

It was encouraging to discover that, in one way or another, indentured men managed to gain possession of weapons.

"You got any belongings to unpack?"

Jared took a razor and a spare pair of stockings from his pocket and placed them on the table.

Marshall was not surprised. "Come along," he said. "It's nigh time for dinner."

The other indentured men were gathered around a circular stone-lined pit, and all of them were taking a hand in the preparation of their meal. Jared had been hungry for weeks, scarcely able to eat the unappetizing food on board the brig, and he soon discovered that in one respect, at least, his life had changed for the better. The men began their dinner with a soup they called chowder, which they poured into gourds. In it were potatoes, leeks, milk and butter, large quan-

91

tities of corn and whole oysters, as well as a tougher native shellfish known as clams.

The soup, however, was only the beginning of what Jared regarded as a feast. While they were waiting for their main course to finish cooking, some of the men ate raw oysters, while others fried oysters and mussels in a pungent fat that the newcomer later learned was the grease of bear bacon. At last the roast was done, and every man hacked himself a smoking, dripping chunk of venison, which he cut into smaller pieces with his knife as he ate. There were ample quantities of a coarse brown wheat bread, too, baked in heavy round loaves, and some enjoyed raw marsh onions, which they had picked in swamps near the river.

No one used plates, the seemingly all-purpose knives were the only eating utensils, and table manners were nonexistent. Nevertheless, Jared found the indentured men were infinitely better behaved than the prisoners at Newgate. Some of these men had served terms at Newgate, but experience had taught them the code of the New World. No one pushed or shoved, no one tried to snatch a choice morsel before someone else could take it, and, above all, no one displayed greediness. The reason for their behavior, Jared decided, was that food supplies were so ample in the colonies that there was no need for a man to fight for his share.

Each indentured man drank strong, bitter ale from a battered mug, and it alone appeared to be rationed. After someone finished his ale, he had to drink water if he was still thirsty.

Jared's biggest surprise was still in store. At the conclusion of the meal the men carefully rinsed their faces and hands with water drawn from a well. Never had the new arrival known people of the servants' class to be so meticulous, but Marshall offered him a logical explanation. "There are flying critters that'll bite your flesh clean off your bones if you got any food left on you," he said. "They're called mosquitoes."

The reason for serving such a large meal soon became evident: The men more than earned their keep. Marshall put Jared to work weeding in a cornfield, and within an hour the former cavalryman's back was aching. He had no tools except a sharp, pointed stick that someone had whittled, and he quickly learned he was expected to labor without pause. Rest periods were unknown, and although Marshall was personally sympathetic in his attitude to the men whose activities he supervised, dawdling was not permitted. Long before the end of the day, Jared was stumbling. It was agony for him to kneel and then stand again, and to his surprise, his hands were trembling. He had always taken his physical strength and endurance for granted, accepting them as a natural endowment, but he knew when he saw the other indentured men working that he had no reason to feel proud of his stamina.

No one laughed at him, however. Each of the others had gone through a grueling period of training, and everyone seemed to understand how he felt when, at sundown, he was scarcely able to make his way back to the cabins. The supper the men prepared for themselves was similar to that which they had eaten at noon, except they substituted wild boar for vension. Jared thought himself too tired to eat, but the first taste of food made him realize he was ravenous.

A short, swarthy man with the letter *T* branded on the back of his right hand came up to the newcomer, and Jared knew the man had been convicted, either in England or the colonies, as a thief. Marshall deliberately turned away from the pair and became conspicuously busy in a conversation with others.

"You ain't goin' up t' the main house for nothin' t'night, be you?" the short man asked.

Jared shook his head. It was unlikely, he thought, that he would ever see the inside of the mansion.

The man's broad smile revealed his toothless gums. "Mistress Murtagh would whup you herself if she smelled your breath." With the air of a conjurer he produced an ale mug. "Me and some of the lads made this out in the forest. We put up a shed out there that nobody ain't goin' t' find."

Jared saw that the liquid in the mug was colorless.

"Go ahead, try it," the thief urged. "We're givin' it to you 'cause you need it."

Cautiously swallowing a small amount of the liquid, Jared thought his mouth and throat were on fire. He gasped, and tears came to his eyes.

"That ain't the way t' drink," the man said reprovingly. "Take as much as you c'n swallow, fast, and it won't be near as hurtful."

Aware that most of the others were watching him and that he would be judged by his willingness and ability to drink the raw liquid without flinching, Jared raised the mug to his lips and drained it. He was in agony but continued to stand erect, his face reflecting none of his misery.

His reward was the obvious admiration of his new colleagues.

The thief, deeply impressed, grasped his elbow. "I'll show you down the line t' your house," he said, and started toward the huts.

Jared's first night in the New World was dreamless, and for the first time in months he enjoyed an uninterrupted sleep.

Polly White was the object of endless speculation on the part of Caroline Murtagh's male indentured servants. Some boasted of their hopefully all-but-accomplished aim of seducing her at the first opportunity, while a minority, rather wistfully, expressed the belief that she was the type they wanted to marry when their bonded service ended. None, however, met her, spoke to her, or even had the chance to flirt with her. The chasm that separated the field workers from the household staff at the mansion was broad and was bridged only by the overseer, Marshall, who could think of nothing but the property on which he intended to settle the following year and who had no interest in attractive young serving maids.

Jared kept silent when the others spoke of Polly, and nothing in his manner indicated that he had enjoyed a brief affair with her. He had no idea whether others might find it easy to match his success, but felt it his duty as a gentleman to keep quiet. He knew his real motives were selfish, however, and that he, like the others, hoped to find or create the opportunity to spend more time alone with her.

More than a month passed, however, and still he did not see her. He spent all his daylight hours in the fields, where his physical strength and resilience doubled, but at no time did Caroline or anyone else in the house send for him. In a sense, he had no cause for complaint, and life was infinitely better than it had been at Newgate. He worked hard but was enjoying robust health, ate heartily, and slept well. His comrades had accepted him as one of their number, and those who realized he had been a member of a higher class bore him no resentment. Indentured servants were equal, and only the few, like Marshall, who had served the better part of their terms were granted special privileges.

As Jared became accustomed to life on the farm, a sense of restless dissatisfaction came alive within him again, and he recognized it as the feeling that had prompted him to gamble away his inheritance. He and other indentured servants shared few interests, and he knew he was bored, but he could no more fill the vacuum in his life than he could assuage the yearnings for a woman that welled up within him. It did him no good to dream of spending a night in London, and he had no desire to apply for permission to go off to New Castle for an occasional Saturday evening. From what he had seen of the drab little town, he was happy to avoid it.

He had little desire to learn anything about local conditions, either, but he was given no choice.

Marshall, long starved for an intelligent companion, spent several evenings each week talking to him, and in spite of himself, Jared obtained a general idea of the area's political affairs.

Apparently the three Lower Counties, or Delaware—Jared certainly didn't care what they were called—had little chance of retaining an identity of their own. New Jersey wanted to annex the northern county, New Castle, while Maryland cast covetous eyes at the others, Kent and Sussex, her neighbors, from which she was separated by a border she considered artificial. The most substantial claim, however, was that of a large and powerful neighbor to the north, Pennsylvania. The governor of Pennsylvania also served as governor of Delaware, although the Lower Counties had administered their own internal affairs for more than three decades through a separate legislature and executive council.

Jared was surprised to learn that more than half of the inhabitants of Delaware were not full-blooded Englishmen. The Dutch had settled the area first, in 1631, but had been wiped out by the local Indians. Then, in 1638, the Swedes had arrived, although they in turn had held the region for no more than seventeen years before the Dutch, under Peter Stuyvesant, had retaken the area. Only later had the English arrived.

The Lower Counties, Marshall said proudly, were different. The Dutch Reformed Church flourished, and so did the Swedish Lutheran Church. Quakers from Pennsylvania were well represented, as were Catholics from Maryland.

There were also large numbers of Calvinists—
Huguenot refugees from state-inspired persecu-
tion in France—and in recent years there had been
an influx of German Lutherans who had originally
intended to settle in the Pennsylvania mountains
but had changed their minds.

"Everybody gets along good with everybody
else," the overseer said. "Now and again somebody comes along preaching hate, but we ride him
out across the border on a sapling. If we can stand
up to the Crown and Pennsylvania, we can hold
our own against anybody."

Jared was faintly amused. "How do you stand
up to the Crown?"

Marshall chuckled. "The Lower Counties were
part of old William Penn's original grant. Under
the law, this here is part of the English proprietary
colony of Pennsylvania. But we've been so mean
and ornery, they've been as glad to get rid of us
as a farmer is to burn out a hornet's nest in his
chimney. The last governor tried to collect
Pennsylvania taxes from us, and when we
wouldn't pay, he sent some tax collectors from
Philadelphia to make us obey."

Jared knew he didn't have to ask questions.
Regardless of whether he wanted to hear the rest
of the story, he would.

"Down they rode in their fancy leather hats and
belts, and quite a sight they were. Well, every man
in Delaware—and that includes all the bonded
men—went off to the wilderness for a little sport.
We took the shiny leather purses the collectors
carried for tax money, and they were lucky we
didn't scalp them. You never saw anybody ride

across the border so fast. Their horses didn't leave hoofprints on our roads."

"Did respectable citizens have a hand in—in hounding them?" There had been many men at Newgate, Jared recalled, who had boasted of their lawbreaking activities.

Marshall laughed. "Every last one of our militia captains was out there in the forest, aiming his rifle about a half inch over the collectors' heads, and so were all the members of the legislature. Do you think they'd miss the sport?"

Delaware, Jared gathered, was even less civilized than the rest of the primitive New World to which he had been condemned to spend a decade and a half.

There were unexpected compensations, however. One day at noon, after he had finished a grueling morning's work in the fields, he found it was his turn to draw drinking water from the main well, which had been dug near the barns. He went to fetch it and suddenly came face to face with Polly White, who was carrying a bucket of milk.

She was less pale than she had been, her face had filled out, and her figure had grown a trifle plump, so that her breasts strained against the fabric of the immaculate white uniform she was wearing. She wore her black hair tied in a loose bun at the nape of her neck, and she looked even prettier and more appealing than Jared had thought her on the long voyage across the Atlantic.

"Well," he said, halting.

Polly flushed and tried to move around him. "Good morning." She sounded nervous.

Jared deliberately blocked her path.

"I'm not permitted to speak to you or any other bonded man."

"That's as chilly a greeting as I've ever been given by a—friend."

"I mean it. I'll be given the lash if I'm caught."

"Have you been whipped?"

"Not yet, and I don't aim to be. Mistress Murtagh has a bad temper."

"So I discovered myself." Jared grinned. "Where is she now?"

"Up at the house."

He looked around and saw they were completely alone. "She's there, and we're here. No one else is around." He spoke soothingly as, taking the bucket from her, he drew her into the shadows of the larger barn.

"What do you want?" Polly eyed him apprehensively.

"How you've changed in a few weeks!"

"Is it any wonder, with that woman standing over me? You've changed too." She softened, looking at him admiringly. "Sometimes, when I've looked out of the windows, I've seen you in the distance, but I was never sure it was you."

Aware that his hair was very long and unkempt, he ran a hand through it in a feeble attempt to comb it.

"You're so sunburned you look as dark as the Indian peddlers who came to the door last week."

Jared realized he was naked to the waist and that Polly, in spite of herself, was looking at the rippling muscles in his arms and torso.

"I guess," she said uncertainly, "that life hasn't been easy for you."

"I've missed you." Placing the bucket on the ground, he put his arms around her, holding one hand against the base of her spine as he pressed her body close to his.

Polly resisted for a moment as he kissed her, and then she yielded, her lips parting.

Jared's hand dipped unerringly inside her neckline and cupped her firm breast.

She wrenched free, her green eyes blazing, and slapped him hard across the face. "Is that all you want? Do you think you can tumble me any time you catch me alone? Well, think again, bonded man!" Picking up the bucket of milk, she flounced off toward the house.

The astonished Jared tried to apologize, realizing that he had moved too quickly and had offended her dignity. But Polly preferred not to hear a word he said.

CHAPTER SIX

"There's a tavern in Baltimore," Adam Marshall said, "that has little rooms, just big enough to squeeze in a man and a woman, and then you pull the curtain closed. I was there one time, but I couldn't find me a wench, so I never did get to sit on one of those benches that has horsehair stuffed under the cover. Up in Philadelphia there must be twenty taverns at the waterfront, and all of them serve a whiskey that's made from potato peelings and colored tea. It rots your insides, if it don't kill you, but the sailors from the merchantmen want to get drunk so bad that they pay no mind to taste. I tell you, the more I travel, the more I say there's no place like this."

New Castle's Crown and Scepter was unique, Jared was forced to admit, but he was careful not to show his lack of enthusiasm for the place. It did not matter that the chairs were fashioned from kegs and that the tables were planks of rough wood supported by barrels. Neither did it bother him that the floor was bare, hard-packed earth. After all, he had been living for months under primitive conditions, and what would have been shocking in London was commonplace in Delaware. There was a single leaded window at the front of the establishment, but its impressiveness was spoiled by the presence of oiled paper rather than glass between the metal strips. The noise was deafening, and the patrons, all of them male, wore either buckskins or rough work shirts and black breeches of linsey-woolsey, making it impossible to distinguish between free men and indentured servants. Apparently such distinctions did not matter; with the exception of a few trappers who had not bathed in a long time, everyone in the crowded taproom earned his living farming.

What made Jared faintly ill was the quality of the spirits the Crown and Scepter served. The mere aroma of the whiskey and the gin made him faintly ill, the rum was raw, and the ale, which he was drinking, was barely potable. Two men whom Marshall identified as plantation owners were drinking brandywine, which looked reasonably good, but at thruppence a glass its price was prohibitive. In fact, Jared was lucky to be drinking ale as Marshall's guest, since he still didn't have a farthing to his name.

"The whiskey in Philadelphia," he said, "must be very bad."

Marshall puffed on a battered pipe. "I've never tried it, and I don't know anybody who has. All I know is that there are so many sailors sleeping on the streets that the constables of the night watch just make sure they're still breathing, and take nary a one off to jail. Not even a town as rich as Philadelphia could afford that many boarders."

Jared thought that if what he had seen of the New World was typical, he couldn't blame the sailors for seeking oblivion. Smiling, he raised his mug just as someone jostled his arm, spilling ale down the front of his shirt.

He turned and glared at a sandy-haired, balding man of about his own age, a brawny fellow with a thick chest.

The colonial did not shrink away. "Keep your elbow to yourself," he bellowed out so that the whole room could hear.

Jared had found no outlet for his frustrations other than his work, and he made no attempt to curb his own temper. "Watch where you're walking. And when you speak to me, don't shout."

The brawny man blinked at him, then put a heavy hand on his shoulder.

Jared jumped to his feet.

The other patrons sensed a fight brewing, and conversation ceased abruptly.

But Adam Marshall, displaying surprising

agility and speed, stepped between the two antago-
nists. "Phil," he said, "it was an accident, and
you blame well know it. Jared, sit down."

The man who had been addressed as Phil
clenched his fists. "First he'll apologize!"

"I'm the one who has the ale wetting his shirt!"
Jared felt his cold anger mounting.

"I'll mix a little blood with it."

"Then it'll be your blood."

Again Marshall intervened, even more firmly.
"Jared, I gave you an order. Sit down. And
Franklin, stop acting like a wild boar trapped in
a pigpen. Get him out of here," he added to the
man's friends as the proprietor and his two sons
moved in to prevent a brawl.

Franklin, still scowling and muttering under his
breath, reluctantly allowed himself to be led away.

"If the night watch arrested you after a fight,"
Marshall said to the still-aroused Jared, "Mistress
Murtagh would be within her rights to forbid you
the privilege of coming into New Castle for a year,
maybe longer."

"I wouldn't be missing much. And it would be
worth it."

"If you want to avoid a beating, stay away from
Phil Franklin. Nobody hereabouts is his match in
a free-for-all."

"The next time I meet him, we'll see about
that." Jared was growing calmer.

"I'm trying to warn you."

"You've been kind to me, Adam, and I'm trying
to return a favor. Put a wager on me—the higher
the odds against me, the better—and you'll win
yourself a fat purse."

Marshall looked at him and saw that his self-confidence was not the outgrowth of anger. If anyone could put Franklin in his place, which was doubtful, it would be a man who was unafraid.

By London standards the parlor of the main house was simply furnished, but from what Jared had seen of the colonies, it was sumptuous. Linen curtains shielded the windows, and he counted three sets of silk drapes. Two chairs were covered in velvet, and another dark, smooth material he was unable to identify decorated a long divan. There were hooked rugs scattered on the polished wood of the floor, and he could tell at a glance that the crystal chandeliers and the two oil lamps in the room had been purchased in England.

Feeling thoroughly out of place in his work clothes, he shifted his weight from one foot to the other as he waited, wondering why Caroline had summoned him in the middle of the day. Marshall, who had brought him the message, had been completely in the dark, so he assumed she was not displeased with anything he had done. Certainly he had given her no cause for displeasure; aside from his one brief venture into New Castle for part of an evening, he had done virtually nothing but work in the fields, eat, and sleep.

After a wait that seemed interminable, Caroline came into the room, radiant in a blue silk gown that matched her eyes. Jared couldn't help wishing she were less attractive, and he told himself that if she were plain he might dislike her less intensely. Marshall had urged him to bow deeply, as was customary for bonded servants, but he found it difficult even to incline his head in a token gesture of respect and greeting.

If Caroline was aware of his cold reaction, she gave no indication of it. "Hale," she said brusquely, coming to the point at once, "you're familiar with horses, I believe."

If the observation hadn't been so absurd, Jared would have laughed. Any officer who held a commission in King George's cavalry obviously knew horses. Reminding himself bitterly that he had lost his commission, he contented himself with a brief "Yes, ma'am."

"I've just bought another gelding and a mare for riding, and there are enough horses in the stable now to justify employing someone as a groom. Do you believe yourself capable of handling such work?"

He had no idea why it seemed more humiliating to be a groom than a field hand. Perhaps, he thought, the days when his own personal groom had been assigned to him in the dragoons were still fresh in his memory. "I have no doubt, ma'am," he said icily, "that I can serve to your satisfaction."

She surveyed him, her eyes as remote as his. "You may begin today," she replied, and dismissed him with a wave.

Jared was relieved to take his departure, but something in her manner, probably her complete indifference to him as a person, made him seethe.

The new position had its unexpected advantages, and there were times when Jared could forget, briefly, that he was an indentured servant with a bleak future. Caroline Murtagh kept only eight horses, so the groom's duties were light, and after a few days working in the stable, Jared realized his luck had finally turned. One of his duties was that of exercising the animals, and, spending several hours in the saddle each day, he began to explore the surrounding countryside.

Gradually, almost unconsciously, he discovered the New World had a rugged appeal that had escaped him when he had first landed at New Castle. Life in the colony was primitive, but no one went hungry, and he was fascinated by the deep silence of the forest. After a time he was surprised to find that the quiet was deceptive. A man who listened carefully could hear creatures moving through the underbrush, and occasionally he caught a glimpse of a porcupine or a raccoon. He found a salt lick, too, only five miles from the Murtagh plantation, but saw no deer in the vicinity, even though he found their tracks on more than one occasion.

He also encountered reminders that the New World was a wild and savage place. One day when he dismounted to explore a marshy area not far from the main house, he almost stepped into what resembled a muddy bog. Something prompted him to test it, and he threw a broken, heavy tree branch into it. To his astonishment, the branch slowly sank from view and was completely enveloped in the bog. Only then did he realize that this was a patch of treacherous quicksand into which an unsuspecting man or animal could stumble and vanish without a trace.

Usually he finished the day's work by noon and, with little to occupy him the rest of the day, spent his afternoons brooding. Often he wished he were working in the fields again, wanting any activity that would keep him busy and prevent him from dwelling on the circumstances that had led him to this remote corner of the world, so far from the life to which he had been accustomed.

Everything in America seemed to be on a larger scale than in England. Distances between dwellings were great, people ate enormous meals, and even the weather was more violent. The rain, it seemed, fell only in torrential cloudbursts. Peering out the stable door one afternoon at the sheet of water that descended from the skies, he told himself that if he should ever be fortunate enough to return home, he would never again complain about the English weather, which he had always thought miserable.

Suddenly a figure appeared a few feet from him, and Polly dashed into the barn, a heavy scarf over her head, a long cloak protecting her dress. "Mistress Murtagh left her best gloves in the carriage and sent me to fetch them," she said breathlessly as, water streaming from her cloak and scarf, she headed straight toward the carriage.

It was obvious to Jared that being alone with him made her apprehensive, so he did not follow her. He could afford to wait, he decided, and he smiled as he closed the barn door.

She climbed into the coach, emerging with the pair of gloves in her hand. "Thank you," she said primly, her eyes growing wary when she saw that he stood between her and the door.

"There's no need to thank me," he replied. "I've done nothing."

Polly made no attempt to explain the reason for her gratitude.

"I give you my word," Jared said, "that I won't touch you—unless you wish it."

She sidled toward the door.

"You needn't run back to the house before you catch your breath, you know." He deliberately folded his arms and leaned against the wall.

The girl hesitated, then relaxed slightly. "I hate days like this. She keeps finding more and more work for me to do. I've polished her silver-backed hand mirror and hairbrush until my arms are ready to fall off."

"Be glad you have enough to keep you busy." Jared was unaware of the bitterness in his own voice.

Polly's green eyes widened. "You really hate living here, don't you, Jared?"

"Of course. Why shouldn't I?"

She sighed, and when she spoke, there was a note of deep sympathy in her voice. "I keep forgetting. I'm always so pleased that I'm not rotting in Newgate, that I have good food and clean clothes and a solid roof over my head. When I think of you—"

"Do you?"

"Naturally. I tell myself how much better it is for you here than it was in prison. But I can't seem to remember the—the grand life you led before you were sent to Newgate."

"I never thought it grand."

"To someone like me, who seldom had two silver crowns to her name, it seemed like a fairy-tale life."

Jared was touched by her genuine concern. "There are no fairy tales that come true in this world." He tried to speak softly, but himself heard the harsh, grating tone.

Polly didn't know what to say.

But words were unnecessary. Her feminine warmth was a solace he desperately needed, and he reached for her.

The barn door opened, and Caroline stood in the frame, water dripping from her bonnet, which was covered with oiled paper, and from her cloak.

Polly saw her, slipped out, and fled toward the house.

"I followed her," Caroline said, "because I've come to know you, Hale. You can't keep your hands off a girl who is unable to protect herself, can you?"

She made him sound cheap and lewd, which infuriated him. She had no concept of human needs, or of the rapport that could bind a man and woman to each other. "You're incapable of understanding what Polly and I have in common." He knew she would find his contempt unbearable, but he was too angry to care.

Caroline brushed a rivulet of water from her face, then snatched off her bonnet and threw it angrily onto a mound of hay. "Are you trying to tell me you love her?"

"No, I'm just saying she's a woman—a real woman—who can feel for a man whose luck has turned sour. Just as I can feel for her, because she's had no chance to live the kind of life she's always wanted."

"Your excuses are flimsy, Hale."

"I make no excuses."

"What's more, you forget your place."

"A place I never sought. I was brought to the colonies against my will—"

"You were in no position to be given a voice in the matter. You seem to have forgotten you're a convicted felon."

"I don't forget it, I assure you. I'm aware of it every waking moment, every day."

"Yet you deliberately break the law. You think that because you're bonded to a woman rather than a man, you can do what you please. You've exhausted my patience, Hale." Caroline opened the tie at the throat of her cloak and was so perturbed she didn't realize the damp garment slid to the floor.

"I work hard to earn my keep, but I won't grovel."

"You're insolent." Caroline glanced in the direction of the wall where bridles and other riding equipment were hung. Her silk petticoats rustling, she snatched a riding crop.

Jared wanted to take it away from her and break it in two, but he knew it would only get him in deeper trouble.

"Under the law," she said, trying to remain calm but unconsciously revealing her tension by speaking a half octave higher than usual, "I'm permitted to punish the transgressions of indentured servants as I see fit. In fact, I'm required by law to establish and maintain discipline."

He stood very still, looking directly into her eyes.

For a moment she seemed to waver. Then

Caroline slashed him across the chest with the riding crop, tearing through his shirt and leaving an ugly red welt on his skin.

He realized he shouldn't have been surprised, but he had thought her femininity would prevent her from resorting to violence.

Again she slashed at him, the riding crop cutting into his shoulder.

The pain was so intense that Jared gasped. Reacting instinctively, he took a step toward her.

Caroline saw the murderous intensity of his expression but stood her ground. "Stand back. If you put a hand on me, I'll have you hanged!"

He realized that legally she could have him put to death if he assaulted her, so he let his hands fall to his sides again.

Caroline struck him again, then a fourth time.

Jared refused to give her the satisfaction of wincing or otherwise indicating that she was hurting him. If he could do nothing to protect himself, at least he could salvage his pride.

Again and again she struck him, the tempo of her blows increasing. She began to breathe rapidly, partly because of the physical exertion, partly because of her own emotional reaction to the punishment. A strange sheen appeared in her eyes, and she scarcely seemed to know what she was doing.

In her inflamed imagination, Caroline saw Osman Murtagh standing before her. Somehow, inexplicably, the bonded man who refused to bow to her will had vanished, and in his place had appeared the husband who had mocked and abused and terrified her beyond measure.

That phenomenon gave her added strength, and she lashed at him repeatedly, the sheen in her eyes now giving way to a kind of temporary insanity.

Jared's agony was excruciating. His torso felt aflame, and it became increasingly difficult for him to curb his own desire to strike back. Each time the riding crop cut through the air he was forced to close his eyes, bracing himself for the blow, and each time the pain was so sharp that he wanted to cry aloud.

Caroline became so frenzied that, no longer seeing her target clearly, she slashed Jared across the side of the face, his ear taking the brunt of the blow.

Suddenly he could tolerate no more. His legs trembling, he stepped forward and grasped the riding crop.

To his astonishment, Caroline allowed it to slip from her hand. Her eyes half-closed, she struggled for breath and stood unsteadily, swaying from side to side.

Jared grasped her by the shoulders and began to shake her, his strong fingers pressing her shoulders. The woman made no attempt to resist and let him do as he pleased.

His fury suddenly changed direction. He no longer wanted to retaliate in kind but felt an overpowering desire to prove to her that no woman, not even one to whom he was indentured and who could have him put to death if she wished, could treat him so viciously. He picked her up, carried her to the mound of hay, and unceremoniously dropped her into it.

All at once he knew, looking down at her, that

he wanted her more than he could recall ever having wanted a woman.

He fell down beside her, and Caroline remained passive as he kissed her savagely. He fumbled with her skirt and petticoats, and still she made no move. Then, unexpectedly, she came to life and returned his kiss, embracing him with a fervor that astonished him.

Neither was able to remember precisely what happened in the next few minutes. Jared was determined to have her, to teach her he was a man, no matter what price he might be required to pay, and Caroline was eager to accept his advances, welcoming his lovemaking.

Finally they became satiated, and after they stopped thrashing, sanity returned.

Jared climbed slowly to his feet, aware now that his shirt had been cut to ribbons when she had whipped him, and that blood from his wounds had smeared her gown, ruining it.

Caroline sat up, making a halfhearted attempt to arrange her tousled blond hair. At last she regained her feet and forced herself to look at him.

He had long thought himself expert in understanding women, but he found the expression in her eyes unfathomable.

"You realize," she said in a low tone, "that every court in Delaware would sentence you to be hanged for what you've done."

Jared's body was aching from the beating he had been forced to tolerate. "I suppose," he said, "that if you care to tell a court what happened, you can then enjoy the pleasure of watching me dangle from a noose."

"How clever of you."

"I'm not trying to be clever."

"Well, I don't care to have your execution on my conscience." Caroline absently brushed hay from her skirt.

He made no reply.

"Come up to the house with me. You'll need an unguent for the cuts on your chest."

"I'll manage without your salves, thank you."

She stared at him, her expression still revealing nothing.

It occurred to Jared that their relationship had been changed for all time. He was still her bonded servant, but the intimacy they had shared had destroyed invisible barriers. He was no longer angry because she had beaten him, and, as nearly as he could judge, she bore him no grudge for having taken her.

Caroline held herself erect, unmindful of the hair tumbling down her shoulders and back. "If you think I'm just another of your cheap conquests—"

"I make no comparisons." He knew he had achieved the upper hand, and he added firmly, "That matter is ended. I'll neither mention it again nor presume on it."

A flicker of surprise showed in Caroline's blue eyes. Apparently she had not anticipated such gallantry. Unable to reply, she inclined her head in a brief gesture of thanks.

Jared wanted to tear off his ragged shirt and rub soft butter on his wounds, but he could not let her see that he was in great pain.

"I had no intention of whipping you so hard," she said.

He was aware of her inner struggle.

"I—I have no idea why I behaved as I did. I'm sorry." How different life would have been, she thought, had she married a man like Jared Hale rather than Osman Murtagh, who had abused and mistreated her so viciously. What abruptly dawned on her—and what she could not tell Jared, now or ever—was that she had hated him unfairly simply because he was the same sex as her hated husband. Yet he bore no resemblance to Osman, and it was high time that she knew it and remembered it.

Jared grudgingly had to give her credit for an exceptionally difficult apology. He recognized the importance of allowing her to retain and nurture what remained of her pride, and himself made a great effort. "I deserved it."

Again Caroline stared at him. Then, donning her cloak and bonnet, she quickly left the barn. The rain pounded on the shingled roof, and in one of the stalls a mare neighed plaintively.

CHAPTER SEVEN

Caroline Murtagh was kept busy supervising the operation of her farm, an occupation she handled with single-minded efficiency. She relieved the tedium of work by going into town two or three afternoons a week on necessary shopping expeditions, but these jaunts did not satisfy her, particularly as a new crisis had arisen and had plunged the British colonies into war.

In October 1740, Great Britain and France renewed their enmity of centuries in a new conflict, which became known in Europe as the War of the Austrian Succession. The real bones of contention were the New World colonial possessions of the two great powers, with each eager to expand its domain in North America at the expense of the other. The French, working out of Quebec, were farseeing and quick acting. Strengthening their great fortress at Louisbourg, on Cape Breton Island, they sent bands of Algonkin, Ottawa, Abnaki, and other northern Indian tribes on raids deep into New York and as far south as Pennsylvania.

The British colonies, stirred by the burning and looting of frontier villages, organized to meet the challenge in what was to become known in America as King George's War. No one responded more energetically than the governor of Pennsylvania and the Lower Counties, George Thomas, an Englishman who had owned and operated a plantation on the Caribbean island of Antigua prior to his appointment by the Crown to his new post. He established large militia quotas, and when the Quakers of Pennsylvania refused on religious grounds to answer the call to the colors, the governor outraged them by issuing a proclamation ordering indentured servants to perform military service.

In Delaware, Thomas faced different but equally vexing problems. Volunteer companies of militia were forming, but the Lower Counties were far from the areas threatened by hostile savages, and their political leaders blandly took advantage of the situation, demanding greater independence from Pennsylvania in return for their cooperation. Their price was formal admission by the governor of rights they had already seized by force—namely, administration of their own internal affairs. Thomas was reluctant to grant such prerogatives under duress, and both sides began to bargain.

The war seemed remote in the Lower Counties, but Caroline was restless and felt the need to discuss it with someone who would understand the implications of the struggle.

Polly, now her personal serving maid, neither knew nor cared about the war, nor did any member of the household staff. As for the bonded men on the property, they, too, lived in ignorance. So she finally settled on Jared as the one member of the staff with whom she could converse.

At least she told herself that it was his background that would make it possible for him to talk intelligently on the subject. In private she wondered whether she was afraid of him because of the treatment she had received at the hands of Osman Murtagh. She had to admit that on the occasion when she had given in to Jared's love-making, he had been almost miraculously gentle and tender, considering the circumstances. She even pondered the question of whether she was falling in love with him. But the whole idea was so absurd that she shrank from it and could not bring herself to consider it seriously.

Consequently she found herself in the paradoxical position of holding him at arm's length even while seeking his company. As a result, their meetings usually ended in misunderstanding and miserable failure.

One day Caroline followed her new practice of inventing a seemingly valid reason to visit Jared in the stables, and after attending to her alleged business with him, she lingered long enough to say, "The war is becoming much worse, I'm afraid."

He was immediately alert. "Are the French actually invading the colonies?"

She shook her head. "No, they don't dare go quite that far. But their Indian allies have conducted devastating raids near Springfield, in Massachusetts Bay, and in New York's Mohawk Valley."

Jared looked blank. His knowledge of New World geography was hazy at best, and he smiled politely, then shrugged. "I'm afraid," he said, "I'm not familiar with those places."

He left her with nothing further to say, and she flounced out of the barn, annoyed with herself for having gone there to speak with him in the first place.

His own problems kept him occupied. Caroline never referred to their intimacy in the barn, but Jared was now required to drive her coach, taking her on visits to her friends in the neighborhood. She had sent to Boston for a suit of green satin livery with pewter buttons, which she ordered him to wear on these occasions, and he was forced to obey. And although he pondered it at great length, he couldn't decide whether she was deliberately humiliating him, a former dragoon officer, by dressing him in a servant's uniform, or whether she simply was insensitive to his feelings.

Caroline herself gave no sign. It was typical of her to order the carriage brought to the door, as she did early one afternoon in December, then nod remotely to Jared as she climbed in and, in an impersonal tone, directed him to drive her to New Castle, where she intended to buy some cloth and make several other purchases.

The air was cold and damp, but Jared, sitting in the open behind the team of horses, was indifferent to the weather. There was one advantage he enjoyed, he thought: America was so remote from England that no one he had ever known could see him wearing servant's attire and the ankle band of a bonded man.

Two young women who, beneath their cloaks, were wearing gowns of what Jared had learned to recognize as bombazine, a stiff fabric found only in the colonies, were waiting for Caroline in New Castle. She went off with them, telling Jared to meet her in an hour's time. He had nothing to occupy him, but it was too chilly to remain seated on the coach box, and curiosity led him in the direction of the village green when he heard a fife-and-drum corps playing a ragged tune.

A number of small boys were racing up and down one side of a field, and several men in bicorn hats and cloaks with beaver collars were standing nearby, stamping their booted feet to keep warm. "We can't lose, I tell you," one of them was saying. "We've held back our share of the governor's wages for two months now, and in

120

another month he's sure to give in. A man bleeds hardest when you hit him in the purse, that's what I always say, so you mark my words. Thomas will grant us every last one of our demands."

Jared was faintly amused but lost interest in the conversation when he saw a spectacle he could scarcely believe. A squad of thirty men was marching and drilling on the green, and never had he seen such a ludicrous sight. Each of the "soldiers" wore a white rag on his upper left arm as a token uniform insignia, but no two were dressed alike. Several carried long frontier rifles that the professional fighting man immediately dismissed as too cumbersome; others were armed with muskets, some of which must have been at least fifty years old, and a few were burdened with ancient blunderbusses with flaring, horn-shaped muzzles. Jared recalled having seen one in the War Office's military museum in London.

The attempts of the militiamen to march in formation were pathetic. No one man kept step with those on either side of him; the guide leaders, or corporals, had no notion of what was expected of them; and the three lines, each consisting of ten men, wavered and rippled. But it was the sergeant in charge of the drill who provided the ultimate absurdity. Phil Franklin, the brawny young man with whom Jared had exchanged words at the Crown and Scepter, was bawling orders, contradicting himself, then cursing the men because they were too confused to obey even the most basic directions.

If this squad was a fair sample of Delaware militia, Jared told himself, the French would win every engagement they fought against the English colonials.

Franklin was walking backward, trying in vain to keep his men in step, when suddenly he lost his balance and went sprawling on the hard ground.

Jared laughed aloud.

Everyone looked at him, and Franklin, hauling himself to his feet, walked swiftly to the side of the green. He halted directly in front of Jared, looked him up and down, and then demanded, "What's so damned funny?"

Jared, bristling, returned his glare. "Your army," he said, "and you."

Franklin grinned unpleasantly. "We aren't working here, on our own time, with no pay, to have a lackey in a pretty suit mock us." He paused, then became deliberately insulting. "A pretty lackey in a pretty suit."

Jared unbuttoned his satin coat, removed it, and, after placing it on the ground, started to roll up his sleeves.

The members of the militia squad, their drill forgotten, surrounded the pair, and the gentlemen in the bicorn hats moved closer, too.

"Move back, lads," Franklin said, a gleam of anticipatory pleasure in his eyes. "Willie, you hold my rifle and see it don't get dirty." Abruptly he turned back to Jared. "Are you carrying a pistol or a knife?"

"No, and I won't need either."

Franklin reached into his boot top for a bone-handled knife. "Hosea, you take care of my knife, and don't get ideas of making off with it. My initials are whittled in the handle, and even if you scraped them off, I'd know the knife anywheres." He tossed aside a scarf that had been wrapped around his throat, then rolled up his sleeves.

Jared saw the size of his biceps and, measuring his opponent carefully, knew he had set himself a difficult task. He and Franklin were approximately the same height, but the colonial outweighed him by at least thirty pounds and appeared to have a slightly longer reach.

"No holds barred?" Franklin asked politely.

Jared was not aware of any wrestling holds that could be of use in a fistfight.

"He don't know what you mean, Phil," one of the men called.

"Then I reckon I'll have to teach him. His face won't be so pretty when I'm finished with him."

"You talk a good fight," Jared said.

With no warning, Franklin lunged at him, trying to butt him in the stomach with lowered head.

Only Jared's training as a swordsman saved him from being bowled over. He instinctively side-stepped, and as the colonial charged past him, he lashed out with a hard short jab that caught Franklin on the cheekbone.

First blood had been drawn, and the crowd roared its approval, apparently playing no favorite and not caring which man won.

Franklin halted his rush, straightening as he turned back to face his foe. There was new respect in his eyes, and a swelling on his cheek indicated that the blow had stung him.

Jared had no intention of losing the initiative he had achieved, and he danced in swiftly, feinting with his left and, as much by chance as by skill, landing a right in precisely the same spot he had planted his first blow.

Franklin winced, then made an animallike sound compounded of pain, rage, and humiliation. Suddenly his right foot shot up as he aimed a kick at the Englishman's stomach.

Surprised, Jared leaped backward but could not completely avoid the kick, which grazed his chest. Outraged by what he considered unfair tactics, he caught hold of Franklin's foot as it descended and, heaving with all his strength, sent the colonial crashing onto the ground.

The crowd was shouting even more loudly, but Jared was scarcely conscious of anyone other than his opponent. He was beginning to realize what Franklin had meant by "no holds barred" and he knew he had to remain alert for trickery that even the thieves in Newgate would have hesitated to use.

He had no way of protecting himself against Franklin's next move, however. One moment the colonial was flat on his back, but in an instant he curled himself into a ball, then sprang from a prone position at the Englishman. Jared could neither evade him nor cushion the impact of the lunge, and he crashed to the ground with Franklin on top of him.

Before Jared knew what was happening, Franklin's knees were pinning down his shoulders, making it impossible for him to move, and heavy fists were battering his face. It would not be enough to ward off the blows, he knew, realizing that unless he could resume his own attack, Franklin would beat him into unconsciousness.

Desperation made Jared inventive. He heaved himself upward with all his might, sweeping his feet in an arc as though he intended to perform a backward somersault. He managed to bring his right leg high enough to hook it around his opponent's throat, knocking Franklin off-balance.

As the colonial fell to one side, Jared pulled himself to his feet, shaking his head to clear it. He could see that Franklin was rising, too, and from the way the man was hunching his shoulders, realized he intended to lunge again.

Several men in the crowd shouted advice to Jared, urging him to move in swiftly. But his opponent had taught him a lesson he would not forget, and he formed a battle plan in his own mind, a scheme that was primitive but that—if he could only bring if off—could be highly effective.

He pretended to be in a daze and stood with his arms hanging at his sides limply. It appeared that one or two blows would knock him out of the fight.

Franklin promptly changed his tactics and waded in confidently.

Jared started his punch at knee level, putting all his weight behind his fist as he swung it upward.

The surprised Franklin had no opportunity to ward off the punch, which seemed to explode at the point of his chin. A lesser man would have dropped, but he stayed on his feet, planting them apart while he regained his strength.

Again Jared lashed out at him, catching him with a hard left to the pit of the stomach that doubled him over, then straightening him with a vicious right to his already tender cheekbone.

The excited spectators were in a frenzy now, expecting one final punch that would end the fight. But they failed to take into account the rugged stamina of Franklin. Even though he was glassy-eyed, he waded forward and began to throw hard punches of his own.

Jared stood up to him, and the two men, almost toe to toe, exchanged a score of blows, rocking each other, fists crashing against flesh and bone. All thought of tactics, of possible trickery, left Jared's mind, and he knew only that his survival depended on his ability to inflict damage while absorbing brutal punishment.

Suddenly he felt his arms being pinned to his sides and discovered that three men were holding him. For an instant he thought his opponent's friends had entered the fight, but he realized that men were also holding Franklin.

"That's enough, boys," a gentleman in a bicorn hat was saying sternly. "No more of this or you'll kill each other."

Jared tried to free himself and vaguely knew that Franklin was struggling, too.

"Listen to the colonel," someone shouted.

"Franklin," the man in the bicorn growled, "I'm giving you an order. Stop fighting now, or I'll haul you before a court-martial board."

"Yes, sir," Phil Franklin muttered, his swollen lips making it difficult for him to speak distinctly.

Jared's left eye was half closed, and he peered with difficulty at the distinguished middle-aged man who spoke with such authority.

126

The colonel saw that Jared had turned to him, and he addressed the Englishman quietly. "You aren't enlisted in my regiment, which is too bad. I can use a man who fights as you do. For the present I still have enough authority under Delaware law to have you put in the stocks for disturbing the peace. As colonel in chief of the colony's militia, I'm responsible for maintaining order, so I advise you to cool off, by yourself, unless you prefer forty-eight hours in the stocks."

Jared made a great effort to control himself, and stopped struggling. Although he knew he had been severely battered, he had accomplished his goal, and he grinned as he looked at Franklin's puffy face. The militia sergeant would treat him with far greater respect the next time they met.

"If you'll tell these fellows to release me," he said, "I can promise you I won't start another fight."

"Let him go," the colonel ordered.

Jared shook himself, wiping a trickle of blood from the corner of his mouth.

Franklin was released, too, and they eyed each other warily, each prepared to resume the fight the moment the other made one hostile move.

"It's customary," the colonel said, "for men who have almost knocked each other senseless to shake hands. I heard your argument, and it's plain to me, even if it isn't to you, that you have no real cause to bear grudges."

Jared and Franklin continued to stand, both reluctant to make the first move.

The colonel became impatient. "Shake hands!"

Jared had been a professional soldier for so long

that he instinctively responded to the older man's crisp voice of authority. He extended his arm just as Franklin did the same, and their hands clasped in a firm grip.

"You're good," Jared said generously. "I thought I'd finished you, but you'd just started to fight."

"Hellfire," Franklin said, "you're the first man I've ever met in the Lower Counties who can stand up to me for five minutes. If I teach you some free-for-all tricks, you might even be able to whup me someday."

"Tricks or no tricks," Jared retorted, "I can do it right now!" He was surprised to hear himself laugh, and realized he bore no real ill will against the man he had fought.

Franklin laughed, too, his swollen lips twisting in a grimace. "I'm ready. Anytime."

"But not now," the colonel said.

"No, sir," Franklin replied, hastily amending his statement. "Not right now." He looked at the crowd still clustered around them. "The squad is dismissed," he called. "Go about your private business, lads."

The group broke up reluctantly, and men moved away from the green.

"My name is Baker, Edward T. Baker," the colonel told Jared. "If you'd like to volunteer for service in the regiment, I'd be pleased to find a place for you."

"In my squad," Franklin added.

Jared's feeling of pleasure vanished as he remembered his status. For a short time he had been on his own in a world of free men, but he was reminded, with a wrench, of his real standing. "I'm in no position to join your regiment, Colonel Baker," he said. "I'm indentured."

The older man registered no surprise. "So I realized from your lackey's suit." He carefully refrained from mentioning the ankle band that identified anyone who was bonded.

Jared appreciated his delicacy but simultaneously became aware of the condition of his clothes. His breeches were torn and dirt-stained, and at some point in the fight either he or Franklin had trampled on his satin coat, ripping it.

The colonel sensed his dismay and patted him on the shoulder. "I'll do what I can for you," he said, and walked away quickly in the direction of the buildings at the far side of the green.

Jared was alone with the sergeant. "I got to admit," Franklin said, "that your suit was prettier a while back. But I reckon I can help you a mite. I'll go to the man who holds your indenture and tell him the fight was my fault." He was genuinely apologetic.

"Thanks," Jared said with a shrug, "but I'm bonded to a woman."

Franklin whistled under his breath, his swollen lips making it impossible for him to accomplish the feat audibly. "The first time I saw you at the tavern, you were with Marshall." He paused. "Is it Mistress high-and-mighty Murtagh?"

Jared nodded.

"You better come with me." Franklin led the way to the rear of the building on the near side of the green.

There they found a well and took turns

splashing icy water on their faces to remove grime and, hopefully, reduce some of the more obvious signs of battle damage.

"I've got to hurry or I'll be late," Jared said.

This time Franklin voluntarily held out a hand. "Good luck," he said. "You can whup any man in the Lower Counties—except me. But I'll be damned if I know how you deal with the woman who holds your indenture."

Jared was equally at a loss and, walking back to the carriage, he tried to brace himself for a fresh storm. The cuts on his face had stopped bleeding but were still ugly, his left eye was almost swollen closed, and his hated lackey's suit was completely ruined.

Caroline was standing near the coach, chatting with another young woman, who left as Jared approached.

He tried desperately to think of something appropriate to say.

"I saw the whole fight," Caroline told him, "from the second-floor window of Mistress Anderson's dressmaking shop. I honestly thought that brute was going to kill you." There was neither disapproval nor sympathy in her tone, and her attitude was impersonally remote.

"I'm afraid I have no way of repaying you for this uniform," Jared said.

"The price is worth the talk. My friends were thrilled."

Jared thought he detected a hint of amusement in her voice.

"I had no idea you could be so ferocious, either, but I suppose it's what I should have expected from someone who felt so much at home in Newgate."

Jared wanted to reply that she had literally no idea how he had felt at Newgate, but he forced himself to remain silent.

"You can work for several hours after your supper every night in the fields," she said. "Perhaps, in a month or two, you'll have paid me for the suit through labor."

Her serenity was as infuriating as the sentence she had imposed. There was no possible appeal to a higher authority, and Jared had no intention of offering an explanation that might persuade her to change her mind. At the very least, he wanted to shake her until her teeth rattled; he knew he wanted to take her again, but he might be less fortunate if he forced her to submit to him a second time. Although she neither knew nor cared whether he preserved some remnants of his shattered pride, he could not afford to destroy hers.

"If you have no more fights to keep you busy this afternoon," Caroline said, "I'm ready to be driven home."

Jared, opening the carriage door for her, wondered how he could preserve his sanity in the years of servitude that lay ahead.

CHAPTER EIGHT

In January 1741, Governor Thomas agreed to meet a commission from the Lower Counties to resolve their differences, but a new impasse immediately developed. The governor assumed that the

Delaware representatives would come to Philadelphia for the conference, but they insisted that he come to their own soil and offered him his choice of New Castle or the smaller but growing town of Wilmington as a site.

George Thomas was outraged and refused to leave his own mansion in Philadelphia. The Lower Counties responded by sealing the border, allowing no one but citizens of Delaware to travel in either direction. Thomas threatened to use royal troops to break the deadlock, but Ian Murray, the chairman of the Delaware commission, laughed when he heard the governor's statement.

"I could imagine that Thomas is angry enough to use troops against us," Murray declared in a brief speech from the steps of the New Castle courthouse, "but he's bluffing. He has no royal troops, not a single company of them. There's half a battalion stationed in New York Town and another in Boston, but those colonies are fighting a real war, and you can wager your last sixpence they won't let Thomas have trained soldiers for no purpose other than to spank us."

Throughout the crisis Colonel Edward Baker remained calm. "I refuse to admit the possibility of a battle between Delaware and Pennsylvania militia," he said. "Governor Thomas is a sensible man who is trying to do his duty. When he realizes we can't be frightened, he'll change his tune fast enough."

Baker was right. On February 2, 1741, the chief executive officer of the proprietary colonies of Pennsylvania and the Lower Counties sent his personal aide to New Castle with word that he would arrive in three days to open conclusive negotiations. The news caused an unprecedented flurry of activity. Politicians from all three counties met day and night, the owners of plantations in the neighborhood offered their houses for the convenience of the governor, and their wives vied with one another in planning dinner parties and receptions.

George Thomas confounded his hosts, arriving at noon on February 5 with an escort of only two men, a legal assistant and a financial expert. Refusing all offers of hospitality, he engaged a small room in a lodging house, and after announcing that he was not interested in social life of any kind, he plunged into his debate with the Delaware commission.

Forty-eight hectic hours later, a formal agreement was signed. Delaware was granted the identity she had been assuming; she was given autonomy in her local affairs, including the right to levy and collect taxes, and New Castle was officially recognized as her capital.

The Lower Counties, in return, promised to submit themselves to the authority of Thomas, provided his decrees were issued in his capacity as governor of Delaware rather than Pennsylvania. The commissioners pledged a portion of tax collections for the maintenance of the executive branch of government and, for the immediate future, offered to raise two regiments of volunteers for the war against France.

Colonel Baker, who had not been consulted, protested vehemently. There were not enough free men in Delaware who could leave their families unsupported, he said, and he insisted it would not be possible to raise a second regiment.

Governor Thomas, equally energetic, offered to issue a decree similar to that which had created a furor in Pennsylvania. Indentured servants who volunteered for military service would be accepted, and all time spent in military service would be included in their obligations under their bonds. Baker promptly accepted the proposal.

The proclamation was issued that same day, prior to Thomas's departure, and within the next twenty-four hours its provisions were read aloud by members of the colonial legislature to all male indentured servants in Delaware.

The bonded men on the Murtagh plantation were eating their noon meal when a member of the House of Representatives arrived and, in accordance with the law, read aloud the governor's offer. As he spoke, the men exchanged glances, trying to weigh the possible advantages of accepting militia service. Most were hesitant, unwilling to commit themselves until they discussed the matter privately.

But there were no doubts in Jared's mind. The one drill session he had observed on the New Castle green had been an absurd display, and he certainly had no respect for the militia. But any respite from indentured service would be welcome, and a year of military duty would reduce his bonded obligation to Caroline Murtagh accordingly.

The moment the representative stopped speaking, Jared raised his voice. "I volunteer!" he called.

After a moment four others echoed him.

The representative looked pleased.

"When do we go?" Jared asked.

The representative had encountered the same problem earlier in the day, and he grew uncomfortable. Governor Thomas, in his haste, had issued an order that actually worked a hardship on plantation owners. "Well," he said, "Colonel Baker wants you right off so he can get the new regiment organized. But it won't be easy for Mistress Murtagh to find replacements for you, so you ought to consider—"

"How soon can we leave?" Jared interrupted.

"Today. Right now." The representative sounded resigned and a trifle weary.

Two more indentured men volunteered.

The representative looked at Adam Marshall, shrugged, and mounted his horse.

Marshall gestured brusquely. "Those of you who are going, line up here," he said, and when the seven volunteers came forward, he wrote down their names. "You'll have to wait until I notify Mistress Murtagh." His left eyelid flickered in a suggestion of a wink as he glanced in Jared's direction.

Less than a quarter of an hour later he returned. "Before you go," he said, "you'll have to sign your names or make your mark on a promise to return as soon as your military duty is finished. Then you'll be free to leave." He went to Jared and lowered his voice. "You're wanted up at the house, Hale."

Caroline was standing at the parlor windows overlooking the withered grass of the lawn, a slip-

135

pered foot beating a rapid tattoo on the hardwood floor. She did not turn as Jared came into the room. "I might have known you'd find a way to trick me," she said.

"The offer was made to indentured men by Governor Thomas, not by me," he replied. "Complain to him, or to Colonel Baker."

She ignored his sarcasm. "May I know your reasons for accepting military service?"

He saw no reason to be less than completely candid. "I find army life more congenial than work as a groom, coachman, and field hand, ma'am."

Caroline turned and appeared surprised to see that he was not gloating. "You may be killed, you know."

"I'm accustomed to risks."

She sighed. "For the present you've beaten me."

"I'm thinking of myself, not you," he told her honestly.

Caroline smiled and held out her hand, the only time she had shown warmth other than the occasion when they had been intimate. "I wish you good luck. I believe you'll find wilderness fighting quite different from the type of military life you knew in England."

Jared formally shook hands with her, resisting an urge to kiss her. A rebuff would spoil the very slight improvement in their relationship. "Thank you for your good wishes. I won't pretend to you that I'm going to war for reasons of patriotism. Any love I felt for England died in prison, and I've no reason to develop a liking for the colonies." He didn't know why he spoke so freely, but he felt that he owed her something in return for his abrupt departure. "You've always thought of me as an opportunist, so your opinion is confirmed."

He bowed low and, not waiting to be dismissed, left the room. He made his way toward the rear of the house, and when he reached the pantry, someone moved in the shadows at the far end of the crowded chamber.

"I've just heard the news," Polly White said.

Jared went to her. "Will you miss me?"

"In some ways."

"What are they?"

"You know them." Perhaps Polly realized he was crowding her, but she made no attempt to escape.

"What are the reasons you won't miss me?" Jared demanded.

She made no reply.

He put a hand under her chin and tilted her face upward. "Answer me."

"I'd rather not." She displayed the same quality of unexpected dignity that she had shown when they had last been alone together, for a few moments, in the barn.

Jared wondered whether she had discovered, or perhaps guessed, that he had seduced Caroline. As nearly as he could judge, however, jealousy was not responsible for her reticence. "I dislike mysteries," he said.

"Sometimes they're unavoidable."

It occurred to him fleetingly that since her association with Caroline she had enlarged her vocabulary and now spoke with a less marked lower-class accent.

"If I die in battle," he said with a grin, "I'll never find out."

"Your kind never gets killed." Polly made the observation quietly, without rancor.

"I'm not sure that's a compliment."

"I mean it as one. You can look after yourself, Jared." Polly glanced over his shoulder toward the pantry door. "I—I don't want to be caught here, talking to you."

"Did she make trouble for you last time?"

She shook her head.

"Polly."

The girl looked at him, her eyes troubled.

Jared knew only one way to handle the situation, and he kissed her.

She yielded to him limply but did not respond.

He released her and walked out into the open without looking back. Between them, he thought, as he stalked past the kitchen, Caroline and Polly were succeeding in sending him away thoroughly confused.

The New Castle green had been transformed, overnight, into a sea of tents. New recruits, including both free men and indentured servants, were arriving at the hastily erected camp in an unending stream, and Jared was surprised and somewhat amused by the informality of the newcomers' reception. Those who could write printed their names on a sheet of rough paper, while a lance corporal performed the task for the illiterate. Two officers, the only men in the bivouac who were in uniform, stood near the

138

entrance to the enlistment tent and administered a brief oath as each newcomer emerged.

Several noncommissioned officers waited nearby, each eager to snare recruits who appeared to be good military material. The entire process was so haphazard, so completely lacking in organization, that Jared again wondered whether he had made a mistake. Perhaps he would have been wiser to remain on the Murtagh plantation.

"I'm claiming that one," a loud voice boomed.

Jared saw Phil Franklin beckoning.

"I've had to give up half my squad to a cadre for a new company," Franklin told him, "and I need men. So I'm claiming you. Go over yonder up to the area of the First New Castle Foot and ask for Corporal Willie Painter. I'll be along after I get hold of a few more lads who look like they won't shrink from a good battle."

Jared recognized Painter, who had witnessed his fight with the sergeant, and Painter, a short, narrow-shouldered man with a thin face, knew him instantly, too.

"This here is a good break!" The corporal pumped Jared's hand enthusiastically as he led him into a tent. "You'll need some new boots," he said, "a buckskin shirt, and some trousers that won't split when you sit on brambles." He made some notes on the same kind of rough paper that had been used in the enlistment tent.

"Do you issue uniforms?" Jared asked him, motivated partly by curiosity, partly by amusement.

Painter shook his head. "We don't wear 'em, and only the officers can afford their own." He lowered his voice confidentially. "When we can't get 'em any other way, we steal what we need. Believe me, you're lucky to get into the First New Castle Foot."

Jared laughed, but he realized Painter was serious.

The corporal's tone changed. "Take off your shoe and stocking."

Jared was surprised by the unexpected order.

"No man in a Delaware regiment wears bonded chains!" Painter produced a thick metal file.

The next quarter of an hour was indelibly etched in Jared's memory for the rest of his life. Painter sawed at the metal band that encircled his ankle and finally, sweat pouring down his face, cut through it. "You'll want the joy of taking it off, I reckon," the corporal said.

Using all his strength, Jared bent the metal sufficiently to remove it. Then, uncertain what to do next, he started to slip it into his pocket.

Painter snatched it from him and tossed it into a bucket in the corner of the tent. "Garbage," he said. "Any man who carries Delaware weapons fights as a free man. I don't reckon you brought along a rifle or musket?"

"I haven't been permitted to own firearms," Jared reminded him.

"You know how to shoot?"

Jared had been in the colonies long enough to know that no one in the New World boasted of his achievements. "I can manage," he said.

The corporal, remembering seeing him in personal combat, heard something in his voice. "Let's find out." He led the Englishman out of

140

the tent and to the far side of the green, where a crude portrait of a soldier in a French uniform had been drawn on a burlap sack nailed to a tree.

A few moments later Jared held a musket of fairly recent make in his hands. He loaded and primed it with swift efficiency, took aim at the figure from a distance of one hundred paces, and squeezed the trigger.

"Not bad," Painter commented when he saw the bullet had lodged itself an inch or two above the French soldier's belt. "Maybe it would have killed him, maybe wounded him real bad. You ever shoot a rifle?"

Jared shook his head. By now a small crowd had gathered around him, and someone stepped forward and handed him a long, slender gun. It was a strange weapon, unlike any he had ever handled. The octagonal barrel alone was at least five feet long, the butt was small and narrow, and the piece as a whole was heavy and cumbersome.

"She has a nice smooth kick, like good whiskey," Painter told him, "and you've got to hold her steady but gentle, the way you would a woman."

The spectators appreciated his humor.

"She won't jump near as far as a musket, so you don't have to allow much for lift," the corporal continued. "You aim her true and treat her right and she'll be the best friend you'll ever have."

Jared soon discovered that it was somewhat more difficult to load the rifle than it was to perform the same operation on a musket, but the crowd was not shy in offering advice. Still uncertain how the weapon would respond, however, he

141

braced himself as he squinted down the long barrel, aiming straight at the dummy's face. He found he needed to apply only a light touch to the trigger and the rifle discharged, the butt recoiling surprisingly little against his shoulder.

When the smoke cleared, he saw he had missed the nose of the dummy by no more than a quarter of an inch. He quickly revised his opinion of the weapon, for which he had felt only scorn. "First rate," he said, realizing a marksman could attain a degree of accuracy with a rifle far exceeding the potential of a musket.

Painter pushed through the throng to join Franklin, who was coming toward him. "Phil," he said, "this here lad is a natural!" He explained what had happened and took the sergeant to inspect the holes in the burlap.

"I reckon we'll have to find you a rifle somewhere," Franklin told Jared.

It was best not to ask whether the weapon would be stolen, Jared decided. The militia apparently had its own unique method of obtaining equipment and supplies.

A sudden thought occurred to the sergeant. "You've been in an army somewhere."

Jared had no desire to elaborate, and nodded.

"I should have guessed it right off. You always hold yourself like you were standing for inspection." Franklin removed his stocking cap and rubbed his balding head. "There's only one thing to settle. We'll go back to our bivouac area."

They returned to the tents of the First New Castle Foot, where a number of men were preparing the evening meal in large kettles. As

142

nearly as Jared could tell, the militia might lack the sinews of war, but there seemed to be no shortage of food.

Franklin led the way into a tent that he shared with several corporals. "Now, then," he said, a familiar light coming into his eyes. "You and me, we fought to a draw. But I like things to be tidy."

"So do I," Jared replied promptly.

The sergeant was pleased. "Once I've whupped you, we'll get along together just fine."

"Suppose it works out the other way?"

The possibility hadn't crossed Franklin's mind, but he considered it. "Nobody can say I'm not fair. Right, Willie?"

Painter, who had followed them, solemnly agreed.

"I've yet to meet the man who can put me out of a fight, but if you do, I'll admit it in front of the whole blamed company."

"That wouldn't be wise," Jared said. "You're the company sergeant major, and you'll have no authority if the men don't respect you."

"Here's a lad who uses his mind! I like you, Hale!" Franklin thumped Jared between the shoulder blades before becoming serious. "We got us a couple of problems, but I know how to solve them. Colonel Baker won't tolerate fights, and he'll scalp us with his own skinning knife if he finds out we've had us a friendly little mix. So we'll have to go off into the woods at sundown, right after supper. We don't want a crowd, seeing somebody might talk, so I'll just bring Willie, and you can bring anybody you like."

The idea of taking seconds to a brawl delighted

143

Jared. "I don't know anyone that well. Corporal Painter will suit me fine."

The corporal was honored, and beamed.

"This time," Franklin said, "we'll fight your style instead of no holds barred."

"Your way is good enough for me."

"Except you don't know the tricks, and I won't have it said I took advantage. Fists only, that's how we'll do it."

"If you wish."

"There's one thing more. Colonel Baker can sniff out a fight from a mile away, like smelling a skunk when there's a high wind. If he sees any marks on our faces, I'll be demoted, and you'll be assigned to permanent sentry duty. So let's make a rule—we'll hold ourselves to body blows only, where they don't show."

It would be difficult to fight under such conditions, but Jared was willing and said so.

Corporal Painter laughed. "Phil her has another reason. He's going off to see a girl tonight, and he won't be able to kiss her if you smash up his mouth the way you did last time."

The sergeant was furious. "You tend you own damned business, Willie, or I'll have to put you in your place."

"No offense meant." Painter backed away.

"Are we agreed?" Franklin asked.

Shaking his hand, Jared realized that Americans were a strange breed who sometimes fought for the sheer joy of violent physical action.

An hour later, after eating a hearty, savory stew, the three men left the camp on the green separately, meeting behind the courthouse. Ostensibly taking an aimless stroll, as were many other militiamen, they made their way to the woods at the northwest side of the town. There Franklin took charge, and Jared marveled at his ability to find seemingly invisible tracks on a dark night. Swiftly, unerringly, the sergeant led his companions to a small clearing.

"We're lucky," he said. "The ground is frozen, so there won't be too much mud on your shirt and breeches when I knock you down."

Jared removed his short work coat of rough wool, which he handed to Painter. The air was icy cold, and he rubbed his hands together, then scratched his arms.

Franklin took off his coat, too, and said, "Let me know when you're ready, Hale."

"There's one thing I want to know," Jared said. "We could fight all night, I imagine, if we really wanted to dig in. How will we know when to stop?"

"Whenever you've had enough, let me know."

"I'm ready," Jared said.

Franklin lunged at him in the style that Jared already knew and rained jarring blows on his shoulders and chest.

The punches were bruising, but Jared knew he could absorb such punishment indefinitely, as could his opponent. Under the rules they had established, each was really vulnerable only in the stomach, so he immediately decided to concentrate, if he could, on the one area.

For the moment, however, he was fully occupied trying to defend himself. Franklin's power was tremendous and he was surprisingly agile, repeatedly slipping inside the Englishman's guard. The speed and precision of the sergeant's blows became greater, and all at once Jared found himself flat on his back.

Franklin stood over him, breathing easily. "I don't want to hurt you," he said. "Had enough?"

Jared sucked in some air so he could laugh. He sat up, and a new problem presented itself; he was being crowded so closely that he would be knocked down again as soon as he stood. So he made an awkward but effective move, scrambling backward like a crab while in the same motion he leaped to his feet.

Franklin rewarded him with a quick smile of congratulations, which faded as he lunged.

Jared did not retreat. Planting his feet apart to help enable him to meet the onslaught, he aimed his first punch, a very hard right jab, at the pit of the sergeant's stomach. His fist found its target, and he followed it with a longer left to the same spot, then another right.

Franklin doubled over, gasping, and Jared quickly reviewed the possibilities of what he might do next. In an ordinary fight he would follow with a blow to the jaw, but since faces were outside the permitted target zones, his choice was limited. A sharp punch to the chest or a shoulder might knock his opponent down, but that would merely give the sergeant time to regain his breath.

So Jared waited until Franklin began to straighten, and then sent another crashing blow into his foe's stomach.

Enraged, the sergeant forgot the rules he

himself had made and sent a wild left sailing toward the Englishman's head.

Jared ducked, wondering how long he could curb his anger if such tactics were repeated.

Franklin regained his self-control at once, however, and still too breathless to speak, let his eyes apologize for him.

Jared accepted with a nod and at the same time resumed his assault. He sent two more jabs deep into the sergeant's stomach and was surprised when a third crumpled the man on the ground.

Willie Painter probably had never seen his friend in such condition and became alarmed. "Are you all right, Phil?" he shouted, running forward into the center of the clearing and peering down at the fallen figure.

Franklin nodded but made no attempt to stand again. It took him some moments to regain his breath, and he sat up, one hand gingerly massaging his stomach. "I wouldn't have believed it," he muttered hoarsely, "but you got a punch as strong as mine."

Jared had no intention of allowing him to chat long enough to recover his equilibrium. "Had enough?"

The sergeant went through a painful inner struggle. "I reckon I have," he said at last, staring dully at the dead, matted leaves on the ground beside him.

Jared extended a hand to him and hauled him to his feet. "Sergeant," he said, "I've never known a man who can fight as you do. I had some good luck tonight, that's all."

Franklin recognized the gesture, which helped

147

ease his humiliation. The experience was new, and he groped for words. "Hale," he said at last, "you and me, we'll make a great team. Between us, I reckon we can whup a whole squad of the best militiamen in these here colonies."

Corporal Painter looked at the two bigger men, still unable to believe that his idol had fallen.

"I have an idea," Jared said, "that we'll work well together against the French."

Franklin raised his hand and threw an arm around the shoulders of the man who had so unexpectedly defeated him. "God help 'em!" he shouted, his self-confidence restored.

Jared quickly learned that the Delaware militia was unlike any army he had ever known anywhere. Its unorthodoxy was normal, rather than exceptional, and rules were elastic, to say the least.

Less than forty-eight hours after his enlistment, he returned to his bivouac area late in the afternoon to find Phil Franklin standing alone, his brawny arms clasped behind his back as he paced up and down, muttering to himself.

"What's wrong?" Jared asked.

"We've been waiting and waiting for London to issue us some new arms, as they promised us, before we go marching off to war. Well, a ship put into the harbor today, and you'll never guess in a million years what they sent us."

"Muskets? Cannon? Rifles?"

Each time Phil shook his head in disgust. "Nothing," he said contemptuously. "Not a blame thing, except a few sabers. Can you imagine that? How in thunderation do they expect Delaware men to fight with sabers?"

Jared's interest was sparked immediately. "I know of no weapon," he said, slightly offended, "more useful in battle than a saber. In the hands of a cavalryman who knows what he's doing, it can be devastating."

Phil looked at him and shrugged. "That may be so in Europe. Only trouble is, nobody hereabouts knows how to use them."

"*I* do," Jared said emphatically. "Can you get your hands on any of them?"

"Sure. All I got to do is to sign out for 'em and I'll have enough for the whole company."

"Then by all means get as many as you can," Jared told him. "We may not be the Royal Dragoons, but I'm sure they'll come in handy someday. And besides," he said, patting his friend on the back and smiling as if at a private joke, "we can always use them to slice melons."

CHAPTER NINE

The Delaware militia regiments marched endlessly through a vast wilderness, and even in the more populated countries there were literally thousands of acres of uninhabited territory. Jared, footsore and always cold and weary, developed a lively appreciation of the infantryman's problems. He and his comrades were awakened at dawn after spending the night on the freezing ground, each man wrapped in a single, inadequate blanket. Breakfast invariably consisted of jerked venison and stale bread, washed down with a hot, bitter beverage made from roasted acorns. The first time Jared tasted the brew he gagged, but eventually a desire for something warm to drink overcame his scruples and the violent protests of his palate.

An hour after sunrise the day's long march began, the men making their way in uneven ranks down frozen dirt roads or through the trackless forests. Everywhere there were hidden snares, from snow-covered roots and fallen branches that tripped the unwary, to thorns and brambles that ripped at the trousers and shirts of those who were not yet fortunate enough—Jared among them—to wear the buckskins suitable for wilderness travel.

A halt was called around noon, near a frozen lake, and the two regiments ate a meal that duplicated their breakfast, except that they had nothing to drink but melted snow. Then the march was resumed and maintained until sundown, sometimes later, when the quartermasters, who traveled ahead of the main body, arrived with food they had purchased from neighboring farms. No matter what they brought, though, the men dined every night on stew, sometimes made with a beef base, sometimes venison or, less frequently, fish. Parched corn, boiled until it became a tasteless paste, was usually included, as were onions and, less frequently, dried beans. At best the evening meal was barely palatable, but Jared and his companions were too cold and hungry to care and did not complain until, stretching out around their fires after dark, they had the time and energy to voice their frustrations.

Jared surprised himself by feeling increasingly

close bonds of friendship with the other militiamen. He was beginning to understand the irreverent humor of Americans, and certainly he shared their lack of respect for Crown authorities. Even the meek, quiet members of the First New Castle Foot were irritated by the monotony of their diet, the harshness of their living conditions, and the apparent belief of the high command that they were impervious to cold, snow, and blisters on their feet.

After spending years in the Royal Army, Jared had thought he had acquired a rich vocabulary, but the Americans proved themselves far more colorful than their English counterparts. Corporal Painter was particularly adept at expressing his feelings, and when timed at a campfire one night, he demonstrated that he could curse for more than five minutes without repeating a single word. No noncommissioned officer in the dragoons had possessed his volatile imagination.

During the first days of the march north, Jared hated the wilderness. After a time, however, he realized he was spending his energy needlessly, and thereafter he made a conscious effort to accept his environment. Certainly the expanse of the forest inspired him with awe, as did the size of ancient trees. Nowhere in England had he seen elm, oak, or beech so huge, and he thought it miraculous that there was always game to be found in the woods and fish in the rivers, even in the dead of winter.

The most pleasant surprise of the march was provided by Philadelphia, which was a smaller, cleaner version of London. The Pennsylvania capital, with a population of almost fifteen thousand, was the largest metropolis in England's New World colonies and had developed a sophistication of its own that in no way resembled the cosmopolitanism of Europe's cities. The town's leading citizen, Benjamin Franklin, published newspapers in English and German, books, and a magazine. A repertory company of actors presented plays, both classical and modern, throughout the year, and the citizens could take their choice of a variety of concerts and lectures at several halls.

The architecture was similar to that of new buildings erected in England during the past half century, but houses were infinitely cleaner and fresher-looking in Philadelphia. Only the waterfront, where merchantmen flying the ensigns of a half dozen nations were docked, was grubby, and only on the streets near the seamen's taverns did Jared see any sign of drunken or disorderly conduct. What made the place most unlike London was the almost complete absence of beggars; he saw only one, an Indian half-breed with a strong smell of rum on his breath.

There appeared to be great wealth in Philadelphia. The homes of the substantial citizens were very large, and around four o'clock every afternoon the traffic on the main thoroughfares was slowed to a crawl by interminable lines of carriages. Philadelphians were conscious of their dress, but Jared did not think it either incongruous or amusing that their styles had been popular in London five or six years earlier. It occurred to him that his own attitudes were changing somewhat and that he was accepting Americans at the values they had established for themselves rather than seeing them through English eyes.

The Delaware militia camped just outside Philadelphia for the better part of a week, and not until the end of that time did they learn that Colonel Baker had been engaging in a quiet war of his own with Governor Thomas, refusing to resume his march until his men received their pay. Baker won, the governor giving him funds for a three-month campaign, and that same day every man in the regiments received wages for thirty days of duty.

That evening Jared, armed with a saber and carrying the rifle he had finally been issued, celebrated at a tavern with Sergeant Franklin and Corporal Painter, relishing the feeling of having silver in his pocket for the first time since coming to America. He paid a shilling for a memorable feast, which started with mounds of roast oysters followed by a peppery tripe soup, and continued with dishes of smoked eel, roasted turkey, and *ascutasquash,* an Indian vegetable that resembled a cucumber. The steak-and-kidney pie was delicious, the salad greens were crisp, and so many cheeses and fruits were served at the end of the meal that Jared and his companions could only sample them. They drank sack flips and a bottle of canary, and each downed two glasses of port; but they had consumed so much food that the liquor gave them no more than a faintly pleasant glow.

Jared felt affluent for the first time in years, and

after the dinner he bought himself a pair of new boots—handsome yet stout enough to withstand the rigors of the campaign—an antler-handled hunting knife, and, with the last of his hard-earned pay, a brand-new set of buckskins.

The march north was resumed through Pennsylvania and New Jersey, and although the men speculated endlessly, no one knew their ultimate destination. Some thought they would be assigned to frontier duty in western Massachusetts Bay, which the French might capture if they sent a strong expedition south; a few believed it more likely that they would push into Canada itself for a direct confrontation with the French. Colonel Baker and the members of his staff listened, the talk swirling about them, but said nothing.

The Delaware troops joined forces with several other units that were already encamped on the western bank of the Hudson River, opposite New York Town. There was one regiment of English-speaking Pennsylvanians in the bivouac, and another of Germans. The New York contingent included a full regiment of light infantry and four troops of the worst-trained cavalry Jared had ever seen. New Jersey had contributed one regiment of infantry. In all, the army consisted of more than four thousand men, the largest force ever raised by the colonies. Colonel Baker, who was the senior officer in both experience and length of service, assumed temporary overall command and should have been promoted to the rank of brigadier, but no one colony had the authority to give him the higher grade.

The men of the First New Castle Foot were

granted permission to row across the Hudson for one evening in New York Town, and those few hours were more than enough for Jared. The place typified all that he disliked in America. Although New York was only the third largest city in the colonies, ranking far behind Philadelphia and Boston, and had few buildings or homes of note, its citizens were boisterous, self-assertive, and grasping. Jared and his companions walked out of three taverns in succession when they learned the outrageous prices the proprietors were demanding for ale and rum. Later they heard, too, that men seeking the company of trollops who clustered in the streets and lanes near Fort George and the Battery at the lower tip of Manhattan Island had paid dearly for their pleasures.

Orders were given to break camp the following morning, but the departure of the militia was delayed when a riot broke out between the German-speaking Pennsylvanians and the New Jersey troops, who were aided by the New Yorkers from the Mohawk Valley. All other units were confined to their own bivouac areas, while the regimental and battalion commanders, led by Colonel Baker, tried to separate the combatants. The brawlers were beyond reason, so the cavalry troops were summoned to ride between them, and Colonel Baker sent for his own First Regiment, too, its men being instructed not to discharge their weapons but to use force short of actual killing, if necessary.

The First New Castle maneuvered itself into the van of the advancing infantry, and Jared was astonished by the sight directly ahead, on a bluff overlooking the Hudson. Several hundred men were struggling on the plateau, as scores of fist-fights and free-for-alls raged. One group pushed another toward the edge of the cliffs, but the defenders rallied and swept back their foes. What made the situation completely confusing was the impossibility of distinguishing friend from opponent. None of the enlisted men was wearing a uniform, so the troops on both sides looked alike.

"Hold your ranks," the First Delaware's officers called. "Hold tight, lads!"

The tactics were simple, Jared saw. With the cavalry in the lead, Colonel Baker intended to put a living wall between the fighting militiamen. But the maneuver failed miserably, principally because the cavalrymen seemed incapable of acting decisively. Instead of riding boldly down on the battling regiments, the cavalry officers timidly slowed their mounts to a walk, and soon the horsemen, as well as the Delaware infantry, were swallowed up in the riot.

Sergeant Franklin promptly and joyously forgot why he had been summoned and waded into the fray with an enthusiasm that the entire First New Castle Foot immediately emulated. Men used the butts of their rifles and muskets as clubs and swung them with impartial abandon at the New Yorkers, Pennsylvanians, and New Jerseymen.

Jared thought the riot was as insane as it was meaningless, and was reluctant to join in the combat until a savage shove from behind sent him sprawling on the ground. He leaped to his feet, enraged, and, snatching up his rifle, looked for the man who had attacked him from behind. In the pushing, shouting mass, it was impossible to locate the culprit, however.

At that moment, just to his right, he saw a cavalry trooper knocked unconscious by a stone that caught him on the forehead. The man slumped in his saddle, and Jared ran up to him in order to catch him before he toppled to the ground. As he lowered the man's inert body, Jared found a simple plan forming in his own mind. He vaulted into the saddle and, after making his rifle secure, waved his saber over his head.

"Troopers to me!" he roared. "Lively, now!"

Horsemen responded to the ring of authority in his voice, and dazed riders who had been edging their nervous mounts toward the side of the plateau finally had a goal. In a short time Jared had accumulated a score of cavalrymen.

"Form in ranks of four," he shouted. "Closer! Now, follow me, lads, and ride like hell!" He spurred to a gallop, the reinvigorated cavalrymen behind him.

Heading straight toward the storm center of the riot, Jared increased his pace, brandishing his sword over his head and shouting at the top of his voice. The other riders did the same, and the brawlers were startled when they saw the troopers descending on them. Losing their appetite for combat, they scattered.

The officers of the First Delaware Regiment were quick to exploit the advantage. Regaining control of their own men, they marched into the gap that Jared and his followers had created. Each double file faced outward, with the men in the two front ranks kneeling, rifles and muskets aimed.

The combatants had been separated from their comrades, and on each side of the cordon there were men from several colonies. Everyone felt isolated, and the threat of retaliatory force had a remarkably calming effect. Battalion and company commanders soon regained control of their units, and the sheepish militiamen were marched off to their own bivouac areas.

The departure of the colonial militia was delayed twenty-four hours, and a court-martial board of senior officers convened to try the ringleaders of the riot. Three men were given dishonorable discharges and were handed over to the Royal Army garrison at Fort George in New York Town for a year's imprisonment, while sixteen others were flogged with a cat-o'-nine-tails in the presence of the entire army.

The much-subdued militiamen retired to their own unit areas, and Jared, bewildered by the inexplicable outburst of violence, tried to grope toward an understanding of what had happened. Had any similar incident occurred in the Royal Army, it would have been considered a mutiny, and large numbers of men would have been executed.

"Why did so many men rebel?" he asked Phil Franklin.

The sergeant looked surprised. "Rebel? Hellfire, Jared, the boys were letting off some high spirits, that's all."

"But at least fifty men were injured!"

"That's not too bad a record for a riot that was stopped before the lads got themselves worked up proper for a fight."

Jared became impatient. "There must have been some reason for the riot."

"Why, sure. Those Pennsylvania Germans stay off by themselves, like they think they're better than anybody else. Then there's the Jerseymen. They got a pretty high opinion of Jerseymen. And the New Yorkers are just plain ornery. They don't think much of the rest of us, and we don't find them even tolerable. If we'd heard earlier about the fight, every last man from Delaware would have been there, showing them all what we can do in a free-for-all. But after the officers got hold of us, we had to obey orders."

"How do you expect to fight a common enemy if the men from every colony hate those from all the other colonies?" The prospects of an army of militiamen were bleaker than Jared had imagined.

Franklin's expression was pitying. "We'll take care of the Frenchies and their Indian friends, don't you fret yourself. What's that got to do with the boys getting some healthy exercise?"

Jared did not consider it "healthy" when a large number of men had suffered cuts and sprains that had required the attention of the army's physicians.

"There's no colony like Delaware," the sergeant continued. "We wouldn't trade one foot of our land for a thousand acres of prime farm country anywhere else. But the trouble with the lads from the other colonies is that they're ignorant. Why, there's dumb animals in our Delaware forests that have more sense than the brightest men from other places. Now and again we have to remind them that we're the best. And one of their worst problems is that they've all got to thinking they're so blamed smart. That's why they get to feuding with each other. But nobody carries a grudge. They'll work together just fine when we start shooting at Frenchies."

Jared found the assessment impossible to accept. Men whose intercolonial rivalries were so intense would be incapable of blending into a cohesive corps of fighting men. The ever-optimistic Americans were heading toward a major disaster, and he wished that rather than participate in a tragic fiasco, he had stayed on the Murtagh plantation and forced himself to endure his drab existence there.

The conversation was interrupted by an excited Willie Painter. "Jared," he called, "you're wanted over at headquarters."

Puzzled, Jared jumped to his feet and brushed dirt from his buckskins.

"One of Colonel Baker's aides was nosing around, looking for you. You're wanted right now."

Franklin was worried but tried to look unconcerned. "If he's got his dander up because we got into the fight for a few minutes, tell him to send for me. I'll take the responsibility."

Jared nodded absently as he hurried to the far side of the camp, toward the complex of tents that housed the senior officers of the colonial militia. Even colonels, he thought as he looked at the limp, patched canvas tents, lived far more modestly than did junior officers in the Royal Army. Colonials appeared to have no concept of the dignity that high rank required.

He revised his estimate slightly, however, when he was admitted to the quarters of the colonel in chief. Edward Baker's well-tailored green tunic and silver epaulets added something to his natural air of distinction, and it didn't matter that he was writing at a makeshift desk in a tent that an English captain would have considered cramped.

Jared stood at attention and, as Colonel Baker raised his head, saluted smartly.

"I'm in your debt, Hale," the colonel in chief said. "You were instrumental in putting down the riot this morning. In fact, if it hadn't been for you, the troops would have remained out of control much longer."

"I only did what seemed called for at the time, sir." Jared was embarrassed; a similar act performed for his own regiment in England would have been expected of him.

"It is obvious you're familiar with horses."

"Yes, sir."

"Sit down, please." Baker looked sympathetic. "Men who have been indentured are always eager to defend themselves before they're attacked. I neither know nor care why you were sent to prison and sold into bond."

Jared relaxed slightly, but remained wary.

"You were a cavalryman?"

"Yes, sir." Jared didn't want to appear surly and reluctantly added, "In the dragoons."

"You were an officer, of course." Colonel Baker made a flat statement that required no reply.

Jared remained silent.

It was necessary for the colonel in chief to dig a little deeper. "What was your rank?"

"I held a troop-grade commission, sir."

"You saw combat duty?"

"In the 'thirty-seven expedition to the Low Countries."

Colonel Baker was silent for a moment. "You're being wasted in an infantry company."

Jared became alarmed. "Please, sir, don't transfer me to the cavalry. That battalion is the most miserable unit of horsemen I've ever seen." The torture of serving with such troopers would be subtle but intense. "They need at least a year of training before they'll be fit to go into battle."

"Unfortunately," Baker replied dryly, "the enemy refuses to accommodate us in that regard. We're being forced to campaign with the men that we've been given. However, I have no intention of letting Delaware lose you. I'm putting you into my own headquarters detachment, which is mounted. My quartermaster is buying a dozen new horses today, and I'll give you your pick of them."

"Thank you, sir." It would be a relief to ride, rather than march on his own feet through the forests. Yet, surprisingly, Jared realized he would miss the companionship of Phil Franklin and Willie Painter, men for whom he had felt only contempt a few short weeks earlier.

"Assuming," the colonel said, "that the members of the detachment know how to ride their horses, is it possible that you can help train them in the techniques of cavalry warfare?"

"Yes, sir!" Jared leaped to the challenge.

"Then see to it," the colonel said, and dismissed him with a nod.

But Jared hesitated. "There's just a point or two I'd like to clear up, if I may, sir," he said. "It'll be very helpful if you can pry away the sabers that were issued to my old infantry company. They'll be required weapons for any self-respecting troop of cavalry."

The colonel grinned at him. "I understand, and you can consider it done. The detachment will be duly armed with sabers."

"And I'd like your authority, sir, to impose a strict training schedule on the detachment. Of course they'll be training on the march every day, but I would also like them to put in at least another hour or two after we bivouac in the evening. Knowing soldiers, I am sure they won't like it. In fact, they'll scream their heads off when they find they have extra work to do, and I'll need your authority to get them to take their training seriously."

"Use my name in any way you see fit, Hale," the colonel told him.

Jared drew himself to attention and saluted. At last he had a mission commensurate with his talents, and the future, at least for now, looked wonderfully bright.

CHAPTER TEN

A regiment of Connecticut infantry joined the army on its march north, and the town of New Haven sent three batteries of light artillery. The nine small guns, all of them firing six-pound shot,

163

amounted to more than half the cannon in the entire colony.

Soon after arriving in Massachusetts Bay, the colonial militia was greeted by two additional regiments, one raised in Boston and the other in the colony's hinterland. The next day, as the army bivouacked near the village of Worcester, a battalion from sparsely settled New Hampshire came into the camp.

The colonial army was now complete, numbering almost six thousand men. Colonel Solomon Hopkins of Massachusetts, in civilian life a prominent fur trader who had often journeyed into French Canada, assumed the supreme command, with Colonel Baker acting as his deputy. Quartermasters went off to Boston and Providence to buy or beg all the provisions and ammunition they could transport, and the militia settled down in the rolling hills near Worcester to await the coming of spring.

Jared found his lot as a soldier completely changed. As a member of the mounted Delaware headquarters detachment, he had ridden with the vanguard on the march north from New York, and now that the unit was being used in bivouac to guard the high-ranking officers, he was discovering far more about long-range plans. Only Colonels Hopkins and Baker and the regimental commanders knew the details of the coming campaign, but the members of the cavalry detachment—who, when on sentry duty, often heard snatches of the senior officers' conversations—felt certain that the army would march into Canada and, perhaps, try to take the city of Quebec.

The lack of activity in winter quarters provided ample time for training, and Jared worked for hours each day with the cavalry unit, demonstrating maneuvers and teaching the men how to ride in unison and wield their sabers in an attack.

What impressed him most was the attitude of his colleagues, which gave him another insight into the New World and its marked difference from the Old. He held the same rank as most members of the detachment, and had this been England, they would have resented his acting as an instructor and would have rebelled against taking orders from him.

Quite the contrary was proving true in America, however. The men had been somewhat hostile at first, but once they had learned that Jared knew his business and had experience as a cavalryman, they were eager to learn everything he had to teach them. Now they obeyed him without question and began their training each day in high spirits and with great vigor. As a result, as the winter wore on, he was increasingly satisfied with the results.

"They aren't Royal Dragoons as yet, sir," he said one day to Colonel Baker in response to his superior's question, "but they come pretty close. I think it's fair to say that they're at least a match for just about any cavalry unit they're likely to come up against."

The ground was still frozen in mid-March, and as anyone who had ever visited the Maine District and Canada well knew, snow was undoubtedly still falling farther north. But the colonels decided it would be imprudent to delay their drive any longer. All commissioned officers were summoned to a council of war that lasted the better part of a day, and the following morning the entire army was assembled in an area that had recently been cleared of trees.

The regiments marched to the gathering in loose formation. No one bothered to keep step, men chatted and joked, and the officers seemed either unwilling or unable to exert discipline. Jared, who was standing guard duty near the tree stump that would be used as a speaker's platform, shuddered as he watched the amateur soldiers taking their places. Never had he seen troops less fit for military service, and he could not understand why the commanders, who appeared to be highly intelligent men, were unable to realize the grave shortcomings of their units. If he were in their place, he surely would not hesitate to disband the army and send the men home to their respective colonies rather than lead them in a major operation that was destined to fail because of its unprofessionalism.

Solomon Hopkins, a short, round-faced man whose dark blue uniform fitted him too snugly, looked more like a bookkeeper than the commander in chief of the largest expedition ever mounted by the colonies. It was difficult to believe he had won three duels—two with swords and one with pistols—or that only two years ago he had escaped from a Quebec prison after being jailed as an espionage agent and had hidden in the wilderness for almost two months, living on roots, berries, and raw fish until his pursuers had given up their hunt for him and he had been able to make his way back to Massachusetts Bay.

166

The militiamen continued to talk, paying no attention to Hopkins as he mounted the tree stump. He smiled benignly, and Jared shook his head. A British commander under similar circumstances would become violently irate.

Still looking mild, Colonel Hopkins quickly took two pistols from his belt and fired them over his head.

The talk halted abruptly.

"That's more like it," he said in a surprisingly deep voice. "I didn't call you together for a sociable jamboree. You're here to listen while I talk." He threw the pistols to an aide, who reloaded them and handed them back to him.

"By now I reckon the enemy has an idea of what we're going to do, so it's high time I let you in on our secrets."

A wave of laughter rolled across the clearing.

Jared was amazed. He had never heard of troops being told the plans of their high command and had been trained to believe that just as it was the place of officers to lead, it was the duty of soldiers to obey orders without question.

"You'll fight better, boys, if you know what Colonel Baker and I have in mind," Hopkins said.

The militiamen were being coddled, Jared thought, and he was disgusted.

"We could wait for the enemy to come to us," Hopkins said in a casually conversational tone, "but that would be a dull sport for the spring and summer. So, instead, we'll march into Canada."

The men greeted the announcement with a roar of approval.

Colonel Hopkins raised a hand for silence, and

when the men failed to obey, he brandished one of his pistols over his head. They laughed and then became quiet. "Our main aim," he said, "is to beat the daylights out of the French and their allies. Now, make no mistake, boys, we've set ourselves a hard task."

"Those Frenchmen are professional soldiers who believe they belong to the best army on earth. We've got to prove them wrong. The Indians they've bribed to help them are plain mean. Some of you who live in seaboard towns have never been raided by a tribe on the warpath. When it happens, you won't forget the experience, and you can't afford to make one mistake. Leave the tribes to the men who know how to deal with them, and do what you're told.

"If any of you are afraid of discomfort, hardships—and danger—the time to leave is now. Apply today, and you'll be discharged without prejudice. But we're going to assume that any man who stays until time for supper tonight will see the whole campaign through to the end.

"We haven't been able to buy any more blankets, and since the weather will stay cold for the next few weeks, you'll have to get along with what you've got. I hope we won't go hungry, but I can't guarantee it. We have enough food supplies to last one month."

Jared was horrified. An army of nearly six thousand men should march with provisions for an entire campaign; he had never heard of a responsible commander taking the field without a heavily laden supply train.

"I've asked every company for hunters and

foragers," Hopkins continued. "Don't volunteer unless you've had experience bringing down game. Later, when we get into French territory and start raiding barns, the rest of you can pitch in and help.

"I don't promise you glory or victory. We're gambling. We have a fairly good idea of the size and condition of the French forces, but we know very little about the Micmac and the Abnaki and the other tribes we may face. We intend to find out all we can, but I am not prepared to swear we'll be successful."

The candor of the new colonel in chief was shocking. Jared knew that if any European commander had outlined the prospects of a campaign in such stark terms, his troops would have become panicky. The Americans, however, listened with apparent calm and seemed undisturbed by the odds against them.

"Colonel Baker and I," Hopkins went on, "aren't going to perform miracles for you. When we go into battle, we'll try to do your planning for you, but you'll have to do your own fighting. The outcome of this campaign will depend as much on you as on us. Battalion adjutants, dismiss your formations."

The militiamen moved off to their own bivouac areas, their informality resembling that of a crowd leaving a theater or church. A few seemed reflective, and the majority were somewhat less boisterous than they had been before hearing the brief address, but there was no general air of depression, no brooding silence.

Jared returned to the headquarters area with

the other guards, certain that the campaign was already lost. Unless the French were equally disorganized, equally indifferent to the basic rules governing military practice—and Jared considered that unlikely—he saw no chance for victory.

Jared's watch was over and he should have been relieved from duty, but instead he was stationed outside the tent to which Colonels Hopkins and Baker had retired. Detachments of reliable infantrymen from Delaware and Pennsylvania were summoned, and when they were ordered to keep all other troops from the immediate vicinity, it became apparent that something out of the ordinary was about to take place.

Nothing happened for several hours, however, and the sentries became as fidgety as they were bored. Then, unexpectedly, an aide ushered a group of new arrivals into the headquarters tent, and Jared stared hard at a small band of the most savage Indians he had yet seen in the New World. They were attired in loincloths and leather shirts, their moccasins seemed molded to their feet, and each wore three feathers in his scalp lock, identifying him, Jared was told, as a senior warrior. Streaks of crimson and yellow paint were smeared on their cheeks and foreheads, making their faces masklike. They carried long knives in their belts, and all were armed with rifles, which they carried with easy familiarity. What impressed Jared was the sense of power they conveyed; although of medium height and slender, they moved with the silent grace of wild animals. Not deigning to glance at the militiamen, they filed into the tent.

"Seneca," said the corporal of the guard, who

170

was stationed beside Jared. "Now we know why there aren't any Yorkers around. Settlers from the Mohawk Valley would start shooting the minute they saw these bastards."

Jared realized his original estimate had been correct. The Seneca, a nation of the Iroquois Confederation, were probably the most universally feared braves in the English colonies. Merciless and courageous in battle to the point of foolhardiness, they had led the fight to prevent the settlement of New York until, faced with the need to throw in their lot with either the English or the French, they had chosen the English.

Jared wondered whether a column of Seneca warriors was going to join the colonial army, but immediately he dismissed the notion. If it was difficult to prevent fights between the militia of different colonies, it would prove impossible to halt a major battle between the New Yorkers and the savages. Remembering what Colonel Hopkins had said about the attempts that would be made to learn more about the Indian allies of the French, he concluded that the Seneca would be used as scouts. In any event, it was a relief to know he would not have to fight either as their ally or their foe. As a civilized soldier, he infinitely preferred the French as enemies.

The colonial militia marched almost due north from Worcester into New Hampshire, then headed east into the Maine District of Massachusetts Bay. Everywhere the wilderness was the same—dense, wild, and, even in early spring, almost impenetrable. In some regions evergreens stretched out across the hills to the horizon, and in others were stands of massive oak, maple, and elm. The beech were tall and stately, and birch were as common as weeds. There were almost no meadows or clearings, so a vanguard of ax-wielding infantrymen marched ahead of the headquarters cavalry, literally hacking a road through the forest.

Progress was maddeningly slow, and at first the column averaged fewer than ten miles a day—less than half its previous rate. Food, however, was plentiful. Hunters brought in deer, bear, and smaller game every day, there were fish in the lakes, and the whole army cheered when flocks of geese and ducks were seen overhead on their spring migration to the north.

Each day Jared found himself more at home in the wilderness for which he had felt such loathing when he had first come to the New World. He was discovering that a man was forced to adapt to the forest, which yielded its treasures and its own comforts to those who were pliable and willing to learn. Insoles cut from birch bark made his boots more comfortable, herbs that he soon learned to recognize improved the flavor of his meals, and when he slept in a carefully chosen hollow, preferably behind the protective bulk of a boulder, his one blanket provided him with ample warmth.

Like everyone else in the expedition, he was impressed by the forest's demand for silence. Men no longer chatted idly as they marched; the deep wilderness imposed its own quiet on them.

Though the Maine District was more rugged than the other territory through which the militia had passed, the column gradually began to move more rapidly, gaining a little additional ground each day. The pathfinders and ax men grew more adept, and the regiments marched at a livelier pace, taking the hardships of living for granted.

By mid-April the last settlements had been left far behind, and the column swung closer to the seacoast, where it would be possible to march without hacking a trail through the woods. Soon they would reach Canadian soil, and the men brightened at the prospect of activity against the enemy. Another month's wages had been paid, and with nothing else on which to spend their money, the men in every regiment, battalion, and company laid large wagers as to the number of French troops each would kill.

Then, one morning about an hour after starting on the day's march, the militia blundered into a trap, and the enemy drew first blood. The trail-blazers and the headquarters cavalry were unmolested, but the First Massachusetts Infantry regiment, which came next in the line of march, was ambushed on both flanks by unseen foes who riddled the colonials' ranks with arrows and musket fire.

The attack was so sudden that the infantrymen became panicky and would have withdrawn to the rear had not the bulk of the cavalry been stationed directly behind them. So with only one direction in which to run, the soldiers raced forward under a continuous hail of lead and arrows.

The Massachusetts Bay officers were having trouble restoring order in their ranks, and Colonel Baker, observing their plight, came forward with a regiment of Pennsylvanians while Colonel Hopkins remained in the rear, holding the bulk of the militia in reserve.

The headquarters cavalry detachment of forty men suddenly found itself in the thick of the fight, and Jared was infuriated by the lack of organization. Each trooper seemed concerned only for his own safety and took refuge for his mount and himself behind the nearest tree or boulder.

It was frustrating, too, not to be able to see the enemy, not to know precisely where to strike back. But, recalling his success during the riot, Jared decided to repeat the same tactics he had used that day. "Cavalrymen to me!" he shouted.

No one responded, and a musket ball whistled close by his ear. An instant later he felt something cut through his heavy buckskin shirt and was surprised to see that an arrow had cut into his arm. He ignored the wound and again shouted. "Cavalrymen to me!"

"You goddam fool," a corporal called from his refuge behind a nearby oak, "shut your stupid mouth!" Paying no further attention to Jared, he peered off into the forest, quickly raised his rifle to his shoulder, and fired.

Another arrow grazed Jared's leg, and when another musket ball sang so close to his ear that he winced, it finally occurred to him that he was the target for more than one of the unseen enemy. Feeling sheepish, he headed his mount in the direction of a huge boulder behind which two other troopers had already sheltered themselves.

Only the inaccurate aim of the foe enabled him

to reach the spot without injury to himself or his gelding.

The other two men were busy and ignored him. Each stared intently into the forest, occasionally raising his rifle, firing, and then reloading quickly.

Jared looked, too, but could see nothing.

The presence of the Pennsylvanians stabilized the men of the Massachusetts Bay regiment, and Jared was astonished by the military spectacle the two units made of themselves. Militiamen of both regiments had thrown themselves onto the ground and, spreading out by crawling on their stomachs, were firing from a prone position into the woods on the flanks.

Growing somewhat calmer, Jared began to study the forest more carefully, and after what seemed like a long time he was rewarded by a glimpse of something that moved behind the thick branches of a pine tree. He lifted his own rifle to his shoulder and fired, but he had no idea whether he hit his target.

The strange battle continued for another half hour or longer, and during that time Jared blindly fired at least a dozen rounds into the forest. Seldom had he known such frustration.

At last the enemy fire dwindled, and just as it was dying away, the men of the Massachusetts Bay infantry redeemed themselves by making a wild charge through the underbrush. There was another brief volley of rifle and pistol fire, then silence. A few moments later some of the militiamen returned, holding up dripping scalps in triumph.

"It's like I thought," one of Jared's companions said. "Abnaki."

The other nodded. "Two hundred of 'em. Three hundred, maybe." He turned to Jared. "Hale, the Almighty was good to you today. When Naturals attack, you don't go calling men into a formal line. You scatter, you find yourself the coziest place to make yourself invisible, and then you wait for a brave to make a move you can see."

The trooper who had identified the attackers as members of the Abnaki tribe gestured toward the underbrush. "It becomes a game. You're waiting, and the Natural is waiting. Sooner or later somebody gets to be a mite restless, and he moves. Then he gets a lead ball or an arrow between his eyes."

"You hear that Indians are patient," the other soldier added, "but that ain't true. They get to feeling they want to squeeze that trigger, the same as we do. So you got to outwait them. If you bide your time, they'll move. They hate pitched battles. It just ain't in their nature to stand up and trade punches. The way they fight, they want to take their enemy by surprise, hit him before he knows what's happened to him—and then make off again into the wilderness as fast as they can get away."

"They won't make a stand unless you back them into a corner and give them no other choice," the first trooper declared. "I've heard it said they're cowards, but don't you believe it, not for one minute. I've known just a few of them to attack hundreds of militiamen at odds that would make me think it would be mad."

Jared was rapidly revising his opinions of American fighting men and their battle tactics.

"What you got to remember," the more articulate of the troopers said, "is that the Naturals have been fighting in these here forests a blame sight longer than we have. They make war the way they do because it fits right. It's the best way to win in the wilderness, you might say. They taught us, and we've been fighting their way. My pa lived in Wilmington when it was just a little village—Christinaham, they called it in those days—and there were Naturals a few miles away.

"Well, those Indians, they got themselves an itch for loot every few months, and they'd get all dressed up in their war paint and make a raid. There was an old militia captain—an uncle of Thomas Willing, I think he was—who fought the French in one of the Duke of Marlborough's regiments, and he made his whole company march out into the open for a battle against the Indians.

"Most of those boys were lucky to get back inside the fort with their scalps still on their heads. The old captain, he died right off, and they took his scalp with the women and children watching from the windows of the fort. Nobody in Christinaham ever fought the Indians that way again."

Jared was grateful for the advice and realized, humbly, that in spite of his experience as a professional soldier, he still had a great deal to learn about New World warfare.

Caroline Murtagh, clad in a negligee, sat in front of her dressing table and methodically brushed her long blond hair. Her lips moved as she counted the strokes, and Polly White, who was putting away into appropriate chests and cupboards the underclothes she had washed, knew Caroline wouldn't stop until she had reached the last of the two hundred and fifty strokes she had prescribed for herself each day.

Caroline surprised her by stopping and turning to her, the brush suspended in midair. "You must miss him dreadfully," she said.

Polly had no idea what she was talking about and looked at her blankly.

"I'm speaking of Jared Hale," Caroline explained. "I've never had a man go off to war, but I'm sure that if it were to happen, I'd be worried day and night about his welfare."

Polly resumed her task of putting away the laundry. "Jared is the type," she said with a slight smile, "who can take care of himself. We used to have a saying in the part of London that I come from that men like him are never killed in battle. They always die in bed."

Her calm was surprising, and Caroline resumed brushing her hair.

Something niggled at Polly, however, and eventually she broke the silence. "If you don't mind my inquiring, ma'am, what made you think I was worried about him?"

Caroline put the silver-backed brush carefully on the dressing table and replied with slow deliberation. "Naturally," she said, a hint of frost in her voice, "I assumed you'd be concerned about the man you love."

Polly astonished her by whooping with laughter.

Caroline stared at her openmouthed.

"I beg your pardon, ma'am," Polly said quickly, her tone apologetic. "I swear I'm not mocking you, but it was just so unexpected hearing you say that I'm in love with Jared Hale, of all men."

For reasons she couldn't explain to herself, Caroline felt strangely relieved. "Apparently I've misinterpreted the situation," she said. "Ever since I came upon the two of you on board ship at an inopportune moment . . ." Her voice trailed away.

At last Polly understood. "Oh, that," she said briskly. "That was just one of those things that happened." She went on to enlarge on the theme, explaining that she had first seen Jared and had been attracted to him when she had worked at the gaming establishment in London, and that he had been quick enough and clever enough to take advantage of her interest on board ship.

"I—I begin to understand," Caroline murmured.

The serving girl shook her head and turned to face her. "I don't rightly think you do, ma'am," she said. "Oh, Jared finds me attractive enough. I'm the type of wench he'll tumble any chance he gets, being a man who never misses the main chance, so to speak. But I gave up any thought of ever having a permanent relationship with him long ago."

"Why is that?" Caroline persisted.

Polly raised a dark eyebrow. "He may be indentured like me," Polly said earnestly, "but he's far too grand for me. Besides, I knew that he had no interest in me—except as a casual bedmate, which I wouldn't permit—once he came to know you."

Caroline's heart pounded in her ears, but she fought to maintain a calm facade. "Whatever makes you say that?" she gasped, just barely able to get the words out.

Polly smiled knowingly. "It's been plain for anyone to see," she said, "that he has eyes for no one on earth except for you, ma'am. He's smitten with you, and he has a bad case of it." She finished putting away the laundry, and grinning cheerfully at the other woman, she took her leave.

Alone in her bedchamber, Caroline began to brush her hair again. It was obvious that her mind was not on what she was doing, and she stroked absently, her eyes looking far off into space, a curious half smile on her delicate lips.

CHAPTER ELEVEN

The casual air of seasoned militiamen on the march was misleading. Cavalrymen and foot soldiers alike seemed carefree and indifferent to their surroundings, but Jared, observing them carefully in the days following the skirmish with the Abnaki, discovered they were actually alert to every nuance of change in the forest. They listened constantly for any faint sound emanating from the brush, and it was common to see a horseman reach for his rifle when he heard a faint crackle, inaudible to the inexperienced, somewhere in the distance.

It was impossible to determine whether such sounds were made by animals or humans, so the veteran held himself ready for immediate action and maintained his guard for periods ranging from a few minutes to an hour or more. Rarely did a trooper give alarm, either. His comrades sensed his tension almost as rapidly as he himself felt it, and no other warning was necessary to put an entire squad on guard.

Jared was pleased by the progress he himself made. Once he would have thought it unlikely that any man could hear a deer, fox, or raccoon making its way through a forest, but he found he was able to train himself, and through practice he was becoming infinitely more proficient. No longer too proud to seek help, he went to his squad leader, Sergeant Ben Greene, a New Castle farmer who had spent most of his life near the wilderness. Greene taught him how to trace a path taken by a person or large animal by noting the direction in which an occasional blade of long grass was bent, and how to listen for the pounding of horses' hooves or the beat of marching feet by placing an ear close to the ground.

He surprised himself by becoming more proficient in finding food in the wilderness, too. Now that spring was at hand, wild onions were becoming plentiful, and there were several plants—none of which the settlers had bothered to name—that had edible roots, and some that could be eaten raw. Berries were appearing on bushes, and although they were not yet ripe, they could be eaten if boiled. So could the sap of trees that the colonists called sugar maples. One evening Greene showed him how to set snares for small animals, and the next morning the two men ate roast chipmunk for breakfast. It was comforting, at the very least, for Jared to know that a resourceful man who knew the forest would not starve in the wilderness.

England became increasingly remote to him on the long march, and so did his existence as an indentured servant in Delaware. He often found himself thinking of Caroline, and he realized that he no longer bore her any deep rancor. He could not analyze his own attitude toward her, but was willing to grant that he had been as much to blame as she for their initial mutual hostilities. She had been decent enough to make an effort to be gracious when he had taken his leave of her, and although she had failed, he gave her credit for trying, under difficult circumstances.

He was even more confused when he thought of Polly. There were times when he wondered whether he was in love with her, whether he had actually succumbed to her warmth and femininity. But he could not be certain; knowing himself, he realized that Polly had inspired his deeper interest by withdrawing from him, by assuming a greater air of dignity than he had believed it possible for her to possess.

He was foolish, of course, to let himself think of either woman. His immediate future was hazardous and uncertain, although admittedly far more exhilarating than he had anticipated. He could not let himself dwell on what awaited him—if he survived—after the campaign came to an end. The very idea of returning to a life of bonded servitude sickened him, and he was afraid he lacked the stamina to live again in slavery.

He could understand now why so many indentured servants, men and women alike, disappeared from the homes of their masters and made their way to the western frontier, where they began new lives under assumed names. Now that he was beginning to understand the forest and was learning to cope with wilderness living, the temptation to run away and establish a home for himself somewhere in the mountains west of the seaboard settlements was almost irresistible.

Jared even toyed with the thought of asking Polly to go with him, knowing, of course, that the risk of being caught, returned, and subjected to severe punishment would be far smaller if he escaped alone. Polly, he told himself, was a Londoner born and bred, and even in Delaware she enjoyed such luxuries as hot baths and a dry roof over her head; she might prove unwilling to adapt to life in the wilderness. He supposed he would be wise to let that aspect of his future take care of itself.

At least he could understand now why most members of the militia took such care to respect one another's privacy. It was unwise to ask too many questions, to probe into another man's background. One evening Phil Franklin had remarked casually that some of the most important men in the colonies were former indentured servants or the sons of the bonded. Jared hadn't attached any

183

significance to the comment at the time, but now he could see that Phil had been suggesting a way out of his own predicament. If others had run away from dreary captivity, evaded the authorities, and created happy, useful lives, so could he.

In the meantime he was a free man, at least for the present, and every day he was learning new skills that would not only help him as a soldier but could be of inestimable value to him when the war ended. He had good cause to find out all he could about the wilderness, to enjoy its benefits.

In fact, Jared had much more time to adapt to the wilderness than he had expected. Colonels Hopkins and Baker had deliberately selected a long route for their march into Canada, following the seacoast, almost to the point of the Maine District's eastern border, and then turning north. Not only did they hope to confuse the enemy by taking an unaccustomed line of march, relatively far from the homes and hunting grounds of most of the Indian nations allied with the French, but, depending on the location of the heaviest enemy troop concentrations, the colonials could either attack Quebec from the east or swing back to the traders' trails that approached the city from the south.

In some ways the strategy paid handsome dividends, although the infantrymen complained that they were being forced to march all over the continent. Settlements were almost nonexistent east of the Penobscot River, and the forests were so rich in game that the men ate a wilderness banquet every night. Fish were running in the rivers, salt licks where animals congregated were numerous, and there was so much food that the quartermasters, who were kept busy preserving meat and fish, actually carried more provisions than they had brought with them from Worcester.

The idyll was too quiet, too pleasant to last. One evening in late April the corps had just completed its day's march and was settling into a bivouac on the rocky heights overlooking a small lake not far from the eastern bank of the Penobscot River. Sentry outposts were established by each regiment, cooking fires were started, and the horses of the officers, headquarters detachment, and cavalry were hobbled and turned loose in a meadow along the shore of the lake. Several men were assigned to keep watch on the mounts and prevent them from straying, while scores of soldiers who had nothing better to do went down to the lake to try out their luck at fishing.

"There's plenty o' lake trout up this way," Sergeant Ben Greene told Jared. "A man needs two or three t' get his fill, but there's nothin' sweeter. Come along."

Jared, knowing that Phil Franklin was partial to trout, suggested they stop at the camp of the First New Castle Foot and invite him to join them. All three made their way down the steep, rockstrewn incline to the lake, where Greene, working quickly, fashioned fishing poles of maple branches, then used vines and hooked thorns to complete the gear.

The sun had not yet set behind rows of giant pines to the west, and Jared, rifle under his arm and fishing pole in his other hand, knew the first moment of complete contentment he had experienced in the New World. For reasons that he made no attempt to explore or weigh, he felt at home.

A movement at the far end of the meadow attracted his attention, and he froze. The militiamen who had been assigned to guard the horses, believing themselves safe far behind the sentry outposts, were watching comrades fishing on the near bank of the lake and were completely unaware of possible trouble.

At first Jared thought that a wild animal was stalking the horses, but then he noticed a second movement in the tall grass, then a third, and then many. Men, probably Indians, had somehow managed to sneak past the sentry lines and were posing a grave threat to more than two hundred horses.

Jared touched Ben Greene on the arm, Franklin became aware of the raid at the same instant, and all three stared in the direction of the irregular, rippling waves in the tall grass. Like his companions, Jared realized the predicament at once: A rifle shot or shouted alarm would alert the entire militia on the heights, but the savages would be able to slaughter, maim, or drive away scores of horses before themselves being killed or driven off.

Other militiamen who had already started to fish or were preparing to cast their lines into the water saw the three unusually still figures, and soon twenty or thirty soldiers were aware of the situation. One took a deep breath, intending to call out, but a comrade clamped a hand over his mouth.

With one accord Jared and Greene started

forward, Franklin a single pace behind them. They ran into the meadow, crouching low as they made their way through the waist-high grass, and without a single order having been issued, the rest of the group followed their example.

Only one plan of action seemed feasible to Jared. The bulk of the herd was grazing near the shore of the lake, so it seemed obvious to him that he and his companions had to place themselves between the marauders and their targets. Franklin and Greene appeared to be of the same mind, and all three raced desperately in an attempt to head off the savages.

As nearly as Jared could judge, the militiamen in the meadow were outnumbered by the Indians by at least two to one, but there were enough soldiers on the heights, of course, to make the ultimate odds overwhelmingly favorable to the militia.

The Indians, cautiously snaking their way toward the mounts, seemed not to know they had been detected, and the lead trio of militiamen, wanting to take no unnecessary risks, halted when they reached a point about fifty or sixty paces from the braves. Then Greene, the senior noncommissioned officer present, took command. He spread out his small force, the men following the example of Jared and Franklin, who had thrown themselves onto their stomachs in the grass.

Jared, peering down the long barrel of his rifle, waited for Greene to give the order to open fire. But the sergeant was strangely silent, and Jared was startled when he turned to look at his superior, who was on his knees, wavering, an arrow buried deep in his shoulder.

Phil Franklin did not hesitate. "Fire whenever you're ready, boys," he called softly.

Jared and someone farther down the line discharged their rifles at the same instant, and Jared had the satisfaction of seeing a shadowy figure crumple.

The sound of the shots caused immediate bedlam in the bivouac above, and the negligent guards in the meadow suddenly remembered their duty, too. But it was impossible for either group to open fire, since neither could distinguish between friend and foe in the tall grass.

The danger to the horses, now alarmed by the gunfire, was not lessened, and the full responsibility for protecting the animals continued to depend on the men who had made the initial reply to the braves' challenge. Jared knew, as did his companions, that it was essential to keep moving; once a militiaman revealed his position by firing his rifle or musket, he had to move elsewhere at once or increase his own chances of being hit.

Crawling quickly away and then reloading, Jared raised his head for a moment, caught a glimpse of another figure in the grass off to his left, and fired again. A piercing scream that sounded high above the din told him his aim had been accurate.

Both sides were firing freely now, the attackers using both firearms and bows and arrows. Scores of militiamen were crowded onto the heights, and many had to be restrained by their officers to prevent them from firing blindly into the grass below. Four or five of the guards were still standing near the horses, trying to herd them away from the fighting, and Jared angrily called out to them to take cover and make a last protective line.

He made his way to them as rapidly as he could, firing once more before reaching them. Not until then did he realize that he had moved far more quickly than Franklin and the others, who were at least fifteen paces behind him.

The warriors, meanwhile, had become bolder and were almost upon him and the guards. He began to reload but had no time as a husky brave leaped through the grass at him.

Wrenching himself to one side just as the warrior landed, Jared brought down the butt of his rifle on the man's head. The Indian went limp, and Jared instantly turned to the other onrushing savages.

"Hold steady, lads," he shouted to the guards. "They've got to pass us to reach the horses."

Another warrior, his face and naked torso smeared with paint, was almost within arm's reach, and Jared on one knee, swung his rifle like a club. He missed, so he dropped the rifle and, snatching his knife from his boot top, grappled with the brave.

The warrior had oiled his body with animal grease and was so agile and slippery it was impossible for Jared to attain a sufficiently firm grasp to bring his knife into play. The rank odor of the Indian's body made him gag, and he was not sorry when the savage, hearing a call, pulled away, crawling rapidly through the grass.

Apparently the other braves decided the odds

against them were too great, and just as Franklin and the other volunteers arrived to reinforce Jared and the guards the Indians retreated.

When the braves reached the far side of the meadow the militiamen on the heights were able to open fire on them at last. But the discipline of the marauders remained intact, and the withdrawal was orderly. Night was falling, making it difficult for the men above to see their targets clearly, and the Indians succeeded in reaching the forest safely. Hundreds of militiamen raced after them, but the Indians managed to escape, slipping past the sentry outposts and vanishing into the wilderness.

They left five dead warriors behind, and a sixth, who was gravely wounded, expired a short time later. Sergeant Greene was the colonists' only casualty, the arrow wound in his shoulder being more severe than Jared had at first realized. One of the militia's surgeons put a poultice of herbs on it and gave Greene a drink of bitter laudanum, a crude opiate, to reduce the pain and enable him to sleep. The patient refused even to consider the possibility of being sent back to a town where he could rest and recuperate, so a litter was made for him, and a number of his friends and neighbors from Delaware volunteered to take turns carrying him on the march north until he could regain his strength.

Only two horses had been lost in the raid, one of them apparently stolen and the other killed. The attack had failed, thanks to the prompt intervention of Jared and his comrades. Sentry outposts were doubled, and Colonel Hopkins made a personal inspection of the lines, relieving the lieutenant of the guard and demoting him on the spot to the rank of ensign. The punishment was harsh, but the men agreed he deserved it. If the militia's bivouac was not secured, the entire expedition would be in great jeopardy, and Hopkins was heard by a number of soldiers to remark that he would rather march to Boston and disband than allow penetration of his sentry lines.

Most of the militiamen who had been fishing quietly returned to their sport, but Jared and Phil Franklin stayed with Ben Greene until the surgeon had treated him and he had dropped off to sleep. By that time most units had eaten, so the pair made a meal of what was left in the headquarters detachment's kettles, augmented by a few freshly caught trout that friends brought them. They boned the fried fish and were still eating when an aide arrived, summoning Jared to Colonel Baker's tent.

Hastily wiping his hands, Jared presented himself to his superior, who looked very tired but brightened slightly.

"Hale," he said, "you did well this evening."

Jared was pleased but knew that no reply was required.

"I've been watching you for some time, hoping we could make better use of your experience. But we could do nothing until you began to adapt to our methods of warfare. There are some men who never learn that the techniques here aren't the same as the formal battlefield tactics used in Europe.

"We've also had another problem. There are

191

men in the detachment who have been members of the militia for a long time, and we were afraid they might resent you if we granted you a promotion. I had a long chat earlier tonight with Lieutenant Swenson, the detachment commander, and he's been talking with the men."

Jared didn't know whether he was being promoted or whether Colonel Baker was offering him excuses.

"Effective as of now, you're acting sergeant of the headquarters detachment."

Jared shook his outstretched hand and was surprised to discover that he felt elated. Had someone told him the day would come when promotion to a noncommissioned rank in the informal militia would thrill him, he would have refused to believe it possible.

"Report to Lieutenant Swenson at once. And good luck, Hale."

Jared went to the bivouac area of the detachment and made his way to its one tent, that of the commander. Lieutenant Erik Swenson, a blond giant of obvious Swedish ancestry, was cleaning his pistols but put them aside as he rose and returned Jared's salute.

"I can see that Colonel Baker has told you the news. Here's your insignia." He handed Jared the threadbare sash of rank that Ben Greene had worn.

Slipping it on, Jared again marveled at his feeling of proud accomplishment.

"You're familiar with the detachment's routines. Come to me with any questions. I'll expect you to bring me word of any major breaches of discipline. Settle minor problems yourself."

Jared returned the officer's grin, knowing Swenson was telling him to maintain discipline with his fists.

"A few of our boys may try you out, although most of them know you stood off Phil Franklin, so you shouldn't have any serious troubles. Everybody in the Lower Counties has respect for Phil."

"I've come to know most of the men fairly well, sir," Jared said. "We'll get along."

Swenson nodded. "If I weren't sure of it, I wouldn't have given my approval when Colonel Baker suggested your promotion." He gestured toward the far side of the tent. "This isn't a general's pavilion, but there's enough room for both of us. Ben slept in here, you know. You can move in your gear tonight."

Jared hesitated for only a moment. "If you don't mind, Lieutenant, I'll continue to sleep with the detachment."

Swenson was surprised. "The most consistent complaint I hear is that the detachment is forced to sleep in the open."

"That's right, sir—and that's precisely why I don't want to move in with you. If there's anybody who hates me because of this promotion, it will take the edge off his jealousy if I stay out of doors with all the rest."

Swenson nodded thoughtfully. "I can begin to see why Colonel Baker wanted you made acting sergeant. You have a real talent for the rank."

Jared smiled at the irony of the words. Apparently Lieutenant Swenson did not know that he had held a commission in the dragoons—

which was just as well. He preferred to earn his way, to be judged exclusively on the basis of his merit and accomplishments.

CHAPTER TWELVE

The wilds of the upper Maine District were so remote, so primitive that Jared found it difficult to believe any other human beings had ever made their way through these woods. The ever-present pines and evergreens were taller and thicker than any he had ever seen; dense stands of beech soared skyward; and in most places sunlight filtered down to the underbrush only in weak patches. Berry bushes and thorny brambles were everywhere.

Nevertheless, the militia maintained a steady rate of march. The Seneca scouts returned with word that two major forces were gathering to oppose the Americans. A regiment of French regulars that had been ordered to reinforce the garrison at Fort Louisbourg, on Cape Breton Island, had been diverted southward to meet the threat and was expected to join forces with one of the most ferocious of the Canadian native tribes, the Micmac, who were led by a fanatical clergyman, Abbé Louis Le Loutre. The precise whereabouts of these foes were not known.

Another even more formidable force was waiting at Quebec and consisted of a large but as yet undetermined number of French troops, strengthened by savages from four of the nearby Algonkin towns. Other Indians were also making their way to Quebec, and the American high command sent the Seneca back into the fields to learn more about them.

Meanwhile a full platoon of scouts was sent to search for Abbé Le Loutre's Micmac and the French regiment that, presumably, had already joined them somewhere to the northeast. Colonels Baker and Hopkins held a council of war, and the officers agreed with their estimates: If possible, it would be wise to head off this force and engage it in a separate battle. Should the Micmac and the regiment reach Quebec, the French might be able to achieve such an overwhelming superiority that the colonials would be forced to withdraw without risking an attack.

The militia now followed the Penobscot River northeastward through a swampy, lake-studded area. Then, turning due north again, they marched for two full weeks along the bank of the Saint John River, halting at last and establishing a bivouac just a few miles from the border of New France. They were a week's march from Quebec, and the colonels apparently hoped they had placed their column somewhere between the main body of enemy troops in Quebec and Abbé Le Loutre's force.

Lieutenant Swenson explained the situation to Jared one evening when they sat together before a small campfire in the new bivouac. "We have a choice," the militia officer said. "We can cut off Le Loutre or wait for him to come to us here. And then we can move on to Quebec."

Jared doubted the wisdom of the strategy but expressed his opinions carefully. "Suppose they decide to attack us simultaneously. We'll be caught in the middle, and they can smash us."

"It's possible, I suppose." Swenson seemed unconcerned. "But it isn't very likely."

"Why not?"

"They wouldn't want to leave Quebec unprotected."

"Couldn't they fall back on the city if we happened to beat them?"

"Maybe, maybe not. Suppose we fought a holding engagement, striking them just hard enough to disrupt their lines to the rear. We might be able to sneak off and reach Quebec before her defenders could get back there. It wouldn't be the first time two armies put on a footrace through the forest, with a town as the prize."

Swenson's ideas were contrary to everything Jared had been taught about modern warfare. "The Duke of Marlborough and Prince Eugene of Savoy proved in their war with Louis XIV that there's nothing more dangerous to a defender than static positioning. A commander should never allow himself to be besieged, especially in his capital. He should march out and meet his enemy in the open, falling back on his city only if it becomes necessary."

"I've heard the theory," Swenson said, "and I reckon Marlborough and Eugene proved it. But they fought their battles in civilized places, where the only woods are the game preserves of the nobility. You said something about marching into the open, Hale. Hereabouts there is no such thing as open country. If I were defending Quebec, I'd make my enemy come to me, and I wouldn't budge a foot from the best natural fortress in America. And I can guarantee the French won't move from Quebec, either."

Once again Jared was discovering that the wilderness created its own rules.

He and the officer were interrupted by Colonel Hopkin's aide, who shouted to them as he ran toward their fire. "It looks like there's trouble brewing between the Yorkers and the Pennsylvanians. Move your detachment over there quick, Swenson, and keep them apart."

Lieutenant Swenson and Jared began to shout orders, and in a very few minutes the cavalrymen were mounted. They rode swiftly along the shore of the lake near which the army had set up its camp, and the men of other units, seeing the cavalrymen's rifles slung across their pommels, knew they were on urgent military business and stared at them curiously. No one made a move to join them, however. It was typical of Americans to remain near their own fires—which were necessary to ward off the chill of a Maine District night—and not to stir unless their own officers sent them into action or a general alarm was raised. They lived according to the precept that no one had the right to interfere in the affairs of others.

Jared, riding a half pace behind Swenson and to his left, could hear a roar as they approached the place where the bivouacs of the New Yorkers and Pennsylvania Germans adjoined, and Lieutenant Swenson instantly prepared for the worst. "Sergeant Hale, make ready for action."

"Yes, sir. Detachment, draw sabers! Squad

leaders, pass the word!" Jared drew his own saber, too.

"Use the flats of blades only," Swenson cautioned. "We want no needless killing."

Again Jared repeated the order.

Campfires were burning brightly along the shore of the little lake, and the detachment increased its pace to a gallop as it drew nearer. There were wild shouts that rang through the forest, and Jared braced himself.

But as the detachment moved into the clearing that the two regiments had made for themselves, Jared became confused. So did Swenson, who gave the order to halt.

Jared brought the detachment to a full stop, and both he and his superior gaped at the scene before them. Scores of Pennsylvanians, who could be identified by the green cockades in their hats, were sitting with New Yorkers, and earthenware jugs were being passed from neighbor to neighbor.

Finally one of the men noticed the newcomers. "This here is a private party," a New Yorker called. "We been making our own liquor and savin' it up for t'night. So get out o'here!"

Several of the Germans raised their voices in a chorus. *"Raus!"*

Jared and Swenson exchanged uncertain glances.

The denunciations, although good-natured, became louder and more insistent.

A captain of the New York infantry and two Pennsylvania Germans walked quickly toward the horsemen, and it occurred to Jared that they were a little unsteady on their feet.

The captain acted as the spokesman for the trio. "We haven't put out the latchstring for the whole corps, Swenson," he said. "The boys have been saving up, and they don't want any outsiders nosing in."

"We're here on Colonel Hopkins's orders to put down a riot, sir," Swenson replied stiffly.

All three of the infantry officers laughed raucously.

"Maybe later," one of the Pennsylvania Germans said, "some of the boys get playful and punch, but nobody gets more than a sore nose or eye. We celebrate with our friends."

Jared was thoroughly bewildered, and he couldn't understand how the animosities that had caused the initial riot could have vanished so completely. All he knew was that there were no hostilities now between the men of the two regiments.

"What shall I report to Colonel Hopkins?" Swenson asked.

"You tell him," the other German lieutenant suggested, "if he wants a drink, he should make his own whiskey!"

His companions considered his remark hilarious.

"We have nothing against you Delaware lads," the New York officer declared. "You don't believe me, Swenson? I'll prove it. Come for supper tomorrow night, you and your whole unit. And while you're at it, bring some whiskey. We won't have a drop left by then." He held out his hand.

Jared thought his superior would be annoyed. Instead Swenson leaned down from the saddle and gripped the New Yorker's hand. "You ought to know my lads have dry throats," he said. "We sleep too close to headquarters to make any liquor of our own."

One of the Pennsylvania Germans staggered. "We invite you now," he said grandly.

Swenson expressed his regrets, explaining that the colonel in chief would expect an immediate report. A moment later the detachment was making its way back along the shore of the lake.

The other cavalry units had been mustered in the headquarters bivouac area, and the atmosphere was tense. Colonels Hopkins and Baker had mounted their horses, too, as had the members of their staffs, and the two senior officers were so eager to learn the details of the situation that they rode forward.

Swenson told them what he had found. "They've burned up their war wampum," he said. "And tomorrow morning the lake is going to be full of heads that need cooling."

Hopkins chuckled, and Baker looked delighted. "We know nothing about any drinking," the colonel in chief said quickly. "It's against regulations." He said something in an aside to an aide, who ordered the cavalry to disband.

Baker sighed contentedly. "It happened sooner than we thought."

Hopkins nodded. "Much sooner. I was afraid we'd need a major battle to pull them together."

The headquarters detachment was dismissed, so Swenson and Jared went back to their own campfire.

The young Englishman had never known such

absurdity. The colonels had been responsible for the regulations against drinking and the making of liquor, yet they were deliberately ignoring a flagrant violation of their rules. Hereafter, he thought, the men would feel no respect for their commanders, and there would be chaos—perhaps tragedy—when the militia eventually met the enemy. He could understand the colonials' relaxed discipline to an extent, but this time they went too far.

"You disapprove?" Swenson asked in amusement.

"It isn't my place to criticize Colonel Hopkins and Colonel Baker, sir."

"But you think they're wrong," Swenson persisted.

"Well, I can't see the reason for making regulations if you purposely encourage regiments to pay no attention to them."

"If any New Yorker or Pennsylvanian is caught drinking tomorrow night, or at any other time, he'll be court-martialed, Hale. You can depend on it."

"But—"

"Tonight is different."

"Why should it be?"

Swenson was patient with a man who knew so little about the New World. "Most of the men in this army," he said, "have left their homes for the first time in their lives. I doubt if many of them have ever traveled more than fifteen to twenty miles from their own farms or towns. They're uncomfortable around strangers, you might say. I'm sure that's why we've made this roundabout march north instead of going straight up into Canada through New Hampshire. Hopkins and Baker are crafty old foxes. They knew the boys would get acquainted fast enough when all of them were suffering from the miseries of blisters on their feet and aches in their legs."

Jared began to understand.

"One of my sisters," Swenson told him, "lives in Wilmington with her husband, who comes from Yorkshire. He's the most stubborn man I've ever known, and won't speak to my other brother-in-law, who comes from Lincolnshire. He says no self-respecting Yorkshireman would lower himself. People over here are the same way, but much worse. I've always mistrusted Marylanders and Pennsylvanians, mainly because both states claim to own Delaware; but not a single one of the officers I've met on this expedition—from either colony—even knows about the claims. So I can't blame them for the greediness of politicians and royal governors."

"I've found out myself," Jared said, "how isolated a man can feel in America."

Swenson displayed two rows of unusually white, even teeth when he smiled. "If the liquor holds out long enough for a few more regiments to become sociable," he said, "it wouldn't surprise me if those days are ended. Not one of us on this march will ever be the same after he goes back home."

Jared reflected that the observation was particularly applicable to him. His tiny cabin on the Murtagh plantation wasn't home in any sense of the word, but it certainly would be doubly difficult for him to return to an existence without hope as an indentured servant. Others were eager to rejoin their families and return to their farms, but he had no reason to look forward to the end of the campaign.

Only here, in the deep forests, was he truly free. Perhaps that was why he now savored the wilderness as he never would have imagined he could.

Osman Murtagh walked slowly down the dirt road, not bothering to avoid the puddles of water left from a recent rainfall. As he came to the small wooden wharf, he paused, squinting toward the far end, where he saw the Trevor brothers securing their fishing boat for the night. Nodding to himself, he made his way toward them.

The brothers took note of his grim expression—and the fact that he carried the ax used to chop up deadwood from their fruit trees—and they both immediately braced for trouble.

"Afternoon, gents," Osman said pleasantly.

They nodded in reply, but as he approached, they warily separated so that one of them stood on either side of him.

He was conscious of their maneuver, but seemed unfazed. "Night before last," he said, "I heard you boys telling your ma at supper that you have some business in Bristol and that you're taking the boat there later in the week. It so happens I have some business there myself, so I'm going with you."

They stared at him, and Arthur said coolly, "You better explain yourself."

"I'll be delighted," Osman said, licking his dry

gums. "You and your mother took advantage of me, but you'll have to admit I've never complained. I worked for you diligently, like a slave out of darkest Africa, and I've repaid the little money that you spent on me many times over."

"You've also drained the cask of hard cider in the cellar, which is worth a tidy sum of money," Alvin interjected.

Osman's grim expression remained unchanged. "I know a little something about the cost of labor," he said, "and a hired man would have cost you one hundred pounds for the months of backbreaking work I've done. I'm still not complaining, however; I'm just notifying you that I'm terminating my employment as of today, and that you boys are taking me back to Bristol with you."

Alvin plucked a blade of grass, popped one end into his mouth, and chewed it slowly. "What are you aiming to do there?" he asked.

"If it's any of your business," Osman replied roughly, "I'm going home to my own property in the New World—and you aren't going to stop me or even try to stop me. I've regained my full strength by now, and all I need to do is walk into town and tell my story to a magistrate, and he'll send you lads to prison for forcing me into servitude."

The brothers again exchanged looks, and Alvin shrugged. "If that's the way you feel. I reckon Ma will just have to go back to work herself in the vegetable fields."

"That she will," Osman told him, a grin of triumph on his grizzled face. "You're sailing me to Bristol and I'm going home, and there are no two ways about it!"

The colonial militia remained camped on the shore of the little lake. No one knew why, and the members of the high command kept their own counsel. The men were free to hunt but were ordered not to stray more than five miles from the bivouac. No one was surprised when several Marylanders and a group of New Jerseymen ignored the regulation, since Americans considered it their inviolable right to hunt where they pleased. But the regiments were shocked when the offenders were summoned before a court-martial board and received sentences of ten lashes each for insubordination. Evidently Colonels Hopkins and Baker had their own valid reason for issuing the order.

Fish were too scarce in the lake and nearby streams to feed so many men, so a joint party of frontiersmen from Pennsylvania, New York, and western Massachusetts Bay went out, with special permission, on a foraging trip. The hunters returned after two days and nights laden with sacks of parched corn, beans, and smoked venison, and word quickly spread through the camp that they had found and surprised a village of Abnaki and had driven out the inhabitants.

The men were pleased—even though the venison had a slightly rancid taste—but the high command was disturbed, presumably because allies of the French now knew for certain that the expedition of British colonials was in the vicinity. That same afternoon a firm order was issued by headquarters, forbidding the building of fires at any time of day or night, for any purpose. That same evening sentry outposts were doubled.

The men grumbled after eating their first cold meal, and in the days that followed the complaints became louder. The prospect of action against the foe had prevented the regiments from becoming unruly, but there was no indication that Abbé Le Loutre's Micmac or the French regiment diverted from Louisbourg might be anywhere in the area. Occasionally scouts appeared in the camp to make secret reports to the colonels, slipping away again before anyone else could question them.

The waiting period dragged on, and tempers slowly rose. The days had become warm, and men accustomed to outdoor living chafed under the restrictions placed on their movements. But the nights were the cause of far greater dissatisfaction. The weather remained surprisingly chilly after sundown, and since there were few hollows offering protection from the wind, men deprived of their warm fires became increasingly restless.

There was a near mutiny when the food rations were cut in half, and a company from Connecticut threatened to return home at once. Troops from Massachusetts Bay and Delaware who were loyal to Hopkins and Baker were instructed to encircle the camp and open fire on any who tried to desert, either singly or in units. The insubordination came to an abrupt end, but tension continued to mount.

Probably no group suffered more intensely than did the headquarters detachment. Its members were under standing instructions to keep everyone at a distance from the scouts, which created hard feelings between them and the men of the regiments. They were annoyed, too, by incessant requests for information from friends and acquaintances, who refused to believe they were as much in the dark about developments as the rest of the militia.

Colonel Hopkins insisted, too, that they set an example for the other militiamen by bathing in the lake and shaving daily, and keeping their clothes and persons clean. They accused the colonel in chief, behind his back, of being a martinet. Jared, feeling much as the others did and unable to understand why the high command was being so mysterious, was conscious of the detachment's surliness and went to Lieutenant Swenson.

"Sir," he said, "there's trouble in the making. One of these days the men are going to refuse to obey an order."

"Have you heard anything specific?"

"No, sir. But they're ugly. They feel it's unfair that everyone else is allowed to go hunting while they've got to stand duty. They're the only unit in camp that hasn't tasted fresh meat in more than two weeks, and a diet of parched corn and that sour venison can get tiresome."

"I know." Swenson grimaced. "I find myself swearing I'll never take another bite of that swill, but I get so hungry I keep eating it. If you and I can survive on it, so can the men."

"The question isn't their survival, Lieutenant. It's their temper."

"It would be a disgrace if any man in the headquarters detachment was sent before a court-martial board, Hale."

Only in the American militia would it be possible for men who held posts of honor to revolt, and Jared nodded apprehensively. "I've tried talking to them, Lieutenant, just as you have, but they've stopped listening."

"I'm sure you realize that Colonel Baker's personal reputation is at stake. He's known these boys for years, and some of their fathers have been his friends for a lifetime. He'll be merciless if one of them embarrasses him, and it will mean a sentence of at least twenty lashes. For their own hides as well as his good name, we can't let it happen."

"What do you suggest, Lieutenant?"

Swenson made a fist and stroked it with the palm of his other hand. "Officers aren't allowed to fight enlisted men, and I'd be cashiered and sent home if I did what I've got in mind."

Jared knew what was expected of him. "There's no regulation that prevents sergeants from acting on behalf of their commanding officers."

The lieutenant gazed into space, his pale eyes innocent. "In a situation like this, Hale, I couldn't tell you what to do. I'd be party to a conspiracy. But I believe that when a brushfire is smoldering, it should be stamped out before the flames leap up and cause real damage."

As Jared left the tent he realized he would have to take the initiative—if necessary forcing a quarrel so he could create the opportunity to demonstrate his authority. He wandered toward the base of a giant fir tree where several members of the detachment not on guard duty were sprawled listlessly on the ground. No one bothered to glance in his direction as he approached.

"I figger my stummick can take this garbage we're eatin' for two more days, mebbe three." The speaker was Ray Bronson, in civilian life the New Castle blacksmith, a hulking brute whose only redeeming qualities were his physical strength and his ability to ride a horse with surprising, graceful ease. "So I'll wait another two days, mebbe three. And if old man Baker don't give us the chance t' shoot ourselfs some red meat, I'm headin' for the Lower Counties. I didn't sign up t' starve in the middle o' plenty."

There was a general rumble of agreement.

The situation was even more serious than Jared had thought. If members of the headquarters detachment deserted, the regiments would be totally demoralized as soon as they found out. He looked down at the man and found the excuse he was seeking. "Bronson," he said, "you haven't shaved today."

"No, and I don't aim t' put a razor to my face tomorrow, neither. You know what I'll say if old man Baker comes fumin' at me? I'll tell him right out I've got so weak from eatin' rotten Indian food that I ain't got the strength t' lift up that there razor."

"You know the orders," Jared replied, cutting through the laughter of the others. "Get yourself a bowl and some soap and shave. Now."

The former blacksmith rubbed the black stubble on his chin. "Boys, would you know it, lookin' at me, that I got a delicate hide? I ain't one t' ask for fancy livin', but my hide just plain shrinks when I start t' shave with cold water."

Jared privately sympathized with him but could not admit it. "If you wanted hot baths and dinners of beef-and-kidney pie, you shouldn't have joined the militia. But you did, so you'll do what you're told."

"Who tells me?" Bronson demanded.

"I do." Jared was relieved; not only had his stratagem succeeded, but the quarrel was based on a legitimate military issue.

"Just b'cause you're wearin' Ben Greene's sash don't make you no sergeant, Hale." The big man propped himself on one elbow. "Me and the boys here is havin' a private talk. Nobody asked you t' stick your nose in, so take yourself somewhere else."

Jared continued to stand over him, just out of reach. "I didn't make the regulation, any more than I gave myself Ben Greene's sash. But it's my duty to see that orders are obeyed. So you'll be saving both of us a great deal of trouble if you'll do what you're told."

The man yawned, then winked at his friends.

"You've been directed to shave." Jared still addressed him in a calm, civil tone. "That's a military order."

"You goin' t' make me do it?"

"Yes, if necessary."

"He was lucky," Bronson announced, "when he had hisself a fight with Phil Franklin, so he's got t' thinkin' he's somebody special. But no bonded man with his fancy gentry talk is goin' t' make me do anythin' I don't want t' do. I'm growin' me a beard, and I'm takin' me t' hell back t' the Lower Counties." He deliberately turned his back to Jared.

The other men nudged one another.

Jared knew that no matter what the outcome of the dispute, he would never again be in a position to exercise authority in the detachment if he hesitated. So he moved forward quickly, caught hold of the former blacksmith under the arms, and jerked him to his feet. Bronson was even heavier and more solidly built than he looked.

"That there," Bronson said, eyes narrowing beneath shaggy brows, "was downright unfriendly."

Jared wished they could fight in a spot farther from headquarters, but it was too late to suggest they adjourn to a more secluded place. The issue would have to be settled in the open, and they would have to run the risk of being seen by Hopkins or Baker.

They sparred, circling, each looking for an opening.

Jared realized that his opponent was slow on his feet, far less agile than Phil Franklin, and infinitely less skilled. But his sheer strength was that of a bull, so it would be impossible to stand up to him in a slugging match. In fact, it would be wise to avoid his blows, giving him no opportunity to inflict damage.

Jared knew what had to be done. Crouching in order to present the smallest possible target, he held his fists near his face, his elbows pressed close to his sides, and began to circle more rapidly. When he saw that Bronson was having difficulty keeping pace with him, he darted closer and landed a single sharp jab that caused the man's nose to bleed.

The former blacksmith was more humiliated than hurt and struck out blindly, his fists thrashing wildly.

Jared had moved out of reach.

"Fighting of any kind within the militia is strictly forbidden," someone said in a cold voice.

The men stiffened to attention.

Jared turned to see Colonel Baker glaring at him and hastily placed himself between the deputy commander and Bronson. "I take full responsibility, sir," he said at once. "I provoked this man, and I'm prepared to take any consequences."

Something in his tone caused Baker to hesitate. "Report to my tent in a quarter of an hour," he said, and turned away abruptly.

Before facing Bronson again, Jared saw that the colonel was heading in the direction of Lieutenant Swenson's tent. Swenson could not admit that the encounter had been planned, however, so it would be impossible to count on any help from that quarter.

Bronson was ready to resume the fight.

But his friends had suffered a change of heart. "Hold on, Ray," one of them said. "Sergeant Hale here, he's all right. Did you hear him takin' the whole blame?"

Bronson brushed the man aside. "He ain't no sergeant, and I'm goin' t' hurt him—bad."

Several of the others came up behind him, pinning his arms to his sides. His strength was so great that he almost broke away from them, but they managed to hang on.

"Damn you, Ray," one of them shouted, "Hale has offered t' take the whole punishment from Colonel Baker. You got no call t' fight somebody who acts that decent-like t' you!"

Gradually the former blacksmith subsided.

Jared held out his hand. "No hard feelings?"

"I reckon not," Bronson mumbled.

"Then the incident is forgotten—provided you shave."

Two or three of the men laughed, and Bronson gaped. "You're the most stubborn damn cuss I ever—"

"Use your head! I've already told the colonel I'll take responsibility, and so I will. But if he calls you in for your version, he'll skin you alive if he sees you haven't shaved. You call me stubborn?" Jared said scornfully. "Lad, you're asking for serious trouble."

Bronson scowled as he considered the matter. "Mebbe," he said at last, "I c'n warm some lake water in my hands b'fore I start shavin'." He wandered off, strutting slightly in an attempt to convince his friends that if he hadn't won the argument, perhaps he had not lost.

The other men, Jared saw, were looking at him with new respect. As nearly as he could judge, he had achieved his goal, although he might be required to pay a considerable penalty. "Boys," he said, "if I were you, I wouldn't think of deserting. If you're captured by sentries, which is likely, Colonel Hopkins will have you hanged. And if our own people don't get you, these forests are full of savages who'll be hunting for your scalps. I don't think I'm more courageous than most. In fact, perhaps I'm more cowardly. All I know is that I wouldn't want to make that long march all the way back to Delaware alone, or even with a few friends. I prefer to keep my hair attached to my head."

Giving the men no chance to reply, he walked away quickly. It was almost time to report to Colonel Baker, so he braced himself as he went toward the compound occupied by the members of the high command. He could not tell the truth to the colonel, he thought, without creating difficulties for Lieutenant Swenson and the entire detachment, difficulties that would cause unnecessary complications now that the problem seemed to have been solved.

He presented himself to an aide and was asked to wait. After standing outside the tent for a long time, he heard, "Come in, Hale!"

Colonel Baker was seated behind his makeshift desk, studying what appeared to be a crude map. He seemed preoccupied and did not look up.

Jared stood at attention until he was recognized.

Baker dipped a quill pen into a jar of ink and scribbled something on the margin of the map. "Yes, Hale?" He sounded slightly vexed. "What is it you want?"

"You directed me to report to you, sir."

"I'm busy." The colonel spoke indistinctly.

Jared didn't know whether to wait or leave and return later in the day.

Colonel Baker raised his head, and his face was expressionless. "There seems to be a misunderstanding, Hale. Unless you have something to discuss with me, you're dismissed."

Saluting smartly, Jared left the tent. As he raised the flap he realized the colonel was still looking at him, and saw a faint hint of amusement—and something more—in the deputy commander's eyes.

CHAPTER THIRTEEN

Nothing out of the ordinary happened all day, any more than it had in weeks. The regiments awakened early and then had long hours to idle away. Breakfast consisted of two handfuls of parched corn, augmented here and there by venison and other meats that had been heavily salted. The high command still refused to allow cooking fires to be built, but self-styled humorists pointed out that the order was unnecessary, since there was so little to cook.

Hunting parties went out into the forest, taking care not to stray behind the limits set by Colonel Hopkins, but game was becoming increasingly scarce in the vicinity, and only a few groups were fortunate enough to return with meat. Those who had enjoyed good luck were kept busy. They and their comrades spread thick layers of salt on the meat, pounding it with their rifle and musket butts, then setting it out in the sun to begin a long drying process.

Even though food supplies were running low, the officers had issued strict instructions to the effect that any meat accumulated through hunting was to be preserved for future emergency use.

This was a new concept to Jared. In his experience, troops who were inadequately fed ate heartily as soon as food finally appeared. But that did not seem to be the American way. Here, they were reserving supplies for a still worse situation that they might face at some future time. Their foresight was little short of remarkable.

One afternoon two scouts appeared at headquarters, and the commanders of regiments, independent battalions, and other separate units were summoned to a conference that lasted for several hours. Rumors swept through the camp but died down again after the commanders returned to their bivouac areas and resumed their normal routines.

As was becoming usual, everyone was famished long before sundown. Some units dined early, their evening meal consisting of the familiar parched corn, a handful of beans, and one thin strip of rancid venison. The regiments that had already used up their ration of the dried venison were uncertain whether they were better or worse off than the rest.

A short time after sunset most of the militiamen retired for the night, cursing quietly as they wrapped themselves in their damp blankets and prepared to endure the chill that would not be dispelled until the sun rose again the following morning. The officers in charge of the guard made their rounds of sentry outposts, and the cold and hungry militiamen in the camp finally dropped off to sleep.

Shortly before midnight, however, there was a commotion at headquarters. An aide awakened Lieutenant Swenson, who spent a few minutes with the colonel in chief and his deputy, and then went in search of Jared.

"Listen carefully," Swenson said as his acting sergeant sat up. "All units are to be alerted. We're breaking camp in one hour. The colonels want absolute quiet, and commanders are to be notified that any man who talks or makes other noises will be flogged first thing in the morning. We're to use the detachment as messengers, and there's no time to waste."

All armies were alike in one sense, Jared thought. After weeks of fruitless inactivity, the men were being urged to move quickly. "What's happening?" he asked.

Swenson shrugged. "I haven't been told. All I know is that Hopkins and Baker are in an almighty hurry."

The men of the headquarters detachment were roused and went off to deliver the orders. Here and there men swore sleepily, but in the main the regiments observed the rule of silence imposed on them. Then, at precisely one o'clock in the morning, the first of the regiments moved out of the encampment, leaving the site with few regrets.

The scouts who had met with the unit commanders led the column. In the vanguard was a battalion of riflemen from western Massachusetts Bay, directly followed by all of the cavalry, which included the headquarters detachment. One of the regiments of Pennsylvania Germans, long accustomed to frontier duty, divided into two groups

217

and was strung out along the flanks for protective purposes, while Mohawk Valley riflemen brought up the rear. The small train of artillery, as Jared observed in amazement, had actually been disassembled on the spot, each heavy iron cannon slung between pairs of sturdy horses, so that it was possible to proceed through the forest without having to clear a road.

Although the night was dark, with heavy clouds obscuring the stars and moon, the scouts maintained a lively pace, first skirting the lake to its western bank, then plunging into the forest on a northwestern course. At best the footing was difficult, but even townsmen had become sufficiently experienced on the long march to manage without undue strain. Occasionally, however, someone tripped over a hidden tree root, caught his breeches or shirt on brambles, or slipped on the carpet of damp leaves and pine needles.

But no one cursed or spoke aloud, and the men maintained tight self-discipline. No one knew why the army was moving, or where, but it seemed unlikely that a move would be made in the middle of the night without an accompanying threat of enemy action. And almost without exception, the militiamen welcomed the prospect of a battle after their long weeks of boredom. Rifles, muskets, and pistols had been loaded and primed before camp had been broken, and firearms were ready for immediate use.

Jared noticed that the scouts were leading the troops onto higher ground; but because it was difficult to see more than a short distance ahead, and since he was totally unfamiliar with the terrain, he felt as though he were groping blindly in the dark. At daybreak, however, a halt was called, and the commanders moved their troops into prearranged positions. The sky turned gray, and by sunrise the men could look around at the surrounding countryside.

The regiments had moved into battle formation, in depth, along the length of an open ridge that rose approximately one hundred feet above the densely wooded area they had marched through the previous evening. Toward the west, at the bottom of a long, less heavily wooded slope, a swift-running river churned and frothed as it tumbled over rocks, and Jared, viewing the scene from the heights, realized that it made the right flank of the colonial army almost completely secure.

To the south—the direction from which they had come—stretched the omnipresent forest, and even after the sun was well over the horizon, Jared found it impossible to see more than a few yards into the dark, murky wall of trees facing him. North of the ridge, however, the land was unlike any Jared or his companions had seen for many weeks. The ground fell away from the crest gradually, giving way to a rolling plateau that continued to fall as it stretched toward the horizon. There was not a tree in sight, except for a few smoke-blackened skeletons of trunks and branches that apparently had survived a forest fire.

Long knee-high grass and scrubby brush had grown to cover the scorched earth, but Jared, so long accustomed to deep woods, found the sector barren. Strangely, the regiments had been moved into line to repel attackers from the south and east, and the few cannon had been reassembled and placed so they faced in those directions. Once again he was confused by the unorthodoxy of New World military thinking. Were he in charge of an assault force, he would probably advance from the north, where the absence of trees would make the movement of large bodies of men much easier to control.

But he had taught himself not to criticize Colonel Hopkins and Colonel Baker. Although no European commander would anticipate an attack from the south or east, Jared took it for granted that the high command had valid reasons for turning their backs to the most obvious avenue of approach to the heights. Americans had their own ways of performing military maneuvers, and those ways invariably proved right for New World warfare.

The infantry regiments had already arranged crude barricades a short distance below the top of the ridge, and the cavalry units had been placed in reserve, along with several battalions of foot soldiers, behind the crest. The troops not directly behind the barricade hid themselves in the grass and brush, some of the more experienced men putting small branches, leaves, and twigs in their hats.

Colonel Baker made an inspection while the troops ate their tasteless, inadequate breakfast of parched corn and a little venison, and he offered each regiment an explanation of the mystery that had bedeviled them. "Our scouts couldn't locate either the French regiment commanded by

Colonel de Broussac or Abbé Le Loutre's Micmac," he said. "So we decided to offer them very tempting bait—our entire corps. But we didn't want to reveal our exact position for fear they might move too rapidly against us and take us by surprise. We deliberately left signs indicating the general area of our camp, but we tried to keep its exact location a secret.

"We realized, after our attack on the Abnaki, that the enemy would soon know where to find us. De Broussac and the Micmac joined forces, and since they started moving down toward the Maine District four days ago, our scouts have kept them under constant observation. We had already chosen this site for a battle, and moved here when they were half a day's march away. If they follow us, as they must, we'll fight them before nightfall this evening."

Jared was surprised by the care Colonel Baker exercised to make certain that the men of every unit knew what was happening. He found it equally unusual that the troops accepted the explanation as their due. He was continuing to learn that Americans believed it was their right to be kept informed by their commanders, and that a self-respecting militiaman would consider himself degraded if he were forced to fight blindly.

One thing continued to bother him, however, and when Hopkins and Baker finally sat down to their own meager breakfast a few paces from the headquarters detachment's position, Jared decided he had nothing to lose by asking questions. Leaving his mount with one of his men, he

221

walked to the spot where the commanders were sitting.

"Sir," he said to Colonel Baker, saluting. "I beg the colonels' pardon, but I wonder if you'd clarify something I find strange. Why are we preparing for an attack from the south, when clearly the best avenue of approach is from the north?"

Baker exchanged an amused glance with Colonel Hopkins. "What may be good tactics in Europe would be a pitfall here."

Jared didn't understand.

"The open field to our north," Hopkins added, pleased to give information to someone eager to find out more, "is as much a protection to us as the river to the west."

It was difficult for Jared to believe he was serious.

"The first maxim of wilderness warfare is that no attack should be made over open ground—under any circumstances," Hopkins went on. "The Micmac know it would be suicidal to advance against us across an unprotected field. I assume Colonel de Broussac's troops are also aware of it, and if they're not, well, they'll find out fast enough."

Even the most experienced of British generals, Jared thought, would be thoroughly bewildered by New World tactics.

"There's another aspect of the situation that's equally important," Colonel Baker said, lowering his voice. "Many of our troops are raw recruits, townsmen from Boston and New York and Philadelphia who have never fought a real battle. If they panic—and they well might when they come under heavy, accurate fire for the first time—they have nowhere to retreat. We've put them on the west, where the river will cut off a retreat—and they'll sober up fast enough if they try to run away across an open field. They'll have no choice, you see. They'll have to hold firm."

Jared thanked his superiors and, still marveling at their flagrant disregard of every rule he had been taught to hold sacred, started back toward the detachment.

"By tonight," Colonel Hopkins called after him, "you'll be revising some of your own ideas, Sergeant."

Through the long hours of the morning, time passed slowly, and the militiamen remained tense. But the heat of the sun made them drowsy, the failure of the enemy to appear caused them to relax, and by now they were grumbling quietly, complaining they felt cramped after holding fixed positions for so long. Some argued that there was game in the nearby forest, and company commanders were again forced to threaten severe punishment in order to prevent would-be hunters from wandering off in search of deer, wild turkey, and bear.

Then, suddenly, a single rifle-shot from the south changed the atmosphere. Men who had been sitting or standing threw themselves flat in the underbrush, all conversation stopped abruptly, and it was unnecessary for the senior officers to order an alert.

Jared, sitting his mount directly behind the crest, peered over the lip of the ridge for some sign of the foe but found none. The forest, in the valley below, appeared completely deserted, with no hint of movement that would betray the presence of men in the thick tangle of trees and bushes. Unless the shot had been fired by a skirmisher ranging far in advance of the enemy troops—or accidentally by one of the colonial militia's own scouts—it was safe to assume that there were hundreds, perhaps thousands of professional French troops and their Indian allies now facing the militiamen. Yet the forest remained serene.

The American regimental and battalion commanders cautioned their men to hold their fire. No one stirred, and it occurred to Jared that the enemy, from their hidden positions, probably found the defenders invisible, too. This prelude to battle was so weird, so unlike anything he had ever experienced, that he shivered.

An explosive outburst shattered the silence, and a ripple of rifle fire sounded to the south and east as enemy marksmen discharged their weapons. It was evident that the French and Micmac scouts had done their work well, the main body of enemy troops apparently having moved into a position from which it was relatively safe to launch an assault. Colonel de Broussac and Abbé Le Loutre were displaying admirable caution, too, having opened fire from a considerable distance rather than trying to storm the heights before they could gauge the strength of their foes.

Colonel Hopkins had no intention of providing them with gratuitous information, however, and his regiments wisely refrained from replying to the challenge, even though some militiamen found the temptation to respond almost irresistible.

Again a volley sounded below, and Jared began to understand the enemy's tactics. Probably two hundred men were taking part in the initial assault and were creeping closer to the heights with each volley they fired. Presumably the rest of the Micmac and French force was on the move, too, directly behind the skirmishers.

Colonel Hopkins refused to become panicky. He remained calm when a third volley was fired, and nodded smilingly to Colonel Baker when a fourth volley sounded from nearly halfway up the slope.

This, Jared thought, was the decisive movement. If the French and Micmac established a foothold on the hill itself, it could become difficult to dislodge them.

Hopkins seemed in no hurry, however, and not until the fifth volley revealed that the enemy shock troops had moved to within fifty feet of the colonial line did he stir. Then, in a crisp, clear voice, he gave the command every man had awaited. "Fire at will, boys, and make your shot count!"

The crest of the ridge erupted in a blaze of fire, and the thunder of the cannon added to the din. The French and Micmac had no intention of giving up ground they had gained, however, and held steady, remaining behind cover and returning round for round. Now, at last, it was possible for men on both sides to determine the position of their foes, even if they could not actually see one another. The flash of a discharging rifle or musket, the curling of smoke from an empty barrel were enough, and the Americans trained their weapons on the semidistinguishable targets.

The French and the Micmac, equally adept at wilderness warfare, used precisely the same technique. Here and there a man screamed as he was wounded, but the sounds of human voices were drowned by the rattle of musket and rifle fire, so it was impossible for commanders on either side to judge the effectiveness of their own or the enemy's fire. They were, Jared thought, like two swordsmen dueling blindfolded.

But Colonel Hopkins apparently possessed an instinct for battle of this sort. "Pass the word," he shouted to his aides. "Increase the pace of fire!"

Within a few moments rifles and muskets were firing more rapidly, and the enemy fire appeared to slacken somewhat. This was the first discernible lull on the French-Micmac side, and Jared was surprised when he realized that the enemy seemed to have been driven down to the base of the slope again.

A moment later, however, he had to disabuse himself of the notion that Hopkins was in complete control of the situation. The enemy had apparently employed a sly trick; while fifty or so marksmen had been firing volley after volley at the Americans to hold their attention, scores of Micmac warriors had been creeping up the slope, their approach undetected by the defenders.

Not until a shrill war cry, shouted simultaneously by large numbers of braves, betrayed the proximity of the Indians did the Americans learn that their foes had nearly reached their front-line position. At almost the same instant the enemy fire from below halted abruptly so as to not hit their own allies.

The Micmac, using tomahawks and knives, threw themselves at the militiamen, who were soon forced to discard their unwieldy rifles and defend themselves in hand-to-hand combat. Colonel Hopkins, ordering the front lines to hold firm, quickly called for reinforcements to join in the fray. Jared, watching from just behind the ridge, caught glimpses of vicious struggles only twenty or thirty yards away but could gain no overall impression of the trend of battle. As nearly as he could judge, the Americans far outnumbered the attacking Indians and probably would manage, in due time, to beat off the assault.

Meanwhile both sides were suffering heavy casualties. The troops in the front rank were in the main frontiersmen who had been forced to deal with savage raiders on many occasions, and they gave as good as they received. Militiamen and paint-smeared Micmac alike were viciously slashed, but gradually, as the reinforcements charged to the barricades, the assault was blunted.

Jared, who was beginning to fear that his mounted troops would see no action, was itching to join in the fight, but realized there was no place for horsemen in the struggle below. He was beginning to understand, at last, why American militiamen employed so few cavalry units; horsemen were at a gross disadvantage in the forest, and commanders were wise to rely on their foot troops.

What bothered him even more than his own inactivity, however, was his inability to understand why the Micmac had been sent forward, under cover of musket and rifle fire, to almost certain death. Too few of the savages were being used to give the enemy even a fair chance of success, and Jared knew that either the size of Abbé Le Loutre's command had been exaggerated or else he had sent only part of his force to create a diversion.

Both possibilities had already occurred to Colonels Hopkins and Baker, who had sent word to the unit commanders at all other parts of the line to be alert for a surprise attack from some other quarter. Their vigilance was finally rewarded, but the enemy still managed to surprise them.

A breathless infantryman ran to the command post behind the crest of the hill and, pointing toward the west, gasped, "They're sending hundreds o'men across the river. Frenchies, Naturals, all of 'em are comin'!"

The colonel in chief did not hesitate and sent his deputy to repel the invaders, committing all the reserves to the new attack in the one sector where trouble had been least expected. The head-quarters detachment escorted Colonel Baker, who rode at a gallop, and the other four cavalry units followed close behind, with the reserve infantry battalions from Connecticut and New York trying in vain to keep pace with the horsemen.

Coming in sight of the river, Jared found that a company of New Hampshire infantry marksmen were disrupting the enemy operation but had not succeeded in preventing the French from gaining a foothold on the near bank of the surging stream.

Half a squadron of French cavalry had already completed the crossing, and there were more men swimming their mounts across the river. Behind them were French sappers in dark green tunics, who, displaying great ingenuity, were hurriedly fastening together two narrow log rafts, securing them at either bank to bridge the river. French infantry and hordes of Micmac were massed together on the other side of the river, all waiting to be first across the floating bridge.

Jared knew, even before Colonel Baker gave any orders, what needed to be done. It was imperative that the bridge be destroyed before the enemy expanded their hold on the near side. Unfortunately, to accomplish that objective the colonials first had to deal with the French cavalry—the elite hussars.

Lining up eight abreast at the base of the hill, the hussars, in perfect unison, drew their sabers and began to advance.

This at long last was the kind of warfare Jared best understood, and he felt a sense of wild elation, a fierce anticipatory joy unlike any emotion he had experienced since coming to the New World.

Lieutenant Swenson, who was riding a few paces to Jared's right, looked worried, and Jared couldn't blame him. The combined American cavalry outnumbered the French horsemen, but it was almost too much to expect mounted militiamen who had never fought a cavalry battle to hold their own against seasoned, superbly disciplined hussars.

Twisting around in his saddle for a moment, Jared caught a glimpse of the captains commanding two of the militia cavalry troops, and realized they were slowing from a gallop to a canter. Unless they increased their pace again, they would suffer almost certain defeat.

"Smash the cavalry," Colonel Baker shouted, "and I'll move the infantry battalions in behind you!"

His direction was sound, but obeying it was another matter. The headquarters detachment dutifully headed straight toward the oncoming French squadron, but the rest of the colonial cavalry, bringing up the rear of the charge, was hesitating.

Jared realized he had to assume greater authority than his rank permitted. "Lieutenant," he called, "hold the detachment's fire until we close, then give them a blast aimed low and draw sabers."

Swenson's face cleared. "By God, you're right, Hale! Ride the bastards down, boys! Follow me!"

The detachment swept more quickly down the long slope, and when it became apparent to the commanders of the other colonial cavalry units that they were being separated from the vanguard, they increased their own pace in order to close the gap.

The French continued to advance up the hill at a trot, drawn sabers held at precisely the same angle. Others might have flinched or turned aside from the horses thundering down toward them, but the French ranks did not waver.

Jared had long felt professional admiration for French hussars, the inheritors of a great military tradition. The proud troops in white and gold uniforms, black boots, and gleaming helmets had met the English in scores of battles over the centuries, always fighting valiantly. A battle with them now, in the midst of the North American wilderness, was no fair test, but Jared felt his excitement mount again. At last he was face to face with men who were his true military equals.

At sixty paces the commander of the French squadron, a major, coolly drew his pistol and put a bullet through the forehead of Lieutenant Swenson, deliberately killing the man who was the obvious leader of the onrushing force.

The officers of the troops to the rear outranked Jared, but for all practical purposes he was now in command of the charge, and he knew at once that unless he acted decisively, the militiamen would become panicky and would scatter.

"Fire!" he screamed, leading the charging column past Swenson's sprawled body. Steadying himself in the saddle, Jared raised his own rifle and squeezed the trigger. He was rewarded by seeing the French major slump, a bullet in his shoulder.

Quickly sheathing his rifle, Jared drew his saber and began slashing furiously to left and right as he reached the front rank of the enemy squadron. The rest of the detachment, close behind him, followed his example, and their marksmanship more than compensated for their inability to hold a straight line as they advanced. There were holes in the French ranks, and wounded or riderless horses bolted back toward the river, disrupting the French lines as the Americans continued their wild charge.

The militiamen were no match in the saddle for their professional opponents, but the effect of their rifle volley had been devastating, and Jared exploited to the full the momentum he had gained. Cutting his way through the thinned ranks of the French squadron, he set an example that the horsemen of the headquarters detachment were quick to follow. Those who had sabers used them, and the others grasped their rifles by the barrels and used the butts as clubs.

The startled French troopers at first seemed uncertain how to respond, but rallied by the captain who was second in command of the squadron, the white-clad soldiers fought valiantly. They found it impossible to close their ranks, however, before the other colonial cavalry units swept into the fray, subjecting the hussars to a second, then a third barrage of rifle and pistol fire.

Jared, threading his horse through every opening he saw, continued to work his way toward the riverbank, parrying the thrusts and cuts directed at him while he slashed viciously at every white uniform within range. Twice he slowed to a canter, but he spurred his mount to a gallop again.

Finally Jared broke through to the riverbank, but there a new obstacle presented itself. It was relatively easy to drive off the French sappers, but Jared and his companions made perfect targets for the French infantrymen and Micmac warriors who were waiting on the far side of the river for the bridge to be completed. One American cavalryman toppled from his saddle, another slumped forward, badly wounded, and Jared heard a lead ball whistle by uncomfortably close to his head.

The rest of the colonial cavalry began arriving at the shore in large numbers now, and Jared realized they would be slaughtered, virtually unable to defend themselves, if they lingered in the vicinity.

Turning, he waved his saber overhead and started up the slope again, his own men and the other colonial troops following blindly. It was difficult to attain enough speed to prevent the French squadron from regrouping, but Jared knew he had to do whatever was necessary to keep the enemy off-balance until the colonial infantry arrived. "Reload!" he called once he had led his men safely out of range of the French and Indian riflemen, and then managed to prepare his own rifle for action again. "Fire at will, and don't miss, boys!" This time there was no volley. Instead each colonial took aim when he was ready and then fired at the most likely target. If the Americans had not already demonstrated that their effectiveness reached a peak in individual combat, they proved it now, taking an even higher toll of their foes than they had on the downhill ride and at the same time successfully keeping the French sappers off the bridge.

The squadron of hussars fought on grimly, but their pistols and sabers proved no match for the deadly frontier rifles, and gradually the survivors were forced to retreat toward the bridge.

To Jared's relief, the infantrymen from New York and Connecticut finally started reaching the base of the hill. As the foot soldiers arrived, Jared and his men moved aside, and the militiamen opened a ragged but steady fire on the enemy. Under cover of this operation, a number of volunteers managed to slip into the river and cut the lines holding the rafts to the near bank. The uncompleted raft began to swing downstream, and then, gathering speed in the swift current, it smashed against a boulder, where it lodged itself securely.

The enemy threat was ended, and the Micmac in the forest across the river vanished from sight, the French infantry bringing up the rear. The white-clad hussars, who were now completely isolated, turned their mounts around and splashed back into the river. The militiamen were so inexperienced that the thought of taking prisoners did not occur to most of them, and the hussars made good their escape, most of them succeeding in swimming their mounts across the river to the safety of the far bank.

Jared tried to encourage the American calvary to continue to fire at their retreating foes, but the militiamen had already won the engagement, and in their exuberance they showed no interest in prolonging the fight. A few wounded Frenchmen were rounded up, a surgeon was summoned to treat them, and the major whom Jared had shot asked to see his conqueror.

Riding to the spot where the officer had fallen, Jared dismounted and looked down at the pale face of a surprisingly young man. "Here, sir," the squadron commander said in excellent English, and struggled to reach his sword.

"Keep your weapon," Jared replied gruffly. "You'll need it when you're sent back to Quebec on parole."

He turned away, hoping no one was aware of

the pity he felt for a vanquished enemy, and supervised the rounding up of the riderless French horses.

He was still busy with this task when someone rode up beside him.

"That was well done, Hale," Colonel Baker said. "No one else could have managed it so neatly."

Until that moment it had not crossed Jared's mind that he might be commended for his leadership. He had been pleased with his accomplishments for their own sake and was faintly surprised that his efforts had been recognized.

When the colonel rode back up the slope toward the command post on the ridge, Jared called the detachment together and followed, a number of men leading the captured French horses. Not until he reached the top of the slope, however, did Jared finally realize that all the firing had ceased.

The repulse of the attempted river crossing had broken the impetus of the French attack. Colonel de Broussac had withdrawn hurriedly, while Abbé Le Loutre's savages had seemingly vanished.

Small groups of colonial militiamen advanced cautiously into what had been the enemy position, but no attempt was made to follow the French and smash them. Jared understood, without anyone having to explain it to him, that it would be next to impossible for men who had marched all night and then fought a hard battle to pursue their vanquished enemies through the wilderness.

The small units that had gone off to search for survivors and spoils returned in triumph. Colonel de Broussac had retreated in such haste that he had left most of his supplies behind, and the militiamen were promised their first satisfactory meal in weeks. Jared found his mouth watering at the prospect of salt cod and pork, coarse wheat biscuit, and even the inevitable parched corn and beans on which all troops in the New World—even the French—were forced to subsist.

Guards were assigned to keep watch on the supplies, strong sentry outposts were established to prevent a surprise counterattack by the Micmac—a favorite post-battle trick of the savages—and for the first time in many days campfires were lighted. Men bathed in the river, washing away the grime of battle, and two companies were assigned to escort the wounded from both armies to Boston.

The members of the headquarters detachment received half a bag of wheat flour, and several men began to make unleavened bread on heated stones. Water, beans, herbs, and salt pork were heated in a kettle, and although Jared once would have considered such a plebeian meal beneath contempt, he ate with gusto, refilling his container twice. The men had become raucous, but they did not include him in their merriment. At first he found this strange, but he finally realized they were treating him with a distant respect they had never before accorded him. He was flattered but at the same time felt somewhat disturbed.

Sitting alone, he tried to think of some natural way to enter the conversation of his comrades, and he was so engrossed that he failed to see Colonel Baker approach.

"I see you're paying the price of leadership, Hale," the deputy commander of the expedition said.

Jared scrambled to his feet.

"Don't let me interrupt your meal."

"I'm finished, sir."

"Are you quite sure? Come along, then." Colonel Baker led the way to the command post, where the captains commanding the four cavalry troops had gathered, as had the senior officers of the infantry regiments from the Lower Counties.

Everyone, Colonel Hopkins included, was smiling rather strangely, and the colonel in chief's grin became broader after he returned Jared's salute and held out his hand. "We are all indebted to you, Hale. These gentlemen," he continued, indicating the cavalry leaders, "are still stunned by your grasp of a very complicated situation."

Jared knew now that he had been summoned to receive a commendation, and felt his face growing hot.

"I think you'd like to do the honors, Ed," Hopkins said. Colonel Baker nodded. "Hale, raise your right hand and swear you'll support the Crown, the proprietary colony of Delaware, and her laws."

Jared obeyed the solemn request.

"Swear you'll obey your superiors in all things and that you will never act contrary to the welfare of Delaware."

Again Jared repeated the oath.

"Under the powers conferred on me by Governor Thomas as commander in chief of the militia of the Lower Counties," Colonel Baker said, "I hereby grant Jared Hale of New Castle the temporary rank of lieutenant, assigned to calvary. Effective as of now, you will take command of the headquarters detachment."

The granting of a brevet commission was so unexpected that Jared didn't know what to say, but he saluted before he could stammer his thanks.

Everyone present congratulated him, and Colonel Hopkins said, "We hate to lose Erik Swenson, but it doesn't pay to be sentimental in war. He's been replaced by an officer of talent."

It was almost impossible for Jared to think of himself as a commissioned officer once again.

"Ben Greene is recuperating," Colonel Baker told him, "and should be able to resume at least limited duties as your sergeant." He glanced at the Englishman, and his eyes were shrewd. "I have a notion," he added quietly, "that you'll need no lecture on the responsibilities and obligations of your new rank."

"I'll do my best, sir." Even under these happy circumstances, Jared was reluctant to admit that he had previously held a military commission.

Baker preferred not to dwell on the question. "You'll report direct to me, rather than to either of the Delaware regimental commanders. Junior officers usually don't attend war councils, but we'll want you there."

"Yes, sir."

"Aren't you wondering why?" Hopkins interjected.

"Well, Colonel," Jared replied, "the protection of headquarters will be my responsibility, so I take

238

it for granted you'll want me to have some idea of what's happening."

"Quite right." The colonel in chief chuckled. "Far be it from me to fan a young man's vanity, but after your exploits today, we'd be foolish not to take advantage of your talents in the planning of future operations. I can promise you one thing: You're going to be kept quite busy during the rest of this campaign, Lieutenant Hale."

As Jared walked back to his own unit from the headquarters tent, he found himself wishing that Caroline Murtagh had been present to learn of his commendation and promotion to the rank of an officer. He scowled, dismissing the thought as foolish. For some reason, though, he could not get the idea from his mind. He realized that he was actually anxious to have her think highly of him.

Continuing on his way, he suddenly stopped short, shook his head, and rubbed his jaw in perplexity. Why had he thought of Caroline rather than Polly? He had no idea.

Osman Murtagh marched purposefully down the narrow cobbled streets of Bristol toward the port area. He had landed in the town earlier in the day, thanks to his insistence that the Trevor brothers provide him with transportation from the Isles of Scilly, and now his heart beat faster as he realized that he was at last approaching the goal he had sought for so long. Clenching and unclenching his callused hands, he paused and looked at the four or five ships lying at their berths in the harbor. All of them, he had been told, were bound for the New World, and without exception they would be delighted to give him passage for the sum of ten pounds—the exact amount he had demanded and received from the miserly Trevors.

His senses suddenly alert as he smelled the redolent fragrance of ale, he realized that he was standing outside a tavern. He looked in the open doorway and was sorely tempted to celebrate his return home by indulging in a drink of the rum that he so badly craved.

Stroking the full beard he had grown during his forced sojourn on the Isles of Scilly, Osman wavered for a moment; finally, however, his common sense prevailed over his thirst. He had not consumed a drop of liquor for nearly a week— since the night he had finished off the last of Mary Trevor's hard cider—and he knew that it would be prudent to wait a little longer. If he started to drink now, he would not be able to stop, and the ten pounds he intended to use to pay his passage would vanish in rum instead.

There would be ample opportunity to celebrate once he reached his own home. Chuckling coarsely as he considered the prospect, he continued on his way toward the waiting ships.

CHAPTER FOURTEEN

Jared had almost forgotten the privileges that commissioned officers enjoyed. He no longer cooked his own meals, he slept in the tent that had been Lieutenant Swenson's, and his name was removed from the sentry roster. He still curried, fed, and watered his own horse, however, and earned greater respect from his detachment as a result.

There were innumerable differences between holding a commission in the Royal Army and one in the colonial militia, as he soon discovered. In England there had been a wide, permanent gulf separating enlisted men and their superiors, but in America officers frequently ate with their troops, relaxed with them, and even shaved in their presence, which would have horrified the gentlemen who had been Jared's colleagues in the dragoons. The separation of officers and men was subtle. No one who held a commission went hunting or fishing with his troops except on official parties, and had the militia marched through any towns, officers would not have accompanied their troops to taverns.

The American concept of the commissioned ranks was unique, Jared was learning. Officers were regarded as skilled men who held higher posts because of their greater knowledge. But they were not considered better than enlisted men as individuals, and only a few of the senior colonels and their immediate subordinates were held in awe.

The greatest advantage of his new status, Jared found, was that he was no longer kept in the dark as to the high command's plans. He attended the staff conference at which it was decided to remain for a few days at the ridge, pending receipt of information on the enemy's movements. And he was summoned to Colonel Hopkins's tent for the council of war, which was attended by all unit commanders.

So many officers were present that only Hopkins, Colonel Baker, and the regimental commanders sat. The others, including lieutenant colonels, stood, crowding together near the center of the sloping canvas structure so they wouldn't have to stoop.

"We have news of sorts, gentlemen," Hopkins said, sounding almost too cheerful. "I'll ask the quartermaster to give his report first."

Major Josiah Adams, in civilian life a merchant in the employ of the enormously successful Thomas Hancock Company, clasped his bony hands behind his back and looked distressed. "I see no sense in pretending that we're in good condition when we're not," he said, speaking in the nasal drawl that distinguished most residents of Boston. "We have just enough food to last us another forty-eight hours. Then our stores will be depleted."

A lieutenant colonel from New York broke the silence. "What's left, I suppose, is parched corn and that damned venison."

"There's no more of the venison, I'm sorry to say," Adams replied tartly.

Again there was a long silence.

Colonel Baker coughed behind his hand. "Our hunting and fishing parties have enjoyed only moderate success. I wouldn't be surprised if our battle frightened game away from the area. And your guess is as good as mine as to the reason the fish aren't running."

Tension began to mount, Jared noted.

"Charley Duncan has just come back from some explorations he and his scouts have been making,"

Colonel Hopkins said. "Lieutenant Duncan, tell these gentlemen what you've just reported to Colonel Baker and me."

Duncan, a rawboned man whose leathery face almost matched his faded buckskins, did not enjoy the limelight. "Not much to tell. De Broussac's regiment is marching to Quebec. The damn Micmac have disappeared. Not even my Seneca can scare up their trail. Maybe they've gone off to reinforce Port Royal, or maybe they've had their bellies full of fighting and have gone home. But I doubt it. That damn Frenchie priest had them stirred up good, and I'll lay odds they're still hungry for scalps." Embarrassed by the longest speech he had ever made, the woodsman closed his mouth and stared down at the ground.

"There are some other developments worthy of our consideration, gentlemen," Hopkins said. "Colonel Baker, would you care to summarize the letter we received by courier from Boston this afternoon?"

The deputy commander removed a folded sheet of closely written vellum from his tunic pocket and scanned it briefly. "Governor Shirley of Massachusetts Bay is launching an ambitious project. He's proposing that all of the colonies join in a naval expedition against Louisbourg on Cape Breton Island. This information is to be kept confidential for the present."

Jared was even more surprised than some of the others. Everyone knew that the French fortress of Louisbourg was the strongest citadel anywhere in the New World, its fame having extended to

England and Europe. It was madness to think that British colonials could reduce it.

Baker smiled. "It will take at least a year, perhaps two, to prepare for such a campaign," he said. "Colonel Pepperell of Massachusetts Bay is being given the overall command, with the rank of major general, and his deputy will be Colonel Waldo of the Maine District."

It would be insanity to place militia officers in charge of such a venture, Jared thought.

"Governor Shirley is—ah—inviting the Royal Navy to join forces with him, and members of this expedition also will be asked if they would care to volunteer."

Many of the officers looked at one another in shocked surprise, and the lieutenant colonel who commanded the regiment of Pennsylvania Germans lost a battle to keep a firm grip on his temper. "By Gott," he declared, "we already wear out our boots marching this far from home, and now they want us to wait another year or two for a real war? My boys and I, we fight now, this summer."

There was a rumble of agreement from the other commanders.

Colonel Hopkins appeared to ignore them. "We have two choices, gentlemen. The first is to march to Boston and disband. We'll have accomplished a limited objective, but it is nevertheless an achievement. We'll have put the enemy on the defensive."

"For how long?" demanded a lowly captain, the commander of one of the cavalry troops. "Maybe we have the bastards on the run right now, because we can't be too far from the border of New France, and the authorities up in Quebec must be mighty upset. But they'll start sleeping better the very day we march south. And it won't be long after that," he continued, his voice rising, "a fortnight—three weeks, at the most—before the Naturals start raiding us again. The western frontiers of every last colony will be burned and looted, men will be scalped, and the savages will take our women and children into captivity. I can't speak for any unit except my own, but I can promise you that my boys and I aren't going home until we teach the Frenchies to leave our wilderness settlements alone!"

Colonel Hopkins ignored his outburst as well. "Our second alternative," he said, "is to march against Quebec itself."

The idea was so bold that for a moment the startled officers neither spoke or moved. Then, simultaneously, several of them began to speak.

Hopkins raised a hand for silence. "We're only a day's march from New France. Keep in mind that our provisions are running low. In less than another day after that we'd be in farm country, where we could find all the food we'd need. Charley Duncan tells me the farmers along the Saint Lawrence are growing bumper crops this year, and they've never had more cattle and poultry."

Duncan nodded, a gleam in his eyes.

"That would solve our supply problems," the colonel in chief went on. "If we head for home, we may go hungry for a week or two."

Jared suspected that Colonels Hopkins and

Baker had already made a decision and were simply manipulating their men in a clever but none too subtle manner in order to obtain their concurrence.

"So a campaign against Quebec has certain advantages," Hopkins said. "But I don't want to mislead you, gentlemen. Charley, tell them what you learned about the defenses of the city. Lieutenant Duncan," he added casually, "spent several days there, posing as a fur trapper."

Duncan had no desire to enlarge on the role he had played as a spy. "The Frenchies have three regiments in the town. Another is garrisoned just outside the fort, and de Broussac's regiment should arrive there any day. They have more cannon in the fort than I could count, most of them twelve-pounders. They keep the Naturals a safe distance up the Saint Lawrence from the town, but I'm sure the main body of the Algonkin—and I don't know how many other Indian nations—will join them if they're attacked."

"If any of you has forgotten it," Colonel Baker interjected in a quiet, dry tone, "one regiment of French regulars is equal in size to almost three of ours. Count in their Indian friends, and they heavily out-number us. And don't forget that the citadel in Quebec stands on a cliff more than three hundred feet above the Saint Lawrence and is an easily defended fort. The history of our attempts to take the place isn't very encouraging. More than fifty years ago Sir William Phips, the governor of Massachusetts Bay, led a major expedition there, and was beaten. In 1711, when Marlborough was whipping the French in Europe, a major campaign to take Quebec also failed."

Jared realized that as the junior officer present and a newcomer to the group, he should remain silent. But he could not tolerate what appeared to be shortsighted stupidity. "If our chances of capturing Quebec appear to be slim—and they do—I can't understand what we'd gain by launching an attack on the town." Even though New World military concepts had turned upside down nearly everything he had ever been taught, he had yet to hear of an army deliberately courting defeat.

"We refuse to admit the possibility of defeat until we're actually beaten," Colonel Hopkins replied. "But even if we should lose, we believe we could strike hard enough to disrupt the enemy so badly that they would have to concentrate on rebuilding their defenses rather than on sending their Indians to harass our frontier settlements."

"What's more," Colonel Baker said, "within the next few months they're certain to learn of Governor Shirley's expedition against Louisbourg. You can be sure their espionage agents pay regular visits to Boston and Philadelphia. So, between repairing the damage at Quebec and preparing for a siege at Cape Breton Island, they'd have no opportunity to wage an offensive campaign against us."

Jared was forced to admit, reluctantly, that the thinking of the colonels made sense. It was always sound strategy to keep the enemy off-balance, to force him to devote his full attention to protecting himself.

"If there are no further comments, gentlemen," Colonel Hopkins said, "I'd like to learn your pleasure in this matter."

The leader of the Pennsylvania German regiment shouted, "We attack Quebec!"

A roar of approval greeted his words.

"Does anyone disagree?" The colonel in chief smiled as he looked straight at Jared.

Trying to conquer his remaining misgivings, Jared replied, "I'm in favor of going on to Quebec, sir."

"It would appear that the decision is unanimous, gentlemen." Hopkins took a thick gold watch from his pocket. "We still have three or four hours of daylight left today, so we'll begin our march this afternoon. Tell the men that the sooner we start, the sooner they'll eat a full meal, and I'm sure no one will object to a march on empty stomachs."

The rugged hills diminished in size as the colonial army drew nearer to the basin of the Saint Lawrence River, and at last the vanguard emerged from the wilderness into gently rolling farm country, where thrifty French settlers had created a land of plenty that resembled parts of Normandy and Brittany. There were fields of wheat, rye, and oats; patient coaxing of the rocky soil had produced an abundance of vegetables; and on the southern slopes of hills there were small orchards, principally apple trees, and even some sheltered grape arbors. As Lieutenant Duncan had predicted, the cattle were sleek, as were the sheep, and every farm had a well-stocked poultry run.

The cavalry units were assigned to foraging details, each accompanied by a half battalion of infantry. The headquarters detachment went out with a contingent of Delaware infantry, and Jared was pleased to discover that Phil Franklin, of whom he had seen little of late, had also received a battlefield promotion, to the lowest rank of commissioned officer, that of ensign.

The men from the Lower Counties visited four thriving farms in a single morning and returned to the bivouac area with carts—also commandeered—piled high with foodstuffs. The troops were unusually silent as they made their way across the open fields and remained unresponsive when they were cheered by the militiamen of other regiments who had gathered to watch the much-needed supplies arrive at the camp.

Jared turned over to Quartermaster Adams and his assistants the produce and livestock he had collected, and when he turned away he found Franklin waiting for him. "Come over to the detachment's area for dinner, Phil," he said. "It will be a good one today."

"I will, thanks." Franklin jammed his huge hands into the pockets of his tunic and stared down at the ground. "But I'm not really hungry."

"Neither am I." Jared was silent for a few moments. "I keep thinking of the first family we visited. The man is ruined."

Phil nodded glumly. "I pretended not to see one of his storage bins, and we left him his old milk cow, so there's enough to feed his wife and young 'uns for a spell. Still, they won't have an easy time of it this winter if they don't get help."

"Nobody in the neighborhood can give it to them, that's certain. Everyone else has been hit just as hard. We've scoured the area like a plague of locusts." Jared raised his voice defensively. "There's no choice in war. I hate to see civilians suffer, but the men need food."

Phil kicked a rock out of his path. "What bothers me is that he and his family live pretty much the same way we do down in the Lower Counties. So do all the others hereabouts. They've built their own houses, with no more help from France than we've had from England, and they've had to keep a sharp watch for Indian attacks. I feel like I've been robbing folk who live right down my own road."

The New World had done a great deal to blur the differences between English and French colonists, Jared thought, and they resembled each other more than they did the people in their homelands. "I know what you mean," he said, hoping to offer some solace to his friend. "They're Americans, too—that's what makes it so distasteful." It did not occur to him that he was classifying himself as an American, as well. "All the same, we have orders to obey."

"Oh, I'll do what I'm told, Jared, just like you will. But this is one part of the campaign I damned well don't like, and I'm not ashamed to admit it."

Jared had no reply. Perhaps Phil was right, he thought. If England and France wanted to fight each other, they had ample opportunity to do so in Europe. It was hard enough for a man to make a living in the New World without having to suffer the depredations of war.

Not until much later did Jared realize how much the forests of America had already influenced his own thinking.

The little town of Sainte-Jeanne was unusual, to say the least. Located on the south bank of the broad Saint Lawrence River, it sat on a low, open bluff almost directly opposite the city of Quebec. Inhabited mostly by fishermen and fur trappers— men accustomed to rubbing elbows with their English neighbors to the south, and too independent to submit to the authority and civilizing influences of Quebec—Sainte-Jeanne did not panic as the colonial militia drew near. In fact, the town's few stores, which served anyone reluctant to take a boat across the river to buy such staples as salt, blankets, and cooking utensils, remained open for business and even in some cases eagerly awaited the newcomers. These establishments for the most part were run by retired fur trappers who had spent the better part of their lives alone in the wilderness and who valued the right to live as they pleased, without restrictions.

There were only two small churches in Sainte-Jeanne, both poorly attended and somewhat ramshackle. However, there were five thriving taverns—a surprisingly large number considering the size of the town—all of them serving the raw corn whiskey common everywhere in North America, a vile grade of rum, and a potent ale that became palatable only after the third swallow.

The colonial militiamen, who were amazed at the welcome they received, were also delighted to discover that Sainte-Jeanne boasted more than its fair share of brothels, all of them staffed by young women who had come to the New World from France. Here they would earn substantial sums in but a few years and, enriched by suitable dowries, either settle in Quebec or return to France to find themselves husbands. The smallest of these establishments, which had once been the house of an eccentric merchant, resembled a miniature chateau and ordinarily catered to the wealthier trappers, high administrative officials from Quebec, and officers of the garrison across the river. It was too expensive for the purses of most of the militiamen, who were discouraged by the proprietor, and it soon came to be patronized almost exclusively by the militia's officers.

The high command wisely decided not to restrict the appetites of men who had spent a long time in the wilderness, and both the taverns and brothels did a thriving trade. Colonels Hopkins and Baker were surprised they had been able to reach Sainte-Jeanne without encountering any opposition and were somewhat puzzled when Quebec's garrison—whose sentries were plainly visible from the south bank on a clear day—made no attempt to drive the colonials away from the doorstep of the principal city of New France.

Apparently the French were awaiting reinforcements before launching an attack on the invaders. The commanders of the colonial militia, however, were in no position to force the issue. Too sensible to assault the citadel with an army neither large enough nor powerful enough to conduct a major siege, they realized that they had to wait until their foes came out into the open to fight a battle.

In the meantime they were content to give a well-earned rest to troops who had marched hundreds of miles through the wilderness. The army had ample supplies now, and Major Adams won the goodwill of Sainte-Jeanne's storekeepers, as well as that of the area's farmers, by paying in silver for the food he wanted. The most comfortable bivouac the troops had enjoyed since the start of the campaign was established, and the men, two regiments at a time, were allowed to sample the dubious delights of the town, with one company from each regiment standing duty on a rotating schedule to prevent brawls and riots.

With the enemy directly across the Saint Lawrence, however, the militia's vigilance remained high. Sentries stationed along the river and at all approaches to Sainte-Jeanne from the south, were prepared to sound an alarm well before the French could approach to within striking distance. Colonel de Broussac's regiment had already joined the other troops in the citadel, and Lieutenant Duncan's scouts found no trace of any Indian war parties.

Jared, unexpectedly idle for the first time since he had come to the New World, had an opportunity to reflect on the bewildering predicament in which he found himself. He could not face the prospect of returning to the life of an indentured servant after enjoying the prerogatives, stature, and authority of a militia officer. The idea of disappearing into the wilderness and making a new life for himself somewhere on the frontier was a constant temptation, yet he continued to reject the notion and couldn't quite understand his reasons for feeling opposed to what seemed eminently sensible.

He supposed that, at least in part, he found the prospect of becoming a fugitive from justice distasteful. The long months of his incarceration at Newgate seemed like a far-distant nightmare to him, and he had no desire to live for the rest of his days in fear of sudden arrest, fresh disgrace, and a new term of imprisonment in the colonies. But there was something more at stake than his dislike of lawbreaking, and he realized that both Caroline Murtagh and Polly White were influencing his feelings.

Was he in love with one of them? He didn't know, but thought it odd that he couldn't decide which of them attracted him more. And it was absurd to contemplate the possibility that he might be in love with both of them. He was a civilized man, and although he had never considered marriage, the very idea of having more than one mistress seemed unthinkable. His dilemma made him feel foolish.

Distance, he realized, minimized the shortcomings of both women and made them both seem more appealing. It was easy to forget Caroline's hot temper and arrogance, as well as Polly's strangely secretive sense of independence. It was also possible that he truly cared for neither of them but was merely hungering for the affectionate warmth and sympathy of any woman. No matter how hard he tried, however, he found he was unable to dismiss either woman from his thoughts.

His predicament was very much on his mind one afternoon when he sat around a campfire with a number of officers from the Lower Counties. They had just dined on beefsteak-and-mushroom pie, corn bread, and fried trout, and, comfortably full, were speaking of the day they would return to Delaware. Jared made several attempts to change the subject but failed, and eventually he wandered off alone to a boulder from which he could watch the majestic waters of the Saint Lawrence sweep eastward toward the open ocean.

After a while Phil joined him. "Is something ailing you, Jared?" he asked.

"Not really," Jared said. "I don't particularly enjoy talk of home, that's all. My own future in New Castle isn't very bright."

"It could be worse."

Jared failed to appreciate his friend's optimism. "I suppose," he said bitterly, "I could be shipped back to England in chains and condemned to serve out the rest of my term in Newgate."

"I'm not mocking you," Phil protested, sitting beside him on the peak of the boulder. "You're worried about your indenture, right?"

"Of course. If you had years of slavery ahead, you'd feel as I do."

Phil spat over the edge of the boulder. "Like I said, you could be a heap worse off."

Apparently he had something specific in mind, and Jared turned to look at him.

"Me, now, I've had a niggle almost the same as yours. I've been saving up my money so I can buy the bond of the girl I'm aiming to marry."

"You mean an indenture can be bought by anyone?"

"Sure. A rich man can buy the bonds of fifty

servants, if he has a mind to, and if he'll put up the money. I reckon I'll have most of what I need to set my girl free, and I'll borrow the rest."

The point was interesting, but so irrelevant to his own case that Jared shrugged.

"What's to stop you from buying up your own bond?" Phil demanded.

Jared laughed. "A lack of funds, my friend. Aside from my wages—which wouldn't pay for more than a good suit of clothes, a horse of my own, and a sword when I'm discharged from the militia—I haven't a copper to my name. And I couldn't borrow."

"Why not?"

Jared felt a flicker of an old irritation. New World farmers could be almost incredibly thick-headed. "You're a property owner," he said. "A merchant or a plantation owner takes relatively little risk when he advances money to you. But I have nothing to offer as security for a loan."

Phil pondered this for a while. "Maybe," he said, "it won't be easy. But there has to be a way."

"Do you have any suggestions?"

The burly giant again fell silent. "Not right off," he admitted at last.

There was nothing else to be said, and Jared smiled bleakly at his friend, then stood and climbed down to the ground. Wanting solitude, he strolled off alone in the direction of Sainte-Jeanne, his mood black. He had learned something new when he had discovered that theoretically it was possible for him to buy his own bond, but the information was of no practical value. Not only was he virtually bankrupt, with no prospect of obtaining a substantial sum of money, but he also had no reason to believe that Caroline would permit him, or anyone else, to purchase his bond. She could, if she chose, force him to spend years working out his obligation.

Walking aimlessly, he soon found himself on the main street of the town, Rue Saint-Louis, and heard a roar from the tavern frequented by officers. The thought of drinking strong, raw liquor did not appeal to him, and he had no intention of becoming involved in the card game of twenty-and-one that began at noon each day and lasted until midnight. Never again would he succumb to the lure of gambling, and it was a minor satisfaction to realize that his suffering had made him aware of his weaknesses.

Then, suddenly, he caught sight of a young woman approaching him on the cobbled street, and he forgot all else. She was slender, tall, and handsomely dressed in a gown and matching cloak of green silk trimmed with black velvet. He studied her closely as she drew nearer, and his interest was sparked still more when he saw her fine-boned features, wide-set hazel eyes, and, beneath a feathered, broad-brimmed hat, a mass of auburn hair.

A tiny, provocative beauty patch had been pasted high on her left cheekbone, and he couldn't determine whether her full lips were naturally bright or rouged. In any event, she was by far the most sophisticatedly appealing young woman he had seen in the New World, and he had almost forgotten that such creatures existed.

The woman became aware of his interest, and

a chill seemed to envelope her. She looked straight through Jared, not seeing him, as they drew nearer and passed each other.

He felt deeply embarrassed, wanting to apologize, to explain it was difficult for a member of an occupying army to remember there were ladies in the town.

Not slowing her pace, she turned in at a gate set between two high stone pillars.

Jared blinked and stared harder. Incredible though it seemed, the woman was going into the chateau, Sainte-Jeanne's most expensive brothel. On impulse, his heart pounding, he followed her.

A middle-aged woman admitted him, leading him into the tastefully furnished great hall, but he was disappointed to find that the girl had vanished.

"You have an appointment with someone, *mon capitaine?*" the wife of the proprietor asked.

"I'm a lieutenant, and I'd like to see the young lady who just came in a moment ago."

The woman hesitated. "She is new to us, so I cannot promise you a pleasant afternoon."

"I'll take my chances."

The woman asked him to wait, went off, and finally reappeared, beckoning.

He followed her up a broad, winding staircase to the tiny parlor of a suite on the first floor, where the girl was sitting on a divan. She had removed her hat and cloak, and a single heavy strand of hair fell forward across her shoulder, accenting the deep cut of her pale green gown.

"Mademoiselle Le Brun, you have a visitor,"

258

the woman said, and left, closing the door behind her.

"How do you do, monsieur." The girl extended her hand.

Jared bent over it, still treating her as he would a lady. "Jared Hale, ma'am."

"And I am Elise Le Brun." She regarded him unsmilingly. "Let me offer you a glass of sack." She stood, looked around the room uncertainly, and finally located a carafe and glasses on the shelf of a bookcase. Filling two small glasses, she handed one to Jared.

Her manner was still so remote that he continued to feel uncomfortable. Certainly nothing in her attitude indicated that she was a courtesan, and he decided to satisfy his curiosity directly. "May I ask why you were so cool to me on the street just now?"

She returned to the divan and, instead of asking him to join her, motioned him to a chair opposite her. "I do not walk the streets, sir!" she said indignantly, speaking English with only a trace of a French accent.

"I assure you, mademoiselle, it didn't occur to me that you do."

She accepted the apology with a graceful nod and relented slightly. "I have arrived here just today."

He thought it unlikely that anyone wearing such finery could have been living in a small frontier town. "From Quebec?"

Her reply was casually evasive. "I have spent a little time there, but I know Paris better. Also your London."

"Why do you call it mine?"

"Because your speech is that of an Englishman, not a colonial, monsieur."

He was aware of a shrewdness behind her innocent hazel eyes. Still intrigued by her recent arrival, he thought it almost impossible that she could have crossed the Saint Lawrence by boat without being apprehended by the militia's sentries. "May I ask how you arrived here?"

"When one has friends, one can accomplish much." She seemed bored, and to end his questioning, she assumed the offensive herself. "With what regiment do you serve?"

"I command the headquarters detachment."

The girl stirred slightly. "The headquarters of Colonel Hopkins?"

"You know his name, I see."

"Who does not?" She thawed appreciably, smiled, and lifted her glass. "To you, Jared, and to me."

He sipped his drink, noting that she, too, consumed very little. "I hope you'll take this as a compliment. I mean it as one. You seem—" He stopped, groping for the right words. "You seem alien to the chateau."

Elise shrugged prettily. "One must live." Making a place beside her on the divan, she beckoned. "But I want no one to feel sorry for me."

He realized that her bid for sympathy was so smooth it made up for the lack of subtlety in her approach. Fascinated by this exceptionally attractive young woman who he was sure was no ordinary harlot, he joined her.

"You must hate the New World, as I do." Elise

let her hand trail down his arm, seemingly unaware of the gesture.

Jared wanted to protest that life in America provided certain advantages and pleasures that were difficult for the typical European to appreciate. But she apparently was leading up to something, so he decided to encourage her. "I've been happier elsewhere," he said.

"Perhaps we could leave together."

The suggestion startled him; after all, he had spent only a few minutes in her company. But he felt increasingly certain she had something specific in mind. "Our countries are at war with each other," he reminded her.

"I wouldn't mind going to London." Elise moved almost imperceptibly, leaning against him without applying pressure. "The British are a gallant people; they'd let me stay, I'm sure."

"It's a tempting idea," Jared said, slipping an arm around her waist. "How would we go about it?"

"Perhaps you would take me with you to Boston, and we could sail from there. Perhaps there are other ways."

Jared eyed her meaningfully, then moved his free hand inside her low-cut gown, his fingers closing over her breast. "Passage to England is expensive."

Elise made no attempt to free herself. "I believe I could find the funds."

She was contradicting herself, having indicated earlier that financial difficulties had forced her to come to the brothel. Saying nothing, he began to unhook her gown at the back.

261

Elise seemed to sense her error. "I don't have the money myself."

"I couldn't put myself in your debt."

"You wouldn't." She helped him remove the gown and petticoats. "I have friends who would gladly provide the cost of transportation—and perhaps much more, for both of us."

"How could I repay them?"

Making no immediate reply, she pulled him down onto the divan beside her.

Their talk could wait, Jared told himself. Although it was evident that she was a calculating wench, it had been a long time since he had been with a woman, and her wanton beauty aroused him.

Elise freely gave herself to him, her ardor matching his, and either her ecstasy was genuine or she was the most artful and convincing actress he had ever known.

Then, as they rested, she gently ran her fingers through his hair. "As such an important officer," she said casually, "you must know a great deal. Perhaps your knowledge could be very valuable to my friends—the ones who could help us go to England."

Jared wasn't surprised. "Well, I'm not really taken into the high command's confidence," he replied, temporizing.

Elise's caresses were light. "But you could find out anything you wanted to know."

Returning the physical gestures, he pretended to consider her suggestion. "I suppose I could," he replied, trying to sound a trifle uncertain.

The girl sat up abruptly and reached for her clothes. "Shall we meet again tomorrow?"

"I'd like that very much." To that extent, at least, he was being honest.

Elise dropped the subject and chatted about inconsequentials until Jared was ready to leave. She offered him another drink of sack—which he turned down—and then, significantly, she refused to accept money from him. "I—I couldn't take it," she said, simulating pretty confusion.

He accepted the role she had assigned him, that of a somewhat dense and greedy suitor. He kissed her, finding real satisfaction in her physical appearance. "I'll be here at the same time tomorrow afternoon," he promised.

Not until he walked out through the chateau gate onto the cobbled streets of Sainte-Jeanne did he smile, grimly.

CHAPTER FIFTEEN

Colonels Hopkins and Baker listened without interruption to the story of Jared's encounter with Elise Le Brun. Finally, when Jared had finished, the deputy commander walked to the parlor windows of the little house that had been commandeered for the expedition's headquarters.

"It would appear," he said, "that the French expect something unusual in the way of an attack. I wonder why."

The colonel in chief drummed absently on the table behind him. "I suppose," he said, "they think we're insane to challenge them with a force as small as ours. So either they believe we're intending to use elaborate trickery of some sort or that we are waiting for reinforcements."

"The Comte de Maricourt is a man of imagination." Baker chuckled. "He probably sees himself being promoted from major general to marshal. We mustn't disappoint him."

Jared joined in the laugh. "What I don't understand is how the woman was spirited out of Quebec and into Sainte-Jeanne."

"The simplest way," Colonel Hopkins said, "would have been to take her up the river several miles, beyond sight of our sentries, and then send her into town hidden in the produce wagon of a farmer. I'll instruct the sentries to examine the contents of every wagon passing through our line hereafter."

"It was accidental, I think, that she picked me," Jared said. "She probably chose the particular approach she used when she heard my English accent. I think she would have taken a different tack with someone else."

Colonel Baker was still smiling. "I daresay she's congratulating herself. She well might have had difficulty finding an officer with a headquarters connection."

"You'll keep your appointment with her tomorrow, Hale," Colonel Hopkins said. "You'd be the envy of the entire army if this assignment became known, but you'll mention nothing of the matter to anyone."

"Of course, sir. I'm just wondering if I shouldn't force her to wait an extra day. If I hand over information too quickly and easily, the French generals might become suspicious."

The colonels exchanged glances. "True," Baker said. "You might refuse to bed her tomorrow, and insist she give you more specific information about her offer to meet you with the money. Even a very stupid officer would realize that the girl is an espionage agent maneuvering him into playing a traitor's role."

"That's what I meant, Colonel," Jared said. "Tomorrow afternoon I'll be worried, and I'll balk at cooperating with her. Then, the next day—"

"We don't dare wait that long," Colonel Hopkins interrupted. "The Comte de Maricourt may have set a deadline for her operation. Let her reassure you with whatever details she may invent, and then return tomorrow evening with the false information we decide to pass along to her."

Jared carefully followed his superiors' instructions. He returned to the chateau the following afternoon and feigned deep concern, but pretended to be soothed by Elise's promise to return within seventy-two hours with the necessary funds for transportation across the Atlantic. All he had to do was bring her the military information she sought. He went away, still seemingly troubled, telling her only that he would find out what he could.

Four hours later, soon after sundown, he presented himself at the chateau again. Several other officers were there, waiting to see the girls, and were surprised when Jared was escorted almost immediately to the suite on the first floor.

He insisted on making love to Elise before discussing anything of substance with her, and although she was obviously tense and impatient, she humored him. Finally, with what he hoped would appear to be a blend of triumph and chagrin, he handed her a sheet of paper, written in his own hand.

"This is a copy of a letter that one of our couriers brought in just today."

The girl scanned it quickly. "Who is Colonel Waldo?"

"The militia commander of the Maine District," Jared replied truthfully. "Your friends will know his name."

"He expects to arrive on Thursday, the day after tomorrow?"

"So he says."

"How many men is he bringing with him?"

"Most of the Massachusetts Bay militia and the two new Maine District regiments. More than three thousand men, I know, but I can't tell you exactly how many more."

Elise began to dress hastily. Precisely as Jared and his superiors had thought, she was impatient to take the news to Quebec. If reinforcements were arriving in less than forty-eight hours, the French would be anxious to launch an attack before that time. The false schedule allowed little margin for error, but as Colonel Baker had pointed out, General de Maricourt could not be allowed the opportunity to send out scouts of his own for the purpose of verifying the report that a fresh column of British colonials was marching toward Quebec.

"I'm afraid this is all I could find out for you, Elise."

"It is enough, my dear." Obviously she was in no mood for a protracted conversation. "I shall meet you here the day after the new men arrive, and then we can decide whether we want to leave at once or wait until you have fought your battle. I'll leave that decision to you." She kissed him but urged him toward the door.

Jared couldn't resist dawdling. "Oh, I'll want to fight, provided I'm positive you'll wait here for me. I wouldn't want to be charged with desertion."

"You're right, my dear." She half led, half pushed him to the door.

He finally took his leave, wondering what would happen to her when the French high command learned that their espionage agent had been completely fooled. Reaching the street, he halted, straightening his hat—a sign to Lieutenant Duncan, who had been ordered to surround the chateau with several of his best scouts. Then, seemingly unconcerned, he strolled back to the house that served as headquarters for the militia.

A few minutes later a scout reported to Colonel Hopkins. "She left the house disguised in boy's clothes," he said. "She walked to the market, where a farmer was waiting with an empty cart, and they're riding along the river trail to the west. Lieutenant Duncan and the lads are following them."

Jared settled down with the senior officers to wait, but the better part of three hours passed before Lieutenant Duncan appeared.

"There's no two ways about it—she was a spy, all right," the scout said. "They drove a couple of miles along the river path, maybe a little more, and when they came to a grove of birch they lighted a lantern and signaled. Sure enough, somebody, was keeping watch on the other side of the river, and pretty soon four men rowed across in a fur trader's *bateau.* The girl got in, and I knew for certain she was a girl because she took off her hat and her hair came down. They headed straight back across the river, but it was too dark to see where they landed on the north side."

Colonel Baker thanked Duncan and dismissed him.

"Right about now," Colonel Hopkins said, looking at his watch, "Mademoiselle Le Brun— or whatever her name may be—is reporting to the Comte de Maricourt and his staff. You did well, Hale."

Jared found himself feeling sorry for the woman who had sold herself for purposes of espionage. Her speech and manner had been those of a lady, even if her behavior had not, and he wondered what desperation had led her into such a precarious and degrading profession. He hated to admit to himself that he was becoming more tolerant of others' weaknesses, and preferred to think he felt a natural sympathy with the wench because he had been intimate with her.

Colonel Baker ordered a doubling of the guard at all sentry outposts and assigned two full companies to maintain a close watch on all enemy movements out of the citadel.

"We're fairly certain their regiments will leave

the city by a gate that can't be seen from Sainte-Jeanne," Colonel Hopkins explained to Jared. "But they won't want to strike until they've made a rendezvous with their Indians. We still haven't located any of their warrior allies, but it would be fairly easy to hide them in the deep forests north of the city. As we see it—and we're giving the French the benefit of every doubt in our estimates—it will be physically impossible for the enemy to mobilize, cross the river, and launch an attack in force before morning. One of our problems is that we don't know how many other agents the Comte de Maricourt may have in Sainte-Jeanne."

"The people who operate the chateau must be working for him," Jared said, "and if there's one agent posing as a farmer, there could be others. For that matter, every French subject in town might be eager to betray us if he's given enough money."

"I'm afraid you're right, Hale. That's why we don't want to reveal too soon that we're ready for a fight. All we can say with any certainty at the moment is that Maricourt believes reinforcements will reach us by the day after tomorrow, so he'll be itching to attack us as soon as he can before then. In as delicate and dangerous a situation as this, I'll have to ask you to keep quiet a little longer about the events of the past two days."

Life in Sainte-Jeanne, for all appearances, remained quiet, and only officers and men assigned to extra sentry duty realized that a storm might be brewing. The night passed uneventfully,

269

and in the morning campfires were lighted, as usual, in the bivouac area just outside the town. The troops ate the hearty breakfast to which they had lately become accustomed, and anyone looking across the river from the citadel certainly could see the smoke curling up into the warm, late summer air.

The men were still eating when members of the headquarters detachment were dispatched with a special order of the day, which commanders read to their troops. The town was declared out of bounds; each unit was restricted to its own immediate bivouac area and was instructed to prepare for action as unobtrusively as possible.

The guard was changed, and two cavalry troops were sent along the bank of the Saint Lawrence on either side of Sainte-Jeanne to search for any indication of enemy activity. Scouts arrived at headquarters, each bringing the same discouraging message: nothing unusual to report.

Jared had no assignment to occupy him, and in midmorning he climbed to the top of the boulder that afforded the best view of Quebec. A lieutenant and two ensigns were there, keeping their glasses trained on the fortress and city across the river, and the senior member of the group handed his glass to Jared.

The French flag, a white banner emblazoned with gold lilies, floated high above the ramparts. White uniformed sentries, muskets on their shoulders, continued to pace up and down behind the parapets, and in his few glimpses of the city behind the high walls, Jared could see citizens strolling calmly, apparently going about their normal day's business. Nothing at all seemed to be happening in the wake of the news delivered the previous night by Elise Le Brun.

Either the Comte de Maricourt had discovered the ruse, or, like his foe, he was playing a cleverly deceptive game.

Jared returned to headquarters, arriving at the house just as Lieutenant Duncan was leaving, and they stopped on the steps for a word.

"They're on the move," the scout said. "My Seneca discovered that five hundred Algonkin, and maybe two hundred to three hundred Abnaki and Micmac are drifting down from the forest. The French regiments have been leaving the city by the rear and are meeting the warriors at a rendezvous off to the west, where they'll cross the river."

"How soon will they be organized for battle?"

"The way I figure it, by early afternoon. They plan to make a swing around to our rear, I reckon, and take us by surprise." Duncan squinted up at the sun, obviously impatient to leave.

"It'll be a warm day," Jared said as they shook hands and grinned at each other.

The militia's headquarters, which had been quiet for many days, was in a ferment. Staff officers hurried from room to room, conferring, and there was a stream in and out of the parlor, where the colonel in chief and his deputy made their office. The commanders of regiments and separate battalions began to arrive, and Jared waited, certain that his turn would come.

When he was summoned, his superiors wasted

no words. "You've heard, no doubt," Colonel Hopkins said.

"Yes, sir."

"We'll stay right here in Sainte-Jeanne as long as we can—until noon or thereabouts. Then we'll move to a battleground of our own choice, once the enemy is completely committed."

Jared was disappointed. "I've been hoping we'd meet them at the riverbank and try to prevent them from crossing."

"Too risky," Hopkins replied. "For one, we lack the mobility—we can't chase them up and down the river to see where they'll land. For another, we're afraid they'd retreat into the citadel again—and stay there. We've got to tease them into fighting before the cold weather comes and we're forced to make the long march home in the snow."

Jared realized at once that his reasoning was sensible.

"Since we'll be outnumbered," Colonel Baker said, "we're planning a fight that will give us every possible advantage. You're outranked by the captains of the cavalry troops, but we feel we've got to consolidate our cavalry into one unit, operating as a full squadron. Now—are we correct in assuming that you held a commission in the king's cavalry at one time?"

More was at stake now than personal pride, and Jared knew it would be wrong to try to conceal his past. "Yes, sir," he said.

"You weren't dismissed for military reasons?"

"No, Colonel. I was a damned idiot in the way I handled my personal life."

The two senior officers exchanged quick glances. "Under the circumstances, then," Colonel Hopkins said, "you're the obvious choice for overall cavalry command. We'll promote you to equal rank with the troop commanders for the battle. On your way out, pick up a captain's cockade from the adjutant."

"Thank you, sir." The responsibility was so great that the temporary promotion, as such, meant nothing to Jared.

"At noon," Hopkins directed, "mobilize all four troops and take them, along with your own detachment, to the pond that lies next to the Moreau farm about two miles to the west. You'll be joined by one regiment of Delaware foot, which we plan to use as assault troops. Have your men fed and ready for battle. You'll be given specific instructions after we've found our lines."

Jared saluted and left the room. The adjutant had already been notified of the temporary increase in rank and gave him the blue feathered cockade of a captain to wear in his hat in place of his red lieutenant's insignia. To Jared's surprise, the man also handed him a pistol—apparently the prerogative of a captain of cavalry. Only an hour remained until noon, so Jared, wasting no time, hastily stuck the pistol in his belt and dashed out of the house. Immediately assembling the headquarters detachment and telling Sergeant Ben Greene—who had rejoined the unit a few days earlier—to make certain the men ate a light meal, Jared rode off to the bivouac of the cavalry troops.

There he called a meeting of the officers. "Gentlemen," he said, "some of you may resent

273

the way I've been given command, over your heads. If you do, I can't blame you, All the same, we have work to do today, and its success depends on our ability to get along together. I didn't ask for a squadron command, but it's been given to me, and I intend to fulfill my obligations."

The senior troop commander, in civilian life a prosperous farmer, stood and looked around at the group. "As far as I'm concerned, I'll be proud to take orders from you. Anybody who doesn't feel that way doesn't deserve to hold a commission in the militia. It's been plain to me for a long time that you know more about cavalry than any of us. And I'm sure everybody else agrees. Am I right, men?"

The officers answered with a cheer.

"Thanks for your confidence," Jared said. "I'll do my best—for all of us. Now, then. I don't know our specific assignment yet, or what the high command will ask of us. But there are two things I want to make clear: First, unless told otherwise, hold your troops together. When cavalry is scattered, it loses its effectiveness. Second, make certain that all orders are obeyed at once. Cavalry has two advantages—speed and mobility. Don't forget it.

"We worked together once before as a squadron, and we did well. We can do it again. We must. We're going into battle against some of the best trained, best disciplined fighting men on earth. Hesitation means failure. Confusion means failure. We're being used in some way with a regiment of light infantry. As soon as I'm told the details, you'll learn them, too.

"I'm sure of only one thing at this moment. We have a hard afternoon's work ahead. That's all, gentlemen. Feed your men quickly, and be ready to ride in a quarter of an hour."

The headquarters detachment had arrived while Jared had been speaking, and as soon as the men of the other troops had eaten, he rode at the head of the combined units toward the south. Now, for the first time, the significance of all that was happening began to become clear to him.

It was almost unbelievable that he, an indentured servant, should have been given a post normally held by an officer with the rank of major. Colonels Hopkins and Baker were demonstrating their faith in him by giving him a position of great trust, and provided he conducted himself honorably, his life would never be the same, no matter what the outcome of the battle. He had, in brief, justified his existence in the New World, and now he was being given the opportunity to prove that he could earn the distinction he had been given.

Riding across the open field of the Quebec farms and seeing the frightened faces of the householders and their families peering out the windows of their homes, he found his thoughts turning to the Lower Counties rather than the England he had sorely missed for so long. England, he discovered, no longer mattered to him. What was important was that he be respected here, in the New World, as a man of substance and accomplishment.

Pondering this unexpected shift in his own feelings, he realized that the changes within him had been gradual rather than sudden. And he knew, too, that he wanted and needed more than just the good opinion of his fellow militiamen. It occurred to him, belatedly, that his sleazy affair with the French espionage agent who had called herself Elise Le Brun had jarred him, bringing into focus that which was really important to him.

There had been a time when his relations with a woman—any woman—had been casual and had meant no more to him than a hearty meal eaten to satiate his appetite for food. But his memories of his relationship with Elise were distasteful, and now he understood what had happened to him.

He felt a deep emotional attachment to a woman in the colonies and wanted no one else. He still liked Polly, but the image of Caroline's face kept appearing in his thoughts, and in her eyes was that certain wonderment he now recalled seeing in her after they had made love in the hay. It had been as though she was feeling something for the first time. Yet he knew she had not been a virgin.

There were still too many obstacles preventing him from envisaging a future with her, yet somehow he was buoyed by a new optimism. He had already risen so much higher than he had dreamed possible, and now, in a totally uncharacteristic way, he dared to hope he might be able to find personal happiness, too.

First, however, the battle loomed ahead, and he had a duty to perform.

Osman Murtagh was tired, hungry, and thirsty. He had landed in Baltimore after an uneventful crossing of the Atlantic Ocean, but not having a penny in his pocket, he had been forced to travel on foot for the final portion of the journey to his farm. Well, by rights it was his wife's farm, since her money had paid for it—but it was his under the law, and he meant never to do another day's work as long as he lived. His unpleasant experience in the Isles of Scilly had seen to that.

It was astonishing how much had changed since he had been gone, he thought. As he drew nearer to home, he passed occasional local travelers on the road, and although he recognized them, they didn't know him. His full beard, unkempt hair, and tattered clothes were responsible, he supposed, as well as the fact that he had lost considerable weight during the months he had been forced to earn his living on the Trevor farm, working for that greedy old woman.

Arriving at last at the property he called home, he opened the front gate, then stood still for a moment as he looked ahead. The quarters occupied by the indentured servants were dark for the night, which was not strange, considering the late hour; but he was surprised to see that an oil lamp or a candle was still burning in the front bedchamber. Apparently Caroline was still awake, and if he remembered her habits correctly, she was reading.

He assumed she was alone in the house; but as he drew nearer, he noted that a light also flickered in a third-story window. The chambers on the third floor were tiny and cramped; perhaps Caroline had a servant sleeping in the house. This was a fair enough guess, he figured, since she was probably nervous living alone in a place that large.

As Osman had anticipated, the front door was

bolted. Rather than knock and bring Caroline downstairs, he went around to the rear, and congratulated himself when he found the door to the kitchen outbuilding unlocked. He went in, his hunger getting the better of his desire to let his wife know he was still alive. Lighting a candle he found on a shelf along with a tinderbox and flint, he rummaged around until he discovered what he had been seeking—a cut of rare beef and a loaf of bread, which, judging by the feel of it, had been baked that same day. Just what he needed.

Further investigation revealed a jug of rum, and he was elated. At last! After months of total abstinence, he could really celebrate his return home! He carved himself a slab of beef and tore off a hunk of bread, but he was far more interested in the rum, and his hand trembled as he filled a tumbler to overflowing with the strong drink. He raised it to his lips, sniffed avidly, and then gulped down the better part of the contents, not pausing for breath.

Chortling, he quickly refilled his glass before he took a single bite of the meat or bread. The rum seemed to fulfill his deepest needs, and he discovered that his interest in the food had waned.

He had no idea how long he stayed in the kitchen outbuilding, but the jug of rum was almost empty by the time he shoved back his chair, rose, and stumbled through the passageway that connected the kitchen to the main house. Unable to open the door, he returned to the kitchen, where he found a heavy knife, and taking it with him, he used it to hack away at the wood of the door. His efforts availed him nothing, and in exasperation he put his shoulder against the door and pushed with all his might. He was stronger than he knew, and the door gave way. He grinned and entered the house.

He had been wrong, Osman thought hazily, when he had told himself that everything was changed. Everything was just exactly as it had been when he had last lived here. He needed no lights to find his way in the dark, and he tiptoed quickly, though unsteadily, to the front bedchamber on the second floor.

Raising the latch, he entered. As he had expected, he saw his wife, lightly clad in a peach-color nightgown, reading a book by the light of an oil lamp.

Caroline, startled by the intrusion, looked up, saw the man across the room, and opened her mouth to scream.

Osman laughed heartily, drunkenly.

She peered at him more closely and sucked in her breath in a series of short, spasmodic gasps as she tried to regain her composure.

"You're surprised to find I'm still alive, eh?" he demanded. "I'm like a bad penny—I always turn up." He laughed coarsely at his own humor.

"My God," she whispered. "My God." Her fingers clutched the sheets convulsively, and her knuckles turned white.

Osman teetered back and forth on his heels, peering hard at her.

A feeling of horror, mingled with absolute terror, filled Caroline's whole being as she saw the familiar, hated expression of his lust appear in his bloodshot eyes.

"Thought I drowned, didn't ye?" he demanded as he advanced toward her.

Too terrified to speak, she could only nod.

"Well, I didn't. And now you got your chance to prove how glad you are to see me." Reaching down with his large hand, he caught hold of her nightgown and tore it from her body.

For the first time in years, Caroline screamed. She knew that such an act only infuriated him and would make her plight worse, but she was unable to help herself, unable to curb the fear and loathing that overwhelmed her.

Unfortunately, Caroline was right. The enraged, drunken Osman threw himself at her, simultaneously cuffing her with all his might on the side of her head.

Again she screamed.

He ignored the sound. "You need to be taught some manners. I been away too long," he said as he began the all-too-familiar routine of subjecting her to physical abuse.

She struggled in vain, but her strength was no match for his.

Neither of them heard the door open or saw Polly enter the bedchamber, clad in a robe and slippers.

The servant girl took in the scene at a glance and reacted instantly. Looking around wildly, she found a twelve-inch-long dagger that Caroline used as a letter opener lying on a desk near the door. Seizing it and giving no thought to what she was doing, Polly raced across the room and drove it with all her strength into the intruder's back.

Osman Murtagh stiffened, and as he expired he made a strange gurgling sound in his throat.

Caroline managed to extricate herself from beneath his body, and she stared at him. "You killed him—you killed him," she said. "He—he's dead."

The realistic Polly saw no reason to belabor the obvious. "Are you all right?"

"Yes. Thanks to you." Caroline, gradually recovering her wits, hurried to a clothes cupboard, where she covered her almost nude body with a robe, then fumbled for slippers. "We've got to get rid of him at once," she said.

Polly stared at her. "Shouldn't we leave his body where it is and report to the constabulary? This man was an intruder who would have raped you if I—"

"You don't understand," Caroline said. "I'll explain later. Help me."

Together they lowered the body to the floor and hauled it to the stairs, where they dragged it, facedown and feet-first, to the rear vestibule. Fortunately—although they were not thinking in such terms as yet—the letter opener still protruded from Osman's back, and he bled very little.

Panting for breath when she reached the bottom of the stairs, Caroline leaned against the wall. "We—we need—wheelbarrow," she said.

"There's one behind the smokehouse," Polly replied. "I'll fetch it." She hurried off, still perplexed by the inexplicable events but taking her mistress at her word that she would explain everything in due time.

Polly returned with the wheelbarrow, and together they managed to hoist the dead man into it. This took almost all their combined strength, and Caroline, still nearly out of breath but very much in charge now, said, "Open the door, Polly. We've got to be rid of him before anyone knows he's been here."

"Yes, ma'am," the young woman replied, and her bewilderment increased.

Together they pushed the wheelbarrow down the narrow path that ran behind the stable and other outbuildings. They entered the marshy section that stretched down to the river, and at last Caroline halted abruptly. "Be careful," she said, catching hold of the other woman's arm.

Polly heard the alarm in her voice and stopped short.

For a moment Caroline Murtagh looked down at the body of the man who had been her husband. She had long believed him dead, and now that he was truly dead, she could still feel no sorrow, no pity for him. He had earned his fate, and she would never mourn him for a moment. "Don't step any closer to the bog ahead of you, Polly," she said, "but help me. I'll count to three, and we'll both push the wheelbarrow with all our might. One . . . two . . . three!"

The wheelbarrow moved a short distance, and then, to Polly's amazement, it began to sink, its front wheel gradually disappearing from view.

"Quicksand," Caroline said, completely in control of herself now.

Polly felt chills chasing up her spine as she

stared at the body of the dead man, already half sunk in the mire.

"That was Osman Murtagh, my husband," Caroline told her in a hoarse voice. "I thought he drowned when he was swept overboard at sea on our last trip to England, but obviously he didn't. He appeared tonight, and you know the rest."

Polly blinked at her. "But he—he was attacking you," she murmured.

Caroline nodded. "Yes," she said. "That was his way."

Comprehension flooded Polly. "How awful for you," she said, and instinctively embraced the other woman.

They clung together, both of them averting their eyes as the remainder of the wheelbarrow, with its grisly cargo, was sucked beneath the surface of the quicksand.

Supporting each other, the two women slowly made their way back to the house. They saw the glow of the half-guttered candle flickering in the kitchen outbuilding, so they went there first and, lighting another taper, discovered the remains of the meal that Osman had partly consumed. With one accord they cleaned up the evidence and went into the house itself, where they paused just long enough to inspect the damage to the back door.

"We'll have one of the indentured men repair this tomorrow," Caroline said.

Polly nodded agreement.

They did not speak again until they reached the bedchamber at the front of the house on the second floor, and there Caroline turned to face the servant girl. "Polly," she said, "you've saved me from a life so dreadful that I can't even contemplate how horrible it would have been. The very least I can do for you in return is to grant you your freedom from indenture."

Polly grinned broadly, and they embraced again.

"If it's all right with you, ma'am," Polly said, "I'd just as soon keep on working for you until the army comes back. Until then I have no place to go; and I'd rather not return to the kind of life I led before you found me at Newgate prison."

"Of course," Caroline replied instantly. "Stay as long as you like." Her new feeling of euphoria vanished, however, and she believed with all her heart that contrary to what Polly had told her previously, the girl was in love with Jared Hale and was awaiting his safe return.

CHAPTER SIXTEEN

Major Carl Hector, a Wilmington shipowner and farmer, was reputedly one of the wealthiest men in the Lower Counties, but no one would have guessed it from his appearance. Unlike most senior militia officers, he wore no uniform, instead contenting himself with greasy buckskin trousers and shirt. He had no need for insignia, he said, because the men of his regiment knew him well, and he didn't care whether anyone else recognized his rank. He was of medium height, and his manners were deceptively mild, yet he had made a standing offer to his troops: He was willing to meet any dissatisfied militiaman in a fistfight at any time. His reputation was such that not one of his four hundred and fifty men had chosen to accept his challenge since leaving Delaware.

Hector and his troops were already waiting at the rendezvous near the pond, the men sprawling on the ground at their ease. Most were chatting quietly, some were checking their rifles and muskets, and a few were actually dozing in the sun, even though it had become clear that they would see action against the enemy before the day ended.

Jared, leading the combined cavalry, halted the horsemen and rode forward with the four troop commanders to report to Hector, who was speaking quietly with members of his staff.

"You're right on time," Hector boomed in a deep voice as Jared and his companions dismounted and saluted. "Colonel Hopkins says you don't yet know your mission. It was just outlined to me a few minutes ago, and I don't mind telling you we're going to have our hands full. Sit down, boys."

Jared and the others squatted in a semicircle around him, and he drew a rough illustration in the dust with the point of his dagger. "The main body of the militia," he said, "will take up its battle line in the deep woods about a mile and a half southeast of here. It will anchor its left flank on the crest of a high hill and its right on a small river. The enemy can't be prevented from crossing the river—it's more like a fast-running brook—but they'll be slowed down. So the main body will be relatively secure."

Jared immediately recognized the tactics being

employed by the high command. Since the militia was inferior in strength to the French and their allies, the colonels had chosen to fight a wilderness battle, in which the odds would be equalized somewhat, and had cleverly selected the one location in the nearby area that was suitable for such combat.

"The problem," Major Hector continued, "is that the Quebec garrison will never willingly meet us in a forest. They haven't been trained for that kind of warfare. They'll want to fight in the open."

That, too, made sense to Jared.

"So we can't let them know in advance that we've picked ground favorable to us. You—and we—have been chosen to fool them. We've got to commit them to battle, to lead them toward the militia. And we've got to move quickly, so they'll become involved before their scouts learn the position of the main body."

Jared's mind raced. "In other words, sir, we've got to meet them as they land on the south bank of the Saint Lawrence, is that correct?"

"Colonel Hopkins is leaving that to us. Frankly, I'm afraid to commit a regiment of infantry to an engagement five miles from the spot where we hope the main battle will be fought. My companies will be cut to shreds."

The commander of one of the regiment's battalions started to speak, but Major Hector silenced him.

"My men," Hector went on, "have enough discipline and common sense to look after themselves for about a half hour in the open when they're fighting professional soldiers. If we can arrange it, I'd like to make a sally or two and then fall back on the main body."

Jared pondered the matter. "Then if I understand correctly, sir, you want to arrange a double enticement. My squadron would lead the enemy to you, and then your regiment would fall back as though in retreat and lead them to Colonel Hopkins."

"Precisely." Carl Hector looked at him searchingly. "This is asking you to perform the miraculous, Captain Hale, by getting them to take the bait. Can you do it?"

Jared carefully weighed the odds before replying. Then, after looking at each of his troop commanders in turn, he said, "I'll try, Major. The whole squadron will do its damnedest."

Jared and a group of twenty volunteers rode through the forest toward the Saint Lawrence River, the horses picking their way cautiously over a trail that extended past the cultivated fields west of Sainte-Jeanne. The French had chosen their landing place with great cunning, electing to cross the river where their operations would be shielded by trees and underbrush on both shores. But, in true wilderness style, Jared was taking advantage of the cover that the foe was using.

Now, in the distance, he could hear the sound of voices and the splashing of feet in the water as the French vanguard came ashore. Raising a hand, he halted his little unit, signaled for quiet, and waited. It would be premature to reveal his presence to the enemy before an appreciable number of troops came ashore, yet he could not delay too long, either, for fear the French scouts and their Indian allies might find him and cut him off.

Time dragged, and Jared's tension mounted as the rumble of voices in the distance grew deeper and louder. By now perhaps anywhere from two hundred to five hundred of the enemy had landed on the south shore of the Saint Lawrence, but he could only guess their number. His volunteers were looking at him, their own anxiety mounting, but he knew he had to wait as long as he dared, and shook his head. It was possible that none of them would emerge alive from the forest, but their role had been explained, and they were taking the risk knowingly.

Finally they heard crackling sounds in the underbrush, and Jared knew that the advance scouts of the French force were beginning to fan out in the forest. As nearly as he could judge, they were on foot rather than mounted, and if the noise they made was any criterion, they were French, not Indians.

Jared took his pistol from his belt and quickly and silently primed and cocked the weapon. Then, after another seemingly interminable wait, he caught a glimpse of a white uniform in the under-brush and fired. The shot echoed through the forest, and for an instant there was no sound, no movement. The Battle of Sainte-Jeanne had begun.

The shot missed and was returned by the French soldier, but he, too, missed. Jared had accomplished his initial mission, however, and gave the signal for a withdrawal. As he had more or less anticipated, the scout was not alone, and a crossfire of arrows cut through the air. Algonkin or other warriors made up a party of the vanguard.

"You're on your own, boys," Jared said in a quiet tone.

Rifle fire punctuated the silence, and several screams indicated that the colonial marksmen were finding their targets. After firing, the cavalrymen withdrew a short way, then stopped and reloaded their weapons at a sedate, almost leisurely pace. For the moment it was important that the French think they were facing a small unit of scouts, and contact had to be maintained until the enemy learned better. Jared had decided to extend the previously devised tactics by one further logical step. A small group of cavalrymen would provide the bait that would lead the foe to the whole squadron.

From the direction of the river he could hear orders being shouted, and he knew that one or more French units were being sent in pursuit. After his men had fired a second volley, Jared ordered them to continue their withdrawal at a trot, which was rapid enough to maintain a healthy distance between them and the main body of enemy troops. It was not fast enough to shake off the Indians and most of the French advance guard, however, and the cavalrymen, needing no instructions, fired a third volley, then a fourth, to disperse the warriors.

Heavy boots crashed through the underbrush, and Jared was relieved. He had not dared to hope that the enemy would send foot soldiers rather than cavalry to catch him, but they had, and his horsemen consequently maintained a distinct advantage. Very gradually he continued to increase the platoon's pace in order to shake off the Indians on his flanks while remaining almost within reach of his pursuers.

After leading the French and their allies on a circuitous route for almost another quarter of an hour, which gave General de Maricourt time to land that many more of his troops, Jared rode toward the area where his headquarters detachment and the four other cavalry troops were waiting. As he approached he gave a signal to one of his companions, a frontiersman, who emitted a shrill birdcall.

Almost immediately a trumpet sounded from one sector of the forest, followed by a second, then a third, from distant, scattered points. The crashing footsteps of the foot soldiers stopped instantly, and the Indian warriors fell back, leaving the withdrawing French platoon to its own devices. The ruse had succeeded, and the enemy thought that a large body of British colonial troops awaited them, the blaring of the trumpets having given them the impression that the militia had gathered in force.

Jared rejoined his troop commanders, and as the trumpeters rode in from their stations, he quickly gave his officers an idea of what had happened in the action. One member of the platoon of volunteers had suffered a slight hand wound, but the others had escaped from the encounter unscathed. Jared congratulated himself but knew he could not continue to enjoy such good fortune.

There was a lull while the enemy organized a new, enlarged pursuit force to deal with the situation, and meanwhile their Indian allies cautiously advanced again to probe Jared's sentry lines in an attempt to gain a more accurate estimate of his strength. Occasional bursts of rifle fire told him that the men at his outpost positions were encountering difficulties with the braves, who by now were undoubtedly trying to penetrate his perimeter in strength. At last Jared decided he could tarry no longer.

"Ben," he said to Sergeant Greene, "let's go someplace where we can breathe easier."

Greene took a trumpet from the side of his saddle and blew three sharp blasts on it. He was no musician, and the high-pitched notes were sour, but it had a galvanizing effect on the squadron. Reacting as though they had worked and fought together for years, the cavalry swung toward the rear and moved into the open fields.

Jared had given his own detachment the place of honor, as the rear guard, and his men spread out in a double file as they emerged into the open from the woods. There was no sign of the enemy now, so Ben Greene was ordered to give another signal, and four discordant blasts on his trumpet slowed the entire squadron to a walk.

Riding forward along one flank and then dropping back again along the other, Jared found the men prepared for anything that might develop. Aware of their heavy responsibility, the militiamen were riding in straight lines, their rifles across their pommels, their sabers loose in their scabbards. In a real emergency, it appeared, Americans were capable of demonstrating that they, too, could behave with the crisp aplomb of professional soldiers.

Suddenly a rider in the rear rank of the headquarters detachment raised a cautious shout. "Naturals!"

A party of Indians, about one hundred and fifty strong, emerged from the woods at a trot. They split into two groups, and as they fanned out in opposite directions it grew evident that their purpose was to harass the cavalry's flanks. Jared was reluctant to break away from them; however, his ultimate purpose would not be served unless he managed to engage a considerable French force as well.

"They're Algonkin, Cap'n," Ben Greene said cheerfully. "The meanest scoundrels that ever drew breath. I reckon I'd better take me a scalp or two for souvenirs." Not waiting for permission to fire, he raised his rifle to his shoulder, aimed, and sent a brave sprawling to the ground.

The whole detachment cheered as the warrior collapsed, and within moments the entire unit was joining in the deadly sport. Rifles cracked, and so many braves dropped that their leaders faltered, then fell back. It was true, then, as Jared had heard, that Indians had no heart for fighting in the open. He couldn't blame them, of course; men armed with bows and arrows and tomahawks were no match for marksmen whose prowess with their long rifles would frighten the most battle-hardened troops in any army.

The squadron made its way across a wheatfield, some of the men grim-faced as their mounts trampled the growing stalks of grain. Jared, bringing up the rear with only Greene beside him, half stood in his saddle as he peered back at the woods. There was still no sign of the French infantry, and he was afraid he had failed.

Then, but a moment later, French troops poured out from behind the sheltering cover of the forest into the open. Two troops of white-clad cavalry were in the lead, followed by what appeared to be at least two or three regiments of infantry, with bayonets affixed to their muskets.

"Full gallop!" Jared shouted, and the headquarters detachment responded before Ben could blow the appropriate call.

The entire squadron increased its speed, and no attempt was made to lure the enemy now. The French were in headlong pursuit, and Jared's one concern was that of holding his units' formations. The men realized the need for self-discipline, however, and never had they ridden better. Each troop held its lines intact, even when moving from a canter to a gallop, and Jared felt a surge of pride. Cavalry who could perform this delicate a maneuver under pressure were capable of meeting any challenge.

The French horsemen began to gain on the squadron, however. Mounted on fresher and better-trained animals, and themselves far more experienced, the hussars in the white tunics and gleaming helmets slowly closed the gap between them and their quarry. Behind them, at a considerable distance, came the infantry at a trot, and Jared, calculating as coldly as he could, made a major decision. He would stand and fight, then withdraw again before the infantry could join in the skirmish.

"First and Second Troops break to the left, Third and Fourth to the right," he ordered two members of his own command who acted as couriers.

Spurring their mounts, the two horsemen moved away to deliver his command. A few moments later the American force split into three sections, apparently disintegrating. The headquarters detachment, alone now in the center, was almost within rifle range of the enemy, and Jared gave a hand signal to Greene, who blew a series of calls on his trumpet.

The troops on the left and right swept out in wide half circles, then headed back toward the enemy, while the headquarters detachment, coming to an abrupt halt, simultaneously turned their mounts, then unslung and raised their rifles.

The commander of the French hussars realized at once that he was outnumbered, and slowed his riders, hoping to give the infantry time to catch up to him.

But Jared gave him no chance. His own men raked the front rank of the French cavalry with a wicked volley of rifle fire, while almost at the same time his flanking troops halted and poured their own fire into the enemy lines. Then, before the French could recover, Jared's entire squadron turned again and moved together into a single body, continuing their escape route across the wheatfields.

The battered French cavalry reorganized, forming its lines again, by which time the infantry had overtaken it. The chase was resumed, with the mortified French hussar commander determined to prove himself more competent than he had appeared in the brief flurry of opposition. He remained close to his infantry support, however, so that the colonial cavalry could not repeat their previous maneuver.

Jared had succeeded in putting enough distance between his own force and the enemy to feel relatively secure, and he kept his squadron moving at a slow canter, tantalizing the French by remaining just out of reach. What bothered him was the possibility that other enemy cavalry units would move forward as soon as the Comte de Maricourt learned of the skirmish, and Jared knew his troops were not capable of holding their own against an overwhelming force of horsemen.

Each passing moment brought him closer to the place where Major Hector's regiment of Delaware infantrymen was awaiting him, however, and he breathed an inaudible sigh of relief when he reached the crest of a small hill and saw the colonial foot soldiers lined up in battle position just over the crest of the next.

Jared's squadron thundered around the left flank of the waiting regiment, halting in the rear of the position for a brief respite. Jared reported at once to the major. "They're sending two or three regiments of infantry after us," he said, slightly surprised to discover he was breathing hard, "and they've got a pack of Indians with them. There are a couple of cavalry troops in the vanguard, but we've mauled them once and can do it again, so the horsemen will be no problem."

Hector immediately alerted his men for instant action.

Phil Franklin was moving up and down the line of kneeling men in the front rank, encouraging the members of his platoon, and he waved cheerfully to Jared. If his attitude was any indication of the men's morale, the foot soldiers from the Lower Counties were looking forward to their first taste of combat against a foe that was feared all over Europe.

"How soon will your squadron be ready for action again, Captain Hale?" Hector asked.

"We're ready right now, sir," Jared replied promptly.

"All right. I'll open some lanes for you on the left side of our line. How many do you want?"

Jared thought he would achieve a maximum effectiveness by attacking on a broad rather than a narrow front. "Eight."

Hector raised an eyebrow but made no comment. The cavalry was not under his command but had been assigned to work with him. "As you please," he said dubiously, and gave the necessary order to his adjutant. "I'll let you know when we need you, Hale."

Jared rode to the rear, where he rejoined the horsemen, arranging them in eight columns. "When we move, lads," he said, "I want you to ride like hell. Whatever you do, stay in formation. And you'll have to trust my judgment. I'll turn us aside if I see we're going to take a beating; but unless I give the signal, I want no one to deviate from a direct assault."

His last words were drowned by the sudden

sharp rattle of rifle fire. The French, with their two battered cavalry troops in the van, had just reached the crest of the adjacent hill, and the Americans had struck first.

The white-uniformed professionals halted in surprise, and then a high-ranking officer rode forward to survey the situation. He was accompanied by his standard-bearer and several staff officers, and took care not to move forward across the top of the hill, where he would be fully exposed to American fire. His flag, fluttering in the light breeze, indicated that he was a brigadier general, and Jared looked at him with interest. He had a hard, lined face, and he gestured crisply as he spoke, pointing toward the lines of the regiment he faced. It was obvious he was a man who knew what he wanted done and who knew how to go about doing it. The colonials' first real test was at hand.

The French cavalry moved aside, and the infantry started forward, the men in lines four deep, plumes bobbing above the tops of helmets, bayonets gleaming in the sunlight. Meanwhile the Algonkin warriors, advancing very cautiously, fanned out along the flanks of the attacking regiment.

Jared expected Major Hector to open fire again, but the colonial commander elected to hold off, wanting to achieve a maximum effect with a concerted volley at close range. Not until the French had reached the base of the hill on which the regiment had taken up its position was the order to open fire given.

Here and there a French soldier dropped, but

the line of white uniforms continued to move forward. Clearly these men were professionals not flustered or deterred by expected casualties.

Jared, telling Ben Greene to accompany him, galloped forward to the regimental command post just behind the crest. "Major," he said, "now is the time for me to hit them."

The militiamen had reloaded and were now firing at will, each man acting on his own initiative.

It was apparent that Hector had no real faith in Jared's squadron, but he faced two choices: either agree or withdraw without delay. "Try it," he said at last, without conviction.

Ben Greene had already raised his trumpet to his lips, and he gave the signal for a charge.

The American horsemen, in eight columns, galloped forward through the lanes opened for them on the left side of the infantry line, gaining speed as they rode.

"Cease fire!" Hector ordered as the horsemen moved out beyond the infantry's position.

Jared, at the head of the foremost column, smiled over at Ben Greene, who was leading the column directly to his right. Green and the other column leaders were taking a grave personal risk, Jared knew, exposing themselves to the brunt of the enemy fire, yet Jared felt it essential that he himself, together with his best men, set the pace. His maneuver, he knew, could succeed only if it was so ferocious that it completely disrupted the enemy formation. This was the basic function of cavalry in battles fought in the European manner; and although Jared wasn't certain that colonial cavalry were capable of living up to an obligation that required great courage as well as skill, he would certainly make sure they at least tried.

The thought passed through his mind that perhaps he was still a gambler—that he was taking risks with human lives now rather than with stacks of gold and silver coins. But whatever his own inner motives, he was convinced he was doing the right thing in the highest military sense.

The French infantry, flanked closely by the hussars, braced themselves and began to fire at the swiftly approaching foe. But the colonial cavalrymen, thundering down on them in single-file columns, were almost impossible to hit, presenting relatively small targets.

The situation called for swords rather than rifles, Jared knew, and he called over his shoulder, "Steel!" Setting an example, he drew his own saber and, vaulting his horse straight into the first line of French infantry, began to hack his way through the ranks of the startled French soldiers.

His tactic of attacking in columns soon proved itself correct, even though the French infantry were tightly packed in the orthodox European square formation, moving in lines four deep that literally made a square. The American columns smashed several gaps into the front wall, scattering foot soldiers and disrupting the formation.

This was the critical moment. An infantry commander familiar with such a cavalry charge could counter it by ordering the remaining sides of his square to close in, thus surrounding the horsemen and making it difficult for them to escape. But Jared was well aware of the danger and anticipated it, swerving sharply to his left.

The men in his column needed no orders to follow him. They knew he had achieved unexpected success so far and were ready to follow wherever he led.

A French battalion commander frantically ordered the men on the flank of the square to hold steady, but the command was given too late. Slashing viciously, the cavalry broke out of the square, piercing the lines in so many places that the infantry troops lost all semblance of an organized formation.

Jared was aware that his men bringing up the rear would offer inviting targets if he headed back up the hill toward his own waiting infantry, so instead he rode in a sweeping curve around the base of the hill. Despite the bloody fracas he had just been through, Jared could not help but chuckle when he noticed that the French hussars—who should have prevented such a maneuver on his part—were nowhere to be seen. He realized that they had belatedly ridden to the front of the French squares in a futile effort to cushion the colonial cavalry charge.

But Jared soon forgot the hussars, for straight ahead of him he saw the Algonkin warriors, who had been advancing on Major Hector's flank. Jared spurred his mount, and he and the men following him quickly regained their momentum. The savages saw the saber-wielding horsemen coming directly at them and promptly scattered, dashing off in all directions to avoid direct contact with foes who seemed possessed by demons.

Elated by the unexpected additional success, Jared led his squadron to the rear of the hill and then slowed to a more leisurely pace. To his relief, he noted that all eight of his columns—amazingly, still in near-perfect formation—had made it back to the colonial lines. Enthusiastic militia foot soldiers were cheering, but he and his men were too tired to appreciate the applause. The moment was anticlimactic, and Jared's arm felt heavy as, wiping off his blade on a cloth, he slipped the gleaming steel back into its sheath.

Major Hector was waiting near the crest. "By God, Hale, you did it!" he shouted. "That was the most beautiful ride I've ever seen!"

Jared muttered his thanks and dismounted to stretch his legs.

"Look yonder," the infantry commander said, pointing.

The French had retreated beyond the top of the lower hill, and from the command post Jared could see they were waiting for additional reinforcements to arrive. His one squadron had so thoroughly disrupted a force many times its own size that the regiment of Delaware foot soldiers had been given no opportunity to play a significant role in the skirmish.

The troop commanders came forward to report, and Jared enjoyed his greatest pleasure of the afternoon. Casualties had been far lighter than he dared to hope: Two cavalrymen had been killed and their horses were lost; five others had been wounded, but none seriously. So, for all practical purposes, the squadron was intact and after a short rest would be ready to resume the fight.

"I owe you an apology," Carl Hector said, his manner indicating the difficulty a strong, independent-minded man felt when admitting he had been wrong. "I thought you were committing suicide and taking all these boys to their death with you. But you did something I'll never forget, and neither will anyone else who saw it."

As far as Jared was concerned, he had only done his duty, and it was still too early to celebrate victory. But Major Hector seemed to read his mind.

"Right now," Hector continued, "we've done what we were ordered to do. You've done it, Hale. We'll have the whole French army chasing us, which is just what Colonel Hopkins wanted. So I suggest we start to move while we're still alive— and I can boast about the greatest cavalry charge ever made in the New World!"

CHAPTER SEVENTEEN

Major Hector's regiment pulled out of its hilltop position in good order, the cavalry squadron acting as a rear guard, and marched rapidly across the open fields toward the forest south of Sainte-Jeanne. The French, trying to reorganize as they waited for reinforcements, were slow to follow, and Jared deliberately tarried with his cavalrymen, not wanting to lose contact with the enemy.

The Algonkin took heart again, moving forward far more swiftly than their allies, and when they were joined by a large number of Abnaki and Micmac braves, Jared summoned one of his men. "Ride forward to Major Hector," he said, "and tell him we may have a full-scale Indian battle on our hands before we reach Colonel Hopkins."

The trooper rode away, returning in a few minutes with a laconic message. "The major wants to see you," he said.

Jared was reluctant to part from his squadron, even temporarily, but he had no choice. Leaving the senior troop commander in charge, he spurred his own mount past the ranks of the infantrymen to the place directly behind the vanguard where Hector was riding. To Jared's surprise, the major greeted him with a hearty laugh.

"Hale," he said, "I've never seen anyone perform tricks of magic with cavalry as you did, but I can still teach you a few things about Naturals. Don't give them another thought."

Jared was irritated. "Perhaps my courier garbled the message I sent you, sir. The Indians are moving up on both flanks of my squadron and must outnumber us by about three to one."

Hector nodded complacently. "You wouldn't be safer behind the walls of the citadel in Quebec."

"I suppose it's your privilege to trust them, sir. But I assure you that I don't."

Again the major laughed. "Who said anything about trust? The French will pay them a bounty for every one of our scalps they bring to General de Maricourt."

"Then I'm afraid I don't understand."

"They won't attack in the open. They'll stay at a safe distance on your flanks, like a pack of wolves. But they won't open a real fight until we reach the cover of woods or night falls."

It was impossible to dispute the word of an expert, but Jared felt dubious.

"I won't ask you to take my word for it, Hale. If I'm wrong, if they do something unlike the way Naturals have always acted, I'll turn the regiment back and come to your aid. You saved our hides, and that would be the least we could do in return. But it's a cheap promise, make no mistake about it."

Jared returned to his own place at the rear of his squadron and saw that the Indians had crept closer but were carefully remaining beyond rifle range. Major Hector had been right, he thought, to the extent that he had likened the savages to wolves. They were stalking their prey, waiting for precisely the right moment to strike.

Sergeant Greene chuckled quietly and jerked a thumb in the direction of the Abnaki and Algonkin on the right flank. "I've got me a notion," he said, "that we won't have any stragglers this afternoon. Any man who drops out of line will have his hair separated from his head before he hits the ground."

Far to the rear a cloud of dust rose slowly into the air, and Jared knew that the French had resumed their pursuit. Only horsemen kicked up that much dust, so he believed it likely that the main body of French cavalry had joined the enemy vanguard. General de Maricourt now had far greater mobility, and the threat from his cavalry was far worse than that posed by the Indians.

Again Jared rode forward to keep Major Hector aware of the developments.

This time Hector nodded soberly, then turned

to his adjutant. "Direct the battalion commanders to march at double time!"

The infantrymen broke into a trot, and Jared, once more dropping back, moved his squadron closer to the rear of the regiment. He kept watching the dust cloud, which grew nearer with each passing minute, and it seemed that the Indians, sensing that the time for their own assault was approaching, were edging closer still to the retreating Americans.

The long march seemed endless, and Jared, coldly weighing the chances of Major Hector's and his own units, knew they both could be totally destroyed if the enemy struck quickly and in force. Neither his own small squadron nor the regiment could last even ten minutes against the bulk of the French army.

Major Hector was wise to flee, and the only question was whether the two commands could reach the relative safety of their own lines in time. The retreat created no strain for the cavalrymen, who were riding easily, but the foot soldiers ran grimly, not daring to halt or slacken their pace to regain their breath.

The pennants of the French cavalry squadrons could be seen in the distance now, and Jared estimated there were at least six units, the equivalent of a full brigade of horsemen. It would be useless even to try to put up a fight when the odds were so great.

For the third time he spurred forward for a word with the major and explained the situation to him.

"We knew from the start that we were taking

this chance," Hector said, "but all the same, I hate to sacrifice men needlessly." He made a quick decision and once again addressed his adjutant. "Order the battalions to run as though they had Beelzebub nipping at their heels. To hell with dignity!"

The infantrymen began to sprint, and although the French cavalry continued to gain on the Americans, they moved closer at a somewhat slower pace.

Jared felt deep sympathy for the struggling foot soldiers, who were burdened by their blankets and other personal gear. Occasionally a militiaman found it impossible to keep up with his fellows, but the cavalry, acting on their own initiative, helped them ease the burden. When an infantryman dropped out of line, exhausted and panting, he was hauled up onto the saddle of a horseman, where he could rest and regain his strength before moving back into position with his own unit.

The French continued to edge nearer, and Jared counted eight cavalry squadron pennants in the closely massed formation. The situation was even worse than he had thought, and there was no doubt in his mind that his own troops would be incapable of putting up more than a brief, token defense against such powerful foes. Nevertheless, he had to do what he could. The rendezvous area with the corps was still half a mile away, and the entire infantry regiment could be annihilated unless he slowed the French.

"Sergeant," he said to Green, "instruct the troops to prepare for action."

Ben blew a single, sour note on his trumpet.

Infantrymen who had been riding with the cavalry jumped to the ground and hurried forward to their own ranks, some of them hobbling painfully. The cavalrymen methodically made sure their rifles were primed and ready for immediate use, and as an additional precaution loosened their sabers in their sheaths.

Jared knew he was about to employ the most difficult of all maneuvers, but he had no alternative. His men would be required to close near enough to the pursuing enemy to unleash a deadly hail of rifle fire while themselves continuing to retreat in good order. Even the most proficient of seasoned British dragoons would be hard put to execute such a move, and he thought it unlikely that colonials could give a good account of themselves, even though they had so far performed superbly.

He pondered the problem, realizing that time was short, and then came to a decision. Signaling his troop commanders back to his own place at the rear of the column, Jared rode with them in tight formation. He had to shout to be heard over the thundering hoof-beats.

"No time for formations," he called out. "At my signal, break ranks and slow down enough for one shot. Don't miss. And don't spread out too far. Just follow my example."

The officers nodded quick acknowledgment, everyone conscious of the approaching French horsemen.

"Good luck!" Jared shouted.

The captains rode back to their troops and

relayed the instructions to their own subordinates. The men accepted the orders calmly, and no one appeared to panic.

The French cavalry was now well within rifle range. Several of the nearest hussars drew their pistols and fired.

The American squadron appeared to fall apart. The rigid formation broke, and individual horsemen twisted in their saddles while continuing to ride forward. Their seeming demoralization encouraged the enemy; French trumpets sounded, and the Indian warriors moved still closer to the flanks.

Jared was the first to return the fire. He saw an officer in the enemy front rank, although he was not able to identify the man's insignia, and aimed his rifle carefully. There was a sharp report, and the white-uniformed figure toppled to the ground.

Most of the militiamen held off their own fire until the French moved closer still. More French pistols crackled, but still the Americans held off, and Jared, sheathing his rifle, drew his own pistol and fired again. Another hussar tumbled from his horse.

Here and there a militiaman was wounded, and at least one was killed, hurtling headfirst from his saddle as his horse collapsed under him. But the others remained steady, and only when the enemy came perilously close did the colonials open fire, each trooper sighting his target carefully. Although both groups were in motion, the fire of the militiamen took a much deadlier toll, each fallen Frenchman disrupting the tightly packed formation of the hussars.

The open fields now began to give way to a partly wooded area, and Jared hoped the terrain would also help slow the French. Suddenly, however, his own horse halted abruptly, pitched sideways, and crashed to the ground. Realizing the animal had been struck by an enemy bullet, Jared managed to throw himself into the clear, tumbling head over heels. He quickly took shelter behind the fallen animal as the first line of French thundered past. He grabbed his rifle, and with his sword still in its sheath at his side, he knew he was not completely helpless. All the same, he was in an open area, and there were enemy cavalrymen all around him, within easy pistol range, so he could not tarry. Fifty feet away was a small thicket, and Jared knew it was his only chance. Bending low to the ground and picking the right moment, he sprinted in an erratic, zigzag course in order to discourage any French marksmen who might be aware of his relatively helpless condition.

He relaxed somewhat as he reached the heavy underbrush, but quickly tensed again when he saw that he was not alone. Lying on the ground not ten feet from him was a French ally, a half-naked Indian warrior.

Jared drew his sword, at the same instant realizing that one of the brave's legs was covered with blood and that this foe was not a grown man, but a boy in his mid-teens.

The youth, armed with only a knife, looked up at Jared and braced himself for the inevitability of death.

But something made Jared hold back his blade. He simply could not kill the boy.

Their eyes met and locked, and although the young Indian's stolid face seemed devoid of expression, Jared nevertheless saw the look of relief that crept into the dark eyes when the boy realized his antagonist had spared his life.

Jared ran on another twenty paces, then paused to take stock of his situation. He had little opportunity to do even that, however, for as he turned he saw a horseman in a gold-and-white uniform crashing through the underbrush, bearing straight down on him. The horseman must have seen him escape into the thicket, Jared realized.

He acted quickly. Sheathing his sword, he gripped his rifle by the end of the barrel, and as the French sergeant raised his own saber, Jared jumped aside and swung his rifle like a club, striking with all his might.

The butt glanced off the descending saber and caught the French soldier full on his face, and at the same moment his frightened gelding shied. The combination threw the sergeant to the ground, and he appeared to be unconscious.

Jared did not linger in the vicinity to make certain of his fallen enemy's condition. He leaped into the saddle and, mastering the jittery mount, spurred the animal back through the underbrush and into the open field.

Major Hector's infantry regiment, he could see in the distance, was already disappearing into the sanctuary of the forest, so he had a few moments at best to save his own men now that they had completed their mission. He set off at a full gallop, threading and fighting his way through the pursuing hussars. At last he reached the stragglers of his own lines. Several of his men had drawn their sabers and seemed reluctant to break off the engagement, but without exception they obeyed instantly as Jared signaled them to retreat toward the safety of the forest. Their flight looked like an inglorious rout, but Jared didn't care—and he knew Colonel Hopkins wouldn't either. He could not pause to think about it, however, as he himself was still in the open, so he bent low in his saddle and rode hard, the pursuing French cavalry sending a heavy fire after him.

The instant he reached the sanctuary of the forest, Jared knew he and his men had succeeded in their mission. The entire colonial militia, virtually invisible up to this point, materialized from behind trees and bushes. The three regiments that formed the front rank opened fire, sending a murderous volley into the lines of the white-uniformed foe. No sooner had the front rank fired than the second rank rose and delivered another thundering volley.

Too late the French realized they had been lured into a trap. The militia's few cannon had also opened fire, and at such close range they found it impossible to miss their targets.

Jared, however, was unaware of the progress of the battle. He followed his unit toward the rear, where he found Major Hector and Colonel Baker calmly sitting astride their mounts. When the bone-tired Jared approached and saluted, both officers grinned at him.

Jared sheathed his saber. "I believe we've accomplished our mission, sir. I'll have a casualty report for you as soon as I can."

Baker reached into his hip pocket and produced a silver flask of brandywine. "The casualty report can wait."

Jared gratefully swallowed a long drink, and as the warm brandywine spread through him, he was able to relax slightly.

"Carl tells me you were responsible for bringing the enemy to us, Hale."

"The whole squadron did it, Colonel. Give the credit to every last one of them."

Colonel Baker leaned forward in his saddle and patted the young cavalryman on the back. "You need a breathing spell, Hale. Take it while you can." Not waiting for a reply, he moved off through the trees.

Jared rode on another thirty paces and found the tired squadron assembled, the men having dismounted. The troop commanders and Ben Greene gave him the casualty figures, which were lighter than he had feared, and he made a mental note of them so he could report later to the high command. Then he said, "I don't know how soon they'll want us to go into action again, so keep the men ready for another fight."

Major Hector rode up, his right hand extended. "Hale," he said, "you went through hell for my boys and me, and I won't forget it. If we live until we reach the Lower Counties, I owe you the biggest dinner of roast oysters and beefsteak pie you've ever eaten."

Jared for some reason felt no desire to conceal his true status. On the contrary, he felt it important that he make his position clear. "I'm

312

not sure you'd want me, Major, or that I'd be allowed to come. I'm indentured."

Hector was startled but recovered swiftly. "If you were a prisoner in jail," he replied, "I'd burn the place down so I could entertain you at my table."

They were interrupted by a courier, who brought them word they were both wanted at the command post. It became increasingly difficult to talk as they drew nearer to the scene of battle; rifle and musket fire from both sides was incessant, and the American artillery added to the din.

Colonel Hopkins was watching the developing conflict from a pine-studded hilltop, while Colonel Baker gave orders in an unending stream of messengers from the various units taking part in the battle.

"We've committed the whole corps except for your two units," the colonel in chief shouted. "So far we've managed to hold the French in the open, and only a few Algonkin have skirted our flanks and moved into the forest. But I don't know how long we'll be able to hold."

"The cavalry is ready for action, sir," Jared replied.

"My boys haven't done a thing today except exercise their legs," Carl Hector said. "Their rifles are a mite rusty."

Hopkins shook his head. "There's no more than an hour of daylight left. It's time we begin our retreat, and I simply want to know whether the Delaware regiment and the cavalry feel strong enough to move."

"Yes, sir," both officers replied in unison.

"Very well. Hector, I'll give you the rear-guard position. Your men can relax for another quarter of an hour before moving into the line. Hale, I want you to cover the flanks. Duncan's scouts will root out the Indians for you, and then it will be up to you to disperse them."

Jared and Major Hector rode off, and the colonel in chief devoted his full attention to the battle again.

The French had by now thrown all their regiments but one into the fight, and although they had brought no artillery with them, their greater strength was making itself felt. The Comte de Maricourt's cavalry was relatively ineffective and had retired to the rear, but undoubtedly it would see vigorous action again if the colonial militiamen became flustered and allowed their lines to break.

Casualties on both sides were heavy, but the French were taking the worse beating, their troops being plainly visible in the open. Their marksmen were superbly disciplined, however, and men stepped quickly into the ranks of the fallen to maintain a steady, unyielding pressure against the militiamen, who were shielded by the trees. So far the American high command's battle plan had been carried out almost to the letter, but the final test was still to come. If the militiamen could retreat in good order, taking a continuing toll of the enemy, the goal of Hopkins and Baker would be realized. If the retreat became a panic, however, men might be slaughtered by the hundreds, perhaps thousands. Indeed, it was still too early to tell whether the Battle of Sainte-Jeanne would end in a victory or a debacle.

"Unless it's absolutely essential," Jared said, "I don't want to divide the squadron into two groups, one for each flank. We don't have enough men to beat off attacks in force."

His troop commanders were in unanimous agreement.

Lieutenant Duncan wiped the palms of his hands on his buckskins. "From what I hear tell," he said, "you boys ride like deer escaping from a wolf pack."

Jared acknowledged the compliment but still was concerned. "Are you suggesting we swing around the vanguard from one side to the other, as we're needed?"

"That's the general idea."

"We're badly outnumbered by the Indians."

"There's things you don't rightly understand, Jared." Duncan waved his skinning knife, jabbing it into the trunk of a birch tree to emphasize each point he made. "First off, the Algonkin are such proud bastards they won't fight alongside any of the other tribes. And the Abnaki think the Micmac are scum. So we'll have to worry about only one tribe at a time. They may march near each other, but they won't share scalps.

"Second, they have no common sense. If they worked together, we'd be in real trouble. But the Algonkin will come at us first, seeing they have more braves than the others. The Abnaki will wait their turn, hoping the Algonkin fail. Then, maybe, the Micmac will rush in, provided the other braves don't squeeze them out."

"Will there be any time between assaults?"

315

Duncan considered the question. "If you scatter one set of warriors good and proper, the next won't be in a hurry to strike."

"Then it will be our duty to hit them hard," Jared said.

The scout ripped off a strip of bark with his knife, then shredded it. "Squash them," he said, showing deep emotion.

"How will we know where to turn?" Jared asked.

"You leave that to my boys and me. We'll ferret them out for you." Recovering his poise, Lieutenant Duncan sounded calmly sure of himself again.

The infantry regiments were moving off through the forest now, heading south, with Hector's regiment and another from Massachusetts drawing the French into the forest. Patches of sunlight filtering through the trees were slanted from west to east, so it was apparent that dusk was not far off. The time had come for the cavalry squadron to perform its new task.

"We'll ride just ahead of the vanguard so we can swing either way," Jared told Duncan. "Let me know when you want a helping hand."

The scout drifted off into the wilderness without bothering to reply.

The cavalrymen moved forward past the marching foot soldiers, and Jared was impressed anew by the problems horsemen faced in deep woods. The cavalry squadrons of the French would be of little value in such obstructed terrain, where it would be impossible to maintain even the semblance of a battle formation. But his own men, displaying the nimble facility of wilderness dwellers, were picking their way through dense underbrush, making detours around bramble patches and separating when their path was blocked by mammoth fallen trees.

He was pleased by the discovery that he could hold his own with them, and he knew more than ever that the forests had become his home.

A scout in disreputably greasy buckskins materialized out of the forest ahead so suddenly that Jared reached for his rifle.

"Algonkin are gatherin' in force on the left flank, Cap'n," he said, wasting no words. "They're aimin' t' strike any time, and Lieutenant Duncan says not t' dawdle."

"Left flank," Jared told Sergeant Greene. "Pass the word quietly."

A moment later the column of horsemen moved off to the left and turned back, riding parallel to the foot soldiers marching in the opposite direction. Fighting savages in the depths of the forest called for a technique far removed from a formal battle, but Jared understood what was required and felt confident of himself and his men.

It was unnecessary to give any orders now. Every horseman knew what was expected of him, and when the first shower of arrows startled the mounts, the cavalry troops charged hard toward the unseen foe. Waiting until they actually caught sight of the enemy, Jared's men held their fire until they were almost on top of the main mass of warriors, then discharged their weapons with deadly effect.

Jared, like his men, rode down every warrior he

could locate, using his rifle or pistol when he had a chance to reload, his saber when there was too little time. Rank no longer mattered; in a fight with savages, officers and men were equal in every sense, and each waged his own personal struggle against an enemy who was both cunning and courageous.

The battle lasted for no more than a quarter of an hour, and at no time was the outcome in doubt. Armed for the most part with crude weapons that were no match for the cavalrymen's long rifles and sabers, the warriors could not hold out for long. The few braves who did carry firearms were prime targets for the colonials, and after a spirited exchange the Indians moved off, carrying their dead and wounded with them.

The cavalry squadron returned to its place with the vanguard, but its respite was brief. The Abnaki were threatening the right flank, and Jared spurred there with his men, fighting an even briefer but equally conclusive skirmish. Thereafter the Algonkin, about an hour or two after nightfall, made another sally on the left, and when they were forced to withdraw, the Micmac finally moved in. But Abbé Le Loutre was not there to inspire them, and having seen what had happened to the other tribes, they had little heart for battle.

The tired cavalrymen called on their reserves of strength and beat off this fourth assault so viciously that the Micmac, showing little desire for close combat, quickly withdrew.

"I don't think they'll be troubling us again," Lieutenant Duncan said when he joined Jared at the head of the column. "They had to attack at least once for the sake of their honor. If they hadn't, the other tribes would have called them old women, and as sure as I'm telling it to you, the Micmac homeland would have been invaded before the snow falls."

Jared nodded wearily, yawning. His assignment on the hazardous retreat was the most grueling he had yet been given, yet he knew that to the rear, the battle between the main forces was still raging.

Colonel Hopkins had sent two relatively fresh regiments to relieve those in the militia's rear guard, but the French showed no sign of wanting to break off the engagement, even though the hour was growing late and their casualties were mounting. The parade boots and other formal gear of the French infantrymen made it difficult for them to march through the forest, and when they tried to move closer to their retreating foes, their white uniforms revealed their proximity, and they suffered heavily from the musket and rifle fire of the militia's rear guard.

Colonel Baker moved from unit to unit late in the evening to explain the situation and encourage the men. "We're doing even better than we expected," he told the cavalry troopers when he finally reached the head of the column. "We've been killing and wounding so many in the French vanguard that they'll soon have to fall back. Our own casualties have been fairly light, and we're carrying the wounded on litters near the supply wagons, where they're safe. So keep up your spirits, boys! We're crippling the French so badly they won't be able to take the field again for a year, at the earliest!"

Jared indicated that he wanted a private word with his superior, and they rode ahead to a place behind the screen of scouts, out of earshot of the cavalrymen. "How much longer are you planning to march tonight, sir?" he asked.

"As long as we keep killing the enemy, and as long as he still has an appetite for battle."

"Thank you, sir." Jared's voice was expressionless and his face blank.

"Now it's my turn to ask a question. How much longer can your squadron operate efficiently?"

"As long as necessary, Colonel."

"We realize your men are tired, Hale, and we're not expecting the impossible from them."

"The squadron isn't complaining, Colonel."

Baker started to speak, then changed his mind and rode in silence for some minutes. "I was wrong just now, Hale. The whole corps has been doing the impossible. Now it's just a question of stamina—whether we or the French will buckle first." He turned and moved back through the lines toward his own place in the column.

The sound of rifle and musket fire continued, but the cavalry saw no new action until midnight, when the stubborn Algonkin launched their most desperate and sustained assault yet. For a time Jared thought he might have to ask for infantry support in order to drive off the savages, but his men eventually succeeded in dispersing the braves unaided.

The casualties in the engagement were the highest the colonial cavalry had yet suffered: five troopers killed and eight others injured. Among the wounded was Jared, who was struck by an arrow in his upper left arm. He refused medical attention, however, although the wound bled profusely for a time, and instead washed it himself with brandywine supplied by Major Adams and then asked Sergeant Greene to bind it for him with strips of cloth.

The French continued to maintain their pressure until the small hours of the morning, when it became inconceivable to the colonel in chief and his deputy that the entire enemy force could be on the march. Lieutenant Duncan's scouts were sent to make a cautious investigation, and they returned with word that only two French regiments, augmented by several hundred warriors, were still in pursuit.

Colonel Hopkins immediately ordered the entire column to halt and fight a pitched battle. But the outnumbered French declined the invitation to further combat and withdrew. The scouts who followed them said they were breaking off all contact and starting back toward Quebec. The Indians also withdrew, vanishing into the depths of the forest, and the militia knew its first peace in many hours.

The regiments that had seen the least action were assigned sentry duty, and strong outposts were established in a cordon around the force. Most of the militiamen were so exhausted that they threw themselves onto the ground, rifles and muskets within reach, and dropped off to sleep at once.

But the throbbing of the wound in Jared's arm

kept him awake for a time, and he stared up through the trees at a small patch of dark, clouded sky. Rubbing the stubble of his chin, he tried to make himself comfortable on the hard ground, and not until he began to grow drowsy did it occur to him, belatedly, that the Battle of Sainte-Jeanne was at an end.

Barring an unlikely attack later in the morning, the militia had achieved all its objectives. Technically the battle had been a draw, with neither side winning, but for all practical purposes the Americans had been victorious. Perhaps the greatest French army ever assembled in the New World had been severely mauled, and henceforth the Comte de Maricourt would be forced to remain on the defensive both in Quebec and at the fortress of Louisbourg. His Indian allies would be far less inclined to raid the frontier settlements of the British colonies to the south, too, when they realized that no French regulars would come to their aid if they found themselves in serious trouble.

It was even possible that the savages had gained enough respect for the prowess of American militiamen that they would not want to risk a future challenge. That, however, remained to be seen. For the present Jared felt satisfied with his squadron's accomplishments and his own efforts, and at last he slept.

The makeshift camp began to stir soon after dawn, even though the men had enjoyed only a short rest. There was no reason to keep the location of the camp a secret, however, so trees and underbrush were cleared away, cooking fires were started, and the militiamen enjoyed their first meal since noon of the previous day. Major Adams complained that sacks of flour, sides of beef, and barrels of salt fish and pork were disappearing at an alarming rate, but no one, including the members of the high command, paid any attention to him.

The army remained in its bivouac until noon. Then, unshaven and grimy, the regiments started on the long march home.

CHAPTER EIGHTEEN

Caroline Murtagh woke up out of sorts one morning, but as the day passed, she had no idea why she was so restless. She thought she was hungry, but none of the dishes served to her whetted her appetite, and she sent them all back to the kitchen virtually untouched.

She spent the morning at her desk, but to her increasing annoyance found it almost impossible to concentrate, and at noon she gave up the effort. That afternoon she went for a long horseback ride but succeeded only in tiring her horse and perspiring heavily herself, with little enjoyment. After she returned home and bathed, she discovered that her restlessness was in no way alleviated.

At last, after she undressed and sat at her dressing table in her nightgown, she stared at her reflection in the mirror and said aloud, "Enough of this nonsense, Caroline. What ails you?"

The surface reason was not hard to find. She was young and a widow, but no potential husband loomed large in her future, and she faced the strong possibility that, even though she was exceptionally attractive, she might remain a widow for the rest of her days.

That was utter nonsense, and she well knew it. She was making excuses to avoid thinking about Jared Hale and how much she missed him. There! At last she was being honest with herself!

She missed Jared terribly and well knew it. There was an ache inside her that was caused by his absence and that only his return would end. Or would it? If he indicated that he preferred Polly when he came home—as she suspected he well might—there would be nothing she could do about it, and she would feel crushed.

Staring soberly at her reflection, Caroline faced reality. She had fallen in love with a man who was her indentured servant and who probably loved another woman.

If he should be killed or severely wounded in battle, she knew she would be devastated. In fact, no matter how she viewed her situation, it seemed extremely unlikely to her that she and Jared had any chance of getting together.

Nothing she said to herself discouraged her, however, and she knew that she would continue to care for Jared, no matter what might happen. That was the burden she would be forced to bear, and even though she could find no solution, no way to reach an accommodation with him, she knew she would not change. For better or worse, she loved him.

Additional food supplies were commandeered at two French villages as the militia marched south, and halts were made at lakes and rivers so the troops could bathe and wash their battle-fouled clothing. Bands of Algonkin and Abnaki followed the militiamen but remained at a distance from the column, and the scouts, ever alert, reported every move they made. The pace maintained by the column was slow, almost leisurely, although many of the troops were impatient to return to their homes after so long an absence.

The precarious health of the wounded, however, dictated the slow rate of march. The high command was tempted to assign the injured to the care of one regiment and allow the rest of the army to proceed more rapidly, but the danger posed by the trailing savages made that idea unworkable.

The fastest and shortest route would have taken the militiamen south by way of Lake Champlain, but Lieutenant Duncan felt that the area was too heavily populated by France's Indian allies, and the colonel in chief, after holding another council of war, accepted the scout's advice. So the army headed back toward the seacoast with the intent of returning the way they had come.

Food was no longer a problem, but new difficulties arose when the weather unexpectedly turned very cold. Many of the men had discarded worn-out woolen garments during the warm months, and they suffered now, particularly in the bitter chill of early morning. Since the location of the column was already known to hostile Indians, each unit was permitted to light as many campfires as it needed, and the dispensation, unusual in time of war, was helpful.

Jared recovered slowly. Although he was never incapacitated by the wound in his arm, he did run a fever for several days. Phil Franklin applied a poultice of the inner bark of the ash tree, mixed with ground acorns, to the open sore, and in forty-eight hours the fever dissipated. Jared's arm remained tender, however.

One day, shortly after the column had reached the coast, a fishing fleet was sighted at anchor in a small cove, and when some of the men from Massachusetts Bay recognized several of the schooners, signal shots were fired. A party of fishermen came ashore to investigate, and when they discovered the identity of the army, they contributed almost their entire catch of cod to Major Adams, as well as one of their boats to transport the most seriously wounded men to Boston. For the next forty-eight hours the militiamen had fresh fish for their meals.

Hundreds of citizens from every part of New Hampshire came to the little town of Portsmouth to greet the victorious troops, and for the first time the militiamen realized how quickly news of their exploits had spread through the colonies. A great feast was prepared and served near the waterfront, every prominent local official delivered an address, and a reluctant Colonel Hopkins was required to say a few words. After dark there was a fireworks display—which the officers of the army, mindful of the shortage of gunpowder throughout the colonies, deeply regretted.

The following day the New Hampshire troops were scheduled to be dismissed from service, so a review was held in their honor. Boots were cleaned, and the men who wore uniforms polished their brass. About an hour before the parade began, while the cavalrymen were currying their horses, Jared was summoned to the house in which Colonel Baker had been an overnight guest.

"Hale," the senior Delaware officer said, "Colonel Hopkins and I want the cavalry squadron reassembled. You'll ride today as a unit."

Jared was surprised, the four troops and headquarters detachment having gradually separated in recent days. "Yes, sir."

The colonel concealed a faint smile. "Perhaps we've been remiss, but we've made your promotion permanent, and until the corps disbands, we want the squadron to remain a unit."

Jared became slightly flustered, having assumed he would revert to his previous rank now that the danger had passed.

"We considered making you a major," Baker continued, "but there are officers senior to you who might resent too many rapid promotions. So we're doing the next best thing and making your captain's pay retroactive to the start of the campaign. I have an idea you'll be able to enjoy yourself in Boston."

The Bunch o'Grapes was one of the most renowned taverns in the British colonies. Although the wealthy Boston merchants who ate there daily took it for granted, Jared and the other cavalry officers, who had been given a private room for their banquet, dined on delicacies unlike any food they had ever eaten. Certainly Jared had never tasted anything comparable in the taverns and coffeehouses of London.

The oysters were sprinkled with garlic and tiny bits of toast before being roasted, and then coarsely ground pepper was added to the finished dish. The soup was a creamy chowder of minced clams, to which onions and celery had been added, and the poached fish was so light that no one in the party recognized it as cod. The venison had been marinated and simmered in an excellent French red wine, which Jared learned had been supplied by Thomas Hancock, Boston's leading merchant, who was an expert at smuggling French goods into the city by way of the West Indies. Even though Great Britain and France were at war and the colonies were deeply involved in the struggle, Hancock's fellow citizens applauded his efforts and were pleased whenever he succeeded in slipping contraband past the customs inspectors.

The main dish of the meal was roasted wildfowl, and Jared, who had been ravenously hungry at the beginning of the feast, discovered he was unable to do justice to the turkey, duck, partridge, and goose that the barmaids brought to the scarred oak table. The turkey was served with a chestnut dressing that was delicious, as were the turnips, which had been mashed and prepared with butter and pepper.

Most of the officers preferred plum pudding for dessert, but Jared tried a Boston dish he had never before tasted, pumpkin pie, and he liked it so much that he ate three pieces. He thought himself incapable of eating the fresh apples and New England cheese that concluded the meal, but remembering the many days he had gone hungry during the campaign, he accepted both.

He and his companions were in a lazy, amiable mood after drinking a final tankard of ale, and several members of the party broke into song as they strolled through the streets of Boston. Evening had come, there was the bite of autumn in the air, and the merchants, storekeepers, and artisans of the city were making their way to their homes. The cavalrymen, enjoying the bustle of the second-largest English-speaking city in the New World, eventually found themselves on Treamount Street, Boston's principal thorough-fare.

Hungry for the amenities of civilization after their long months in the wilderness, they watched the carriages of the wealthy rumble past on the cobblestones, grinned at the attractive young women, and stared curiously into the shop windows of booksellers and wine merchants. Wandering aimlessly, four abreast, they were startled by an angry shout.

"Out of my way, you louts!"

They found themselves gazing at a captain of Royal Infantry, his face almost as red as his scarlet tunic. With him were two British lieutenants and an ensign, all of them also glaring unpleasantly.

No one moved, and the British captain became still more annoyed. "Do what you're told, by God!"

Pedestrians began to gather, sensing a brawl.

Jared, who had been walking arm-in-arm with two of his troop commanders, stepped forward. "I'll take care of this, lads," he said, and slowly looked the redcoat up and down. "It's customary," he drawled, "for brother officers to exchange the courtesies of salutes."

"You consider yourselves officers?"

One of the other redcoats had realized that Jared's accent was English, and he commented aloud on the fact.

"I'm an American," Jared snapped. "And I was speaking to your senior officer. We're members of the colonial militia, and we not only hold the king's commission, but we've done more fighting in the past four or five months than you've done in all your life. So, on behalf of Colonel Hopkins's expeditionary corps, I demand a full and immediate apology."

The British captain laughed scornfully, but the sound died on his lips when Jared whipped his knife from his boot top.

The blade hovered a fraction of an inch from the redcoat officer's throat. "Soldiers," Jared said, "don't take kindly to insults from stuffed scarecrows."

The other British officers looked as though they intended to intervene, but one of the colonial troop commanders drew a pistol and cocked it, moving so swiftly that the men opposite him had no chance to take their swords from their scabbards. "This is a friendly little argument. We'll let them settle it their own way."

"Apparently you command a company in the Second Guards," Jared said. "Perhaps you were with them four years ago when Brigadier Lord Taswell threatened to disband the regiment because its officers were lazy incompetents incapable of maintaining discipline in their ranks. I can sympathize with him."

The British captain, conscious of the knife at his throat, stared at this grim figure in buckskins and cockade-decorated hat who, it seemed, knew one of his regiment's most shameful secrets. "Who are you?" he demanded hoarsely.

"I have the honor to command Colonel Hopkins's squadron of cavalry, the finest group of horsemen on earth." Jared waved his free hand to indicate the crowd, which had become dense. "For the sake of our good friends here, I urge you to acknowledge the supremacy of my squadron."

"This is outrageous."

"Not at all, my dear sir. Surely you know it's the policy of the War Office in London to send only inferior officers and a few malcontent troops to fill ceremonial posts in the colonies. When there's real fighting to be done, Americans do it."

The British captain sputtered incoherently.

Someone in the crowd laughed, and several men began to applaud.

"I don't suppose you've seen any Indians except the nice tame ones who come here to peddle furs and the like." Jared's smile was amiable. "Scalpings are interesting. You just lift up the hair, and if you're expert, you can perform the whole operation in one quick move. It's sometimes a bit more difficult to scalp a living man, of course. He's inclined to move around and jerk away. But it can be done. I've seen it, many times, and I need the practice."

The British officer turned pale.

"Boys," Jared said to his companions, "maybe one of you will make certain he holds still."

"You'll be hanged for this," the redcoat muttered.

"Who'll arrest me and put me in prison? The town constables? Your token detachment of troops that stands guard duty outside Governor Shirley's office? My dear sir, there are thousands of veteran fighters in our corps. We've fought together, suffered together, and won a great victory together. Our regiments will support me to a man, especially when they hear that an outsider who should know better has insulted the militia. There isn't a force in all the New World that has the strength of authority to put me into prison for something as unimportant as cutting the hair off the top of your head."

"My God," one of the British lieutenants gasped, "they're all savages here."

Jared remained unruffled. "We'll take care of you after we've finished with your friend. Lads, let's get this done. We've been enjoying our little walk, and we want no more interruptions."

The redcoat captain wilted. "I—I offer my apologies to your squadron, and to your whole damned—to your whole corps. Does that satisfy you?"

Jared pretended to consider for a moment. "Fair enough, I think. Are you satisfied, lads?"

The cavalry officers, scarcely able to hide their mirth, assented.

"Now all we'll need will be a few words from your friend over there." Jared's knife moved even closer to the captain's throat. "Lieutenant?"

The British lieutenant quckly muttered an apology.

Jared stuffed the knife into his boot top and deliberately linked arms again with his companions, forcing the British group to the side of the road. The militiamen started to saunter off down Treamount Street, and the crowd cheered wildly.

It hadn't occurred to Jared until now that Crown representatives might be unpopular in the colonies, but it was obvious that he had struck a responsive chord in the citizens of Boston.

Phil Franklin came forward through the throng, stuffing a brace of pistols into his belt. "A few of us just happened to be on hand," he told Jared, "and we were ready to step in if any trouble developed."

"It was easy enough to handle," Jared said. "I had no intention of shaming them in front of a crowd at first, but I refuse to let anybody look down on us."

Phil grinned at him. "You've really cut your last ties to England, haven't you? I reckon you've become an American."

Jared thought about the observation for a moment. "I reckon I have," he replied.

The officers of the colonial militia were summoned to an assembly on the Boston Common directly opposite the Massachusetts Bay government building and the governor's mansion. Sentries were stationed around the outside of the area to keep private citizens away, and Colonel Hopkins arrived with a middle-aged gentleman in a curled brown wig and sober but expensive clothing.

Mounting a low stone wall, Hopkins held up his hands for silence. "Gentlemen," he said, "you know I'm not one to make speeches. But I've come home, and my own regiments are disbanding, so this is my good-bye to you. I'm proud of you, and you have reason to be proud of yourselves. We know what we've done together, so I won't dwell on the past. What I'm hoping is that we'll see each other again, sooner than many of us expected."

Beckoning to the gentleman in the wig, Hopkins introduced the governor of Massachusetts Bay.

William Shirley was an accomplished orator, but he realized this was no occasion to show off his talents. He made a brief, graceful address expressing his gratitude for the achievements of the army and then launched into the real reason for his presence. A campaign was being planned for the following year, he said, and if it was successful, it could bring the war in the New World to an end.

Although he did not mention the French fortress at Louisbourg by name, virtually everyone knew he was referring to the great enemy stronghold.

"Our need for experienced officers and seasoned troops will be great," Shirley said. "If you'll join the colors again, your men will follow you. I realize, however, it may be premature to ask you now to volunteer your services. Only in the past few weeks have I written to the governors of other colonies, and neither they nor your assemblies have yet voted their approval of a campaign or authorized the expenditures of funds for such a purpose.

"Some colonies may not agree to take part. If they don't, Massachusetts Bay will guarantee you a commission at your present rank and will pay your wages. We make the same offer to your men.

"One way or another, we want and need your help.

"I understand that you're eager to return to your homes and attend to your own affairs. Normally we wouldn't ask you to think of another campaign that won't start for many months. But I beg you to remember, gentlemen, that the war may drag on forever, unless we bring it to a proper end. You may be called to duty many times, year after year, unless we act once and for all to destroy the French capacity to wage war in North America. I needn't tell you that we can and must solve our own problems without England's assistance."

There had been a time when Jared would have been astonished to hear an Englishman, the chief representative of the Crown in the most prosperous and important of Britain's colonies, express such indifference to the mother country. But it was apparent that William Shirley, like Jared himself, had been changed by the New World and thought of himself primarily as an American.

"I'm not asking you for a final commitment at this time. But it would be helpful to gain some idea of the support you'll give us. How many of you believe you'll be able to join us in this coming campaign?"

Scores of hands were raised, and Jared was the only man in his immediate vicinity who did not indicate a willingness to serve. His cavalry comrades looked at him in puzzlement, and so did a large group of officers from Delaware who were standing nearby. He reddened and stared down at the ground.

Only Phil Franklin and Carl Hector knew he wasn't his own master and had no right to plan his own future.

CHAPTER NINETEEN

The column dwindled slowly. The majority of the Massachusetts Bay militiamen left the corps in Boston, and the Rhode Islanders were dismissed at Providence. The remainder of the Massachusetts Bay troops—those from the western frontier—waited until they reached the mouth of the Connecticut River and then traveled upstream to their homes.

The first selectman of New Haven made a long address of welcome to the remaining regiments, a divine worship service was held at Yale College, and the troops, rapidly regaining the weight they had lost in the wilderness, were guests of honor at an outdoor feast attended by people from many Connecticut towns.

Some of the Pennsylvanians, in a hurry to reach their homes in time for an election of the colonial legislature, said their farewells to their comrades at New Haven. The army was now reduced to a small fraction of its maximum strength, and

Colonel Baker accepted an invitation to billet the men temporarily at Fort George in New York Town.

Jared found that New York was infinitely more hospitable to commissioned officers than to enlisted men. Remembering the few bleak hours he had spent in the town at the beginning of the campaign, he was surprised by the hospitality of merchants and attorneys, shipowners and physicians who entertained him at lavish dinners at their homes. The British commandant of Fort George held a reception for the militia officers, and ladies and gentlemen of New York appeared in finery worn with an air that would have put some Londoners to shame.

Although there were bigger and more prosperous cities in the colonies, Jared came to the conclusion that New York was the most sophisticated place he had visited in the New World. And for that reason he disliked it. He had grown accustomed to the wilderness and longed for its tranquility.

The troops from New Jersey were so close to their homes that they refused to linger at Fort George, so their officers had to cut short their merrymaking and depart. The men from Pennsylvania and the Lower Counties left a few days later.

Pennsylvania greeted the veterans with an aplomb that appeared to verge on boredom. The streets remained empty, there were no ceremonies of welcome, and the regimental adjutants found it difficult to arrange for adequate lodging for the men. But Governor Thomas paid a visit to the troops mustered under his authority, and every enlisted man was given a bonus of two pounds, every officer a purse of five pounds. The money had been raised by the citizens of Philadelphia, and they had made no distinctions between Pennsylvanians and troops from the Lower Counties.

A few Delaware cynics believed the ultimate aim of the donors was the improvement of trade relations between the two colonies, but the majority of men from the Lower Counties accepted the gift in good faith. Governor Thomas was careful to issue two official proclamations of welcome, and even his critics in the Delaware militia were forced to admit he was being scrupulously fair.

The two Delaware regiments of infantry and the headquarters detachment of cavalry marched on alone, making their way down the west bank of the Delaware River. Many farmers closed and bolted their doors when they saw the column approaching, an unnecessary precaution. The men were veterans now, well disciplined and imbued with too much dignity to steal pigs, chickens, or vegetables.

The farmers could not be blamed, however, for thinking they might be assaulted by this exceptionally large band of unusual-looking ruffians. Certainly the troops no longer resembled soldiers—if they ever had. The majority had spent a large portion of their bonus and wages in Philadelphia on new clothing and had discarded their ragged linsey-woolsey shirts and breeches, their homespun stockings and drab cloaks for the gaudiest finery available.

Only the members of the headquarters detachment still wore their buckskins, which they regarded as uniforms of honor. They did not think it accidental—nor was it—that Colonel Baker, whom they escorted, also dressed in buckskins.

No matter how understandable the fear of the inhospitable Pennsylvania farmers may have been, many of the men resented their reserve; as a result, the goodwill created by the gifts from the wealthy Philadelphians was quickly dissipated. But there had been changes since the troops had departed, and they soon discovered they could not turn back the clock. Relations between Pennsylvania and Delaware had entered a new era, and after plunging into the forest near the border, the men were astonished to discover there were no guards stationed on either side.

A strong wind began blowing up off the Delaware Bay, and soon after entering the forest the militiamen were drenched by a cold, driving rain. They made camp on the bank of the river, trying in vain to protect themselves from the elements, and by the following morning, with the rain still falling, everyone was in a foul mood. Breakfast was soggy, clothes and boots would not dry out, and the officers, themselves miserable, listened to the low, insistent grumbling they had heard for so many days on the long march.

It was early afternoon when the bedraggled column finally reached the town of Wilmington. The Delaware, Christina, and Brandywine rivers, which met there, were swollen. Streams of muddy water ran through the deserted streets, and all doors were closed. Shopkeepers had locked up their establishments for the day, the few farmers who had brought their produce to market had vanished, and the British flag had been taken down from its pole above the courthouse, indicating that justice was not being dispensed for the rest of the afternoon. The troops heard nothing but the tramping sound of their own muddy boots; and a mongrel dog, standing on a protected porch, barked at them.

Then, suddenly, Wilmington seemed to explode. No one knew how the town discovered that her men had returned, although a niece of Thomas Willing subsequently claimed the credit. "The roof over the parlor was leaking," she said, "and just as I started out to the pantry for a bucket, I happened to look out the window and saw my husband marching past with his platoon."

Wilmington immediately demonstrated its supreme indifference to the elements. Doors were thrown open, and citizens of all ages streamed out, completely interrupting the march. The men who lived in the town were dismissed at once, and the others were escorted in triumph to the fort, where makeshift quarters were prepared for them. Housewives emptied their larders of delicacies, and meals were served in Old Swedes Church and the recently completed First Presbyterian Meetinghouse. A fife-and-drum corps of teenage boys serenaded the returning heroes, and masters from two of the ships tied up at the waterfront invited the militiamen to drink their fill of ale and other spirits on board. The town's one inn was slightly more cautious and charged a token fee for refreshments.

About one third of the members of the headquarters detachment lived in the Wilmington area and went off to their homes. Jared accompanied the others to the fort, where he saw to it that accommodations were made available to the men and stalls found in the barns for their mounts. He was just completing this task when he felt someone tug at his sleeve and turned to see a boy of about ten who looked vaguely familiar.

"You're Captain Hale," the child said.

Jared nodded.

"My pa says you're to come with me."

"Who is your father?"

"Major Hector, of course," the boy answered proudly.

They rode together on Jared's gelding to the Hector mansion, a three-story dwelling of stone and white clapboard on the edge of town. There Carl Hector, happily reunited with his family, was expansively entertaining a group of officers after having said farewell to the remainder of his regiment.

Mrs. Hector was feverishly supervising the activities of the kitchen staff as they prepared a meal for so many unexpected guests, but she nevertheless found time to give Jared a warm greeting. "From what my husband tells me, you saved his regiment from annihilation, Captain."

"He exaggerates, ma'am. If my men and I had any success, it was because we had your husband's regiment supporting us."

The atmosphere was festive, everyone was

drinking hot toddies of buttered rum and sack, and Hector's two daughters, both of them attractive girls in their late teens, were very much in attendance. Platters of oysters and smoked ham appeared, and the guests, prodigiously hungry and thirsty, drank steadily and ate huge quantities of food.

Jared found himself unable to enter the spirit of the occasion, however. He had no appetite for the toddies or the food, and although the pretty Hector girls devoted far more attention to him than they did to the older men, he had no desire to flirt with them.

His host finally became aware of his withdrawn silence. "Cheer up, lad! We're home!"

This was not the moment to remind him that they had far different concepts of home, and Jared tried to smile politely.

Carl Hector pointed a thick forefinger at his elder daughter. "Frances, look at him."

The dark-haired girl was embarrassed.

"Do as I tell you. Study him, Frances, and tell me if he's in love. Is that what ails him?"

Jared was mortified by the feeling of color rushing to his face.

Frances Hector took pity on him. "If he is, Papa, she's a fortunate girl."

Jared's smile became still more strained, even though he was grateful to Frances for her help. The realities of the present were demolishing his past dreams. In another twenty-four hours at the most, he would arrive in New Castle and resume his life as an indentured servant, and he realized how stupid he had been, in the distant wilderness of New France, to imagine that he could find happiness for himself. He had enjoyed his freedom, which had been precious to him, but the interlude was ended, and soon he would return to his bleak existence as a bonded man, condemned to spend many more years paying for the folly of his youth.

The following morning the remaining units of Delaware militia, save for the New Castle contingent, were disbanded. The paymaster's strongbox, as usual, was half empty, and each man received only a portion of the wages due him. Colonel Baker promised, however, to take up the matter with Governor Thomas and the colonial assembly in the immediate future and swore he would not rest until the wages were paid in full.

The members of the headquarters detachment said good-bye to their commander, telling him they would gladly enlist again for another campaign if he would lead them. Jared was grateful for their confidence and, buoyed by it, went for a last farewell of his own with the head of the colony's militia.

"Colonel," he said, "I'm turning my horse over to you. He won't bring much of a price on the market, but whatever you get will help pay the men's wages."

"I won't hear of it," Edward Baker replied flatly.

"Sir, the animal isn't mine. I didn't start the campaign with a mount, I never paid a penny for one, so I certainly don't own one now."

Baker frowned. "We have at least a dozen animals in the common pool because of casualties.

I dispose of them as I see fit. The horse you've been riding belongs to you, Hale. You earned it. When I make my formal report to Governor Thomas and the legislature, I'll inform them that the Lower Counties have made you a gift of a horse."

"Thank you, but I don't really know whether an indentured servant has the right to own private property."

"Your rifle, pistol, and sword also belong to you." The colonel was firm.

"Isn't it against the law for a bonded man to own arms?"

"Laws are made, and laws are changed. As far as I know, you've commanded the first intercolonial cavalry squadron in our history. It would be an insult to every man who marched to Quebec if your weapons were taken from you. I won't hear of it!"

"I believe the law is intended to prevent an indentured servant from escaping. We're supposed to be dangerous if we own weapons."

"You proved to the French and their Indian friends how dangerous you could be," Baker said with a grin.

Jared smiled, too, but remained dubious.

"I plan to post a fee guaranteeing Caroline Murtagh's reimbursement if you should run away. Carl Hector would do the same, and so would half a dozen others."

Jared wondered whether the colonel was actually encouraging him to disappear. "I give you my word that you won't lose your money, sir. I've thought about going out to the frontier, but I can't spend the rest of my life as a fugitive."

Baker laughed aloud. "I hope you realize that the task of finding and returning escaped bonded servants is the militia's. Can you imagine any of the men who went on this campaign making you a prisoner and bringing you back? Frankly, I can't."

Jared's feeling had been right. Edward Baker was definitely suggesting that he vanish and begin life anew elsewhere. "I'm sure none of the men who knew me would arrest me, but there will be other campaigns and other wars. There will be newcomers who go to Louisbourg next year. And if the war isn't ended, still others will be recruited. Sooner or later someone who can use the reward offered by the assembly—it's ten shillings, I believe—"

"Twelve."

"—would be tempted by the money. I can't spend the rest of my days in hiding, under an assumed name. I've made enough mistakes in my life, sir, and I can't start making more now."

"Your value as an officer is that you have an independent mind. I'm afraid that same mind is going to cause us troubles we haven't anticipated." Edward Baker sighed. "I admire your honesty, Hale; however, we'll have to review the circumstances. . . ."

Jared didn't know what he meant.

The colonel started to say something more but refrained.

Perhaps, Jared thought, he was merely being polite in an embarrassing situation. There was nothing that Baker, Hector, or anyone else could do for him. Indentured servants had been granted a special dispensation by Governor Thomas to perform militia duty, and now that their service was concluded, they would revert to their previous standing. His own case was somewhat unusual, of course, because he had moved up through the ranks to a post of considerable responsibility and trust. But if an exception was made for him, every other bonded man who had taken part in the march to Quebec could go into the courts and claim freedom, too.

"Perhaps, sir," he suggested, "men in my position will be permitted to take part in the Louisbourg campaign. If they are, you can be sure I'll volunteer."

"And you can be sure that I'll get you a permanent commission as a major from Governor Thomas—even if every last veteran of this march has to lay siege to Philadelphia!" The colonel held out his hand. "Good luck, Hale. If you become discouraged in the days ahead, try to remember you have friends."

"I'll never forget any of you, Colonel." Jared was surprised to hear a huskiness in his own voice. "All of you—and this country—have changed my whole way of thinking."

Turning away abruptly, he mounted his horse and rode off toward the Wilmington waterfront fort. For one more day he would be an officer and a free man, and he wanted to savor the last crumbs of his liberty.

CHAPTER TWENTY

The militia contingent from New Castle marched slowly on the last segment of the long journey home. Habit kept the men in columns four abreast on the road, with the officers riding at the head of the line, and even though no one was hurrying unduly, a steady pace was maintained. Other militiamen had passed the same way the previous day, and farmers stopped working in the fields to offer the troops food. In the villages people raced out into the streets to cheer, and one enthusiastic plantation owner, who had been enjoying a quiet but apparently concentrated hour in a small tavern, emptied his purse and threw a shower of coins at the men. Two sergeants quietly gathered the money from the road and returned it to him.

The weather had improved, a surprisingly strong autumn sun had dried the ground, and the air was crisp. Leaves, which had already disappeared from the trees in New England, were just beginning to turn yellow and red and brown, and the men sang lustily, each step bringing them closer to their ultimate destination.

Jared, riding beside Ensign Phil Franklin, remained silent, unable to share the lighthearted mood of his comrades. He was keenly aware that the day was sparkling, however, and he wished it were still raining. It would be far easier, he thought, to give up his freedom in miserable, gloomy weather.

Phil reached over and touched his shoulder.

"We'll stop off at the Crown and Scepter for a last tankard of ale."

"I wish I could," Jared replied.

"Why in thunderation can't you? If you've spent your wages, it will be my treat!"

"There are rules, Phil." Jared forced a smile. "If I report to the Murtagh plantation with the smell of ale on my breath, I might be whipped."

"The boys and I wouldn't need much encouragement to burn every building on the property down to its foundations!"

Knowing his friend meant it, Jared became alarmed. "You can't interfere with a system that has been in effect ever since the colony was founded!"

Phil's smile was tight-lipped. "Who says we can't?"

"I forbid it!"

Looking at him, Phil shook his head. "There are times I can't rightly figure out what goes on in your head, Jared. But you're my friend. I know a little something about the problems of bonded folk myself," he added, then paused.

Jared wanted to question him, but it was apparent that Phil intended to say nothing more on the subject.

"There's no law says the boys and I can't put the fright of the Almighty into the Murtagh woman and her hired help!"

"If you get rough with her, Phil, you'll have to fight me again, and this time it won't be a friendly match!"

"I reckon you can trust me enough to know I

won't go hurting women! All the same, I'm going to handle this in my own damned way!"

Jared could not stop him from dropping back in the line.

Phil conferred briefly with the members of his own platoon, and they in turn spread the word to other units. Moving forward again, he muttered a few words to the other officers and then rejoined Jared, chuckling. "You'll come to the Crown and Scepter for a tankard of ale if we have to tie you up and force it down your throat," he said. "After that the boys and I will take charge. So relax, Jared. You don't have a worry in the world."

Some of the New Castle militiamen who were married went off to join their wives and children the moment the column reached town, but the vast majority marched to the Crown and Scepter. Never had the tavern done such a thriving business in a single day, and the crowds were so dense it became necessary to pass mugs, cups, and tankards of ale to men in the street who were unable to crowd their way into the establishment.

Meanwhile New Castle itself went wild with joy, and virtually everyone in the town headed toward the Crown and Scepter to greet sons, relatives, and friends. Shops closed for the rest of the day, as did the produce market, and volunteers began to dig roasting pits for what would become a communal jamboree. The excitement became so intense that no one could work; the county court adjourned, and when children of all ages raced out of the one-room schoolhouse without asking permission, the master tried to salvage what was left of his dignity by belatedly proclaiming a holiday.

The leaders of the militia did not forget that they had a final task to perform before disbanding, however. Promising to return as quickly as possible for the celebration, they mustered the troops. A few men who had managed to drink too much in a short period of time were weeded out. Then a protesting Jared was escorted from the tavern and lifted into his saddle. Ben Greene blew a familiar sour call on his trumpet, and the troops began their last march.

The remaining cavalrymen formed the vanguard, as usual, and behind them came the infantrymen, marching by platoons. The foot soldiers who had comprised the prewar fife-and-drum corps had decided that some martial airs would not be out of place, and they played with spirit, if not in unison. Scores of civilians who did not want to miss the festivities followed, and a number of small boys raced up and down the side of the road beside the column, accompanied by most of New Castle's dogs, whose barks occasionally drowned the efforts of the musicians.

Jared's sense of apprehension mounted, although he tried to reassure himself that his companions were jovial and that no one showed signs of vindictive unpleasantness. "I hope you realize," he said to Phil, "that anything you do now could be hurtful to me later, after you go back to town."

"I have me an idea," his burly friend replied, "that everybody is going to treat you just fine."

"But—"

"Look here. You didn't have to scalp every last Micmac and Algonkin in the woods south of Quebec to make the Naturals behave, did you? Well, I reckon civilized folks can take a hint a heap faster than savages. We're aiming to let the whole county know—especially the people on the Murtagh plantation—that you have good friends who'd grieve if you weren't treated right. You'll see; they'll be mighty anxious to spare us the grief."

They were moving now through countryside that was familiar to Jared, and in spite of the future that awaited him, in spite of the additional tensions the well-meaning militiamen were causing, he felt the vague stirring of a sense of pleasure. Soon he would arrive at the only home he had ever known in the New World.

Plantation owners, tenant farmers, and even indentured servants heard the fife-and-drum corps, saw the marching men, and came from all directions to join the still-growing throng. At least two hundred civilians were following the troops now, in what was quickly becoming the largest demonstration ever seen in the county.

At last the vanguard came to the main gate of the Murtagh estate. It was thrown open, and the troops marched in, followed by the crowd, while the fife-and-drum corps played loudly in order to attract the attention of everyone on the property. The vanguard drew nearer to the main house, and Jared saw curtains move at windows on the ground and first floors. It was impossible to see the faces hidden behind them, however.

Then Adam Marshall, looking leaner and grayer

than ever, ran toward the front of the house. Behind him were Caroline's indentured men, most of them carrying rakes and sickles. They halted in astonishment, gaping at the procession.

It had not occurred to Jared that he might be pleased to see Marshall, particularly under these circumstances, but he felt a lump in his throat when Adam, smiling in obvious delight, waved to him.

Phil called the marching militiamen to a halt.

The troops straightened their lines, then stood stiffly at attention.

Ben Greene blew a long, seemingly meaningless call on his trumpet, and a captain of infantry, the senior officer present, came forward to Jared and saluted. "Sir," he asked in a loud, clear voice that undoubtedly could be heard by everyone in the house, "will you accept a review?"

Jared had never been accorded such a great honor. His eyes became misty, but he was able to reply, "It would be a great privilege, sir."

"Mixed battalion, stand to review before Captain Hale!" the infantry officer called.

An honor guard led Jared to a place on the front lawn of the Murtagh mansion as the drummers beat a tattoo. Then they left him, returning to their place in the line. Battle flags were unfurled, Sergeant Greene blew lustily on his trumpet, and the fife-and-drum corps broke into the most popular of the tunes sung by members of the expeditionary force on their long march: "We'll Hang King Louis by His Scrawny Little Neck."

The song snapped Jared's tension. He grinned,

then drew his sword and held it at salute before him.

The cavalry rode past him first, Sergeant Greene at the head of the detachment, and Jared could not recall ever seeing the horsemen dress their lines so accurately. Ben barked a command, and every saber was whipped from its scabbard at the same instant.

"Salute the reviewing officer!" Ben called.

The cavalry saluted and then, in a spontaneous gesture, raised their blades high above their heads. "Hurrah for Captain Hale!" one of them shouted, and the others repeated the cry.

The infantrymen came next, displaying a precision in their marching they had not shown previously. They carried their rifles on their shoulders, and as each received the command "Salute the reviewing officer!" the slap of hands on barrels and butts could be heard. Again, after presenting arms, the foot soldiers emulated the horsemen. Raising the weapons high above them, they sent cheer after cheer echoing across the lawn.

The onlookers from New Castle and the surrounding countryside stood silently, scarcely daring to move. They all seemed to realize that they were watching an unusual tribute, and even the small boys, aware of the solemnity of the occasion, were still.

Ensign Phil Franklin, riding alone, brought up the rear of the column. He saluted Jared with his sword, then searched the windows of the house. He made no effort to conceal what he was doing and refused to be rushed. His face expressionless, he seemed oblivious to the crowd. Finally he turned back to Jared. "Captain Hale, sir, what are your orders?"

A lump had formed in Jared's throat and refused to dissolve. The next words he spoke might be the last military commands he would give in his life, and he took a deep breath. "Mr. Franklin," he said, surprised at the steadiness and depth of his own voice, "you may dismiss the militia!"

"Very good, sir. Unit commanders, dismiss your troops."

Orders were shouted, but the militiamen, facing Jared, had one more surprise in store for him. The men in the front rank lifted their rifles and fired a volley into the air. Those in the second line did the same, and finally those in the rear broke the silence for the third time.

Then, without a backward glance, the veterans of the Quebec campaign moved off, some of them escorting civilians who had come all the way from town to watch this last parade.

Jared continued to sit his mount, watching until the last of his comrades had departed.

A stir at one end of the lawn reminded him of the present—and the future he dreaded. The other indentured men who had been members of the militia were being greeted boisterously by those who had remained behind. He started toward them.

As he drew near, they fell silent, all of them clearly ill at ease.

Adam Marshall stood apart from the others, a faint smile on his weathered face.

Jared sheathed his sword and dismounted.

Deliberately, slowly, he extended his hand. "Adam, it's good to see you," he said.

The overseer's smile broadened. "I'm not sure I'd have recognized you," he said. "You're as dark as a Nanticoke or Lenape warrior."

"I haven't seen myself in a mirror for so long that I wouldn't know." Jared felt he had to break down the reserve of the others. "Harry, you sure haven't changed. You still have the ugliest face I've ever seen. And Ned, you've put on weight. I reckon you've been eating our share of the vittles while we've been gone."

There was a hushed pause, and then one of the men muttered audibly, "My God, he even talks like us now!"

Jared led the roar of laughter.

"The front lawn," Adam Marshall said gently when the merriment subsided, "isn't a place for the likes of us."

The entire group started off toward the rear, with Jared leading the gelding.

"That's a fine-looking animal," Adam said.

"He's mine."

"So we heard. Colonel Baker sent a messenger to Mistress Murtagh today. She's had the groom—the lad who took your place—clear a stall for him in the stable."

Jared was too dumbfounded to reply.

Adam reached out and touched the barrel of his companion's rifle.

"These weapons are mine, too."

The overseer patted him on the shoulder. "I don't reckon Mistress Murtagh will try to take them away from you. It might be dangerous," he

355

added with a chuckle, "seeing you're so handy with them."

"How do you know?"

"The whole colony has been talking about Captain Jared Hale for the past couple of weeks. The boys who can write sent letters home, and every blamed one of them had something to say about you."

"A man's friends sometimes exaggerate what he's done in a war. It makes their own exploits more daring. Although I've got to admit I've never seen anyone fight—anywhere—the way our militiamen fought. People can be proud of them."

"We are. And of you." Adam paused. "So are the troops. That was a grand tribute to you."

"It was a way the lads had of saying good-bye to a bonded man."

They had arrived at the stable, where a youth of about eighteen took Jared's horse. "I'll curry him good, sir," the boy said.

"Thank you." Jared was silent again until he and Adam were alone. "They'll have to learn not to call me sir. I'm no better than anyone else."

"There's some might argue with that." Adam led the way toward the shacks of the indentured servants, but they paused when they heard a commotion back at the stable.

A few minutes later the youth reappeared, sitting on the box of the coach, which was driven by a team of matched bays.

"What's happening?" Adam called.

"Blamed if I know, Mr. Marshall. Mistress Murtagh sent word from the house that she had to go into New Castle right away."

Adam shrugged and would have walked on, but Jared put a hand on his arm. "Wait."

They stood, neither speaking, as the groom drove to the front of the house. After a few moments two young women emerged and climbed into the coach. Polly White looked unexpectedly elegant and ladylike in a dress and matching cloak of pale violet wool, and Caroline Murtagh was patrician and beautiful in dark red silk.

Jared was staring hard, his face pale beneath his tan, his fists clenched. He had been prepared for almost anything, but it was an unexpected agony to see only from a distance the woman he loved. She was unaware of his proximity and did not glance in his direction as the coach pulled out of the driveway.

Adam was deeply sympathetic but thought it wise not to comment.

After a moment or two Jared shook himself, and they resumed their walk toward the indentured servants' quarters. "I suppose I'm to have my old hut?"

"Not exactly."

"When is a new ankle band put on me? Now, or after I formally report to Mistress Murtagh that I'm alive and back at work?"

Adam couldn't blame him for the bitterness in his voice, but smiled. "I'm not heating a proprietary band for you, and no one else has the courage to do it, either. For one thing, it would be a shameful way to treat a war hero, and for another, I'm sure your friends in the militia would tar and feather any man who laid a hand on you."

"But the law—"

"There are times it's sensible to ignore the law," Adam said. "It's healthier, too."

Jared had no intention of disputing the matter. His badge of indenture had always distressed him, and it was a relief to know that, at least for the present, he would not be forced to wear the symbol of his degradation. It was possible, of course, that when Caroline learned of the situation she would have other, positive ideas and would insist he wear the band.

"I don't believe," Adam said, "that a bonded man has ever caused so many people to wonder how he should be treated. You were head of a cavalry troop—"

"A squadron!"

"Whatever. All I know is that Colonel Baker and the colonel from Massachusetts Bay had enough faith in you to give you a place of importance in their army. It would reflect badly on the Lower Counties if we treat you like scum from Newgate."

"You forget that I am scum from Newgate." Jared spoke lightly to hide his pain.

A new cabin had been erected a short distance from Adam's own dwelling. It was considerably larger than the other huts, and greater care had been taken in its construction. Clay filled the chinks between the logs of its walls, a layer of pine tar had been smeared thickly under the shingles on its sloping roof to keep it dry in bad weather, and, like Marshall's house, it boasted real panes of glass instead of oiled paper in its windows.

Adam opened the door, and Jared was startled when he saw the interior. The cabin boasted a floor of pine planks and consisted of two large rooms, both of them comfortably furnished with plain but sturdy chairs, tables, and chests of unpainted wood. The most astonishing sight was the real bed in the inner chamber, on which sheets, blankets, and a pillow had been laid.

The overseer chuckled when Jared turned to him for an explanation. "Everybody on the plantation worked on it for you," he said. "The boys and I put it up and made the furniture, the glass came from Mistress Murtagh's own supply, and the housemaids came out and gave it a scrubbing when we were done. It was Polly who made up the bed for you."

The little house was far more spacious and solid than most frontier homes Jared had seen on his long march. In fact, it was a place that any wilderness dweller would have been proud to own. "Does Mistress Murtagh know about all this?" he demanded.

"Of course. You don't think I'd steal the glass without her knowledge? She came every day to see how we were making out while we were putting it up, and she made a last inspection, you might call it, after everything was finished."

"She doesn't object?" Jared said feebly.

"How can she? We've heard tell that you're one of three or four men who are going to get a special vote of commendation from the colonial assembly. Think how she'd be made to look if she put you in one of those huts!"

Caroline, Jared thought, was probably seething, but she could do nothing until the excitement over the return of the militia subsided and Delaware returned to normal. She would have to wait before reducing him to the place she considered appropriate.

Adam closed the door behind them and sat down in a chair that boasted a cushioned seat. "I can't rightly tell you what she has in mind. But it was just this morning that she called me up to the house and told me not to put you to work in the fields, the stables, or anywhere else."

"I think it unlikely she's going to give me a holiday."

Adam shrugged. "It's my feeling that she'll want you to replace me as overseer when my indenture ends. You're the natural and proper choice."

"I refuse to become a slave master."

"It's better than being a slave."

"Not when a man has been one. At least it isn't for me."

"You'll refuse if she offers you the place?" Adam asked incredulously.

"I will. I'm opposed to the whole practice of indenture. The system is barbaric, and my conscience won't allow me to do anything that will help perpetuate it or make it successful."

"Sometimes," the overseer said, "I think you have too much of a mind of your own. Don't let the praise you've been getting give you wrong ideas of your importance."

"I've already learned that one man can't stand alone to fight things that are wrong with Crown justice. It would take all the American colonies banding together to do that."

Adam was shocked. "Are you preaching treason?"

"No, only justice. A man learns his real inner worth in the wilderness, Adam, and I say that no matter what he's done to break the law, he shouldn't be robbed of his dignity."

"You've come back from the war with some mighty strange ideas. They may get you into worse trouble than you realize."

"Maybe so. But I'm willing to take that chance. If the New World teaches men anything, it teaches them the real meaning of liberty. When I was in the middle of the Maine District wilderness, nobody put a guard on me to watch me and make certain I didn't run away. I was given all the privileges and responsibilities of freedom. And no matter whether I fought well or poorly, no matter whether I was a hero, as you call it, or a coward, I'd fail as a man if I didn't live up to what I learned about myself—and what I learned about this land."

"I can't help wondering if you're drunk, even though I know you're sober."

"You've spent fifteen years earning your freedom, Adam. Will you go to England when your indenture ends?"

"Are you mad? I aim to find myself a piece of land I can farm, and claim it! Right here in Delaware!"

"Exactly what I'm saying to you. Here you can hold up your head and enjoy the liberty that men have wanted and dreamed of for hundreds of years."

Every word he had just heard was true, Adam

knew, but still he was afraid that a clash would be inevitable when Caroline Murtagh discovered it was no longer possible for Jared Hale to live as a humble bonded man.

CHAPTER TWENTY-ONE

The plantation's indentured servants, in order to celebrate the return of Jared and the other bonded men, had prepared a feast that was a triumph of ingenuity. Two of the servants had somehow got hold of a boat and had sailed down to the bay the previous night, returning with baskets filled with oysters, mussels, and clams. Others had concocted a savory stew of wild rabbit and root vegetables from the forest; and there was a huge bluefish that had been hooked near New Castle in the Delaware River, as well as venison and bear steak and a potent wine made from the fermented juices of berries picked from bushes in the forest. The entire meal had not cost a penny in cash.

Though Jared ate and drank more than his fill, when he finally retired he found he could not sleep. At first he blamed the comfortable bed in his new house and thought he would have felt more at home rolled in a blanket under the stars. But he realized he was fooling himself; after months of anxious anticipation he was only a hundred or so yards from the woman he loved, and the tension of waiting to see her, to find out if they could resolve their mutual problems, was becoming unbearable.

He rose at dawn with the others, but at breakfast

Adam Marshall reminded him that he was not allowed to engage in work of any kind for the present. So at the end of the meal he wandered over to the stable and, lacking anything better to do, saddled his horse and exercised the animal for an hour. He rode down familiar roads, finally plunging into the forest, and thought how easy it would be to follow Colonel Baker's advice and run away. No one would follow him, and he could begin a new life, under an assumed name, wherever he pleased.

But, having made his decision, he felt no sense of inner struggle as he turned back toward the plantation.

He returned his horse to the stable, feeling a trifle uncomfortable when the young groom there insisted on taking charge of the animal. At loose ends, Jared had nowhere to go except to his own cabin. He wanted to visit the main house, but protocol was important, and he realized he would be presumptuous if he went before being summoned.

For some minutes he wandered back and forth between the two rooms of his house, thinking that had he known he would be inactive, he could have bought some books in Boston or Philadelphia. At least his future was assured to the extent that he could start a new library, and it was good to know he had enough money to purchase a number of volumes.

Lost in thought but restless, he continued to pace until a tap sounded at the door. He opened it and saw Polly White on the threshold.

He could not remember when she had looked

more attractive. A trifle plumper than she had been when they had first met on board the ship that had brought them to the New World, she was wearing a honey-color dress of wool, its low-cut neckline accented by a single large curl of dark hair that fell forward over her shoulder. Her eyes were radiant, and it was evident at first glance that she was supremely happy.

At first neither spoke; then Polly stepped into the little house, smiling as she removed her short cloak.

Directly behind her was Phil Franklin, looking pleased with himself. He kicked the door shut, leaped at Jared, and pounded him on the back. "It's done!" he shouted. "Everything is settled!"

It was impossible for Jared to escape from his bear hug without knocking over furniture.

At last Phil released him. "I was rarin' to ask you to lead a cavalry charge on the assembly, but it won't be needful."

Polly had to raise her voice to be heard above Phil's roar of laughter. "You look contented, Jared," she said.

"So do you. I've never seen you so pretty."

"She ought to be," Phil boomed. "The papers were signed early this morning. She's free now— free to marry me." He beamed at her.

The girl returned his smile.

Jared was so startled he didn't know what to say; but seeing them together, he immediately sensed they had achieved a rapport he had never been able to find with Polly.

"I wanted to tell you about Polly for months," Phil said, "but I couldn't. There were too many things in the way, and I was afraid that talking about them might spoil everything."

For an instant Polly looked directly at Jared, silently speaking to him.

He understood at once. She had kept her affair with him a secret and had not mentioned it to Phil. He wanted to reassure her and said, "It's my right to kiss the bride."

His lips touched Polly's, gently, and he patted her on the shoulder.

The woman's relief was infinite as she stepped back.

"You'll stand up with me," Phil said. "We'll be married in New Castle Saturday at noon. We've waited long enough." He swept a proprietary arm around Polly.

There were so many questions Jared wanted to ask that he scarcely knew where to begin.

Phil anticipated him. "Polly and I started seeing each other a long time ago, when she made trips into New Castle with Mistress Murtagh and was left to wait in the coach. We—ah—kind of struck up a friendship, you might say, and one thing led to another."

All at once Jared knew why Polly had been so distant during his last months on the plantation, prior to his enlistment. It was clear now that she had been trying to avoid him, that she had been terrified of his advances because she had fallen in love with someone else. And he understood, too, why Phil had shown no interest in the women the militiamen had encountered in the various towns they had visited. "I was stupid, I suppose," he said. "I should have known long ago."

Phil was eager to tell him the important part of the story. "Our big problem was getting Polly released from her bond."

Jared's smile faded, and he nodded somberly.

"I told him to let me deal with Mistress Murtagh, and he finally did," Polly said quietly. "I was afraid he'd start roaring at her, the way he does at the soldiers, and that would have been all wrong."

"I've been saving the money to buy the bond," Phil began, "and I had near enough by the time we got home. All I needed was the rest that's due on my militia wages—"

"But Mistress Murtagh refused to accept a ha'penny from him. She tore up my bond and said it was her wedding gift to me."

Neither now nor at any future time would she reveal to anyone the secret of Osman Murtagh's return, his attempted rape of Caroline, his death, and the grisly disappearance of his body. As far as the entire world was concerned, he had vanished forever after falling overboard on the voyage to England.

"Just now," Phil said proudly, "I sawed off her ankle band. She's a free woman."

"But I'm gladly giving up that freedom tomorrow." He would have crushed her in an embrace, but she held him at a distance. "You will come, Jared?"

"If I'm allowed to go into New Castle tomorrow." He averted his face when he saw the sympathy in her eyes. Her own freedom was so new that she clearly remembered how it felt to be at the mercy of another's whims.

"We can always muster the troops if there's any trouble," Phil said, a vein swelling at his temple.

Polly intervened swiftly, calming him. "I'm sure Mistress Murtagh will be sensible about it. She's going into town again this morning on some urgent business, but I'm sure she intends to see Jared later in the day."

Phil subsided, muttering under his breath as she stroked his arm.

"What makes you think she plans to see me today?" Jared asked.

"She was going to send for you after breakfast, but then she got a message and had to ride into New Castle instead."

"Well," Jared said heavily, "I have nowhere else to go, so I'll be right here whenever she finds the time."

Dusk was falling when the young groom came to Jared's snug new cabin to tell him he was wanted at the main house. Jared resisted the temptation to don his sword, knowing it would be a childish sign of bravado, and he walked quickly to the mansion, where a newly hired maid led him into the drawing room.

A fire was blazing in the hearth, tapers in the chandelier had been lighted, and the atmosphere was warm and comforting, reminiscent of the holiday cheer Jared recalled from his youth. A door squeaked open, and he turned as Caroline came into the room.

She had dressed with special care for the occasion, as he quickly realized. Her gown and slippers were the precise same shade of blue as her eyes, her blond hair had been freshly piled in curls on the crown of her head, and glowing touches of rouge perfectly set off her cheeks and her lips.

"Welcome home, Captain Hale," she said.

Jared bowed, uncertain whether she was being intentionally sardonic.

She waved him to a chair by the fire. "Would you care to join me in a glass of sack? Or perhaps you'd prefer something a trifle stronger."

"Sack will be fine, thank you," he replied, dazed because she seemed to be treating him as a guest.

"You've changed," she said, studying him as she handed him a glass.

"And you haven't changed in the least."

Caroline knew he intended the remark as a compliment, and smiled.

Jared realized that a profound change had taken place in their relationship, but he was not yet able to think about it clearly.

"If the parade in your honor was held for the purpose of impressing me," she said, "it succeeded."

"I'm sure that was at least part of the purpose, although I knew nothing about it before it began."

"So I understand."

There was a long, strained silence. Jared supposed he should thank her for his new house, but he had no desire to seek her favor through gratitude. And he knew there would be trouble if she offered him Adam's position as supervisor, which his conscience would not permit him to accept. The cheerful atmosphere she had seemingly established was illusory, and the spell would be broken at any moment. She would lose her temper when she learned of his stand; then he would become angry, and it was impossible to predict how the unpleasant scene would end.

Jared took a deep breath. "Caroline," he said, addressing her by her Christian name and speaking very rapidly, "you'd better prepare yourself for a shock." He wasn't saying what he had intended, but he could not stop himself. "It so happens that I love you."

She became scarlet and almost dropped the glass she held in her hands. She placed it on a table beside her.

"However," he continued, "it appears there is nothing I can do about it. I realize we live in different worlds, and that it's presumptuous of me. An indentured man doesn't pay court to the woman who owns his bond."

Caroline tried to speak, but he gave her no opportunity to break in.

"I would have preferred not to love you. Looking back, I realize I fought myself for a long time, but it was in vain. I could no more cure myself than I could if I became ill with the pox."

"I don't believe I care for your illustration."

"I'm sure you don't, any more than I've enjoyed the way you treated me—and your other indentured servants. You've been capricious, thoughtless, selfish, and cruel. You've forgotten—or haven't cared—that bonded men and women are people, too, and that they have feelings of their own. You've been arrogant and high-handed." He paused for breath.

"Is that all?" Caroline was maintaining superb self-control and sounded remarkably calm.

"Not quite. If I were a free man and could meet you on equal terms, I would never relent until you married me. Then, I promise you, I'd tame you once and for all."

Sparks of anger appeared in her eyes, but she merely murmured, "You're very sure of yourself."

"Not at all. I know what I could do. But it's useless to daydream. I had to tell you what's been going through my mind for months, and I trust I'm gentleman enough to apologize for any embarrassment I might be causing you. I apologize for nothing else, though," he added belligerently. "And if you care to have me whipped, which is your legal right, I can guarantee you that you and the men you assign to do it will have Satan's own time trying to hold me down. There will be a few bloody heads before I'm strapped to a whipping post." Thoroughly aroused now, he glared at her.

She said, "I've never felt as miserable in my life as I did when I—well, went mad for a time and struck you. I swore to myself that I'd never do anything like that again. And I won't."

Jared's anger drained away, leaving him limp. It had not occurred to him that she would have the grace to apologize, to admit without equivocation that she had been wrong, and he realized he was trying to fight a shadow that had suddenly faded away.

"Is there anything else you'd care to say?" Caroline was conscious of his change of mood.

"I've probably said far too much already." He

had not wanted to hurt her, and he felt ashamed of himself.

Taking her time, she refilled their glasses and then returned to her chair. "It seems you have a great many friends in the Lower Counties—and in other colonies, too."

Jared saw no need to explain to her the feeling of brotherhood that existed among men who had faced death together.

"They're ingenious and very talkative. I've spent a great many hours in New Castle yesterday and today, listening to them telling me many things about you."

Jared jumped to his feet, almost tipping over his chair and the table beside it. "My God," he shouted, "if Phil and the boys dared to threaten you, I'll have their scalps, every last blasted one of them!"

"Mr. Franklin didn't take part in the discussions, but if he had, I'm sure he'd have been kind and pleasant, too," Caroline replied soothingly. "I was treated with respect by everyone I saw."

He grunted, partly mollified.

"Please sit down." She smiled at him warmly.

Not quite realizing why he was obeying, Jared sat.

"Your future has been a matter of great concern to Edward Baker and Carl Hector—and others. A gentleman in Boston who was the head of your army—"

"Colonel Hopkins."

"That's the man. He persuaded Governor Shirley of Massachusetts Bay to send a letter to Governor Thomas, requesting that you be freed

371

of your indenture by royal decree, which Governor Thomas could sign as the king's viceroy."

Jared was astonished.

"They want to give you the commission of major in their next campaign, and they believe it would set a bad precedent for a bonded man to hold such a high rank in an intercolonial army."

Jared's mouth and throat felt dry. He hadn't dreamed that his friends would go to such lengths to help him.

"I told them I wouldn't hear of any such proclamation."

If Caroline intended to fight the move, it might take years before the appeals and counterappeals moved through the colonial courts and finally reached the House of Lords in London. Jared's feeling of elation disappeared.

"I also told them I'd be presented to my friends in the worst possible light. My reputation would be destroyed. So I insisted they allow me to tear up your bond voluntarily, which I've already done." Caroline reached into a small velvet purse at her waist and removed the document that was the legal evidence of his indenture. It was already torn into four pieces, which she showed him before she placed them atop the fire, one piece at a time.

"Perhaps you won't want to believe this, but it's what I had intended to do in any case. I had hoped to have a little ceremony yesterday, before Edward Baker sent me a message asking me to meet him at once in New Castle."

"Of course I believe you, and I'm grateful to you." Jared's knowledge that he had been freed from bondage was accompanied by the realization that technically he could ask her to marry him. But too many other obstacles stood in the way. Caroline was a wealthy woman, and he had nothing to offer her.

He jumped to his feet again and began to pace up and down the room. "When I clear some land for myself out on the frontier," he said, "I'll build a cabin. It won't be very big, and it won't be comfortable. It may be years before I start making money. I can't ask you to share hardships with me."

Caroline tried to speak.

"And I refuse to live on your money! What's more, I don't approve of indenture. I couldn't spend my life with a woman who earns an income from the work of bonded men, slaves."

Caroline remained tranquil, waiting for him to stop.

"I've caused you enough trouble, so the biggest favor I can do for you is to clear out and leave you in peace."

"I do wish you wouldn't march up and down. It makes talking so difficult."

Jared halted directly in front of her, hooking his thumbs in his belt as he looked down at her.

"Your friends had another surprise for you, and Colonel Baker was very considerate—he gave me permission to tell you about it. Land is very inexpensive in the hills about ten miles west of New Castle, in the wilderness near the Maryland border. So they've bought you a tract of five thousand wooded acres."

"I—I can't accept!"

"That's what they thought you'd say, so the

Delaware assembly will vote you the property in recognition of your services to the Lower Counties."

He caught his breath and felt dizzy. "I'm going off on the new campaign next spring!"

"To be sure," she replied simply. "You're needed."

For the first time he allowed his hopes to rise.

"Two of my neighbors," Caroline continued, "have been wanting to buy this plantation for a long time." She rose and faced him. "And I've been waiting—almost as long—to be kissed."

IF YOU HAVE ENJOYED READING THIS
LARGE PRINT BOOK AND YOU WOULD
LIKE MORE INFORMATION ON HOW TO
ORDER A WHEELER LARGE PRINT
BOOK, PLEASE WRITE TO:

WHEELER PUBLISHING, INC.
P.O. BOX 531-ACCORD STATION
HINGHAM, MA 02018-0531